"*Hearts Aweigh* is a delightful vacation i
—Angela Ruth Strong, aut

"I'll follow Shannon Sue Dunlap and h(
of a certain age anywhere. Inspirational
ery cozy moment they spend with the Shippers!"
—Bethany Turner, author of *Cole and Laila Are Just Friends*

"With a mischievous group of matchmakers, a mysterious blackmailer, and a toe-curling romance, *Hearts Aweigh* is a delightful read from the first page to the last. Dunlap has woven an intriguing tale of forgiveness and second chances, sprinkled with laughter. A story to savor!"
—Tara Johnson, author of *To Speak His Name*

"*Hearts Aweigh* is an absolutely adorable and engaging story that kept me giggling throughout. I was moved by the threads of family and re-connection. The characters sparkle with relatable charm and quirkiness. And what fun it was to mingle with the Shippers and their matchmaking antics. Readers will be enthralled by every part of this delightfully heartwarming read."
—Jenny Erlingsson, author of *Her Part to Play*

"The Shippers are up to their old tricks again, and I'm here for it! As much as I enjoyed *Love Overboard*, I think *Hearts Aweigh* might be even better. When one of Monarch Cruises' childcare specialists, Abby, re-cruits the Shippers to work their matchmaking magic, she opens the door to their hilarious hijinks, and they don't disappoint. The sparks fly between Abby and Spencer from their first meeting, and the mystery of Daisy's blackmailer adds just the right amount of good-natured sus-pense. This witty, heartfelt romance is an absolute treat for readers. I can't wait to see what Shannon Sue Dunlap comes up with next!"
—Elly Gilbert, coauthor of *Under the Blue Skies*

LOVE OVERBOARD

Love Overboard
Hearts Aweigh

Hearts Aweigh

A NOVEL

SHANNON SUE DUNLAP

KREGEL
PUBLICATIONS

Hearts Aweigh: A Novel
© 2025 by Shannon Sue Dunlap

Published by Kregel Publications, a division of Kregel Inc., 2450 Oak Industrial Dr. NE, Grand Rapids, MI 49505. www.kregel.com.

Published in association with Books & Such Literary Management, www.booksandsuch.com.

The persons and events portrayed in this work are the creations of the author, and any resemblance to persons living or dead is purely coincidental.

The following quoted lyrics are in public domain: "Bingo," folk song; "Down by the Riverside," Negro spiritual; "Glory, Glory, Hallelujah," Negro spiritual; "Just as I Am, Without One Plea," by Charlotte Elliott (1836).

Library of Congress Cataloging-in-Publication Data
Names: Dunlap, Shannon S., author.
Title: Hearts aweigh : a novel / Shannon Sue Dunlap.
Description: Grand Rapids, MI : Kregel Publications, 2025. | Series: Love overboard ; 2
Identifiers: LCCN 2024060020 (print) | LCCN 2024060021 (ebook)
Subjects: LCGFT: Romance fiction. | Novels.
Classification: LCC PS3604.U5523 H43 2025 (print) | LCC PS3604.U5523 (ebook) | DDC 813/.6—dc23/eng/20241216
LC record available at https://lccn.loc.gov/2024060020
LC ebook record available at https://lccn.loc.gov/2024060021

ISBN 978-0-8254-4870-6, print
ISBN 978-0-8254-7437-8, epub
ISBN 978-0-8254-7436-1, Kindle

Printed in the United States of America
25 26 27 28 29 30 31 32 33 34 / 5 4 3 2 1

To one of my favorite traveling companions,
Aunt Donna

CHAPTER 1

MAYDAY. MAYDAY. MAYDAY.

Emily Windsor's seventy-eight-year-old bones sounded a silent warning. She twisted an empty butterscotch wrapper in her wrinkled fingers and tried to pinpoint the problem. Her mission in life was finding lonely people a love as sweet as her own had been. She should be chomping at the bit to have a ready and willing candidate. But this case seemed a little too . . . what was the word?

Easy.

A petite figure sat in a padded chair a short distance away. The pretty redheaded woman picked at the gold lace edge of her lavender ball gown. A lopsided tiara sparkled atop her curly locks.

Emily shoved the wrapper in her pocket and combed a hand through her own unruly mop of gray hair. "I'm sorry, dear. We'll get started soon."

Geraldine Paroo's five-foot-ten frame filled the chair beside her. The retired librarian raised a red pen, crossed through a word in her paperback novel, and straightened the cat-eye spectacles on her nose, more than content to read as they waited for the others.

The ladies faced their new protégé from one side of a long table like a reality show's judging panel. A harried waitress zipped through the MS *Buckingham*'s elaborate dining room with a freshly laundered pile of tablecloths. She cast them a confused look but said nothing. A shout from the pier below drew Emily's attention to the windows. They had mere minutes before a fussy crew member demanded they vacate the ship for zero count. All passengers must be off before the new cruise guests started loading.

No time to waste. But two of the Shippers were missing.

Emily reached under her chair and tugged a walkie-talkie from her large black purse. Static crackled as she pressed the button. "Daisy, have you found Althea yet?"

"Coming," a breathless Southern drawl answered. "We're outside the dining room."

The ornamental wooden doors to their left opened, and fashionable Daisy entered in a black silk blouse and matching skirt. Her chin-length silver hair swung as she towed her smiling roommate, Althea, behind her.

"Sorry, y'all." Althea scrunched her smooth Creole skin into an apologetic grimace. Her generous hips swayed. "I got waylaid by the first mate. Peter kept trying to escort me off the ship."

"Never mind that." Emily waved her over. "Our client is waiting."

Daisy hurried to a seat at the opposite end of the table from Gerry, but Althea swerved and headed for the young woman.

"Just let me grab a hug from our Abby-girl." She squeezed the redhead so tight the tiara slipped onto the young woman's forehead.

Abigail O'Brien adjusted her crown. Her lips parted in a lighthearted smile. "I don't normally dress this fancy for an interview, but I have to greet the children in a few minutes." She brushed her hands down her lap. "Thank you for considering me. Getting help from our ship's famous matchmakers is a real honor."

Althea huffed as she made her way to sit in the middle beside Daisy. "I don't understand why we're doing this. We've never interviewed anyone before. Let's cut the fuss and get to the romance."

"I must admit"—Daisy folded her hands in her lap—"I also don't see the need for a formal inquiry. Why must we go to all this trouble?"

Gerry grumbled. "I was hoping to write another chapter in my novel before we deboarded. Is this really necessary?"

Emily remained silent because she didn't have an answer. This meeting was a last-ditch attempt to shush her cantankerous bones. The charming young woman in front of them was not only willing but asking for assistance. After setting up multiple uncooperative couples, Emily should count it a blessing to have someone enlist their services.

Am I being contrary, Lord? You deposited this precious child in our laps. I should be raising the sails, not dropping anchor. What's the matter with me?

No voice from heaven, angelic choir, or burning bush answered. Even a gentle whisper would've been sufficient. Emily tapped her thumb against the table. She didn't care for the silent treatment.

Abby zeroed in on the head Shipper's agitated thumb. She didn't know them well, but these ladies used to like her. Had something changed their minds?

The silver-haired tribunal stared her down. She averted her gaze from the long table of senior citizens to the muddy brown waves of Galveston Bay outside the windows. Why had she assumed they'd jump at the chance to orchestrate her happily-ever-after?

"What makes you think we can help you?" Gangly Gerry at the end thumped her polished black oxford on the floor like she was marking the seconds it took their examinee to answer.

Abby fidgeted. The cruise ship's dining room waited in all its pristine glory for the new passengers making their way through security. No one should be in here less than an hour before boarding time. But nothing deterred these four women. This boat was their home, and even the captain quailed at telling them no.

Abby gulped. "You . . . you're the Shippers. Experts at relationships. If anyone is lacking in the romance department, you ladies are the ones to call. Everyone knows that."

"Oh mercy." The dainty Daisy on the opposite end pushed a glossy silver lock of hair behind her ear. Her soft-spoken tone hearkened back to humid summer nights and sweet tea on the veranda. "Our work is supposed to be a secret. Did you say everyone knows?"

"Maybe not everyone. Just"—Abby tilted her head—"most people employed on the MS *Buckingham*. You ladies reconciled our last cruise director with his long-lost sweetheart and even caught a rogue detective smuggling cocaine into the States. It's hard to keep that kind of success under wraps."

Emily, the short but commanding woman in the center, drummed her fingers on the table. Her hair stuck out from her head like it was boycotting conditioner. "This might make operations more difficult if the general public is aware of our intentions." Swatting a drooping curl, she continued. "We need to exercise more stealth. Gerry, make a note."

The tall woman flipped open her laptop and began typing at lightning speed. "If the cat's out of the bag, there's no sense trying to stuff it back in. You'll just end up with a scratched face."

"I hate cats." Althea unwrapped the waxed paper from a gooey, chocolate-covered caramel and took a bite. "They always act like they know better than me."

"I'm inclined to side with the cat." Gerry raised her hands from the keys. "Even with my allergies."

"Don't get my dander up." Althea crumpled the candy paper and tossed it on the table.

"Better than cat dander."

"Ladies." Daisy reached down the table to quiet her squabbling compatriots. "We have company." She fetched the discarded litter and tucked it in her purse.

Abby repressed a chuckle. It wouldn't do to offend her interviewers. An uninformed person might mistake these women for a doddering, unfocused quartet, but she knew better. They were clever enough to spend their golden years on a cruise ship instead of in a retirement community. Smart and savvy, the Shippers made the impossible happen.

For Abby, finding true love was proving to be the most impossible of quests.

Emily studied her. "Most clients resent our interference. At least in the beginning. You're the first person who's ever sought us out."

"I really want to get married," Abby admitted without a hint of embarrassment.

"Why?"

"I haven't thought too much about why." She laughed. "Don't most little girls love to stick a curtain on their heads and pretend to walk down the aisle? Not very women's lib, I know. But true. I guess I want to get married because"—she wrinkled her nose—"it's lonely by myself. I'd rather have a partner. Someone to share things with. That guaranteed one person who's always on my side. My best friend."

"Not all husbands are friendly," Daisy drawled.

"Another reason I came to you." Abby waved at the line of ladies. "I need the experts to help me choose wisely. Past experience has shown my taste isn't always trustworthy."

The dining room door whooshed open, and a white-blond head poked through. "Mrs. Windsor!" First mate Peter's frantic blue eyes widened in horror as he scurried to their table. "Why are you still on board?" He skittered around Emily's chair like a nervous hamster. "Ladies, I'm begging you. Please vacate the ship for zero count."

"Forgive us, Peter." Emily slid her walkie-talkie into her roomy handbag. "We had important business."

The statement warmed Abby's heart. Her love life was important to these ladies, even though they barely knew her.

"But it's turnaround day," Peter said.

"Sorry, baby." Althea side-eyed Emily. "We'd have been off the boat an hour ago if *somebody* hadn't called an emergency meeting."

He gaped at his phone. "It's 11:54 a.m. The VIPs are boarding in six minutes."

Daisy flipped open the miniature pendant watch she wore on a gold chain around her neck. "My timepiece says 11:52. Have no fear, Peter. We'll make it." She rose from her seat with the noble grace of a queen.

He sputtered. "I'm not sure that antique—"

Althea wiggled a finger. "Don't discount something just because it's been around awhile. Daisy told me that Masterson heirloom has kept time for a century without losing a second."

Daisy's lips quirked. "It wouldn't dare."

Emily folded her hands on top of the table. "You see, Peter. We have eight minutes. More than enough time. Why not let us stay aboard on turnaround day? You know we're going to walk down the gangplank and come right back up again."

The finicky employee shook his head. "It's not protocol. Because you've received special permission from the owners, you ladies are allowed to leave your belongings in your cabins. But zero count is a nonnegotiable. We can't let the new passengers onto the ship until the old passengers are off."

"Are you calling us old?" Althea's eyebrows puckered, along with her mouth.

Four pairs of Shipper eyes drilled into him.

"N-no, ma'am." Peter retreated. "I meant, I . . . I—" His gaze moved in a wild circuit and landed on Abby. "Aren't you supposed to pass out refreshments to the VIPs while they wait to board?"

"Yes, sir." She hopped from her chair. "I'm sorry."

"We can't risk offending our first-class patrons. Hurry!"

Abby wadded the skirt of her voluminous ball gown and prepared to run.

"Wait." Emily lifted a hand.

Abby flopped back onto her seat.

The older woman glared at Peter as if chastising him for the interruption. "Abby, we'll get more details from you later, but give us a twenty-second summary of what you want in a man."

Abby grinned. "How about a carbon copy of the last husband you found. The guy you matched with my buddy Lacey was a dream come true. Sweet. Considerate. Funny."

"Tall, dark, and drop-dead everything." Althea sighed. "If Jonny had been a few decades older, I'd have kept him for myself."

Abby pointed at Althea and winked. "I'll take one exactly like him, please. Except for the tall part." She stood to her full height of five foot two. The fact she wore tennis shoes under her billowy satin dress didn't help. She rotated in a slow circle. "I'm vertically challenged. I want to look up to my husband in the figurative sense, not the literal. Someone *medium*, dark, and dreamy is fine with me. No one over five foot ten, please."

Spencer Masterson's six-foot-plus frame allowed him to see over the stares of the waiting passengers. He tugged the lapel of his charcoal-colored business suit. A determined sea breeze whipped from one end of the pier to the other, attacking the straight black locks of his carefully styled hair. He pushed the wayward strands into place and smoothed the knot on his navy-blue silk tie.

A man in a floral shirt and Bermuda shorts grumbled beside him. "Who goes on a Caribbean cruise in that getup?"

"I wish *you'd* wear that kind of getup." His female companion tittered.

Spencer rolled his shoulder and pretended he didn't hear their unguarded conversation. A flimsy velvet cord separated the preferred customer line from the teeming mass of regular passengers. The Monarch Cruises VIP experience lacked a few finishing touches.

He checked his watch and sent another text to the office. It took two people to cover his caseload during this little excursion. His jaw clenched as his to-do list ran through his mind. If he concluded this business on the first day at sea, they could charter a plane in Cozumel and fly to New Orleans in time for the trial on Friday. He stuffed the phone in his pocket and shifted the bag of legal briefs to his other hand.

"Excuse me, sir." The woman behind him in the austere gray suit spoke. "The child is hungry." She motioned to the five-year-old at her side.

He glanced at the blond-haired girl in the intricate lace dress who looked nothing like him. His daughter. One hand held the diamond-studded locket around her neck as she grasped her governess with the other. Her confused blue eyes absorbed the surrounding pandemonium. A twinge of guilt hit him. Had she eaten breakfast? He usually made do with a cup of coffee.

"Madeleine"—he crouched to her height—"did you eat this morning?" She blinked. "Y-yes, sir."

Did she think he was reprimanding her? They'd spent only holidays together for the past two years, and he knew next to nothing about being a father. How did one go about communicating with children?

He brightened the pitch of his voice. "Would you like a sna-ack?" The last word squeaked like a cartoon mouse.

Madeleine covered her mouth and giggled.

Heat singed Spencer's neck. He stood up and gestured to Ms. Blanchet, the expensive caregiver his executive assistant had hired from the most prestigious agency in New Orleans. "You're the governess. Didn't you bring any food?"

"Of course I did." The woman straightened her already rigid shoulders. "But you made it clear mealtimes were nonnegotiable."

Spencer stared. Ms. Blanchet's poise remained unruffled. And Spencer stared more. She wavered and tugged open the large leather satchel at her side.

"Perhaps one granola bar won't spoil her lunch." She unwrapped the all-natural, sugar-free snack and passed it to the child. "You said we'll be on the boat for no more than two nights. Correct?"

"Yes. I should complete my business soon. We'll fly from Cozumel to New Orleans."

"Thank you," the little girl murmured.

Spencer's gaze took in the pocket-size stranger below him. His ex-wife's decision to live in New York during their two-year separation meant he'd had few opportunities to spend time with Madeleine. Now that the divorce was finalized and Priscilla had agreed to give him sole custody, he would do everything in his power to make sure his daughter was happy. But how?

Madeleine chewed on her granola bar without complaint.

At least she's quiet. Unlike her mother.

One dubious benefit of his ex-wife's constant criticism had been that it left him in no doubt of her desires. Spencer had been a full-time father for all of three days and still hadn't a clue what his little girl wanted. Would Madeleine tell him if she needed something? Or would their relationship resemble his own childhood? Always passing messages through a bevy of servants and employees.

God?

Spencer swallowed. The awkward sensation of seeking help from an invisible Creator rankled his Masterson pride. He'd been taught to never show weakness to anyone. But he'd recently realized the value in relinquishing things to Someone greater than himself.

I'm new at this whole prayer thing. If you're listening, I could use assistance. Please help me be a father she can trust and depend on. I have no idea where to start.

A musical voice sounded behind him. "Welcome to the MS *Buckingham*, dear honored guests."

He turned to find a diminutive young woman dressed in a long purple gown like a princess from a fairy tale. Her fiery hair curled around her face, and her smile beamed with a warmth to match. She held a silver tray with bottled water.

He would have responded, but she wasn't looking at him. Her twinkling eyes were fixed on Madeleine. She dipped in a curtsy and held out the tray to his daughter.

"Would you care for water, Your Majesty?" She spoke the words in a fake British accent and without a trace of irony, even though her own tiara listed to the side.

Madeleine shook her head. "No, thank you, ma'am."

The wannabe princess stood tall, if five foot two could be considered tall. Her compact but shapely figure turned his way as she lifted the tray. "Water, sir?" The pesky breeze whipped her red hair, and she twisted her full pink lips to puff it away. "Sir?"

"No." He'd paused for only a second, but it bothered him. Why was he so distracted? As the most reputed lawyer in New Orleans, he was never at a loss for words.

She moved to the next passenger in the VIP line. Spencer forced his attention away and focused on the mammoth ship in front of him. The pristine white sides towered above them. Crew members rushed along the decks with armloads of miscellaneous items. A twisting mass of tube slides rose from the pool at the front end of the ship. Near the gangplank, a mariachi band stood in black suits with gold embroidery and wide red ties, filling the air with spirited music. It was a giant, floating amusement park.

Spencer squinted at the festivities. "It baffles me why Daisy is living in a place like this."

CHAPTER 2

THE SHIPPERS STOOD ON THE pier. Semitrucks rumbled in the distance as forklifts unloaded pallets of perishables. The crowd of excited cruisers undulated like an ocean wave, jostling each other in carefree abandon.

A random elbow bumped Emily. She tottered forward, the hard pavement rushing to meet her.

Gerry grabbed her in a death grip. "Careful, now." She hauled her up and blocked Emily's smaller frame from the crowd. "Where's your cane?"

"I don't need that sissy stick."

Gerry had honed the art of silent disapproval during her many years as a librarian. Her thin lips pinched. She eyed her friend like she would an overdue book.

Emily shuffled her feet. "I'm fine. Truly."

"A few months ago, you were in the infirmary with a heart arrhythmia. You should take precautions."

"I can lean on one of the railings for support."

"Forget the railings, honey." Althea slipped a soft hand around Emily's free arm. "Lean on me. I'm much cushier. We can chat about cute little Abby."

Daisy raised her perfectly plucked eyebrows. "What do y'all think of our latest candidate?"

Althea shrugged. "I like her."

"Liking her isn't the problem," Emily said. "Can we help her? Our last match required so much effort, we took a break after the wedding."

"I'd hardly call two weeks a break." Gerry snorted. "And we all saw you making mental notes. I bet you already have a list of prospects for Abby."

Emily didn't bother denying it. The other ladies knew her well. She lived and breathed her mission.

Daisy opened her clutch purse and withdrew an embroidered hand-kerchief. "It makes it easier if she fills out her own background information and preferences. Saves us hours of legwork. My vote is yes."

"You normally don't say much when we choose a client, baby." Althea looped her other arm around Daisy's. "What's different this time?"

Her roommate considered before she answered. "She's spunky but with a gentle spirit. Plus"—the short lady looked up at Althea—"I know how it feels to be a buttercup in a world of long-stemmed roses. My late husband loomed over me. I suggest we find her someone height-appropriate so she doesn't spend the rest of her life with a permanent crick in her neck."

"Sounds good to me," Althea agreed. "I vote yes too."

Emily bounced on the rubber soles of her orthopedic sandals. "What about you, Gerry?"

"It's obvious you're itching to get started." Gerry dragged the strap of her computer bag over her shoulder. "Let's quit lollygagging."

"Mrs. Masterson!" a voice laced with a thick Russian accent beckoned above the clamor. One of the ship's spa employees, Magda, weaved through the passengers. She approached them and extended a black envelope. Her glittery gold nail art sparkled against the dark, heavy paper. "Someone asked me to bring this to you."

Daisy's brow wrinkled. "Who?"

Magda rested her arm on top of her head and scratched her opposite temple. "I do not know. He is not from the boat."

She presented the envelope again. Daisy took it with hesitant fingers and surveyed the crowd as if she expected to find the sender. Magda gave a curt nod and left.

"Pssssssttt."

The airy sound drew their attention. A guard with a freckled bald spot on the back of his head sat facing away at the check-in counter. His lazy gaze swung to them. He gestured with a wink. The Shippers brandished their passports and slipped past the line.

"Thanks, Barney." Emily patted his chubby cheek before heading up the gangplank.

They passed another guard at the ship's threshold. Mr. Everson stood with hands on hips, feet spread apart. He eyed every passenger from behind gunmetal sunglasses. His honey-brown hair was streaked with gold from hours patrolling the outer decks. Though he wasn't more than five foot ten, his black polo shirt stretched across toned muscles, the word SECURITY emblazoned in white letters on the fabric.

"Good morning, Mr. Everson." Althea waved. "Keep up the good work."

His chin jerked down.

Daisy whispered, "I've yet to see that man smile. He's quite intimidating."

"We should find him a wife," Emily said. "She'd soften those rough edges."

"Let's finish the case we've got first," Gerry said. "The girl is hankering to get married. I doubt Abby will take long though. It might not hurt to prep our next client."

The Shippers entered the enormous vessel they'd chosen as home base. Opulent marble floor tiles reflected the light from the crown-shaped crystal chandelier hanging overhead. A winding staircase covered in deep-purple carpet connected the three-storied room. Balconies revealed art-laden hallways stretching in all directions. A musician sat at a baby grand piano, and sweet melodies drifted from under the glossy black lid.

"Home sweet home." Althea spun in a slow circle. "Hey, Daisy. Take a video of me in this dress. I want to show my granddaughter I got her present."

Daisy tucked the envelope in her pocket, then accepted Althea's phone. She murmured pose suggestions, and her friend complied. Behind them, a few couples in understated but elegant vacation clothes wandered through the doors.

Emily grasped her purse handles. "The Sovereign Club members are boarding." She assessed each man walking through the door. "I wonder if any might do for Abby."

Gerry shook her head. "Cruise ship employees aren't allowed to date passengers. That could get her thrown off the boat."

"Like I always say"—Althea unzipped her red, sparkly fanny pack and fished out a piece of candy—"the cruise line can't dictate who you love. If Abby wants to get married, that's her prerogative. She can work somewhere else."

Emily continued to make mental notes of the arriving VIPs, but it was unlikely any of them would be a match for their new client. Not many eligible gentlemen cruised alone.

Gerry sat in a chair and pulled a novel from her bag. "Monarch Cruises knows how to pamper the fancy folks. I wonder how much money big shots pay for the luxury suites and VIP perks."

"More than I got." Althea plopped onto a couch. "But thanks to my frequent-traveler miles, I get almost the same perks for free." She motioned to Daisy and patted the cushion beside her. "Sit down, baby. This will take a while."

Daisy lowered herself onto the seat and straightened the hem of her pleated black skirt. "I wouldn't trade the fanciest accommodation in the fleet for the cabin I share with you."

"Awwwww." Althea wrapped Daisy's slight figure in an embrace and jiggled her back and forth. "I love you too."

Daisy gripped her. "You're shaking me to pieces."

Althea stopped jiggling but kept hugging her. "I can't help it. My best friend is so sweet, I want—well hellooooo, handsome. I haven't seen a gentleman that fine since we left N'Orlins."

The other Shippers turned to the entrance as a tall man in a business suit strode through the lobby. He scanned the room and settled on Daisy. His shiny dress shoes clicked against the floor like a soldier in lockstep. She drooped as he neared and stopped in front of the couch.

Emily didn't care for his calculating gaze. She inserted herself between the stranger and her friends. "Can we help you, young man?"

He ignored her, looking to the shrinking woman seated beside Althea.

"Hello, Daisy." A polite smile crossed his grim face. "Or should I say Mother?"

CHAPTER 3

SPENCER APPRAISED HIS LONG-ABSENT progenitor. She didn't appear any the worse for wear. On the contrary, her cheeks lacked the gaunt pallor he'd noted the last time they'd met.

One year and six months ago. At his father's funeral.

The woman standing in his way moved to a nearby chair.

"Mother?" The full-figured woman beside his parent sat forward. "Is this your son, Daisy?"

"Yes, I . . . he . . . this is my son, Spencer Randolph Masterson." Daisy lifted a trembling hand his direction.

"He's a young thing. You must have had him late."

"I was in my forties."

The stranger shuddered. "I bet that hurt. But what a good-looking boy you produced." She popped off the couch and grabbed his waist. "Hello, baby. Give me some sugar." She bussed his cheek with her wide lips. "Any child of Daisy's is a child of mine."

Spencer leaned away. Who was this woman? And what relation did she have with his mother?

She laughed. "You act just like your momma used to. Guess I'll have to train you too. It's good to see family."

His real family remained on the sofa, her posture as stiff as the spine of a law book. They had never been close, but maybe Madeleine would be the much-needed catalyst that brought them together.

"Did your wife come with you?" Daisy asked.

"I no longer have a wife. We've finalized our divorce."

"Bless your heart"—the lady still holding him patted his back—"I'm sorry to hear that."

Daisy looked anything but sorry. Relieved, in fact. "What are you doing here?"

Spencer disengaged himself from the overly affectionate woman. "I was worried about you. You vanished after the funeral, and no one has seen you since."

"How long did it take you to notice I was missing?" Her delicate eyebrows rose.

Spencer gritted his teeth. Did she have to paint him as an unfeeling robot? Of course he'd known his mother was on an extended holiday. He'd checked with her housekeeper more than once since Daisy had taken off. But starting an argument wasn't the most amicable way to begin a reconciliation. Safer to change the subject. "I've been aware of your lengthy vacation for a while. Don't you think it's time to come home?"

The hugger settled on the couch again, as if she had a say in the conversation.

"Home?" Daisy scoffed. "And where would that be?"

"In New Orleans. With your friends and family."

"I have both right here on this ship."

"That's right, baby." The woman beside his mother wrapped an arm around her. "We take good care of your momma."

"I beg your pardon." Spencer glowered. "Who exactly are you?"

"Althea Jones." She held out her hand. "I'm your mother's roommate. We share a cabin."

"You . . . you share?" He made no move to take her hand as he laughed at the absurd notion. Daisy Randolph Masterson, the woman who reserved two seats in first class on a commercial flight because she didn't want to risk sitting by a talker, was sharing a cabin with this woman.

A *cabin*?

"It's cheaper with two in a room," the newly introduced Althea said.

"She and I can stretch our dollars further. Between the four of us, we manage to save our pennies on the extras."

"I'm sorry. The *four* of you?" Had his mother gotten involved in some crazy cult?

"We wondered when you'd introduce us." A voice spoke behind him. Two older women watched from the seats nearby. The tall one grasped an open novel.

The other lady with the frizzy hair, who'd blocked his way, gave him a once-over and shook her head. "I'm afraid we're going to have trouble with this one."

Three unfriendly faces and the still-smiling Althea stared at him. He hadn't expected his mother to have bodyguards.

The noise level increased as a new wave of passengers walked through the doors. Bodies filled the lobby. Staff members in pristine white uniforms with purple accents rushed to assist them.

"Excuse me, sir." Ms. Blanchet joined him with her young charge. "We've finished in the restroom."

Madeleine! He'd forgotten her again. No one would be nominating him for father of the year.

"Can we wait for you in the suite?" the caregiver asked. "It's getting crowded here."

Daisy's attention fixed on the little girl. Her brow wrinkled, and she leaned forward slightly. Did she recognize her granddaughter? Madeleine had been three when they'd last met.

His daughter's hand rested on her stomach. Was she still hungry? Had the granola bar been enough? Spencer opened his mouth to ask, but a cheerful greeting stopped him.

"Welcome to the MS *Buckingham*." The redhead from the pier approached their group. She still wore the billowing purple ball gown and carried a basket piled with gold crowns and rhinestone-studded tiaras. She retrieved one, set her basket on the floor, and crouched at eye level with his daughter. "Hello again. Is this your first time sailing?"

Madeleine's head bobbed. "Yes, ma'am."

"Oh my. You have such lovely manners. Are you nervous?"

Another nod.

"I have just the thing." The woman extended the golden tiara with both hands. "This is a courage crown. Any girl who feels a bit scared can place it on her head, and her bravery rises. Would you care to try?"

A third nod.

The employee set the crown gently on top of Madeleine with all the solemnity of an actual coronation and clasped her hands to her chest. "You look like a princess!"

His daughter grinned. Spencer couldn't remember the last time he'd seen her so happy. This woman had a way about her.

The child whisperer adjusted the tiara. "What's your name, sweetie?"

"Madeleine."

"Madeleine!" Daisy sprang to her feet.

The little girl jumped and scooted behind the gray-skirted legs of her governess.

"Yes." Spencer glanced at his mother. "As you may have gathered, this is your granddaughter, Madeleine Rothschild Masterson."

The redhead craned her neck in an exaggerated arc to make eye contact with his daughter. "What a perfect name. Did you know there was a famous queen of Scotland named Madeleine?"

The child emerged from her hiding place and gave a slight shake of her head.

"She was one of the most courageous queens who ever lived." The woman leaned forward. "Madeleine is the perfect name for a brave girl like you."

His daughter's full smile broke out, and Spencer's heart cracked. He contemplated the person who'd caused the miracle, and her answering smile beamed.

Who *was* this woman?

Abby possessed a certain talent. A gift. Something that came in handy in her line of work. She could read a child in ten seconds. A quirk of the eyebrow or curl of the lip alerted her to troublemakers. And an overly innocent appearance or sweet-as-sugar simper didn't hide a bully's intentions. But this little girl . . .

This little girl broke her heart.

She was dressed in expensive pink lace, and a gold locket with a diamond bigger than most engagement rings dangled from her neck. She obviously lacked nothing material. Yet her anxious eyes told Abby she was missing all the important things that made a child feel loved and at ease.

Abby took stock of the gentleman beside her. "Is this your father?"

Madeleine paused, then nodded.

Abby observed the man. Her talent for reading people didn't extend to adults. Once a person passed into maturity, they grew better at hiding themselves. His suit was out of place in this festive environment, and his handsome face gave nothing away. Two dark, almost black eyes returned her scrutiny. But he didn't look cruel. Cold and reserved, yes. But not a monster.

Abby rose from her crouched position. "I'm Abigail O'Brien, a member of the childcare team. Have you enrolled Madeleine in our day care service? We offer many different activities."

"There's no need. I've brought a governess to care for her."

Sourpuss. The thought came unbidden to Abby's mind. She wasn't sure if she meant the dad or the nanny. It applied to both.

"I see." Abby spotted another young girl entering the lobby and slipped a fresh tiara from her basket. "If you change your mind, she's always welcome." She tapped his daughter's nose. "Glad I got to meet you, Madeleine. I hope to see you again."

"Bye." The child waved with her hand held close to her body.

Abby waggled her fingers, reclaimed her basket, and turned to leave.

"Just a minute," the father said. It was a command, not a request.

The crowns clattered as she faced him. He stood still without saying anything. The seconds ticked, and the silence crackled between them. She fingered the rhinestones.

He finally spoke. "How much do I owe you for the tiara?"

Abby opened her mouth but closed it as her mind filtered her first response. The customer was always right. "No charge, sir." She winked at Madeleine. "Every princess deserves a crown."

Emily flashed her eyebrows at Gerry. It appeared finding a match for their latest client might be easier than they anticipated. An interesting marriage prospect had presented himself in short order. Daisy's divorced son, no less. Their fellow Shipper could fill in the required information sheet and save them the trouble of a background check.

Thanks for minimizing the paperwork, Lord!

Spencer Masterson cut a striking figure. His honed physique filled out his tailored suit like a modern-day Cary Grant. The prepossessing visitor refocused from the departing Abby to his mother. But Daisy's attention was glued to her grandchild.

"Madeleine." Her voice cracked.

Her son adjusted the pristine cuff of his dress shirt. "For heaven's sake, don't make a scene."

Daisy's body tightened. She elevated her chin the slightest bit and pointed dry eyes at him. "You remind me of your father. I can't recall how many times he admonished me with those exact words. I admit it's difficult to compose myself when the granddaughter I've met only three times stands before me, but I'll do my best."

Emily rose halfway from her seat. A hand restrained her. Althea had slipped alongside, an unusually pensive expression on her usually jolly face. She shook her head. "Let them duke it out on their own."

Madeleine shifted from one foot to the other. Her dress swayed around her slender legs. She patted the ridges of the tiara atop her head and hummed to herself.

Daisy's gaze returned to her. "She's beautiful."

"Yes." Her son's face softened when he looked at his daughter. "As a baby, she had dark hair. It's lightened, like strands of sunlight."

"Do they offer poetry classes on this boat?" Spencer took inventory of his mother. "I don't recall you being so effusive."

Daisy ignored him. "Her hair. Her delicate cheekbones. She inherited nothing from the Masterson side of the gene pool. I hope that's also true of her personality."

She reached to touch Madeleine's face, but her granddaughter jumped in surprise. Daisy halted. She fumbled in her pocket for the envelope and then fanned her flushed cheeks. "What brings you here, Spencer?"

"Would you believe I've missed you?"

Daisy's makeshift fan stilled, and her refined mask slipped a fraction. "I wish that were true."

A shrill laugh sounded from the entrance. A woman in a floor-length sundress and floppy, oversize hat was recording with her phone as she explored the lobby. Children squealed. Mariachi music drifted from a balcony. The joyful melody contrasted with the silent standoff between mother and son.

Emily weighed Daisy's offspring in the balance and found him wanting. How dare he come aboard their ship and upset the sweetest member of the posse? She'd like to give him the spanking he deserved, but that might embarrass his mother.

The sugary scent of fresh-baked cookies wafted from a nearby table. A tourist in a rainbow tracksuit and straw fedora jostled Spencer as he headed for the fragrant display of snickerdoodles. The crowd swelled around them, and a teenager bumped Madeleine's shoulder. Spencer caught her in his arms and used his body to protect her from the swarm of people.

"Are you hurt?" He scanned her from head to toe.

"No, sir." She ducked as another surge of passengers passed.

He placed a hand on her shoulder and turned to Daisy. "Let's discuss the reason for our reunion when there are fewer distractions. If you give me your number, I'll call you."

Daisy resumed her fanning. "I don't have a phone."

"You don't have a . . . Do you expect me to swallow that?"

Althea sprang from the sofa. "It's true. She's the most untechy person I ever met." After scuttling to her friend's left side, she put a protective arm around Daisy. "How 'bout I give you my number? We're always together anyway."

Althea exchanged phone numbers with him. Emily rose and drew close to Daisy's starboard side, and Gerry filled the gap behind them. They flanked Daisy like a protective guard.

Her son eyed their cluster with the lift of an eyebrow. "I'll call you, and we can meet for supper."

"I'm sorry." Daisy's unconcerned face belied the words. "I'm dining with my friends."

"What about afterward?"

"I have a prior engagement."

He clenched his jaw. "I've traveled all this way to see you. Can't you reschedule?"

"That's impossible. I promised my roommate I'd accompany her to bingo."

"To where?"

"Bingo," Emily interjected. "You must have heard of it. Those squares with letters and numbers where you try to make a straight line."

Althea sang, "*B-I-N-G-O, B-I-N-G-O.*"

He stared at them, mouth open. Daisy reached out and lifted his chin. His teeth snapped shut.

"You may join us if you like," she said. "We're meeting in the main lounge at seven."

"I . . ." He buttoned his suit coat. "Yes. Thank you. Until seven, then."

Althea gave him a thumbs-up. "See you then."

"Yes." Gerry crossed her arms. "*All* of us."

His face communicated his displeasure, but he strode away without another word, the nanny and little girl rushing to catch up.

Emily mentally deleted him from the prospect list. She liked Abby too much to couple her with a grouch like this one. No man that bad-tempered deserved their quality matchmaking services.

Daisy sagged, and Althea caught her by the arm.

Gerry placed a bracing hand to Daisy's back. "You aren't going to swoon, are you?"

Emily fetched her large purse. "I'm not sure how you kept a civil tongue in your head."

"I've had plenty of practice." Daisy clutched the black envelope she'd received from Magda. "Almost fifty years of marriage to an iceberg taught me restraint. I fear his son's visit will be neither pleasant nor caring."

Gerry pointed at the note. "Have you read your mail yet?"

"Hmmm?" Daisy squinted. "Oh! I'd forgotten." She slipped a French-manicured fingernail under the flap and withdrew a white note card with no picture or writing on the cover. She opened it, read for a second, and gasped.

"What is it?" Emily peered over her friend's shoulder.

She barely read anything before Daisy crumpled the paper. The petite woman wavered like a flag in the wind.

"Whoa." Emily caught her around the waist. "I'm supposed to be the unsteady one. Remember?"

Daisy disengaged herself, stepping back with the wadded note behind her. "If y'all will excuse me, it's been a trying afternoon. I should retire to my cabin for a rest."

"I'll come with you." Althea followed her. "A nap would suit me fine."

"Go ahead." Emily waved them away. "We'll see you later."

The two left, and a spot of black on the carpet drew Emily's attention. The envelope. Daisy must have dropped it in her haste. Emily took more time than she liked to crouch and retrieve it. She didn't want to risk a broken hip. Her balance was still a bit shaky since her last health scare.

A quick examination of the envelope revealed it was empty. She studied the unaddressed front. No clue as to who sent it or why. Perhaps she should feel guilty for peeking at the letter's contents, but Emily was too concerned about Daisy to quibble about the propriety of her actions. She only regretted not seeing more of the message. But two important words had caught her eye.

Indiscretion.

Money.

CHAPTER 4

BINGO NIGHT IN THE MAIN lounge held all the charm that Spencer had expected.

None.

Waiters zipped down the aisles with drink trays held high over their heads. Underdressed people packed the navy-blue couches that curved in the shape of horseshoes. They spread their paper cards on the tables in front of them and waited with giant markers poised.

He spotted Daisy and her friends in a corner, sitting side by side. His mother's roommate waved with her hands held high.

"Over here, baby."

Spencer ignored the intrusive glances of other passengers as he joined the older ladies. Was it really so unusual to wear a suit on a cruise? Considering the number of tank tops and flip-flops surrounding him, yes.

Why couldn't Daisy have taken a tour of Europe or rented an apartment in Manhattan? The idea of his prim, well-bred matriarch on this noisy ship didn't compute. And who were these crazy women with her?

He approached the table, and his mother looked behind him. "You didn't bring Madeleine?"

"No. The new environment must be very stimulating for her, and I prefer she spend a quiet evening in our suite. Besides, it was nearing her bedtime."

The frizzy-haired friend sitting beside Daisy quirked an eyebrow. "This early?"

"She has certain nightly routines to fulfill. Listening to classical music. Reading a story. Skin care and brushing her teeth."

The tall, bony one asked, "Who's taking care of her?"

Why was that any of her business? "I hired the best governess in Louisiana."

"Governess?" Sarcasm tinged her response. "Is her name Jane Eyre?"

The one he remembered as Althea butted in. "Most people just say nanny."

His mother placed a hand on the woman's arm. "You must forgive him. My son always uses the most haughty, indistinguishable terms possible. He's like his father in that way."

Which was worse? Being castigated for his speech or compared to his father?

Spencer suppressed the ill-mannered words rising in his throat. In the old days, he'd have answered with a scathing reply, but his recent conversion had changed things. The Bible he found comfort in every morning encouraged him to hold his tongue.

Or try to.

"The *nanny* came with sterling references. Ms. Blanchet speaks Spanish, French, and Chinese, and she has multiple degrees in child psychology and education."

Althea sniffed. "Can she sing a good lullaby?"

Lullaby? Did little girls need those? It had never occurred to him. And from the look on this woman's face, she knew it. Was his incompetence as a father that obvious?

Spencer straightened his tie. "Singing ability was not a requirement."

A Monarch employee wearing a green sequined jacket and matching pants crossed the stage. The audience clapped, and the short, older man with silvery red hair tweaked his face mic.

"I wish you were that happy to see me." An Irish accent tinged the man's words. "But I suspect you're more excited that I'll be calling out the numbers. Am I right?"

People hooted and whistled.

"Look, Spencer"—the small, bossy woman by his mother smirked—"you're not the only one in a suit."

Althea scooted over and patted the couch beside her. "Sit down, baby. We bought you a six-pack."

"You . . . you purchased a—"

"Six-pack." She waved a long piece of paper with bingo squares on it. "That's what they call these game boards that have six cards on them. More chances to win."

"Thank you, but I'd rather not play."

"Don't be so stinkin' stuffy." She grabbed his sleeve and tugged him down. Passing a thick marker to him, she pointed at the paper. "Use this dabber to highlight whatever number Seamus calls. That's the man onstage. He has a crush on our Gerry."

Spencer grasped the unwieldy pen and looked around the table in confusion.

On the opposite side of the couch, the skinny one, who must be Gerry, raised her eyes from the book she was reading. "There's no need to tell tales to strangers."

"It's no tale. Seamus is crazy about you, and you know it. Besides, Spencer's no stranger." Althea rubbed his shoulder. "He's family."

A giant bingo card projected on the screen behind the aforementioned Seamus. He walked to a podium where a computer sat and pressed a button. The round ball on the right of the screen flickered until it stopped on a number.

"B-14," he shouted.

"Woo-hoo!" Althea stamped her paper. "It's gonna be a good night. I can feel it."

Daisy observed Spencer. "You were separated for quite a while. When did the divorce become final?"

He sat with his spine rigid, not touching the back of the couch. "Two months ago."

Murmurs came from all four women.

"N-36." The caller tap-danced across the stage for no apparent reason.

"Has Madeleine been with you since then?" Daisy asked.

"No. Priscilla agreed to give me sole custody, but she asked for time to say goodbye. Madeleine arrived in New Orleans three days ago." The reminder he would never again be subjected to his ex-wife's stifling disapproval still brought an inner peace. Even more so because he could protect his daughter from Priscilla's exacting personality. "I expect we won't be seeing much of her mother."

Althea made a sympathetic face. "Does Madeleine miss her momma much?"

"Never mentions her." Spencer rotated the pen in his hand. "Masterson offspring are used to living without their parents." His gaze cut to Daisy.

Her eyes lowered, and she unsnapped her purse to retrieve a handkerchief.

The frizzy-haired woman frowned. "So who watches over the children, comforts them, gives them love? The governess?"

The man onstage spoke above the audience chatter. "Gerry, do you be needing any particular number? I'm not above rigging the game for you."

Grumbles sounded from the crowd, and he held up both hands.

"Just a joke, friends. A man's got to catch the lady's attention somehow. G-52."

Spencer tried to tune out the bingo numbers being called and checked the time on his phone. Would he get back to the room before Madeleine fell asleep? Althea leaned over his arm and placed a few purple circles on his paper.

"O-74."

"Oooh, oooh, oooh!" Althea bounced. "I'm getting close." She added another purple mark to her paper and sang, "*B-I-N-G-O, B-I-N-G-O.*"

He focused on his mother. This was hardly the ideal time to broach the subject of her return, but he wasn't sure she'd give him another chance. "As you can imagine, it's a new experience for me, raising Madeleine alone. I'm hoping you will come home to New Orleans where you can be near her."

"Why?" Her voice remained cordial. "You didn't want me involved in her life before."

An awkward question, but one he understood. Being married to his father had given her a suspicious nature.

"I feel it's important to—"

"I-22." The Irish emcee pointed to the screen.

"You got it." Althea squinted at Daisy's card. "You got it, baby. You got it!" She thrust her fists in the air like a prize fighter. "Bingo!" Althea pushed him off the couch. "Let your momma out. She won."

He stumbled but managed not to land on the floor. She scooted over, stood beside him, and helped Daisy to her feet.

Spencer watched dumbstruck as his mother, the queen of New Orleans society, made her way to the front amid the cheers and disappointed moans of rowdy cruisers. If he believed in doppelgängers, he might worry she'd been replaced with an impostor. She collected an envelope from the emcee and returned to their table.

"What did you win?" Althea asked.

"A spa day." Daisy flourished her certificate in the air.

"Perfect prize for you." Althea let her roommate slip back on the couch, then returned to her seat. "Don't worry, Spencer. There's another round. We might get 'em yet."

The ding of his phone prevented him from answering. He withdrew the device from his pocket, opened his texts, and groaned.

"What's wrong?" Daisy rose slightly. "Is it Madeleine?"

"No, the governess." He dropped his cell on the table. "She's seasick."

CHAPTER 5

NINE HOURS IN A BALL gown was akin to wearing a satin straitjacket. How did Cinderella do it? Abby tugged at the too-tight bodice. She'd better cut out desserts or she wouldn't be able to fit in this outfit a month from now.

Wait! She wouldn't be wearing this dress then. In three weeks, she'd finish her last cruise duty and trade her tiara for a cardigan and her Monarch name tag for a teacher's ID badge. The thought of reentering the school system shot fireworks to her fingertips. Life was perfect except for one important detail. Being a teacher was only half of her dream. Being a wife and mom was the other half.

Please, Lord. Let the Shippers find my special someone. Caring. Handsome. Dark hair. Not too tall. Sense of humor. Decent job.

She laughed at her own audacity.

Never mind, God. I know you've got this. Forget the list. But please make it soon!

At least her greeter duty was finished. She grasped the remaining stack of royal purple invitations and snuck in the back door of the main lounge. The Shippers had entered earlier, and she wanted to see if there were any updates before she changed her clothes.

People lingered in the aisles. Bingo must be over. She saw her matchmakers at a back table but halted at who was sitting with them. The haughty father from the lobby. How could this snob be the son of amiable Daisy? He'd shed his fancy suit coat, but his crisp white shirtsleeves were still buttoned at the wrist and did nothing to soften his demeanor. The man radiated a potent mix of business and charisma. He was gorgeous in an untouchable movie star way.

Althea noticed her and waved. "Come give me a hug right quick."

Abby hurried over, embraced the loving woman, and greeted the others. "Hi, Shippers." She looked at the father. "Hello again."

He stood from the couch with a slight dip of his head. "Good evening."

His steady dark eyes locked on her ball gown. Was he wondering why she was still dressed like an escapee from an amusement park?

She held out an invitation card. "We're having a Day-at-Sea Jamboree in the play center tomorrow. I'm sure Madeleine would enjoy it. And it would give you and your wife some time off."

"My wife?"

"The woman who was with you in the lobby."

"That's the governess I mentioned. She's taking care of Madeleine." His lip curled. "My ex-wife wouldn't be caught dead on a cruise ship."

"I see." No surprise he was divorced. What woman wanted to live with such a wet blanket?

"And what was your name again?" he asked.

"I'm Abigail O'Brien, a member of the childcare team. It's nice to meet you, Mister . . . ?"

"Spencer Randolph Masterson."

"How do you do, Mr. Masterson?" She longed to drop a snarky curtsy.

"Forgive my lack of manners," Daisy said. "Abby, this is my son."

"Wonderful!" She extended the purple invitation. "If Madeleine is Daisy's granddaughter, be assured I'll treat her like family."

"I appreciate the offer." He made no move to take the card. "But my daughter is shy, and I wouldn't want her to feel uncomfortable. As I mentioned before, I've brought adequate childcare."

Althea elbowed his leg. "You said the nanny was seasick. What if she's still upchucking in the morning? Will Maddie hang out with you?"

Abby's lips twitched at his panicked expression. She poked the invitation closer. "I'll leave this with you, in case of an emergency."

This time he took it. His long, lean fingers brushed hers as the card transferred hands. He jerked away and smoothed his already impeccable silk tie. "Thank you. I'll keep the service in mind, should the need arise."

"Yes, sir." This time Abby did bob a curtsy. "Good night, ladies." She fluttered her stack of cards at the Shippers.

Emily folded her bingo card. "Don't you worry, Abby. I'll have a list of viable candidates completed soon. We're studying the options now." Her gaze turned to Spencer.

"Yes!" Abby twirled. "I can't wait."

A bewildered Mr. Masterson contemplated them. "I'm afraid I'm not following."

"Haven't you heard?" She grinned. "You're hanging out with our ship's most notorious passengers. They orchestrate love matches."

"Pardon me." He bent his head. "They orchestrate what kind of matches?"

"Love matches." Abby's composure faltered at the handsome face so near her own. It was like staring into the sun. She feared she might go blind from the overpowering glory. An inviting scent filled her senses. Probably an expensive cologne no man she'd ever dated could afford. "They helped my friend Lacey find—"

A condescending snort issued from Mr. Masterson. "Are you telling me my *mother* is dispensing advice on *love*?"

Emily scowled while poor Daisy wilted like an overheated orchid.

The man rested a hand on the couch. "I'd hardly call Daisy an authority on the subject."

Gerry raised her pointy chin and glared at him with all the fervor of a retired librarian. "Young man, your mother has helped bring together more than one happy couple."

"Too bad she never used this so-called expertise in her own marriage. Does your little club charge people?"

"Pish-tosh!" Emily stood and tossed her bingo card on the table. "We do it out of the goodness of our hearts."

"Goodness?" He disregarded the older women and addressed Abby. "I can't speak for Daisy's friends, but you'd do well to steer clear of any romantic help offered by my mother."

Abby clenched the remaining invitations. She'd been the cause of the current disharmony, but she wasn't sure how to fix it. "Please—"

Ding.

Mr. Masterson checked his phone, fetched his coat from the back of the couch, and shoved the cell in his pocket. "If you'll excuse me, the governess is still unwell and wants to visit the infirmary. I need to relieve her and take care of my daughter."

He pivoted to Abby. She craned her neck to make eye contact with the imposing man. Was this how David felt when he faced Goliath?

She pointed at the card. "Don't forget. We'd love to see Madeleine at our jamboree."

A short incline of his head was his only answer before he walked away.

Abby released a dramatic breath and turned to the Shippers. "I'm sorry about the slipup. I didn't realize revealing your matchmaking would put Mr. Masterson in such a snit. I mean—"

"Everything puts my son in a snit," Daisy said. "There's no need to apologize for his incivility."

"He's not that bad."

Emily cocked her head. "He's not?"

"I mean, sure." Abby tugged at her sash. "He's not the friendliest person, but he obviously cares for his daughter. And he left right away so his sick employee could visit the doctor. That counts for something."

Gerry scribbled in a small leather notebook, and Abby tried to read over her shoulder. Before she could make out the words, Gerry snapped it shut. The woman gave a quick nod to their leader.

Abby waggled her eyebrows at Emily. "So when do you start setting me up with eligible bachelors?"

The boss Shipper's lips curved upward. "You can rest assured, dear. We're considering every angle."

CHAPTER 6

EMILY WAITED BY THE ENTRANCE of the starboard-side lounge, tapping her black three-ring binder against her chin. A family of four entered. The mother and father gushed about the previous evening's buffet dinner while their two boys hunched over their game consoles. Behind them stood a young couple.

Correction. *Half* a young couple.

The man's close-cropped brown hair hinted of gray at the scalp, where his dye job was growing out. A woman in her twenties wrapped around his waist like a second belt. From the way she giggled and cooed, Emily wondered if they were May–December newlyweds. She checked the woman's left hand. No diamonds. But on the man's ring finger was a slightly lighter band of flesh.

Emily studied him—the wary way his eyes darted around the room as if searching for anyone he knew. The couple sidled off to a secluded table behind a potted plant. Emily shook her head.

"Yep." Althea slid beside her. "A cheater if I ever saw one. I wonder if his poor wife is sitting at home, believing he's on a business trip."

Daisy arrived on Emily's other side. "Perhaps he's recently divorced."

A familiar snort came from Gerry as she joined the party. "Perhaps that's his real hair color too."

"Let's ignore the shameful choices of others, girls." Emily gathered her friends and pushed them toward the windows. "We've got a real romance to arrange."

The Shippers picked a table away from the pedestrian traffic for their strategy meeting.

Emily positioned her chair in the corner—a perfect vantage point to observe the room while enjoying the window view at her elbow. She slid the curtain back to let in more light. Blue water waved hello like an old friend from the other side of the glass.

"Time to draft our battle plan. How many viable candidates do we have for Abby?"

Gerry tapped a few laptop keys. "Three, plus one under consideration."

"That's all?" Althea asked. "She's such a cute, cheerful thing. I'd expect the men would be lining up to date her."

"It's not about who's interested," Emily said. "It's about who deserves her. A man who's kind, dependable, and has a good relationship with the Lord. Those aren't so easy to find."

"Handsome too." Althea stuck a finger in the air. "Might as well go for broke if we're asking for the impossible."

"Not a bad idea." Emily laced her hands together. "Why don't we ask for guidance from the One who specializes in making the impossible possible."

They bowed their heads, and Emily prayed. "Dear Lord, you brought Abby to us for a reason. Help us find the man you intended for her. Let him be honest, trustworthy, and fun."

Daisy spoke reverently. "We ask that he treat her with respect and consideration. Let him be a loving partner who supports her dreams and aspirations."

Gerry prayed next. "Please give him the wisdom of Knightley. The good humor of Tilney. The constancy of Wentworth. And the simmering passion of Mr. Darcy."

Althea finished. "And please, Lawd, let him be easy on the eyes. Someone Abby will be happy to look at across the breakfast table for the next sixty years."

They concluded the prayer, and Gerry slipped her glasses on her nose. She spun her laptop around to the other women. It showed a picture of a slim man wearing ironed khakis with a black leather belt and a button-down shirt, tucked in neat and precise.

"Candidate number one," she said. "Norville Boynton, the honorary chaplain for this voyage."

"Doesn't give us much time." Emily took notes in her binder. "What are his qualifications?"

"Age thirty-one. Graduated from a respected seminary six years ago. Pastors a small Methodist church in Cape Canaveral, Florida. Does missionary work every summer at an orphanage in South America."

The air-conditioning blew from the vent over their heads. Daisy withdrew a handkerchief from her purse and pressed it to her nostrils. "He fulfills the height requirement Abby gave us. Tall enough that she can wear heels, but just barely."

"Something's off." Althea's mouth scrunched at the corner. "Don't get me wrong. I'm all for helping the ministry. My son-in-law works harder than any man I know pastoring his church in Chicago. But how did this Boynton guy stay single so long? Thirty-one years is a long time to wait if he's truly walking the straight and narrow. We don't want Abby marrying a cold fish."

"Althea"—Daisy wrung her handkerchief—"that's no way to refer to a member of the clergy."

"I'm inclined to agree with her." Gerry typed away. "No woman wants to crawl into bed with an ice cube."

"Ladies!" Daisy's handkerchief flapped like a signal flag.

Emily's fingers drummed the table. "Deep-six the chatter, girls. We've got work to do. Who's candidate number two, Gerry?"

"Peter." Gerry clicked a button, and a picture appeared of the first mate in his dress whites, a cap tucked under his arm, his blue eyes wide with earnest fervor.

Althea laughed. "Peter? He's skinnier than a Catholic at Lent. And fussy as all get-out."

"He does like to remind us of the rules," Emily admitted. "But he's a good boy. And very accommodating."

"Indeed." Daisy put her signal flag away. "He's always checking on us. And he's a regular member of the staff. That eliminates the time constrictions we encounter with the minister."

"Good point." Emily made a note. "Although Abby's so eager, I don't think she'll mind us rushing her a bit."

"Still not feeling it." Althea held up three fingers. "Next."

Gerry scrolled down her computer screen. "Candidate number three requires a bit of finagling. He's not aboard the ship."

"Say that again." Althea propped a hand on her hip.

"He's a dock manager in Galveston." Gerry spun her laptop again. It showed a burly man with abundant black curls. "I've talked with Diego Gutierrez several times on our turnaround days."

"As have I." Emily nodded. "He's a personable young man. Although he's the youngest of six boys, he takes care of his aging mother, works hard at his job, and attends church every Sunday. I can tell he's on the up-and-up."

"And brawny to boot." Althea whistled. "He must lift a lot of boxes to earn those muscles. Imagine the cute, curly-headed kids he and Abby could make together."

"You said he's in Texas," Daisy said. "How are we to arrange a match if they're an ocean apart?"

"The old-fashioned way." Gerry swiped her finger over the mouse pad. "Or should I say new-fashioned? Back in the day, people corresponded with letters for months before marrying sight unseen. At least now they can talk to each other face-to-face through the internet." An online meeting app filled the screen. "Since Abby's been hinting at us for months, I already laid the groundwork with Diego when we were in port last time. He's seen Abby from a distance and is definitely interested. All we have to do is set a chat time."

Emily steepled her fingers. "I love your forethought, Gerry. This opens a whole new range of prospects."

Althea leaned away. "That twinkle in your eye scares me. We're not going to launch an online dating business, are we?"

"Not at this time. But if things go well with Diego, it's another option to keep in mind for the future."

Daisy tugged her cashmere wrap closer. "What about the last option you mentioned? Why is the gentleman 'under consideration' instead of an official candidate?"

Gerry took off her spectacles and swiped them against her sleeve. "Well, he's a . . . that is . . . Circumstances are a bit difficult to predict with the last one."

"Oh, tell her." Emily swatted her hand. "The last one is your son."

Althea grasped Daisy's arm, but her roomie sat perfectly composed at the revelation. Her expression didn't alter by so much as the flick of an eyelash. Then she cleared her throat.

"This simplifies the process. Please take Spencer off the list, and we can concentrate on the other three. My son is a poor choice for this match."

"Why?" Gerry's eyebrows lowered. "Do you think Abby isn't good enough for him?"

"Quite the opposite." Daisy tilted her head a degree to the right. "Spencer takes after his father. Don't subject a sweet girl like Abby to the same smothering lifestyle I endured."

"Aren't you being a tad harsh?" Emily asked. "Maybe he just needs the right woman to soften his—"

"Isn't a good relationship with the Lord your uppermost requirement for a candidate?" Daisy dropped her wrap from her shoulders and fanned herself. "I can assure you, my son only attends church to establish connections and maintain his social image. He wouldn't heed the voice of the Almighty even if it spoke to him from a pillar of fire."

"God, help me," Spencer whispered.

He stood on the deck and stared at the little girl by his side. Was she hungry? Tired? Should he carry her? His inadequate attempts at caring for his daughter this morning had only confirmed the obvious—he stank at being a father. But Madeleine never complained, even when he'd made an absolute mess of her hair attempting to brush it into a ponytail. Now it drooped from the crown of her head in a loose, flyaway mess with silken bumps protruding on all sides of the rubber band.

Spencer eyed the childcare entrance with distrust. A faux castle stretched above the double glass doors, and a banner proclaiming Kids Kingdom fluttered in the wind. It somehow seemed wrong to leave his daughter with complete strangers. What if the staff was incompetent? What if the other children bullied her?

But he lacked the capability to watch her alone. The last time he'd seen the governess was when she'd pushed past him for another trip to the bathroom. She'd stumbled straight to her room afterward. It was safe to assume she'd be incommunicado for the rest of the voyage.

He studied Madeleine for any signs of panic. She was harder to read than a hostile witness. He hunkered down and placed a hand on her shoulder. "If you don't want to stay here, you can come back to the suite with me."

"Is that Princess Maddie?" A joyous voice drew his attention.

Abigail O'Brien held open a glass door. She'd traded her ridiculous ball gown for a pair of dark-purple shorts and a white polo shirt with the Monarch crown logo stitched on the pocket.

He relaxed at the sight of her. Instincts honed from years of selecting courtroom juries told him she could be trusted. Her candid smile made a person feel welcome.

Spencer rose and extended a hand. "Good morning, Ms. O'Brien."

She hurried forward and squatted in front of Madeleine. Her chin twitched as she studied the girl. "Did your daddy do your hair?"

"Yes, ma'am," Madeleine said. "I don't think he knows how to make a ponytail."

The redhead chuckled. "I think you're right."

Spencer's hand drooped in midair. While he was impressed the woman was so diligent about making young passengers happy, it irked him that the entire conversation had been directed at his daughter. He wasn't used to being ignored. Especially by someone who interested him.

Wait. Not interested. Intrigued.

No. That wasn't the word either.

This woman was . . . unusual.

The unconcerned lady finally stood and focused on him. She clasped the back of her neck and moaned. "Wow. It's a long way up to look you in the eye. What brings you here, Mr. Masterson?"

He made no effort to lessen the distance between them. "Our governess is indisposed, and it's necessary to leave Madeleine here for a few hours while I conduct business."

"Business?" Her mouth twisted. "Aren't you on vacation?"

"My purpose on the MS *Buckingham* is in no way recreational. Once I accomplish my objective, we'll take a flight from the nearest port to Louisiana. I won't leave Madeleine with you for more than today."

"What a shame." She knelt and wrapped an arm around his daughter's shoulders. "We've planned all sorts of fun adventures."

A shadow of curiosity crossed his daughter's face. "Adventures?"

"Oh, so many. A treasure hunt. A water balloon fight with pirates. And even"—Ms. O'Brien lowered her voice like she was imparting a secret—"a giant feast with fifty different kinds of cupcakes."

"Cupcakes!" Madeleine squealed.

"No cupcakes." Spencer shook his head. "I prefer she eat healthy foods."

Madeleine's eyes grew round, and she gripped her dress in both hands. Had he frightened her again? Spencer wished he could rip out his tongue.

"I mean"—he bent—"lots of *delicious* healthy foods that taste better than cupcakes. Yummy, yummy foods."

His daughter's brows formed a skeptical arch. "Like what?"

"Like . . . uh—"

A smothered laugh sounded beside him. Ms. O'Brien patted Madeleine's back. "Don't you worry. We've got all kinds of good stuff." She looked the girl over. "Does she have casual wear? I'd hate to ruin her designer duds."

Spencer hesitated. He had no idea what clothes the governess had packed. Instead of haphazardly grabbing something from the closet, he should have considered the suitability of Madeleine's dress for a play-day. Why couldn't he do anything right when it came to his daughter?

Ms. O'Brien waved her hand. "Never mind. This beautiful outfit is perfect for today. We're having a karaoke talent show. But tomorrow is the water fight. If she visits us again, be sure to bring her in jeans or shorts."

He straightened and nodded once. "Jeans or shorts. Understood." He kept his gaze trained on the childcare worker. "Is there anything else I should do, Ms. O'Brien?"

"Call me Abby." She winked at Madeleine. "Both of you."

Abby wobbled to the left as she got off her knees. Spencer reached out and caught her by the elbow. Her skin felt soft, her bones fragile beneath his fingers.

"Thank you." She moved away from his grasp, took Madeleine by the hand, and walked toward the double glass doors.

Spencer hurried to stop the energetic redhead. "Isn't there a sign-in?"

"No, sir." The smile she gave him was courteous and professional. "The Monarch wristband she's wearing has a computer chip with her health information, dietary restrictions, and stateroom number. It also allows you to keep track of her whereabouts. If you've downloaded the app to your phone, you can see where your daughter is at all times. Rest assured. We'll take good care of Maddie."

She led Madeleine through the castle entrance without another glance his way. Spencer stood still for several seconds. A mountain of emails awaited his response. And the sooner he reconciled with Daisy, the better. Yet, his unsettled mind rebelled against the to-do list.

Spencer retrieved his cell phone and speed-dialed the one person in the world he trusted without reservation. The man who'd shown him that God wasn't a somber character on an engraved altar painting but a loving Father who cared about the minor details of his life.

"Hey, Spence!" The upbeat voice of his pastor and friend answered.

"Hi, Gideon. I dropped Madeleine off at the childcare center like you suggested. She didn't cry."

"She knows you'll come back for her. Was the pretty redhead there?"

Spencer's brow wrinkled. "I never said she was pretty."

"You didn't have to." Gideon laughed. "Your tone said it all when you described her in her ridiculous Cinderella costume."

"And what tone was that?"

"Oh, I'd call it exasperated interest."

Gideon's perception had seen beyond Spencer's social status and polite reserve to the wounded soul underneath. No use hiding his incomprehensible fascination from his friend. Or even himself.

He shrugged. "She's . . . attractive . . . in a wholesome, compact way."

"Compact, huh? You know what they say. Good things come in small packages."

"She has no interest in me whatsoever. She keeps her attention focused on Madeleine. Always." Spencer cleared his throat. "As it should be."

He didn't need a girlfriend. He needed a capable caretaker to watch over the most precious person in his life. Madeleine was all that mattered. Abigail O'Brien's indifference to him was a blessing in disguise.

Abby released a breath the moment they entered the double glass doors of the Kids Kingdom. Parents seldom rattled her, but Madeleine Masterson's father was anything but the usual passenger. His autocratic bearing declared there must be a king or two in his family tree—the kind who put peasants in the stocks. But it wasn't his demeanor alone that flustered her. Not even his arrogance could hide the fact the man was smack-you-in-the-face stunning.

His thick black hair framed a strong forehead, and deep dark eyes glistened like the waves surrounding the MS *Buckingham*. Their depths might have been warm if not for the straight, suspicious brows looming over them. A chiseled jaw and a square chin dared her not to examine his features too long.

Did he sense her nervousness? Her physical reaction? The way her insides flittered when he turned his attention on her?

"Excuse me, ma'am," the girl at her side said. "What do I do?"

What a wretch Abby was. Daydreaming about an off-limits parent when there was an adorable little girl who lacked love and attention. Abby bent to meet her eye-to-eye.

"We have so many choices. There's the karaoke room, the ropes course, or the movie's starting if you want to grab some popcorn."

Maddie surveyed the large play area. A nearby group of children built a fortress with giant sponge blocks. Squeals echoed from the back room where others bounced on trampolines. An alcove with bookshelves and beanbag chairs sat off to one side. The girl pointed to the quiet space.

Abby clapped her hands. "I love reading too. Do you want me to help you choose a book?"

"No, thank you."

Maddie padded to the alcove, slipped a story from the shelf, and sat in a beanbag chair with her dress spread around her like she was posing for a photo. Abby bit her lip. The child was too young to read more than picture books. Perhaps she'd tire of them soon and interact with the other children. Something about her upright posture prompted Abby to keep an eye on this darling child. She got the sense Madeleine Masterson was used to being forgotten. Abby intended to show her how special she was. Even if it was just for one day.

Abby's phone buzzed in her pocket. She pulled it out and found a text from Emily.

What time do you get off? I have a surprise.

Her toes twitched inside her sneakers. If this meant what she thought it did—

A whoop left Abby's mouth. Among the chatter and noise of the playroom, no one noticed. She mouthed a prayer of thanks that singlehood was almost finished. A few more hours, and she'd meet the man of her dreams.

CHAPTER 7

EMILY'S CANE TAPPED ALONG THE deck. She scooted around a passel of oil-slicked sunbathers to a table near the railing, where her friends sat under a purple-and-gold umbrella. Gerry and Althea held playing cards close to their faces like a couple of gamblers in an old Western. Daisy stretched in a lounge chair behind them, studying something.

As Emily drew closer, she recognized the square-shaped note from the day before. Daisy fingered the card, picking at its corner in nervous agitation. She tucked it away in the pocket of her wide-legged black trousers.

"Hello, ladies." Emily approached her fellow Shippers.

Althea waved. "You arrived in time to witness my victory." She pushed her cards together and rapped them against the table. "Knock, knock. Who's there?"

"Button it," Gerry grumbled.

"Oh, you know who's there." Althea spread her cards. "It's Mrs. Big Winner."

While the two squabbled over their gin rummy game, Emily settled in the chair next to Daisy. She rubbed her aching knee. In the distance, a school of dolphins bounced above the waves, following the ship.

Emily gestured to Gerry and Althea. "How long have they been at it?"

"Playing cards or fussing?" Daisy asked. "They commenced their rummy battle twenty minutes ago and their verbal battle one minute later. I'll never understand why they obtain such pleasure from besting each other."

"It keeps their brains nimble." Emily stretched her leg out on the chaise with a wince. "I realize the surprise visit from your family has been a trial. How are you holding up?"

Daisy's mouth formed a moue of distaste. "My son possesses a rare talent for being disagreeable, but any trouble is worth the joy of seeing my granddaughter." Her expression softened. "Madeleine looked precious in her lovely outfit yesterday. I wish I could have taken a picture, but my camera was in my cabin."

"Maybe she'll be the motivation to make you buy a cell phone. I'd welcome the chance to get rid of those walkie-talkies."

Daisy shook her head. "I'm afraid my son would take advantage of the ability to contact me. I prefer to live in peaceful harmony on the MS *Buckingham*—out of reach from anyone in my former life."

"Guess I'd better keep my charger." Emily sighed. "At least you only have to put up with Spencer for a few days. Then life can return to normal."

"Yes." Daisy picked at the polish on her fingernails.

Emily eyed the nervous tell. She'd held her tongue so far, but the curiosity was killing her. What was the meaning behind the ominous card in Daisy's pocket? And what indiscretion had the note referred to?

"You seem a bit on edge lately. And not just about Spencer. Does it have something to do with that black envelope Magda gave you?"

Daisy's fingers stilled. She lowered them to her lap and raised her prim nose. "I'd rather not discuss it."

Emily started to speak, then thought better of it. Before this voyage, Daisy had always been the sweet one. Well-mannered. Careful not to make waves or break protocol. The arrival of her family had unlocked another aspect of her personality.

Despite Emily's impatient nature, she cared enough about her friend to wait. Confidences couldn't be forced.

"Woo-hoo!" Althea's gleeful call interrupted the awkwardness. "I got you now." She slapped an ace on the pile.

Gerry moaned and tossed her cards on the table. "Don't we have matches to arrange?" She pushed away, and the chair legs squawked. "Emily, did you speak with the minister?"

Emily lowered her feet to the floor. "Yes. I talked with Mr. Boynton after breakfast, and he was keen to meet Abby. It probably didn't hurt I kept mentioning what a looker she is."

"Never does." Althea gathered the cards and slipped them into their box. "A truth that never changes is men like a pretty face. When are we going to set the couple up?"

"Very soon." Emily glanced at her watch and stood. "I've arranged to meet Mr. Boynton in half an hour outside the Kids Kingdom. He plans to ask Abby to dinner."

"Oooh, let's all go." Althea bounced from her chair. "I wanna see for myself if there's any sparks."

"I doubt they want an audience." Gerry withdrew her notebook and pen from her bag. "Still, they might require assistance soothing those first-meeting jitters."

"Y'all go without me." Daisy settled on her lounge. "I have some thinking to do."

Althea gave her roommate a quick squeeze. "Don't think too hard. I'll meet you at the cabin in an hour. We can get ready for dinner." She bustled to Emily and Gerry. Standing between them, she slipped her arms around theirs and hurried them in the direction of the children's area. "Let's go, girls. Romance is awaitin'."

Emily peeked over her shoulder. Daisy sat in the same position, her hand resting atop the pocket where she'd placed the envelope. Giving a friend space was one thing, but if someone was trying to hurt one of their own, he'd have the wrath of the Shippers to deal with.

CHAPTER 8

Spencer rushed through the glass doors of the Kids Kingdom. He'd planned to leave Madeleine for only a short while, but an emergency text from the law firm had led to six hours of phone calls, emails, and online meetings. His main objective for coming on the cruise remained untouched. When would he find the time to resolve things with his mother?

Riotous music, along with shouts and laughter, filled his ears. Across the wide playroom, Abigail O'Brien marshaled a crooked conga line of children. She pounded a fervent beat on the colorful drum tucked under her arm as she led a dynamic chant.

"One, two, three. Kick! One, two, three. Kick!"

The dancers snaked ever closer, thrusting their legs to the right and the left in a disjointed rhythm. She orchestrated the movement like an expert conductor who walked the fine line between creativity and chaos. Red curls bounced with every bob of her head. Her joyous, carefree abandon beckoned him.

He took a step back.

She spotted his movement near the door. Abby passed her drum to a coworker and hurried over. "Mr. Masterson, I'm so glad you're here."

His breath stopped. "What's wrong? Is Madeleine hurt?"

"No. No." She waved both hands. "I'm sorry I worried you. Maddie was . . . She—" Abby made a disgusted sound. "Here, let me show you."

She tiptoed to a corner and motioned for him to join her. Maddie sat on a padded bench along the other side of the wall, a stack of books resting beside her.

Spencer's breathing returned to normal. "She looks fine."

"I worry about her."

"Why?" He studied his daughter. "Is she sick?"

"No. But she doesn't do anything wrong."

"Isn't that good?" Spencer sidestepped as a pair of boys raced by them in a rambunctious game of tag. "I presume you value a well-behaved child."

"It goes beyond well-behaved." Abby grimaced. "She sits in one spot with her hands folded in her lap. Like she's afraid I'll scold her if she wrinkles her clothes."

Spencer observed his daughter. She sat separate from the other children, watching them play but making no move to join them.

"It's not natural," Abby said. "Even the best-behaved children get excited and forget to keep their voices quiet. They get tired and cranky and whiny. But Maddie just sits there."

An echo from the past entered his mind—of being five years old with dirty trousers and scuffed shoes, receiving a lecture from his father. One of many.

"You don't have time for this nonsense. Other boys roll around in the dirt. But you're a Masterson. Never forget who you are."

The authoritarian voice in his memory still made him cringe. But what tortured him even more was the thought he might be ruling Madeleine with the same iron fist his father had wielded. How could he make her feel safe and loved?

He crossed to where his daughter waited.

Madeleine stood tall and adjusted her dress. She stared up at him with a timid but eager expression that begged for his approval. "I was good."

Guilt punched him. He forced himself to relax, not wanting Madeleine to think he was angry with her. "Did you enjoy yourself?"

She nodded.

An unpleasant realization hit Spencer that he had no idea how his own daughter's real, uninhibited voice sounded. The few times she'd spoken in his presence, her words were polite but stilted. How could he encourage her to speak without seeming like he was berating her?

"What"—he scrambled for something to say—"what did you like best?"

"The books."

No one would ever call his daughter a motormouth. He tried again. "Did you do anything besides read?"

"I ate lunch." She stepped closer. "I didn't eat any cupcakes. And I didn't spill any food on my dress."

"Oh?" He reached a hesitant hand and patted her arm. "Good. Very good." Should he say more? "You look pretty."

Abby joined them and sank to her knees. "It was fun having you visit us, Princess Maddie." She looked up at Spencer. "Would it be okay if I gave her a hug?"

He blinked. "Why, yes. I suppose it's all right."

She turned to Madeleine. "May I hug you, Your Majesty?"

His daughter giggled.

Abby moved carefully, like a doctor approaching a patient. She wrapped her arms around the tiny body and squeezed tight, rocking her back and forth. "I hope you have the best time of your life on this cruise."

Was it wrong that envy flooded Spencer? If only they passed out hugs to the parents as well as the children. When was the last time someone had shown him affection without an underlying motive?

Abby popped to her feet. "Let me walk you both to the exit. If you need us to watch Maddie again, it will be our pleasure."

They moved to the double glass doors. A group of people entered, and Spencer recognized the gray-headed posse his mother hung out with. Daisy was nowhere in sight. With them was a young man of medium height, dressed in gray cotton pants and a green-plaid shirt tucked in at the waist. He wore a pair of wire-rimmed glasses. His amiable countenance brought to mind a principal greeting visitors on the first day of school.

The ringleader took the stranger by the elbow and led him to the young woman. "Good afternoon, Abby. We have someone special to introduce to you. If you're not busy."

Spencer's eyes narrowed. The matchmakers had chosen their first offering. He'd expected someone a little less . . . mediocre. Was this the best these so-called marital experts could offer? What a disappointment for Abby.

He glanced down to find a sparkle in her eye and an anything-but-disappointed smile on her lips.

CHAPTER 9

Up. Down. Up. Down.

Abby realized she was bouncing on her heels like an over-sugared preschooler and forced herself to remain still. It was difficult when the Shippers stood before her with a man who might very well be the love of her life. She approved of their choice.

An attractive face with glossy brown hair flopping on his forehead. A friendly, open expression that invited her to unburden her soul. The precise pleats in his cotton pants were geek chic at its best. Abby's optimistic heart pounded at the possibilities. He resembled the appealing but overlooked nerd in a rom-com. Would she be the perceptive girl who gave him a makeover?

He held out a hand. "How do you do? I'm Reverend Boynton, the onboard chaplain, but you can call me Norville."

"Hello, Norville." Abby took his hand, careful not to grasp too hard or shake too vigorously. *Must appear ladylike.*

Emily nudged him. "We've told Norville all about you, Abby."

He tapped his index finger against her skin. "Were you the lady in the beautiful ball gown on embarkation day? With that crown on your head, I thought a queen was on board."

Throat clearing behind Abby reminded her of Mr. Masterson and his daughter. She stepped to the side and included them in the group.

Even with her movement, the pastor kept hold of her hand. A promising sign. The Shippers must have really talked her up to him.

A spontaneous party broke out in the karaoke room as the music blared and colored lights flashed. Kids jumped to the driving bass that rattled the glass windows surrounding them. They hooted and sang at the top of their lungs.

Norville gestured with his head at the barely controlled enthusiasm. "I wish I could get that energy in my Sunday morning services. You think they'd come if I invite them?"

Abby mimicked their movement. "I don't know about the kids, but I'll be there with my dancing shoes on."

A rumble like thunder sounded. Mr. Masterson's throat clearing rivaled the pounding beat of the music. He held out his own hand.

"I'm Spencer Randolph Masterson."

"Hello, Spencer." Norville released Abby.

Spencer shook the man's hand once and dropped it. "What brings you to the Kids Kingdom? Do you have children?"

"Oh no, I'm not married." Norville turned to Abby. "Yet."

Her inner thermostat shot up ten degrees. He didn't waste any time. She valued the minister's forthrightness but wished their first meeting wasn't being witnessed by three senior citizens, an attractive father, and his child.

Norville clasped his hands behind his back in a posture more fitting for a grandpa than a man in his thirties. "Tell me, Spencer, will I see you in the chapel too?"

Althea tugged Spencer's sleeve. "Yes, baby. Are you on speaking terms with the Good Lawd?"

A brief but genuine smile lifted the corner of his lips. "Let's just say, he and I are getting acquainted."

"Glad to hear it." Emily elbowed Gerry, who scribbled something in her notebook.

"I'll have a decent-sized congregation for my first service." Norville bent and looked around Spencer to where Maddie stood. "If a beautiful young lady with golden hair came, I'd count myself doubly blessed."

Abby appreciated his attempt to include the shy girl. Some adults treated children as if they were invisible. His acknowledgment of Maddie's presence gave him extra points in Abby's book.

Norville straightened. "I may have a larger audience on the MS *Buckingham* than I do at home. Glad I polished my sermon before I came. My preparation leaves me time to explore the boat." He leaned his head toward Abby. "Now if I can find a guide who knows her way around, I'll be all set."

"That sounds—"

"Excuse me, Ms. O'Brien." Spencer checked his watch. "I apologize for interrupting, but I have a business call in fifteen minutes. You mentioned Madeleine seemed uncomfortable today. It appears the governess will be unable to perform her duties this evening. Are there any other options for childcare besides this public area?"

Technically, her shift had ended five minutes ago, but she couldn't pass Mr. Masterson to another employee when it involved Maddie's welfare. Abby loved kids in general, but there was something about this darling girl that pulled at her deepest heartstrings.

"Yes, sir. Monarch provides one-on-one childcare service for an extra fee, but as a VIP, two hours a day is already included in your vacation package."

He waved to the side. "The cost is of no consequence. What matters is that Madeleine is well cared for and I can trust the person supervising her."

"Rest assured. Every one of our specialists has been through extensive training, including first aid and CPR."

Spencer's jaw firmed. "I don't care how many certificates they've earned. I don't want a random specialist." His head tilted forward, and his voice lowered. "I want you."

CHAPTER 10

WHAT WAS HE THINKING? *"I want you."* Was he aiming for a harassment lawsuit?

Spencer had meant it in a business sense. But what if Abby had taken him the wrong way? The fact she'd agreed to visit his suite and discuss employment in private boded well. He risked a glance her direction. She waited patiently by his side. No shock or offense apparent.

He waved his key card in front of the door and opened it. Madeleine preceded them into the apartment and walked to the couch. After retrieving a book from the coffee table, she sat with her dress spread out as she had in the children's area. Now that Abby had made him aware of it, the posture bothered him. Was his daughter comfortable? Why did she always look like a child model in a magazine spread?

"Thank you for making time to discuss this."

"As long as it doesn't take too long. I have a—*wowzers!*" Abby entered the expansive suite with mouth hanging open. "I've heard about this place from the housekeepers, but this is my first time seeing it in person."

Spencer surveyed the open layout of the lavish two-story apartment with aversion. Shaggy area rugs covered hardwood floors. The furnishings were too modern, and the floor-to-ceiling windows offered an unobstructed view of the ocean that reminded him how far from home this trip was taking him. "It's adequate."

"Adequate?" She held out her arms and spun in a circle. "It's like a luxury penthouse. Oh my word, there's even a piano!"

"Do you play?"

A secretive grin lit her face. "As a matter of fact, I do."

Abby approached the baby grand near the balcony door. Sinking gracefully to the bench, she gave a serene smile. She wove her fingers together backward, stretched her arms out, and then pointed both index fingers.

Plink-plink-plink-plink.

The rudimentary sound of "Twinkle, Twinkle, Little Star" floated through the suite.

"What do you think, Maddie?" she called.

Madeleine discarded her book and moved to the piano. "I like that song."

Abby scooted over to make room on the bench and proceeded to teach his daughter her two-fingered version of the famous tune. Spencer sighed with relief. It appeared that Madeleine would have no trouble adjusting to their new employee.

He went to the dining room table, where his office documents waited in organized piles. The stainless steel desk in the adjoining office had been insufficient. He sat in one of the upholstered chairs, sent a quick text to the office to postpone his scheduled call, then withdrew a blank piece of paper from a manila folder and made a quick list of his expectations.

He spoke as he wrote. "I appreciate your willingness to consider a position as Madeleine's temporary nanny."

Abby stopped playing. "It's no big deal. Our ship offers the special service on every voyage." She rose from the piano bench and walked over. "But I have a previous commitment tomorrow until two. I wouldn't want my coworkers to suffer by having to adjust their work schedules on short notice." She sat on the other side of the table, checking the time on her phone. "You can bring Maddie to the Kids Kingdom again, if you need to"—her tone took on a deriding quality—"work. On a cruise ship. When you're supposed to be on vacation."

He ignored her obvious sarcasm and pushed the piece of paper across the table.

Abby picked it up and read aloud. "'The party of the first part—'"

"That's me," said Spencer.

"'Promises to provide adequate compensation to the party of the second part—'"

"You."

She clamped her lips shut and read the remainder of the document in silence. "Translation, please?" she asked as she set the sheet on the table.

Spencer's brows dipped. "This is my list of expectations, specifying what your duties will be while you care for my daughter, and how I will compensate you."

Abby laughed. "Monarch Cruises provides our nanny valet service. The extra cost will be added to the bill and charged to your credit card at the end of the trip. Easy-peasy, lemon squeezy."

"Nothing in this world is 'easy-peasy.'" He repeated her phrase like it was a foreign language. "The cruise line pays your salary, but I assume you're allowed to accept tips for a job well done. I've missed the last two years of my daughter's life, and I must ensure she is receiving the best care. In this document, you'll find my requirements for you and the remuneration I'm willing to offer in return."

"Is this a legally binding contract?"

"No. But I find that an employee performs better when they are clear on what is expected of them. Naturally, you're free to negotiate any terms."

Abby released a long-suffering sigh and picked up the document. She scanned the items he'd bulleted.

Spencer had made sure everything was spelled out. Bedtime. Dietary restrictions.

Her forehead crinkled. "This says Madeleine must spend at least two hours a day on an educational activity."

Spencer nodded. "We're following the already-established schedule her mother used. I'm trying to make this transition period for Madeleine as easy as possible."

"Two *hours*?"

He nodded again.

Abby tilted her head. "But . . . you're on vacation."

Spencer threaded his fingers together and placed them on the table. "I do not consider this a vacation in any way, shape, or form. My goal is to convince Daisy in the shortest amount of time possible to return home where she belongs. While we are stuck on this ship, I will continue to do my job to the best of my ability, and I expect my daughter to do the same."

"She's five." Abby glanced over at Madeleine and whispered, "She doesn't have a job."

"Of course she does. Her job is to prepare herself for kindergarten next year."

"Ah, yes." Abby sat back in her chair. "That kindergarten is a real killer. Will you hire her a tutor?"

"Please avoid the flippancy. Beyond those two hours, she'll have the remainder of the day to play." He unfolded his hands and tapped the contract. "Is there anything you want to tweak?"

"A few thoughts come to mind."

He'd anticipated as much. Spencer passed a pen to Abby. She took it and added three bullet points to the list of stipulations. The *plink-plink-plink* of the piano continued in the background while he waited for her demands. She slid the paper across to Spencer.

He read her additions, and his eyes shot to hers. "I don't understand."

"You made sure to outline exactly what was expected of myself and Madeleine." Abby pointed at him. "I added what *your* duties will be."

Spencer read aloud. "'The party of the first part promises to spend at least forty-five minutes a day with his daughter in a frivolous, non-educational activity.'"

"I was generous. It really should be an hour, but you said you're busy."

He read again. "'The party of the first part will smile at his daughter at least three times a day.'"

"Again, generous. It should be three times an hour with an adorable girl like Maddie. But you don't smile much, so I'm easing you into it."

He looked to the piano, where Madeleine pressed the keys. "I . . . I smile at my daughter."

"Of course you do. I just meant you could amp up the frequency."

Spencer read the last addition. "'The party of the second part will be given a one-hour break, in addition to mealtimes, for dating.'" His face was still pointed at the paper, but his gaze rose to hers. "Dating?"

Abby grinned.

"Does Monarch Cruises always include dating in your childcare schedule?"

"Not as a rule." She laughed. "But I've recently enlisted the experts to help me with my love life, and I don't want them to forget about me."

"Experts? You mean my mother and her friends?"

"Yes. They'll be arranging different dates for me."

"Can't you attend to these after working hours?"

"I'd like the option of going on a date while the sun's still up. It may not always be at the same time, but I'll give you plenty of advance warning. During that hour you can enjoy your frivolous activity with Madeleine. A two-for-one deal."

"I still can't fathom how Daisy is giving someone else advice about romance." A short, derisive laugh left Spencer's mouth. "You chose quite the expert."

"She and her friends are amazing. The Shippers have arranged multiple happy couples."

"The Shippers? They named their matchmaking service? Do they pass out business cards?"

"Please avoid the flippancy." Abby echoed his words from earlier. "They're called the Shippers because they arrange relation*ships*. I convinced them to take me on by the skin of my teeth, and I'm not going to waste this opportunity."

"Who will you be dating?" Spencer dropped the paper. "The shirt-tucked gentleman they introduced this afternoon?"

"Yes." Her grin reappeared. "Wasn't he cute?"

"I have no idea. So you've decided to marry the minister?"

"Not yet. We're getting to know each other. And that takes time. Thus, my clause about taking an hour off."

"To sum it all up"—he slapped the table—"you're inserting a clause for your blind dates?"

"Yep. And no need to get thumpy. I have two brothers and three sisters who grew noisy at the slightest provocation, so it doesn't affect me in the least. I'm supposed to meet Norville at the Trafalgar restaurant in thirty minutes." She glanced at her phone again. "Are we done?"

Spencer drummed his fingers in a steady tattoo. He hated the third clause. It was unprofessional to include details about her love life. Although he'd written prenuptial agreements with much worse, even down to the number of infidelities each partner was allowed.

Spencer took the pen and scratched through something on the paper.

"Wait!" Abby reached out. "What are you changing?"

"You want me to spend forty-five minutes in a frivolous activity with my daughter while you're on a sixty-minute date. The math doesn't compute. I'm subtracting the extra fifteen minutes. I'll give you an extra daily break of forty-five minutes. You can use it for romance or napping or whatever you choose. If you require any more time, you'll have to arrange your dates for when you're off the clock."

Abby propped an elbow on the table, rested her chin in her hand, and her lips turned upward. "Deal."

Spencer loosened the knot in his tie and stretched his neck. Why did he get the feeling he'd been had?

CHAPTER 11

VIOLIN MUSIC GREETED THE SHIPPERS as they walked through the entrance of the most exclusive restaurant on the ship. When the maître d' attempted to seat them in a booth, they politely declined and headed for a table near the window. It provided a clear view of the action, no matter where Abby and Norville sat on their date.

Emily studied the unfamiliar setup. Though they lived full-time on the ship, they rarely visited its Trafalgar, which boasted an expensive menu. Unlike other dining options, it cost over and above the price of their fare.

"Swanky." Gerry pushed away three forks from the elaborate place setting, then adjusted the window shade to block the sunset's blinding light.

Emily slid her purse under the leather seat. "No wonder they charge extra to eat here."

Althea patted Daisy's hand before picking up the menu. "How 'bout we share something?"

Daisy murmured her assent, and Emily and Gerry decided to split a dish as well. The Shippers placed their orders with the waiter, then watched the entrance for the happy couple.

Daisy spread her napkin on her lap. "Was Abby pleased when she met Norville?"

"Very much so." Emily tapped her fingertips together. "Her smile reached almost to her hairline."

"I noticed one person who wasn't smiling." Gerry chuckled. "He appeared none too pleased at our interruption."

"I caught that too," said Althea. "Methinks somebody has a crush on our Abby. Somebody related to you." She jiggled her roommate's leg.

"Spencer?" Daisy's brow wrinkled. "You must be mistaken."

"No," Gerry said. "He was *not* happy when Abby met the minister."

Althea leaned closer. "What do you say, Daisy? Sure you don't want Abby for a daughter-in-law?"

Daisy crumpled her napkin. "And subject her to the entire Masterson clan? When you marry into our family, you get ten generations of Southern aristocrat baggage as a bonus. No, ladies. Cross Spencer off your list." She tossed the cloth on the table and stood. "I'm sorry, Althea, but one of my headaches is coming on. Do you mind eating the dish we ordered alone?"

"No, baby. Go rest your head."

Daisy gathered her purse and left the restaurant.

Emily had said nothing during the exchange. She waited until Daisy was out of earshot before facing the other two. "She's right, girls. We all witnessed the chemistry between Abby and Spencer, but marriage is about more than two people. There's a whole array of friends and family who come with the deal. If Daisy is against it, then that's that. End of discussion."

Gerry placed a hand to her heart in pretend shock. "Who are you, and what have you done with our full-speed-ahead leader?"

Emily shook her head. "I know I'm usually the first one to steamroll over anybody's objections, but Daisy has a say-so in who joins her family. Our pursuit of true love can't hurt one of our own."

"No biggie," said Althea. "We got plenty of other candidates."

Gerry took a drink from her water glass, Althea waved at a waitress she recognized, and Emily prayed silently. She suspected Daisy was bothered by more than her son's sudden arrival.

Lord, would it be helping or meddling? Am I opening a can of worms?

Without waiting for heaven's response, she dove in. "Tell me, Althea. Is Daisy acting strange of late?"

"Ever since her son arrived, she's been as twitchy as a long-tailed cat in a room full of rockin' chairs."

"I don't mean Spencer. Something else is worrying her. I'm wondering if it had anything to do with that black envelope she received."

"Black envelope?" Gerry set the glass down. "I haven't heard about this."

"Me neither," Althea said. "When did it come?"

"Magda delivered it the day we left port. You were all standing there."

"Now that you mention it"—Althea scratched her chin—"I recall Daisy reading a card as I came out of the bathroom this morning. When she saw me, she slipped it under her pillow."

"Why didn't you ask about it?" Emily said.

"A body has a right to a few secrets. She'll tell me when she's ready."

Chair leather squeaked as Emily scooted forward. "Has Daisy ever mentioned any . . . indiscretions in her family?"

A somber expression settled in her friend's dark eyes. "I reckon that's her business."

"But we should help—"

"Full-speed-ahead Emily is reemerging." Gerry smirked.

A cloud passing over her usual sunny countenance, Althea placed a hand on Emily's arm. "Drop it, baby. If Daisy wants us to know, she'll tell us in good time. We can't let our curiosity cause her pain."

A guilty twinge like the unpleasant pressure of a flu shot pricked Emily. She twisted the cloth napkin on her lap. Was Althea correct? Emily couldn't deny she loved a good mystery. Did she truly wish to help Daisy, or was she just looking for a new thrill?

Gerry tapped the table. "They're here."

Abby and Norville stood at the entrance. Their complementary heights and corresponding smiles lent them the air of newlyweds on their honeymoon. The three Shippers turned their chairs for a better look at their latest match.

CHAPTER 12

ABBY SIGHED IN RELIEF AS the last remnants of the setting sun disappeared behind the windowsill. She could finally stop squinting and enjoy the classy ambiance. A string quartet played on a dais in the center of the room as diners enjoyed the Trafalgar chef's exquisite culinary creations.

A votive candle flickered on the table between her and Norville. She fingered the bouquet of tulips he'd brought. Good thing she'd changed from her work clothes into a simple but feminine sundress. The dim lighting, romantic music, and posh attire of the people around them equaled the fanciest date of her life.

Achoo!

Abby jumped at the eardrum-puncturing sneeze.

"So sorry." Norville took out a clean white hankie and wiped his nose. "I must have caught something. I wasn't sick when I came aboard."

"Uh-oh." Abby winced. "You've fallen victim to the dreaded Cruise Ship Cold. The staff works hard to keep this place sanitized, but every new batch of passengers brings its own germs."

He returned his handkerchief to his pocket. "I hope my sneezing won't disturb you too much."

"No worries. I spent my first two months at sea popping cold-and-flu tablets."

"Abby?" A new voice intruded.

Her workout buddy approached their table. "Hey, Claude. Are you our server? This will be fun. I get to order *you* around for a change."

"You two know each other?" Norville asked the giant man. The waiter's black tuxedo stretched taut against bulging biceps, and his white bow tie was dwarfed by his thick brown pillar of a throat.

"Everyone knows everyone when you work on a cruise ship." Claude chucked Abby on the shoulder. "This girl drafted me as her personal trainer when she found out I used to be a weight lifter."

"I have to be in good shape to keep up with the kids, but I had no idea what I was getting myself into with this guy." Abby moaned. "He's a teddy bear in the dining room but a heartless fiend in the gym."

"Give me some tips, Claude." Her dinner companion made a muscle with his thin, plaid-encased arm. "It's obvious I'm not the bodybuilding type." Norville's nose wrinkled. He covered his mouth with both hands and sneezed. "I could also stand to build my immune system."

Abby chuckled. She liked it when a man didn't take himself too seriously. This date had possibilities. They made eye contact for a few flirtatious seconds before she looked away. A pair of dark eyes met her gaze over Norville's head. Mr. Masterson waited with his daughter at the maître d's desk. What was he doing here? He strode through the room, holding Maddie's hand. His tall body bent to the side to accommodate her short stature. Her temporary employer hadn't been happy when she insisted on having dinner with Norville before reporting as a nanny valet. But the suggestion he let someone else watch his daughter was met with a flat refusal. Her phone lay on the table. She pressed the button and noted the time. There were still thirty-nine minutes before she'd promised to report at his suite. Better to ignore his domineering presence and enjoy her date.

A waitress led the Mastersons to the table directly behind hers. Maddie sat with her back to Abby, and Spencer lowered himself into the chair facing her. He offered his daughter an encouraging smile. It looked like he'd taken Abby's advice to heart. His eyes encountered hers, his mouth twisted, and he lifted two fingers in a salute.

No fair. I'm supposed to be off the clock.

"Abby?" Claude's voice recalled her to the conversation.

"What?"

He tapped his pen against the paper. "I asked if you knew what you wanted to order."

"Oh." She peeked at the nearby table, but Spencer was studying his phone. Probably working again.

Achoo!

Abby focused on her date. "I'm sorry. I guess my attention is kind of scattered."

"May I suggest the chicken Alfredo?" Norville said. "A hostess recommended it to me. She said it was delicious."

Alfredo? Abby considered the pasta with its thick, creamy sauce. "That's a lot of starch. When you're as short as me, you count the carbohydrates."

"What for?" He looked her over. "You're beautiful the way you are. I appreciate a woman with a healthy appetite."

"I . . ." Abby glanced at Claude and then the minister. "I don't know."

"Trust me. You'll love the Alfredo."

Abby searched her brain for a gentle refusal. Nada. Why couldn't she generate a plausible excuse?

She gave a half-hearted shrug. "Okay. Why not?"

"Marvelous." He slapped the menu closed. "Please give us two orders of chicken Alfredo."

"Asparagus or potatoes au gratin as your side?" Claude waited with his pen poised.

Abby laughed. "Do you have to ask? Asp—"

"We'll both have the potatoes," Norville said at the same time.

More carbs.

Abby fought to keep her eyes from rolling up into her head. Instead, they shifted to the next table. Spencer's mouth quirked as if he'd heard her dilemma and was judging her for caving to the pasta peer pressure.

Claude finished writing their orders and left. Norville unfolded the swan-shaped napkin and spread it across his lap. Abby followed suit, keeping her attention firmly fixed on her dinner companion. They chatted about favorite childhood memories until their food arrived.

"I'd like to give thanks." He settled an open hand on the table. "If you don't mind?"

Abby stared at his palm as she processed what he meant. Oh, right. He wanted to hold hands while they prayed. She scanned the dining room. It wasn't that she minded saying grace over the food. She did that anyway. But her family had never been the type to join hands in a big circle at mealtime. They just bowed their heads and prayed. No ceremony about it.

Abby raised her fingers, hesitated, then thrust them into his grip before it got any more awkward.

He lowered his head. "Heavenly Father, we thank thee for thy bounty and those which prepared this meal."

If Abby expected a short prayer, she was disappointed. Reverend Boynton remembered to bless everyone from the cook to the lowliest busboy. His hand grasped hers the whole time, and she tried not to think too hard about why it was wet.

What a sneaky way to hold a woman's hand.

Spencer's index finger tapped the table in a slow, steady beat as he witnessed the benediction. The food arrived, and he cut Madeleine's steak into bite-size pieces, but then his attention returned to the table nearby. A light whimper distracted him. He looked at his daughter, who sat with her fork frozen in midair.

"Do you need something?" he asked.

She pointed at the meat in front of her.

Spencer scrutinized the steak. "I don't understand, Madeleine. What's the matter? Do you want smaller pieces?"

She shook her head. "No, thank you." Her lips pinched tight.

"You have to tell me what's wrong. How else will I know?"

"It's . . . I . . ." Madeleine turned her head and peered wistfully at Abby.

Spencer followed his daughter's gaze.

"Hold on." He winked at Madeleine. "I'll be right back."

Spencer tossed his napkin down and walked to the neighboring table, where the prayer meeting was still in full swing.

"We ask thee to remember those less fortunate than us," the reverend droned.

"Excuse me." Spencer broke into the flowery speech.

Abby jerked her hand from the minister's and turned to her temporary boss.

"I apologize for disturbing your meal." He looked at Abby and motioned to the other table. "Madeleine seems distressed about something, but she won't tell me what it is." He directed his attention to her date. "Ms. O'Brien is my daughter's nanny for the night. Could you possibly spare her a moment? Perhaps she can find out what's bothering Madeleine."

"Absolutely." Abby shot from her chair. "I should help Maddie."

"Will you be returning?" Norville asked. "Our Alfredo—"

"Of course Ms. O'Brien is free to return." Spencer glanced at his watch. "Her shift doesn't start for another twenty-five minutes. Plenty of time to enjoy her pasta." Abby winced, and he paused. "On the other hand—"

Was he being too presumptuous? Just because the woman didn't like the menu didn't mean she wanted to end the date.

Spencer faced Abby. "If we escort Madeleine to the suite, it might be easier to find out what's bothering her. What do you think is best?"

She smiled. "Maddie will be more comfortable in the suite. Why don't we take her back and order room service?"

Norville stood. "Perhaps we can continue this another time."

"Please don't get up." Abby grabbed her tulip bouquet from the table. "You enjoy your meal."

"When might we reschedule our—"

"Madeleine's waiting." Spencer clasped Abby's elbow and steered her away.

"Goodbye, Norville," Abby called over her shoulder.

They collected Madeleine, and the three of them walked through the dining room. They passed a table where his mother's friends sat, and Abby waved.

"Hello, ladies. I had to leave the date for a—"

"Childcare emergency." Spencer interrupted before the meddling senior citizens could ask any questions. No sense encouraging their matchmaking mischief.

He speed-walked them through the entrance and down the hallway. When they reached the elevators, Abby jerked to a stop. Spencer followed suit.

"Let me be clear," she said. "I only let you get away with that because it rescued me from an unpleasant situation. If you ever interrupt one of my dates again, I'll . . ."

Spencer waited, his hand still holding on to her elbow.

"I'll . . ." Abby floundered.

"You'll . . . ?" His eyebrows rose.

"I'm not sure what I'll do, but I promise you it will be painful." She nodded. "Remember my two older brothers? I learned quite a few ingenious torture methods from them."

Spencer released her and took a step back. "Threat received."

He reached around her body, his arm close enough it almost brushed her waist, and pushed the elevator's call button. His face came level with hers in the process.

Abby blinked, moved away, and took Madeleine by the hand. "Did you like the dinner?"

His daughter grimaced. "Not really."

Why did she confide in Abby and not him? Spencer considered the woman at his side. What was it about this pint-size princess that made people want to tell her their secrets? And not just Madeleine. Spencer might unburden all sorts of information if she ever asked.

But she wouldn't.

She was busy dating the minister. Abigail O'Brien showed zero interest in Spencer as a man or even as a human being. If it weren't for his daughter, he imagined Abby would never speak to him.

Logic and order regulated his life. Anything outside of the plan was unacceptable. So how had he found himself on a cruise ship in the middle of the ocean? His friend Gideon had warned him when he became a Christian—God had a way of interrupting the course a man planned with unexpected detours.

Was this woman one of those? Or was she an ill-advised distraction he'd do best to dismiss?

Mr. Masterson's body in no way touched her own, yet Abby experienced the same tingle as her first slow dance with a boy in high school. When her new employer stood this close, she caught again the tiniest hint of his cologne. Not overpowering, it teased her senses and begged her to lean closer for a good sniff.

Ding!

Abby skittered to the side as the elevator arrived. She and Madeleine entered the car, followed by Spencer. The doors closed, and he pressed the button for the suite's floor.

Abby lowered herself to the little girl's level. "What didn't you like about the food, sweetie?"

Madeleine whispered in her ear. Spencer eyed the communication jealously. Abby grinned as she stood.

"Well?" he asked. "What was it?"

"The steak was too rare."

"What?"

She placed a soft hand on the girl's head. "As Maddie put it, she doesn't like food that's bleeding."

"Oh." His bewildered expression shaved a degree of snootiness off his demeanor. He looked at his daughter. "I'm . . . I'm sorry the food was bleeding. We'll order whatever you like when we get to the room."

The elevator door opened, and they walked down the hallway to his apartment. Spencer waved his key card in front of the automatic lock and entered the Imperial Suite. Abby and Maddie followed him.

A large sitting area with pristine white couches and chairs flowed into a dining room with a full-length glass table. At the end sat a compact kitchen with marble countertops and an island. A staircase to the left led up to what Abby assumed was the bedrooms, with a balcony that overlooked the room below.

I wonder where the butler sleeps.

Spencer pointed to a phone on the end table. "Could you please find out what Madeleine prefers to eat and order room service? And feel free to choose something for yourself. Alfredo, perhaps?"

Abby stared. Was he making a joke? It would be totally out of character.

He removed his suit jacket and tossed it on a nearby chair, rolled his sleeves to the elbow, and picked up a pile of documents from the dining room table. "I'll get some work done while you take care of supper." He made his way to the office and shut the door behind him.

Abby looked at Madeleine. "Hungry?"

"Yes, ma'am." She nodded at hyperspeed. "I'm super hungry."

"So am I." Abby grabbed the phone. "Your daddy wants you to eat healthy. We need to make sure you get enough fruit in your diet. How do you feel about pizza?"

"I love it!" Maddie's forehead crinkled. "Is pizza a fruit?"

"Not exactly." Abby waggled her eyebrows. "But there's a certain fruit that tastes really good on it. Do you like pineapple?"

"I think so."

"Yay! My last roommate hated the stuff on pizza, so I never ordered it when we shared. I'm so glad you like it too."

Maddie positively glowed at the affirmation.

They spent the next two hours stuffing themselves with Hawaiian pizza, playing tag barefoot around the swanky living room, and watching cartoons on the giant flat-screen TV. When Mr. Masterson finally exited his office with a file folder in hand, Abby slipped her dress shoes back on and met him at the dining room table.

"We saved you some food."

He looked at the dishes with a frown. "Pizza? Weren't there any healthier options?"

"I thought it was better to offer Maddie something tempting to erase the memory of that rare steak."

Spencer rubbed the back of his neck. "I should have realized she wouldn't enjoy that type of food. Because of me she was unhappy."

Abby leaned her hand against a dining room chair and rotated her foot. High heels were not for work hours.

Spencer's attention zeroed in on her shoes. "And your break was cut short. I apologize."

"No biggie. There's always tomorrow."

"Until we interrupted, how was your date going?"

Abby blinked, surprised he'd asked. "Norville was . . . attentive."

"Cloying?"

This man was quick on the uptake. She'd better be careful how she phrased things. "I wouldn't put it that way."

"Even if it's true?"

"Norville was sweet." Abby felt the need to defend her escort. After all, the man was a minister. "He brought me flowers. And held the door for me. At the restaurant, when I sat in the chair with my back to the wall, he kindly let me know proper etiquette dictates the man faces outward toward the room. It has something to do with keeping watch for danger. He was super mannerly."

Spencer's mouth curled. "Real manners let the lady sit where she pleases."

Abby returned to Maddie's side and dropped onto the plush settee with a moan. "I admit I had the setting sun in my eyes for the first five minutes." She bent and rubbed the toes peeking from the flirty straps of her sandals.

Spencer sat in the chair opposite her and regarded the shoes. "Was he worth the four-inch heels?"

"I didn't even need the boost." She straightened. "Our heights are very compatible."

"If this works out, you can spend the rest of your life squinting at a man on the same eye level as you."

"Are you normally this curious about your employees' love lives?"

"Is it love already?" He thumbed through the folder.

Abby ignored his question and focused on Maddie. The child's head rested on the arm of the couch. Her long golden lashes drooped.

Abby bent and patted her on the back. "Would you like to go to bed?"

Maddie's chin bobbed, but the rest of her body didn't move. Her father sat and studied his folder, absorbed in his work. He'd be no help.

"Looks like someone's too sleepy to walk." Abby placed gentle hands under the girl's arms and lifted her up.

Maddie cuddled close. Her breath regulated as she fell asleep in an instant. A pleasant ache in Abby's heart caused her to squeeze the child tight.

It was good she'd sought help from the Shippers. Good that she'd gone on the date with Norville, even if he was a little fastidious. The sooner she married, the sooner she could have a baby of her own to assuage the longing inside.

Until then, she'd pour her love into this precious girl.

CHAPTER 13

A BRISK, EARLY-MORNING BREEZE ruffled the playful waves rolling past the MS *Buckingham* as the Shippers observed their latest client. The four ladies sat at a shaded table. Abby stood before them, her arms full of picture books. Gerry opened her laptop and signaled for Emily to begin the debriefing.

Emily motioned to an empty chair. "Sit down, dear."

"I'd love to, but I can't." Abby shifted the books to free up a hand. "I'm due at the childcare center in fifteen minutes. Mr. Masterson is meeting me there. I told him he could leave Maddie with anyone, but he insists on turning her over to me before he leaves for his business appointment."

"Who makes business appointments on a cruise ship?" Althea asked. "Are you sure he's not getting a massage?"

"Unfortunately," Daisy drawled, "I can confirm he has a business appointment. Family business. With me."

Emily refrained from giving her opinion on a man who treated his own mother like an employee. She suspected the woman's relationship with her son required more than one conversation to mend, so she'd focus on a more pleasant topic—matchmaking.

Gerry tapped a few keys on her computer. "How did your date go, Abby?"

"Did he kiss you?" Althea wiggled her shoulders.

"What? No!"

"Strike one," Gerry said.

Abby waved her free hand. "Norville was, um, considerate. And he has super good manners."

"Strike two." Gerry's laptop keys clicked in disapproval.

"Manners. That bad, huh?" Althea unwrapped a gooey piece of candy and popped it in her mouth.

"He . . . he's a very nice man."

"Strike three." Gerry snapped the laptop shut.

"Nice? That's the death knell to romance." Emily shuddered. "All the qualities you mentioned are positive but uninspiring. What young woman prays for God to send her a nice, attentive, well-mannered man?"

Abby dropped her gaze and toyed with a book jacket, confirming Emily's suspicions. If the chemistry was missing, there was no use shoving the couple together. Abby needed someone who put a sparkle in her eye.

A bell chimed. Abby pulled out her phone and swiped the screen. The corner of her lips quirked, and she shook her head. "My temporary employer must be anxious to spend time with his mother. He sent a text that sounds like it's straight out of a legal brief." She gathered her mouth in a surly pout, waggled her head, and spoke in a deep voice. "Punctuality is the height of professionalism. Blah, blah, blah."

Emily raised a brow. There it was. A sparkle in Abby's green eyes. If only it weren't because she was meeting the unwelcoming but undeniably handsome Spencer.

Another chime.

Abby checked the screen. "Daisy, your son asked if I saw you to give you a reminder. You're meeting in the tearoom at 8:15."

Daisy sighed. "And y'all wonder why I refuse to carry a cell phone. Can you imagine the unpleasantness I would deal with?" She rose from her chair and gathered her sweater and pocketbook. "I must go to the cabin and freshen my makeup first."

Althea patted her arm. "You hurry along, baby. I'll save your spot till you get back."

Daisy made her elegant way along the deck in anything but a hurried fashion.

Abby lowered her phone. "I'm on my way to meet Maddie. She's one of the sweetest children I've ever met. I just want to squeeze the stuffing out of her."

Emily studied their client. Perhaps her enthusiastic eyes weren't for the man but his daughter. That would certainly make things easier. Even if an obvious chemistry existed between Spencer and Abby, matching them together was impossible as long as Daisy rejected the idea.

But *no* didn't always mean *never*.

CHAPTER 14

ABBY ENTERED THE KIDS KINGDOM and looked at the time—7:57 a.m. If there were a giant grandfather clock on the wall, she got the feeling Mr. Masterson would walk in the moment the gong sounded. She hurried to the employee locker room, shoved everything in, and checked her watch.

7:59.

She hustled to the greeter's desk and ran her tongue over her teeth to eliminate any stray lipstick marks. Twenty seconds later, the Mastersons arrived. Abby chuckled at how predictable the man was. He held his daughter's tiny hand in his with all the comfort of someone carrying a plastic explosive.

Abby bent and hugged Maddie. "I'm so happy to see you. It's been ten thousand years."

The girl giggled. "You saw me last night."

"Did I?" Abby scratched the side of her head. "Maybe it feels like ten thousand years because I missed you."

Maddie beamed. "Really?"

"You betcha." Abby waved them in to the larger room. "Come in. Come in. We're going to have tons of fun today. First, we'll watch a magic show. Then there's a treasure hunt in the Aquarium Room. And a yummy snack when you get hungry."

"Be sure to behave for Abby," Spencer said.

Maddie's smile disappeared. She straightened her spine and nodded at her father.

Abby longed to wag her finger. *Way to ruin the mood, party pooper.*

Spencer held two overstuffed bags in front of him. "I brought the necessary items."

Abby's lips twitched. "Such as?"

"A pillow and blanket. Sunblock. A bathing suit. A sun hat. Allergy medicine."

Exactly what she expected. Nothing useful for a playday indoors. But she gave the man points for trying. Maybe she could convince him to visit the splash pad with his daughter when he returned.

Abby cupped a hand around her mouth and stage-whispered to Maddie. "There's a magician inside."

Screaming erupted from the corner. A pudgy boy with black hair stomped his feet. Tears dribbled down his cheeks.

Spencer frowned at the scamp. "Do you need to check on him?"

"He's fine." Abby laughed at Spencer's shocked reaction. "Did I sound harsh? That's the second fit that boy's thrown this week. The first was yesterday when we wouldn't give him a soda." She tweaked Maddie's cheek. "The truth is, I'm a big softy. When a child is truly crying, I want to wrap them in my arms and shower them with affection. But after years of experience, I can recognize the fakers. Wails. Tantrums. Vomit. One young customer chucked his shoe at me."

She squatted in front of Maddie and gave her a bear hug. "Why can't all kids be as sweet as you?"

Her precious captive giggled in her arms. Abby looked at Spencer. "I reminded Daisy of the meeting. You'd better get going."

His gaze cut to Maddie. "If I forgot anything, call me right away." He reached out. His hand hovered over his daughter's shoulder, but then he withdrew without touching her. "I'll return soon, Madeleine. I promise."

Spencer passed the overloaded bags to Abby. His fingers brushed her arm as he slipped the handles past her wrist. A tickle like static electricity danced across her skin.

Abby gave herself a mental slap upside the head. *Keep it professional.*

"Yes, sir. Nothing to worry about. Maddie and I will have a marvelous time while you're gone." She motioned with her elbow. "Come on, Maddie. Let's check out that magician. We'll sit criss-cross applesauce on the carpet and watch his show. The last time Mr. Seamus was here, he made a whole bicycle disappear."

Abby's words tumbled as fast as her heartbeat. Never had the mere presence of a passenger rattled her so, but something about this man upset her even keel. She could ignore a good-looking guy without a second thought, but what she couldn't ignore was the expression she recognized in this man's eyes. Abby was a sucker for hurting children. And she sensed behind Spencer Randolph Masterson's cultured facade was a lost boy who desperately needed a hug.

CHAPTER 15

SPENCER STRODE INTO THE TEAROOM with five minutes to spare. Not that it made a difference. Daisy always arrived late for everything in order to make an entrance.

British paraphernalia adorned the Royal Crumpets Tearoom. Porcelain cups and saucers painted with the Union Jack decorated each round table, and a portrait of Jane Austen hung on the wall.

He chose a table in the corner where they weren't likely to be overheard. A piano prelude by Chopin played from the speakers. He ordered a cup of coffee from the server and settled in for a long wait. Was this an ideal time to entreat a little heavenly guidance?

Lord, have I come on a fool's errand? I haven't always been the best son, but Daisy hasn't been the best mother either. Is there any way to heal this relationship?

If what they had could even be called a relationship.

Raised by servants. Shuttled off to boarding school at the age of twelve. Spencer couldn't recall a single conversation or embrace with his mother that hadn't been performed in the company of others. Daisy had dwelled on the periphery of his life for as long as he could remember. He doubted she'd even desired children. His father was the only one to pay him attention. And Julius Masterson's particular brand of attention had been painstaking and precise.

Spencer was well into his second cup of coffee before his mother made her appearance. Even in her seventies, she floated across the room with a grace that testified to generations of Southern breeding. He stood as she approached and pulled the chair out for her. Once they were seated, she folded her hands on her lap and offered him a tentative smile.

"It's good to see you, Spencer. I've missed you."

He refrained from voicing the doubt that swelled inside. "Thank you. Have you been well?"

"Very much so. I've made new friends who keep me busy." A twinkle entered her eye. "You might be surprised at the trouble we get into."

He chuckled. "After hearing you've joined a club of matchmakers, I doubt much else could surprise me."

She gave a ladylike titter. "Between matchmaking and bingo, we stay busy."

Spencer hoped bingo was the extent of her roommate's gambling habit. He didn't want anyone taking advantage of his mother.

"You're not loaning them money, are you?"

The twinkle disappeared. "Don't be ugly. Even if I suggested it, my friends would refuse. Not everyone is as calculating as the circle we frequented in New Orleans."

Though she hadn't raised her voice so much as a hair, her indignation was clear. Spencer heeded the irate set of his mother's lips and sent a quick prayer heavenward. Healing decades of hurt was hard enough without piling on new misunderstandings. Perhaps redirection was the best course.

"I had a time tracking you down. You haven't used any of your credit cards since you left."

"As you are aware, those accounts aren't really mine." Her posture appeared relaxed yet ramrod straight at the same time. "Your father kept an iron grip around them during his lifetime, and he passed control to you upon his death. Not even the deed to our house had my name on it."

Spencer fidgeted in his seat. He was well acquainted with his late father's controlling tendencies. "Dad said you were unable to manage your funds. You always bought whatever struck your fancy. Remember when you purchased that modern art monstrosity at a charity auction? You spent twenty thousand dollars."

Daisy fluttered her eyelashes. "And it was worth double when I sold it a year later."

"I concede your point." He fiddled with his coffee mug. "But I worry you'll run out of money with this flamboyant lifestyle. Living on a cruise ship. Buying who knows what? How many closets full of clothes and purses and jewelry are back in Louisiana?"

"Not as many as you think." Daisy braced a hand on the table and rose slightly from her chair. "Thank you for your concern, but I'm capable of supporting myself."

Was she really? What if someone swindled her? She'd never had to fend for herself in her entire life.

He reached to lay his fingers on top of hers. Daisy's gaze softened, and she sat. Spencer tried to convey warmth with his voice. If he could just make his mother understand he was concerned for her welfare.

"How are you paying for this lifestyle? Did you sell the shares Dad left you in his will? Even though his partners run the business now, it might upset our controlling interest if one of them gained the majority."

Daisy yanked her hand away. "Is that your motive for coming? To ask me to sign over your father's shares?"

"Of course not. I'm not a moneygrubbing—" Spencer stopped. He took a swig of lukewarm coffee to give himself a few seconds. He set the cup down and forced an optimism he didn't feel into his demeanor. "If you're happy living in this floating hotel, then who am I to hinder you?"

"I'm glad we agree." Daisy rose once again and pushed her chair in. "If you'll excuse me, I promised my roommate I'd accompany her to bingo."

Bingo again? How many games did this ship run?

He stood opposite her. "Perhaps we can meet later to continue our discussion. Text me when you're available."

"I don't own a cell phone."

He released a long, frustrated stream of air from his mouth. "It slipped my mind. Forgive me."

"I do hope you'll allow me to spend time with Madeleine before the voyage ends."

Spencer inclined his head. "Of course." The conversation wasn't over, no matter how dismissive his mother was. When this boat returned to Galveston, he intended for Daisy to put a permanent end to her cruising career.

CHAPTER 16

EMILY TOOK A SLOW PROMENADE on the upper deck, keeping a weather eye out for their latest client. Had last night's dinner scuttled Abigail and the minister? Emily wasn't quite ready to write off Norville Boynton, but the forecast was dismal. Abby's exuberance had lessened by degrees as the date progressed. She'd seemed relieved when Spencer butted in to claim her help with a childcare problem.

"What do you think, Lord?" Emily stopped at the rail. The easy motion of the whitecapped waves calmed her vexation. "I know Norville is one of your shepherds, but if you don't mind my saying so, he's not very romantic." The edge of her mouth quirked. "Now, Daisy's son? He's like something straight out of a novel—tall, dark, and handsome with a wounded past. Not to mention the Fourth of July fireworks sparking between him and Abby." She sighed. "But if Daisy is opposed, there's no hope." She slanted an eye at the fluffy clouds. "Right?"

A squeal drew her attention to the splash pad where jets of water spurted from the deck. But it wasn't a child's squeal, although plenty of little bodies frolicked through the fountains. No. This sound was feminine and flirty. The clingy woman Emily had noticed in the lounge bounced through the spray in her bikini as if she were barely older than the children.

"Bounced is right," Emily muttered. "There's hardly enough material in that swimsuit to contain anything."

Mr. May–December was stretched out on a sun chair. A bright orange ball cap hid his gray roots as he videoed his considerably younger partner with a cell phone. He ogled her antics like a—

Emily couldn't even come up with an appropriate word.

Gerry joined her at the rail. Her eyes surveyed the splash pad. "You found Abby." She pointed at the pint-size woman wearing a purple rain poncho. Their client was manning a giant overhead bucket, hung between two poles, that routinely drenched the people below with a crashing wave of water.

Emily's lips twisted. "My attention was diverted elsewhere. What's the male equivalent of a hussy?"

Her friend's brow crinkled. "A reprobate?"

"Sounds too cultured." Emily shook her head. "There must be a more humiliating word for a cheater with his tongue hanging out."

Gerry followed her gaze to the man on the lounge. "Who is that?"

"Nobody important." Emily sniffed. "I—"

She paused as a waiter appeared at the man's side with a tall, frosty drink in a decorative glass. The employee passed him the beverage, along with a square black envelope like the one that had ruffled Daisy's feathers.

"Look." Emily clutched Gerry's arm. "It's another black note."

They watched as the man took a sip of his drink before opening the delivery. He slipped the card out and tossed the envelope on the deck. His satisfied leer disappeared as he read. His head jerked like a child afraid of the Big Bad Wolf. Abandoning his drink on the side table, he stuffed the paper in his pocket, scrambled to his feet, and speed-walked away.

"Hey!" his youthful companion called. "Where ya goin'?"

She raced after him, but he didn't slow down until he reached the doors to the interior of the ship.

Gerry glanced at Emily. "Should I be taking notes?"

Emily's jaw set. "Do you even need to ask? It's time we investigate what's in these disturbing envelopes."

Children swarmed past Abby as she and a male coworker manned the MS *Buckingham*'s gigantic splash pad. Positioned dead center, their job was to prevent any accidents from occurring. She stood under a bucket the size of a Volkswagen that rocked over her head. Her shoulders tensed as it creaked. Its lip tilted all the way, and a cascade of cold water doused her body. Abby tugged the hood of her royal-purple rain poncho lower on her forehead. The pad was a popular destination for the kids, but cruise workers counted it a punishment.

"This isn't your usual station." Her friend Amari clenched the lapel of his raincoat closer to his throat as the giant bucket returned to its upright position. "Did you get on the supervisor's bad side?"

"I guess so."

"What did you do?"

"I'm spending a few days as a nanny valet, and Twila isn't happy about being a worker short."

"It's not like you can help it. Monarch makes your assignments."

"I know. She feels— Sweetie, please get off there!" Abby hurried to a five-foot-tall, fluorescent, fake fire hydrant a young boy was scaling. As she drew closer, she recognized Jason, the soda fanatic. He climbed the tower with a superhero beach towel tied like a cape around his neck. He'd almost made it to the top when she grabbed him under his pudgy arms. His chubby cheeks bunched in an exaggerated grimace as she set him on the ground. Abby squatted in front of him. "You might hurt yourself. Please don't—"

He bolted before she finished her sentence. Abby returned to her station, and a little blond head caught her attention. She smiled as Madeleine skipped among the streams of water jetting from the deck floor. At least the child wasn't dressed for a party this time. Her frilled cotton top and matching shorts were still elegant but appropriate for a fun outdoor activity. Her hunky father sat on a nearby chair, close enough to see her but far enough away to keep his laptop dry.

"Doesn't that man ever stop working?" Abby muttered.

"Who?" asked Amari.

A new deluge from above saved her from answering. She shook the streams of water from her plastic coat and moaned.

Amari rubbed his arms. "I wish they'd heat the water."

"It's a splash pad, not a hot tub."

"Jacuzzi duty." He grinned. "Sounds way more my speed."

"Sweetie!" Abby rushed back to the fire hydrant, where Jason was starting his second climb. "I told you to stay off. You might get hurt."

He crossed his eyes, stuck out his tongue, and ran away. Abby groaned. There was one on every cruise. She glanced at Spencer who sat a few feet away. He looked up from his computer.

That's a good enough invitation for me. Time to stick my nose in.

Abby walked over. "You're not exactly dressed for the occasion." She motioned to his white shirt and dress slacks.

"I took my tie off." He waved a hand down the empty front of his shirt.

"By the end of the cruise, you might work your way into a pair of sandals."

His gaze returned to his computer. "Hopefully I won't be here that long."

"Are you going to have your private yacht meet you mid-ocean?"

"Hardly."

"My point is, if you put on a pair of shorts, you could join Madeleine and have some fun."

His left eyebrow rose, but his focus remained on the screen. "Cavorting among ice-cold jet cannons isn't my idea of a good time."

Abby gave up. One voyage wasn't long enough to fix the things that were wrong with this man. She retied the strings at the neck of her slicker and rejoined Amari.

"One more hour." His teeth chattered. "If we live."

"We'll make it. The time will fly—"

A wave hit them from overhead, and Abby staggered to the side.

Amari shivered. "You were saying?"

"Excuse me." Maddie wandered beside them.

Abby crouched down. "Are you having fun?"

She nodded.

"Do you need something?"

"No. I wanted to say hi."

"Hi!" Abby held up both hands and waved them.

Madeleine copied her motion. "Hi."

"Waaaaaaaaa—"

Abby's head snapped up. She zeroed in on the whiny cry. The wannabe mountain climber vibrated in a crumpled heap below the hydrant, tears streaming. Abby raced to help Jason to his feet. Her heart pounded as she took inventory. No blood. She checked his head but couldn't find any bumps. The pathetic bawling was more in line with a toddler than a seven-year-old. She suspected the fall had scared him, nothing more.

"What have you done to my child?" A voice roared from the distance as a woman in a two-sizes-too-small swimsuit and fishnet cover-up barreled over. She examined the boy's arms and legs.

"Ughh, ugh, ugh," he whimpered.

"I don't think he's hurt." Abby laid a hand on his shoulder. "But I can call the doctor if you'd like."

"*You* don't think he's hurt. What do you know? Of course I want the doctor!" She smacked Abby's hand away.

"Yes, ma'am." Abby hurried to the wall phone and placed the call. Afterward, she spotted Jason's superhero beach towel lying in a sodden wad on the ground and retrieved it. She returned to the pair and offered the towel to his mother. "He dropped this."

The woman grabbed it and dabbed at her son's tears. "It's okay. Tell mama where it hurts." She scowled at Abby. "Where is that doctor?"

"I'm so sorry. He is treating an emergency in the sick ward. They're sending one of our registered nurses. She'll be here soon."

"I don't want a nurse. I want the doctor. What if my baby is seriously injured?"

Abby stayed calm. This wasn't the first overprotective parent she'd dealt with. "I promise the nurse is highly qualified to handle this situation."

"Situation! Is that what you call your negligence?"

The woman swung the towel. Wet terry cloth slapped Abby's face with the force of an open hand. Her teeth rattled, and her neck cracked. She grabbed her cheek. A fiery tingling flushed her skin. The towel landed at her feet, and the woman bent to pick it up. Abby cringed, bracing herself for another hit.

"Hey!"

A long arm swooped between them, and Spencer grabbed the towel. He flung it away and slid his large body in front of Abby's. "Excuse me, madam. Have you lost your mind?"

The woman's volume increased. "Me? This lady let my son get hurt. She wasn't doing her job properly."

"I've been at the splash pad with my daughter for"—Spencer checked his watch—"the last hour. In that time, I've observed this employee on two separate occasions encourage your son to get off the hydrant he fell from, even though it was not her responsibility. This may be a supervised area, but parents are still required to monitor their own children." He pointed to a sign posted on a pole. "I witnessed you run over from the opposite side of this large deck. If anyone let your son get hurt, it was you."

"Who are you to tell me I'm a bad parent?" the mother yelled.

"I'm this young woman's attorney."

Abby's eyes widened, as did the mother's.

Spencer retrieved his wallet from the back pocket of his slacks and pulled out a business card. He passed it to the irate parent. "If you can give me the name of your lawyer, we'll know who to contact if she decides to sue you for compensation."

"Comp—compen— What?"

"Assault is illegal, even at sea. If I report this attack to the security team—"

"Mr. Masterson, please," Abby said. "There's no need to go that far."

A crowd was gathering. One passenger had his phone out, videoing the whole humiliating mess.

"See?" The woman grabbed her son. "This worker knows what she did. Forget involving security."

The mother spun on her heel, but Spencer lifted his arm to block her retreat. "If my client chooses to overlook the matter, I won't stop her. On one condition. You owe her an apology."

"For what? My baby is the one who got hurt."

"Your *baby* behaved in a reckless manner, and it was his own poor choices that caused the accident. But *you* physically assaulted Ms. O'Brien, and an apology is the very least you can offer her." He pointed a finger at the business card. "Or you can give me the name of your attorney."

She crumpled the card and tossed it at his feet. Snatching her son's elbow, she jerked her chin at Abby. "Sorry." The woman stomped away with her child in tow.

Rubberneckers dispersed since the show was over.

Spencer turned to Abby. "I shouldn't have butted in, but—"

"Oh. My. Word. That was awesome!" Abby crowed as she grabbed his hand with both of hers. "Can you come and play my attorney every time I have splash pad duty?"

She mentally retracted any unkind words she'd ever thought about his personality or his choice of wardrobe. The man was an overdressed guardian angel.

Spencer looked down at the slim, wet fingers grasping his. Despite her cold skin, an unusual sensation burned where she touched him.

He snatched his hand away and hid it behind his back. "I . . . I'm afraid I . . . have other clients."

"Oh well. My loss."

She pushed the hood of her raincoat from her head. The sun glinted off her fiery red locks. A hint of gold among the auburn strands glowed in the sunlight like sparks from a firecracker and—

What's wrong with me?

He didn't have time to be waxing poetic about a cruise ship worker's hair. "Madeleine!" He shouted louder than he meant to, and his daughter rushed over.

"Yes, sir?"

"Sir" again. Would she ever treat him as a father instead of a stranger? He noted her apprehensive posture, softened his tone, and lowered himself to her eye level. "It's time for lunch. Then we'll check if your governess has recovered. Is that okay with you?"

She gave her customary nod. Had Priscilla prohibited her from speaking? He could barely get a word out of her. The guilt hit him again. If he'd been around more, he might have noticed sooner.

Abby bent to Madeleine. "You're going to love the surprise we've planned at the Kids Kingdom." She met Spencer with a professional smile that was nothing like the effervescent beam she directed at his daughter. "If you come by with Maddie around two o'clock, my required duty will be finished, and I can nanny full-time for the rest of the voyage."

"Perfect," he said. "I've made another appointment with my mother for three."

Abby snickered. "You need an appointment to meet your own mother?"

"When she's Daisy Randolph Masterson, I do."

The pity that crossed her face irked him. He might not have had a conventional upbringing, but he was still a Masterson. He didn't show weakness to anyone.

"Come along, Madeleine," he said. "Let's get some lunch."

His daughter recoiled. "Like last night?"

Spencer chuckled. "I promise the food won't be bleeding this time. You can order whatever you want."

She hopped up and down. "Pizza with pineapple?"

He sighed. "As long as I don't have to eat it, sure." Spencer held out an open palm, and to his great relief, his daughter placed her hand in his. He straightened and acknowledged Abby. "Until two o'clock, Ms. O'Brien."

She jiggled her fingers. "I'll be there with bells on."

CHAPTER 17

A STEADY STREAM OF PASSENGERS dressed in everything from raggedy cutoffs to feather boas traversed the marble-tiled floor of the luxurious lobby. Emily and Gerry stood at the front desk, talking to yet another Monarch employee. The receptionist was their third interview.

"Please tell me you're joking," Emily groused. It had been a frustrating morning following a fruitless trail from the waiter to the bartender to the receptionist. "You found a padded envelope at your station when you returned from the restroom?"

"Yes," Malaya said. "It was sitting on my desk with a sticky note telling me to deliver it to the lido deck bartender. He and I have been"—she simpered—"shall we say, becoming better acquainted? I spend all my breaks with him. I admit I was curious and peeked when he opened it." Her eyes took on a sharp glint. "I wanted to be sure no one was stealing my man. But there was only a smaller envelope inside with another sticky note saying give it to the waiter who works the splash pad."

"It's like a twisted chain letter," Gerry muttered as she scribbled in her notebook.

"Were you there when your boyfriend passed it on?" Emily leaned on the desk.

Malaya giggled. "Boyfriend? It's not official yet. But if you want to slip him a hint, I don't mind."

"Focus, Malaya." Emily tapped the shiny wood. "We can talk about your love life later. What did the waiter find when he opened the message?"

"A black envelope with another sticky note that said deliver it to the man wearing an orange ball cap at the splash pad."

"It doesn't make sense." Emily moaned. "How could the writer be sure he'd still be there? Anyway. Thanks, Malaya."

They moved away from the desk.

Gerry snapped her notebook shut. "Dead end."

"Hello, hello." Barney Bosko scooted to their side, hands in his pockets. "What are you ladies up to today? Making more trouble?"

"Always," said Emily.

"Well, don't leave me out of the fun." He bumped her. "This round of cruisers is calmer than a Sunday afternoon at the public library."

"The library's closed on Sundays," Gerry said.

"Exactly," he grumbled. "I'm about to die of boredom. Be sure and tell me if you find anything interesting."

The familiar form of Mr. May–December approached, his youthful girlfriend nowhere in sight. He swerved around them and charged to the front desk. Gone was the cavalier lecher from earlier. The man placed a shaky hand on the counter. "What will it take to get me off this boat?"

"Excuse me?" Malaya squinted. "We're in the middle of the ocean, sir."

"I'm not blind." He slapped the wood. "I mean, how soon will we dock at a town with an airport? I need to get home. It's"—he glanced over his shoulder—"it's an emergency."

Emily nudged Gerry with her elbow. Her lanky friend opened her notebook once again.

Barney noted the direction they were looking, and his voice rose. "Who's he?"

"Shhh!" Emily whacked him on the arm.

Malaya typed into her computer. "I'm sorry you have to leave us." She explained the customer's options, wrote the information on a sheet of paper, and passed it to him. "Can I help you book a flight?"

"Now you're talking." He eyed Emily and lowered his voice. His words were lost in the drone of lobby conversations.

But no one had warned Malaya to do the same. She responded in her usual vivacious tone. "Will your wife be leaving with you?"

"My wife!" His head jerked as he scanned the lobby.

"Yes, sir." She pointed at her computer screen. "Your reservation is for Mr. and Mrs. Meyers."

"Oh, her." He relaxed. "Nah. She's gonna stay and finish the cruise. She'll probably find a new boyfriend before you sail home."

"Um"—Malaya blinked—"yes, sir."

Emily frittered in her purse so as not to appear interested. After fixing her makeup, eating a butterscotch candy, and studying a wrinkled tourist brochure, she was running out of excuses when Malaya's printer finally buzzed.

The receptionist handed the man his itinerary. "Here you are, sir. Booked on the first flight for Galveston tomorrow morning. You can catch a taxi at the dock. I hope you enjoy your remaining night with us."

He snorted. "Not likely. Any chance you'll give me a refund for the rest of the cruise?"

The tiniest quirk pulled at the corner of Malaya's mouth. "Not likely, sir."

"Figures." He stomped away without a word of gratitude.

Barney turned to watch the man and rubbed his freckled bald spot. "Am I missing something?"

"Sorry, Barney," Emily said. "We'll have to fill you in later."

She and Gerry left without explanation. They tailed the sullen customer through the lobby, careful to keep a healthy distance. When he stopped, Emily slipped a pair of aviator sunglasses on and pointed her face at the ground. The mirrored lenses hid the fact her gaze was still fixed on Mr. May–December. He approached a trash can on the periphery, looked around, and withdrew the black envelope from his pocket. After ripping it into small pieces, he wadded them into a ball, hurled it into the receptacle, and stormed away.

"Gerry." Emily pointed at his retreating figure.

"On it." Gerry tucked away her notebook and followed him.

Emily zipped to the trash can. It was almost empty, and the crumpled remains of the note were easy to pick out. She placed the pieces in her purse and headed for her stateroom.

She always did love puzzles.

CHAPTER 18

Spencer entered the childcare center at precisely two o'clock. Madeleine walked at his side, her fingers twisted together in an awkward tangle. Her young face wore the apprehension of a fifty-year-old woman facing an audit.

He bent and laid his open palm on her stiff back. "Are you okay?"

She nodded.

"Would you like anything?"

She shook her head.

Spencer sighed. Would his daughter ever feel comfortable in his presence? Or was he doomed to repeat the mistakes of his father? Intimidating his family into submission and dominating everyone around him.

Never in a million years. Even if he possessed zero natural talent for connecting with children, he would keep trying.

Spencer moved his hand to his side. "Are you worried about something?"

"I . . ."

She was talking to him! He crouched in front of her. "You . . . ?"

"I'm wearing the shirt Mommy liked. She said it made me look pretty and . . ."

"And?"

"And I don't want to get my clothes dirty."

Spencer leaned back and took in the outfit he'd picked for her that morning. Yes, it was covered in beaded embroidery, but the matching cotton top and shorts were the simplest things in the suitcase.

He pointed at the outfit. "Do you hate getting your clothes dirty?"

"Mommy hates it." Madeleine's eyes rolled up toward the ceiling as if she were reciting a speech. "I mustn't get my clothes dirty. I mustn't scuff my shoes. I mustn't speak too loud or bother the adults."

The words struck Spencer's heart like pointed darts. They so savagely mirrored his own childhood. Always being reminded to act like a Masterson.

He drew an unsteady breath. "Madeleine, I don't care if you get your clothes or your shoes or every single thing you own dirty." Spencer gently placed both hands on her shoulders. "As long as you have fun."

Her bewildered eyes met his. "Really?"

"Really."

For the first time since she'd come to live with him, his daughter gifted him with an unabashed, lip-stretching smile. It knocked the air right out of him.

A jingling sounded, and Madeleine's smile grew. Abigail O'Brien rushed to them in a jester's costume. A three-pronged hat of purple and gold sat on her head, bells dangling from the droopy ends.

"What took you so long?" Abby sank to the child's height and pouted. "I couldn't wait to show you my new hat." She bounced her head, and the bells jangled.

Madeleine giggled with delight. Spencer tried to imagine his ex-wife or anyone in their entire social circle putting on such a show but came up empty. What a bunch of stuffed shirts they all were.

He surveyed his new nanny. "I didn't realize you meant it literally when you said you'd have bells on."

Without a hint of embarrassment, she stood and jiggled her head. "Shows how little you know me." Abby held out her left hand to Madeleine. "We're having a royal dress-up party. Would you like to wear a Cinderella gown and dance at the ball?"

His daughter slipped her hand into Abby's, who bent and gyrated her hat so a bell jingled in front of Madeleine's nose. Spencer suppressed a grin. Abby was his employee, after all. It wouldn't do to let the world discover how charming he found her.

Charming in a professional way, of course. The way people who worked with children were supposed to be. Winning and likable.

Abby straightened with a sober demeanor. "I'll play with Maddie here in case you have business, but please return by four o'clock. I'm taking a walk with Reverend Boynton."

His grinning urge evaporated. "Haven't you given up on the pasta preacher?"

"I don't reject someone because they ordered the wrong thing at dinner." She raised her chin. "If the Shippers chose him, they must have a good reason, and I intend to find out what it is."

Spencer mustered a polite smile. "Please remember your break is forty-five minutes."

"Yes, sir." She spoke in a formal if somewhat mocking tone. "I'll report to my station for duty at the required time." Abby saluted with her right hand. "Come on, Maddie. Let's go to the ball."

They walked away. The sound of bells grew faint, then faded completely. A depressing void replaced the music, and he shook off the silence. Better to spend his energy talking sense into his mother.

CHAPTER 19

A KNOCK INTERRUPTED EMILY'S PUZZLE efforts. She groaned in frustration, shuffled to the door, and opened it.

Gerry entered and walked to the mess of torn papers on the table. "How much progress did you make?"

Emily closed the door and pointed at the partially reassembled card. "He shredded it good, but I've got a portion of the message put together."

Gerry pulled her glasses from her pocket, settled them onto her skinny nose, and read the matched pieces. "'Girlfriend. Wife. Don't want.'" She cocked an eyebrow. "That's all?"

"It's been slow going. But with two of us working on it, we should be done in no time."

No time stretched into three hours. If her cabin had a window, Emily imagined she would've seen the sun dipping ever lower in the sky. But an ocean-view room was too pricey since she lived alone. Still, privacy was worth the sacrifice. She slid the last rumpled piece of paper into place.

Gerry slumped in her chair and massaged the back of her neck. "I need to go to my room and take a nap. That was worse than editing my book for weasel words."

"What's a—" Emily yawned. "Never mind. You ought to finish your novel someday." She pointed to the reconstructed note. "You could add a dash of blackmail."

Gerry read the words aloud. "'Indiscretion equals money. If you don't want your real wife finding out about your girlfriend, it costs five thousand dollars. I will let you know where to drop the cash.'" She clicked her tongue. "If I used this in a book, I'd increase the price or my readers might roll their eyes. What kind of blackmailer asks for a measly five thousand bucks?"

"Good point. He's risking a jail sentence for such a small payout." Emily drummed her fingers on the table. "Maybe it's a matter of quantity over quality."

"How so?"

"Consider how many people must have affairs on cruise ships. If he charged the same fee to twenty cheaters a year, that's a hundred thousand dollars."

"You think he's doing this to more than that lothario and Daisy?"

"I'd bet on it." Emily grabbed her cell phone to take a picture of the completed puzzle.

"Wait till we tell the others." Gerry adjusted one of the paper pieces.

Worry squirmed in Emily's brain. Daisy's happiness trumped any investigation.

Dear Lord, please show me what to do.

Was it really possible one of the blackmailer's victims was their quiet and demure Southern belle? What could Daisy have done to warrant such a threat? It didn't bode well that their friend's note contained two of the same words, *indiscretion* and *money*. If the Shippers hunted down the person responsible for the black envelopes, would it mean exposing one of their own?

CHAPTER 20

ABBY'S CHEEKS ACHED FROM SMILING.

Fake smiling. She'd done her best on her second date with the minister. Norville had been considerate and attentive on their quiet walk around a lower deck. He'd even offered his jacket when it got too windy. She'd enjoyed the gallantry until the overwhelming scent of his musky cologne gave her a headache.

They'd talked of growing up and hobbies and spiritual matters. It was obvious why the Shippers had chosen him. He matched her in so many ways.

But it was hopeless.

There was no spark. No zing. No unnamed something that kept a person awake until three in the morning replaying every interaction.

She checked her watch and hurried. She'd promised to meet Mr. Masterson and Madeleine at the restaurant. Abby broke into a run and arrived outside the ornate wooden doors of Trafalgar with twenty seconds to spare.

"I made it." She held up her hand to Maddie for a high five.

The adorable girl stared at the open palm, paused, and lifted her hand to wave. The poor thing. How had she lived this long on planet Earth with no one giving her a high five? Abby saw she had her work cut out for her. The remainder of the voyage would be spent introducing

Madeleine Masterson to all the wonderful, silly parts of childhood she'd missed so far.

Abby tapped her hand against Maddie's. "High five! You do this when you're happy."

Maddie looked at Abby and then at her father. She pointed back and forth without a word.

"Ah." Abby rose on her tippy-toes. "I'm not sure I can reach, but I'll try." She extended her hand. "High five?"

Spencer Masterson quirked his head. "How is it you have no filter or fear of embarrassment?"

Abby laughed. "When you work with young kids, you chuck your pride out the window. Besides, I take my silliness very seriously." She adopted a stern expression and wiggled her fingers. "High five . . . sir?"

He smacked her hand with his larger one. But instead of pulling away, he bent the tops of his fingers over hers. They dwarfed her own by a good bit. The warmth of his broad palm pressed against her skin.

Zing!

The sensation shot from her toes to her top. It pinballed through Abby's heart and lit her insides.

"Working hard, Abigail?" A mocking voice interrupted.

Abby jerked away and turned to find her supervisor behind them. Twila wore a different outfit than the monogrammed polo and shorts most childcare workers preferred. She stood in her knee-length purple skirt and crisp white jacket, eyeing the trio with one carefully drawn eyebrow hoisted.

She smirked. "I can see why you took the entire second half of the voyage off."

"I'm not taking off." Abby squirmed. "It's part of our nanny valet service. Mr. Masterson brought a governess for his daughter, but the woman's been sick."

"Mm-hmm." Twila waved at the swanky restaurant's sign. "Tough gig."

Abby sagged. She hated confrontation. When she'd been a kindergarten teacher, she'd dreaded parent-teacher conferences.

Her supervisor ignored her in favor of Spencer. "I trust Ms. O'Brien will provide you with the best service, sir."

Spencer inspected the woman as if she were an intruder. A sensitive ten seconds stretched between them, and Twila dropped her gaze, polishing the gold uniform buttons with her sleeve.

"If you have any problems"—she squeaked the words—"don't hesitate to contact me. Good night." With a deferential bob of her head, she was gone.

Abby released a noisy breath. "Great. I'm going to be on splash pad duty for the rest of my Monarch life."

Spencer opened one of the restaurant doors. "Did you do something to get on her bad side?"

Abby took Maddie by the hand, and they entered first. "She isn't too happy with my new side gig as a nanny valet. Most passengers book it for a few hours, not an entire voyage. This extended assignment leaves them short-staffed at the Kids Kingdom."

They checked in with the maître d', who led them to a table by a window. Had it only been a day since she sat here with Norville? The same elegant place settings with more silverware than she knew what to do with lined the linen tablecloth. Folded napkins in the shape of swans rested on the plates. Abby sat at the end of the four-person table on the same side as Maddie. Spencer chose the seat across from Abby. After settling in their chairs, he resumed the conversation.

"As the person who booked your services, I'm the one who deserves her ire. Why is the woman angry with you?"

Abby considered Maddie, leaned closer to Spencer, and lowered her voice. "I suspect Twila doesn't like kids much. Because of me, she'll have to spend more time with them instead of hiding in her office."

"It's a swan!" Maddie ignored the adult conversation and played with her folded napkin.

Abby placed her own cloth swan in front of the child. "Here, now you have two."

Spencer was in the process of unfolding his own napkin. He froze and glanced at his daughter. Taking the swan from the empty seat beside him, he passed it to her. Madeleine giggled at the three cloth figures and pushed them around her imaginary table lake.

Tenderness covered Spencer's face for the briefest of seconds before he turned his attention to Abby. "You keep the children in line with the finesse of a symphony conductor. Where did all that bravado go a few minutes ago?"

She shrugged. "I'm bigger than the kids. But adults are another matter. It's hard to be commanding when you're hobbit-size."

"Size has nothing to do with it. The most fearsome judge I know is five feet tall. Every lawyer in New Orleans quakes when they learn he'll be presiding over a case."

Abby rested her elbows on the table. "How does he do it? Does he speak in a loud, bellowing voice?"

"Hardly. You have to lean close to hear him."

"What's his secret?"

"Should I teach you?"

She clasped her hands together. "I'll be Maddie's permanent splash pad partner in return."

"Permanent? Is that a promise?"

Abby crossed her heart. "I promise."

He cocked his head.

"Sorry. Force of habit. Please tell me, oh Master of Intimidation, how do I make others quake in their boots?"

Spencer stared at her without speaking. Abby smiled. The seconds ticked away.

She twisted in her seat. "What's the secret? Do I grimace? Pound my fist? Wear power suits?"

He remained still.

She fiddled with the button at the neck of her polo shirt. "If you'd rather wait until later, I understand."

Spencer rose slowly. He placed a hand on either end of the table. Abby inched back. He drew closer until he was centimeters away from her face. Her eyes widened.

"Silence," he said.

"What?" Her lashes fluttered.

"The greatest weapon you can wield is silence. When you say nothing, people rush to fill the awkward void. The one who speaks first relinquishes control of the conversation to the other person. Don't be in a hurry to answer."

Abby said nothing. Not because she was following his advice. Her stomach had leaped into her throat. Every muscle in her body clenched. She wished he'd stop scorching the oxygen from the room.

Spencer's gaze made a slow circuit from her forehead to her chin. He moved away. His tall frame settled on the seat. "Was that helpful?"

Abby sucked in a giant breath. "Wow! I pity the people going against you in court." She waggled her shoulders. "I have never been so uncomfortable in my life."

Uncomfortable? Of course she was uncomfortable. He'd dismissed society's unwritten rules of personal space, leaning over his employee in a way her supervisor would've surely misunderstood. He grabbed a menu and held it up to block his face. What had gotten into him? He checked and found Abby sending a tentative glance his way.

"What should I order?" she said.

"Your preferences might be different from mine. But to narrow it down, I recommend either the braised chicken or the caramelized shallot ravioli."

"Chicken. My body aches for protein."

Maddie held a swan in front of her face and asked in a squeaky voice, "Can I have pizza?"

"Look, Mr. Masterson! A talking bird that likes pizza." Abby laughed. "But I think, Mrs. Swan, we should try something new. Why don't you have chicken like me?"

Spencer appreciated her ability to turn Madeleine's request down without making it seem like a rejection. She should try that tactic on the pasta preacher.

"Shall we say grace before or after the food arrives?" he joked.

Abby called his bluff. "Why not now? Let's teach Maddie the important stuff." She bent to the girl. "Saying grace is how we show God we're grateful for our food."

Maddie listened with wide eyes.

"It doesn't have to be long. You bow your head and remember all the things you're thankful for."

Spencer reached out and took his daughter's hand, then winked at her. "This is how the experts do it."

Maddie slipped the fingers of her other hand into Abby's and bowed her head. Spencer held his free hand across the table.

"I learned this trick from the minister."

Abby plopped her hand into his. "He didn't invent it."

Spencer's strong fingers enveloped hers. She shut her eyes and waited. Silence. She peeked at Spencer.

"You'd better say the blessing," he said. "I haven't passed the beginner level in the prayer department."

"I'm a little surprised you talk to God." Her brows winged upward.

"On the contrary"—Spencer's smile was nothing short of angelic—"we used to be close when I was a boy. I'm sorry to say, I drifted as I grew older, assigning him to the same category as Santa Claus."

Abby winced and jerked her head at Maddie.

He cleared his throat. "I assure you. I've seen the error of my ways and am consulting the Almighty on a regular basis now. But public prayers are still a bit beyond my purview. Ms. O'Brien, please say the blessing for us."

She closed her eyes. "Dear Lord, we thank you for giving us a sunny day and healthy bodies to enjoy it. Please bless this food—"

"And remove the calories," Spencer said.

"Bless Grandma Daisy and her friends."

"Keep them from stirring up any more trouble, Lord."

She dug her nails into his palm, and he jerked away. Abby finished her prayer. "And please help the foolish people who can't see your love at work in our lives come to know you better."

"Amen." Spencer massaged his skin. "Who knew praying over food could be dangerous?"

The truth in his words hit him upside the head. This was the second time in the space of ten minutes he'd been unnecessarily close with his employee. Why couldn't he keep his hands to himself?

God, don't let me turn out like my father.

His mind formed the desperate prayer. For years, he'd witnessed his sire treat female employees like they were his own personal playthings. Julius Masterson had flirted with some and carried on actual affairs with others. Although Daisy never once mentioned her husband's philandering in Spencer's presence, she must have known.

Daisy.

She was the reason for this crazy cruise in the first place. *Forget the appealing redhead and keep your eye on the target.* He heard the waiter approach the table. "Bring me the pan-seared salmon."

"Sorry, dear," a sweet voice replied. "I don't work here."

At his elbow, he found not the waiter but one of his mother's friends. The short one with the springy hair. She wore a thick cream cardigan with a flowered print blouse and a pair of khaki pants.

"Emily!" Abby jumped up and gave her a hug.

"I didn't mean to interrupt you." She urged Abby back to her seat and gestured to her own outfit. "I'm not dressed for the Trafalgar. The maître d' wanted to refuse me entry but didn't dare. He's been after the Shippers to set him up with the pretty fitness director. I keep telling him one client at a time. Speaking of clients"—she grimaced at Abby— "it appears our first option isn't panning out, but we have an alternate ready. How would you like to eat lunch with this restaurant's new sous chef while the ship is in port tomorrow?"

"Sous chef?" Abby bounced in her seat. "Is he the guy with the silky blond hair all the housekeepers swoon over?"

"One and the same. His name is Cedric. He wasn't one of our original prospects, but everyone on the kitchen staff speaks well of him, and he's expressed an interest in you."

Abby's delighted squeal told Spencer her reply. Before she could speak, he interrupted. "I'm sorry, but I need Ms. O'Brien's help tomorrow. I plan to take Madeleine for"—he regarded his daughter, who was playing with her family of swans—"some recreation. Ms. O'Brien must choose an age-appropriate activity and accompany us."

A pout formed on Abby's lips. "Sorry, Mrs. Windsor. Romance will have to wait."

"No matter, dear." Emily rubbed her hands together. "I checked with the first mate, and we don't leave port until ten o'clock tomorrow night. How about a romantic walk on the beach with Cedric after your charge has gone to bed?"

Spencer's gaze darted to Abby, who sprang from her seat and wrapped the older woman in another hug. Her joyful laugh enlivened the restaurant's solemn atmosphere.

"That sounds amazing," Abby said. "I owe you and the Shippers a million thank-you notes."

Emily patted her. "Completely unnecessary. Your happiness is what matters. Besides"—the matchmaker's face stiffened—"I have my fill of notes to deal with at present."

The cryptic comment didn't escape Spencer's notice. He studied the woman as she bid them goodbye and exited the restaurant. Even people in their seventies might have underhanded tendencies. Who exactly were these Shippers? Could they be trusted not to take advantage of his mother?

Spencer eyed Abby, who sat in a dreamy coma, her attention pointed at the waves outside the window. He cleared his throat with all the subtlety of a muscle car's engine.

She jolted. "Oops." Her voice sounded the tiniest bit breathless. "What were we discussing? Oh, right. What did you mean by 'recreation'?"

Spencer employed the silence technique as he took a long drink of water from his glass. Truth be told, he had no idea what they were doing or why. He'd made the suggestion on the spur of the moment because Emily Windsor was offering another marriage candidate to Abby. What did his new nanny truly know about these ladies? It was dangerous, yielding such an important decision as marriage to them.

He knew from firsthand experience the soul-crushing tribulation of divorce, and he owed it to his employee to look after her.

Spencer swallowed. "You're the one who pointed out a cruise was for relaxation. I've decided to spend time with my daughter in a frivolous, noneducational activity."

"Excellent decision." She gave him an approving nod. "But where do you want to go? Were you planning to visit a resort at the next port?"

"As to that"—he crossed his arms—"I'd prefer to stay aboard, but I'm unfamiliar with what the ship offers. I assume you must be well-versed in its attractions. What would Madeleine enjoy the most?"

His daughter knocked a swan off the table with her elbow. "Oops!" She bent over the arm of her chair. "I can't reach."

Abby retrieved the napkin and returned it to her. "She liked the splash pad. I bet she'd adore the kiddie pool. It has slides and fountains and everything."

"More water activities?" Spencer cringed. "Isn't there any recreation that would allow us to remain dry?"

"Don't worry." She laughed. "I'll be Maddie's lifeguard. You can stay on solid ground, far away from the pool." Abby wrinkled her nose. "Just don't wear a suit."

Her skin folded in mischievous crinkles between her green eyes. A smattering of light freckles dusted the spot. He forced himself to look away and took another drink of water. As an employer, he was protecting Abigail O'Brien from making bad matrimonial choices arranged by an opinionated group of golden-girl matchmakers. But was that his only reason? He shoved away the suspicion that a tinge of jealousy colored his motivation.

Business. That's all this was.

CHAPTER 21

EMILY PAUSED OUTSIDE ALTHEA AND Daisy's cabin door. Was she doing the right thing? Heaven was silent, so she was going with her gut. This blackmailer needed to be stopped.

No one messed with her family.

She knocked on the door. Gerry opened it and moved away to allow her entrance. With no windows, the inner cabin resembled a spacious closet. The contained space barely had room for the four of them. Daisy stood inside the cramped bathroom, fixing her makeup in the mirror. Althea sat on one of the white-duvet-covered single beds, and Gerry settled beside her.

Emily twisted her purse handles and entreated heaven one last time.

"Girls"—she plopped her bag on the compact desk by the wall—"I have important news." She cast a nervous glance at the Shipper in the bathroom. "A blackmailer has taken up residence on the MS *Buckingham*."

Daisy's hand stilled briefly before she continued applying her mascara. "You don't say. First there were drug smugglers. Now blackmailers."

Althea tsk-tsked. "It's getting so a body isn't safe anywhere."

Emily rapped on the desk. "Just like we tracked down the smugglers, it's our duty to find who's threatening the passengers with these black envelopes. Show them, Gerry."

Gerry produced the taped-together note and passed it to Althea.

"Mmm-mmm-*mmm*." The sassy Shipper hummed in disgust as she read. "Whoever wrote this has a flair for the dramatic. He thinks he's some villain in a Sherlock Holmes novel. 'Indiscretion equals money.'"

Daisy's body drew tight. Emily waited for her friend to confess she recognized the words, but Daisy remained silent. Instead, she replaced her mascara wand in the tube.

Gerry took the note from Althea and walked to the bathroom door. "Do you want to see this, Daisy?"

"No, thank you." Daisy dabbed a spot of her favorite magnolia-scented perfume on her throat. "Althea can tell me about it later."

Frustration boiled inside Emily. Why was Daisy pretending ignorance? Didn't she trust the Shippers with her secrets after everything they had overcome together?

Daisy meandered from the bathroom, picking a single piece of lint from the black sleeve of her jacket. "I'm ready."

"Finally." It took Althea two bounces to maneuver off the bed. "I'm starving. Let's not visit Trafalgar tonight. Those fancy portions are too small."

Gerry tucked the note in her pocket. "Guess this can wait."

A complaint rose in Emily's throat, but she refrained from voicing it. There was plenty of time to discuss the blackmailer. For the moment, they could concentrate on their primary mission.

Matchmaking.

"Speaking of Trafalgar," she said, "I spoke to Abigail a few minutes ago. She was dining there with Daisy's son and granddaughter." She hesitated before adding, "They made quite the familial picture."

Daisy ignored the comment. "Did you tell her about the sous chef?"

"Yes, and she's raring to go."

Althea chuckled. "That's one thing I love about Abby. She's willing to give anyone a try. Her heart's bursting with love to give to somebody."

"True," Gerry said. "Let's make sure her enthusiasm doesn't cause her to choose the *wrong* somebody."

Abigail O'Brien was a dream client. Attractive, amiable, and prepared to follow their direction without argument. Yet a weed of worry refused to be yanked from Emily's brain. Something prodded her like a missing item on a to-do list. Abby deserved the very best, but the best looked different for each person. Who was the man she was meant to be with? Not because the Shippers picked him but because heaven ordained it long before they were born.

CHAPTER 22

SPENCER SCANNED THE LOBBY, BUT there was no sign of his pint-size employee. He switched the bulging canvas bag he carried from one hand to the other. The addition of his laptop to the pile of supplies he'd packed for Madeleine made it heavier. His daughter sat on a purple velvet couch and lightly kicked her sandaled feet.

He dug in his pocket for his cell phone. They'd promised to meet at nine o'clock, and Abby was three minutes late. He surveyed the room again.

"Here I am!" Abby waved from a side hallway. Dressed in shorts and a T-shirt with a cartoon kitten on the front, she carried a polka-dot bag. She raced across the open expanse, swerving around passengers in her haste.

Madeleine hopped to her feet and held out her arms.

Abby skidded to a stop and dropped her bag. She picked the little girl up, squealed, and swung her in a circle. "Oh, I missed you so much. Are you ready to have a blast?"

Spencer observed the enthusiastic welcome with envy. He might as well be invisible. When was the last time anyone had been that happy to greet him?

"You're late," he said.

"What?" Abby set Madeleine down and checked her watch. "Three minutes? I'm not late. I'm fashionably delayed."

"Good thing you're not a lawyer. I doubt that excuse would work on a judge."

"Guess what?" Abby was talking to his daughter again as if he didn't exist. "I saw your grandma at breakfast this morning. She's going to play with us."

"She's what?" Spencer's voice rose.

Madeleine's shoulders bunched, and Abby threw him a warning look.

She squeezed the child closer. "I'm sorry, Mr. Masterson. I didn't think you'd mind letting Daisy spend time with us."

"I . . . I don't mind." He searched for the right words. "It's fine if she comes along. It's just . . . unexpected."

"Oh good." Her smile reappeared. "Aren't you excited, Maddie? We get to hang out with Grandma Daisy today."

Grandma Daisy? Spencer could imagine the wince if his mother heard that description. She'd always been careful to maintain a youthful persona with frequent trips to the Botox clinic.

"Good morning, Spencer." Daisy's genteel voice sounded from behind.

He turned to find not only his mother but her entire coterie of friends. Emily, the frizzy-haired one who approached them at the Trafalgar, wore the same khaki pants with a blue-striped shirt and aviator sunglasses. Her tall friend with her hair slicked in a severe bun wore a gauzy ankle-length skirt and top. And his mother's roommate sported a red scarf over her silver hair to match her outfit. The large woman gathered Spencer in a hug and pounded him on the back.

"Hello, hello, hello!" her robust voice sang. "I'm Althea, in case you forgot."

"Yes." He gave her an awkward double pat and extricated himself from her soft hold. "Althea, thank you for the reminder." He acknowledged his mother. "Daisy, I understand you'll be joining us at the pool."

Althea grinned. "We're all coming, baby." She passed him a leopard-print bag. "My sacroiliac's been hurtin'. Can you carry this for me?"

Daisy handed him a similar-sized black one. "Mine too, if you please. Thank you."

The group stared at him with cheerful expectation, except for the tall one, whose stoic countenance remained unreadable. The four senior citizens began to move, and Abby added her own tote to his ever-growing collection. "Let's head to the pool."

Spencer examined the bags. Since when had he become the porter? Abby was his employee, not the other way around. Who was the boss in this relationship?

CHAPTER 23

A MAN-MADE WATERFALL CASCADED into the crystal clear children's pool as families cavorted in the spray. Mounted speakers played a blend of popular hits, and sunlight glinted off the cheery orange and turquoise tiles surrounding the swimming area.

Emily relaxed on a recliner beside Gerry, who hadn't emerged from her book since they arrived. Daisy and Althea sat on the edge of the pool, splashing their legs at a giggling Maddie, who floated on her back while Abby propped her hands beneath her. A perfect picture—except for one detail.

Emily glowered Spencer's direction. He sat at a table in his starchy khaki pants and crisp white shirt, typing away on his phone. How could the man ignore his family? It was unconscionable.

The desire to meddle surged inside her, but she decided to ask for advice first.

"Lord." She didn't bother praying quietly. Gerry knew her penchant for petitioning their heavenly Father. "What's wrong with that man? He has a beautiful baby girl and a mother who hasn't seen him in a year and a half. Should I say something?"

"Would it do any good?" Gerry snarked.

"I wasn't talking to you."

"I know. But I'm throwing my two cents in anyway. I doubt anything you say would make an impression on that stuffed shirt."

"Mr. Masterson!" Abby hollered from the pool. "Come here. Maddie's floating by herself."

Spencer immediately put the phone away and walked to join them.

"Did you see that?" Emily nudged Gerry.

Her friend poked her nose over the top of her book. "See what?"

"One call from our Abby-girl, and Spencer stopped working to attend the floating lesson. What does that tell you?"

"Tells me he's not completely heartless. He must care about his daughter."

Emily resumed her conversation with heaven. "I don't know, Lord. Am I the only one who's seeing this? Or am I completely delusional?"

"Yes," said Gerry. "And yes."

"Can I go on the slide?" Maddie asked.

"Absolutely, sweetie." Abby helped her climb from the shallow pool.

"Excuse me." Spencer turned. "I need to send another text to my office."

Abby rolled her eyes and walked hand in hand with Maddie to the twisty orange slide.

The little girl climbed the short ladder but hesitated.

Abby called, "Don't be afraid. You can do it. I'll go wait at the bottom for you."

As she spun to head there, her bare foot caught on a waist-high stack of folded lounge recliners piled by the pool's edge. Her body twisted left. Her ankle twisted right. *Pain.* She stumbled and landed on the tiles with a thud.

Quick steps rushed to her side. "What happened?" Spencer knelt beside her.

She motioned to the chairs. "I tripped."

Her boss examined the pile. "Are you hurt?"

"I wrenched my ankle. It—"

"You should be more careful." He reached out to touch her leg.

Abby clamped her lips. "You're right." She moved away before his fingers made contact and stood with effort. "I'll be fine."

He rose to his full height. "Are you sure?"

"Never mind me. Go play with Maddie."

"I have something to do first." He stalked away without another word.

"Probably looking for a phone charger," Abby muttered to herself, and shook her head. "Would it kill you to spend five minutes with your own daughter?"

She took a step and flinched. Sharp jolts shot through her ankle. But at least it didn't feel broken. It was possible to move.

Painful but possible.

"Oh well." Abby leaned her weight on her heel. "Might as well walk it off." Maybe if she put her sneakers on, it would help.

"Abby!" Maddie stood at the top of the slide and waved. "Look at me!"

"You did it all by yourself!" Abby masked her pain as she hobbled over. "I'm right here, sweetie."

Spencer passed his business card to the manager. The man's desk took up most of the space in the narrow office near the main pool. His sweaty forehead gleamed as he bent to read it.

"As you can see"—Spencer pointed a finger at the card—"I'm well-versed in legal matters. You have a situation to deal with before any more injuries occur."

"Any more?" The manager shrank.

"One of your own employees hurt her ankle on a careless stack of chairs near the kiddie pool. My daughter and many other children are playing nearby. I'd hate for anyone else to suffer the same accident. I suggest you tell maintenance to remove them before you find yourself on the nasty end of a lawsuit."

"Oh—oh, yes, sir. Yes, sir!" Sweat beads dripped down his glistening face. "I'll send someone right away."

Spencer headed for the exit. He stopped at the door. The spot where he'd left Abby and Madeleine was empty. Where were they? He inspected the area and spied a glossy mane of red hair by a flower-themed splash pad. Madeleine ran among the jets of water, a sunhat hanging from a string around her neck. Abby stood with hands outstretched. Favoring her right leg, she hobbled after his squealing daughter.

The manager zipped to his side. "I've contacted maintenance, sir. They're on their way to examine the problematic area as we speak."

"Thank you." Spencer stomped out into the sunshine.

The man scrambled along behind. "I'll personally apologize to the injured party."

Spencer wound through the jet streams of the giant splash pad. The blasting cannons doused his khaki trouser legs. He reached Abby, grasped her upper arm, and pointed at her ankle. "Why aren't you resting?" A shot of water hit him in the chest, and he brushed the moisture away with an impatient hand.

Abby tilted her face to him. Her normal exuberant smile appeared a tad forced. "It doesn't hurt as bad with my sneakers on. I'm okay."

Madeleine ran over with a wary expression. "What's wrong?"

"Nothing." Abby smiled. "Everything is good, Maddie."

The manager dashed to their group and began a lengthy apology. Spencer waved him away like a pesky housefly. He steered Abby to a nearby bench and urged her to a sitting position. Kneeling on the deck in front of her, he unlaced her shoe. She winced as he gingerly slipped it off her foot.

His jaw clenched at the colorful bruise forming around her ankle. This was his fault. If he hadn't been caught up in his work, he might have been able to prevent the accident.

The manager flitted in the background. "Oh my—"

"Ugh." Abby wrinkled her nose. "That isn't pretty."

"What happened?" Daisy said, hurrying over, her friends not far behind.

Spencer waved Abby's shoe. "Ms. O'Brien twisted her ankle."

The four women fluttered around them, offering commiserations and advice on how to best treat a sprain.

Madeleine wandered closer and rubbed Abby's heel. "Does it hurt?"

"Don't worry, sweetie," Abby said. "I'm fine."

Emily smacked Spencer's upper arm. "What are you waiting for? You should carry her to the infirmary."

"I should what?" He stood upright.

Abby waved both hands. "Totally unnecessary. I can walk." She pushed herself to her feet and winced.

"See there?" Emily pointed. "You don't want her to injure herself further, do you?"

"But I . . ." Spencer blinked.

"Really, Spencer," said Daisy.

Althea clicked her tongue. "Show them how a Southern gentleman behaves."

Squeals and splashes and the airy gusts of the water cannons told him the other passengers were busy enjoying the pool. So why did it feel like the whole world was watching him? The Shippers definitely were. They stared him down with eyebrows raised in expectation. He sighed and bent, then placed an arm at Abby's back.

Gerry took out a small notebook. "Now we're talking. Maybe I can use this in my novel."

"No, no, no." Abby pushed him away. "I'm fine."

Spencer straightened and glared at the hovering manager. "I assume this ship has a wheelchair somewhere."

"Oh yes," the manager said. "I'm very, very sorry. Let me get you the wheelchair." He scrambled in his pockets. "Where did I put my phone? Let me run to my office—oh, wait. Here it is!" He discovered the cell in his back pocket and went off to place a call.

Gerry shook her head and put her notebook away. "Don't think I'll be getting any material for my book."

"Yep." Althea propped her hands on her hips. "No heroes here."

"I apologize, Abigail," Daisy said. "It's my fault for not raising him better."

"It's coming!" The manager waved his phone over his head. "The wheelchair should be here in ten minutes."

"Ten minutes? You've got to be kid—" Spencer passed the shoe to Abby. "Forget it." He put one hand around her back and the other under her knees.

She hugged her sneaker tight. "What are you doing? I can walk."

He rose in a swift motion. Her petite body settled against his. She weighed hardly more than a child.

"That's more like it," said Emily. "Well done, Spencer."

Althea applauded. "It's about stinkin' time."

"Whoa." Abby threw an arm around his neck and peered at the ground. "I'm going to get airsick up here."

Spencer nodded at his daughter. "Come along, Madeleine."

Abby pressed his chest. "The bags. We left them by the bench."

Spencer ignored the tingling sensation where her fingers rested and addressed the manager. "Get them for us."

"Yes, sir!"

The man skittered away, and Spencer strode off, the Shippers and Madeleine at his heels.

Abby squirmed in his arms. "It looks worse than it feels. You don't have to carry me."

"Madeleine, are you coming?" Spencer made sure his daughter was at his side and kept walking.

"Maddie." Abby craned her neck over his shoulder. "Put your hat on. Your nose is getting sunburned."

The visor dangled from the string around her neck. Madeleine scurried beside Spencer as she pulled it onto her head. He shortened his strides so she could keep up. Even with an injury, Abigail O'Brien was thinking of his daughter first. The motherly concern in her eyes was as foreign to him as the snowcapped peaks of the Himalayas. And just as beautiful.

His nose almost touched hers. From this close, Abby noticed his irises weren't actually black but a really, really deep brown. Like hot fudge. Resting on a six-foot-plus sundae of gorgeousness.

She shook her head. *Professional. Keep it professional.* And make him put her down. Even if she kind of liked the view.

"I can—"

"Hush," he murmured. "It would take you thirty minutes to limp to the infirmary."

Should she take offense? A grown woman shouldn't be hushed, but the man did have a point. She shouldn't inconvenience the group. Her injury had already brought an abrupt halt to their family recreation. Next time, she'd be more careful.

Wait—next time? There wouldn't be a next time. The cruise ended in three days. Spencer and Maddie would return home to Louisiana, and she'd never see them again.

The idea dampened the novelty of being princess-carried for the first time in her life. Abby slumped. As first a teacher and then a child-care worker, she was used to growing attached to the little ones and then having to say goodbye. But this felt different somehow. Was it because of Maddie? Or her attractive father? Or maybe both?

A soft hand squeezed her leg. Emily Windsor contemplated her from below. "Are you all right, dear?"

"Oh"—Abby shook off her melancholy—"don't worry about me. My ankle will be good as new in a few hours."

Emily studied her with eyes that held a lifetime's worth of wisdom. "I wasn't talking about your ankle." Her glance cut to Spencer. "If you need to talk to someone, I suggest the Lord first and me second."

Embarrassment sucker punched Abby. Were her emotions that easy to read? Had Spencer also guessed her thoughts? She sneaked a peek at him, but he was focused on Daisy, suggesting she take Madeleine by the hand.

Abby looked back at Emily. "Thank you. I'll keep that in mind."

Twenty minutes later, she left the exam room with an elastic bandage around her ankle and a bottle of ibuprofen. Her crowd of well-wishers sat in the waiting room.

Abby tottered to the group. "Good news. I'll live. Dr. Grant said to wear this lovely bandage a few days and not to walk too fast." She wobbled over to where Spencer sat with Madeleine between him and Daisy.

"Mr. Masterson, I understand if you'd prefer to have the ship assign you a different nanny."

He stood. "I don't want to overtax you. Will you be staying in your cabin until your ankle heals?"

"Oh my word, no." Abby laughed. "They'll put me on desk duty at the childcare center, but I'll still report to work."

"If that's the case, then I'd prefer you continue as Madeleine's nanny. You can sit in our suite as easily as you can at a desk."

Althea clicked her tongue. "I guess this means no moonlight walk on the beach with Cedric the sous chef. Such a pity. He was raring to go."

"Oh." Abby's mouth drooped. "Bummer."

"Don't you worry." Emily patted her arm. "I've already worked out a plan B."

"Plan B?" Spencer's tone matched his sardonic expression.

"Yes. The best operations always have a backup." Emily dug her phone from her handbag. "I'll text Cedric and have him meet you at Cloud Nine."

"Cloud Nine?" Abby's jaw swung open. "That's the most expensive private venue on the ship. Exclusive VIPs use it."

"I know, dear." Emily winked. "This is when it pays to be friends with the owner's son. After we helped Jon win the woman of his dreams, he said he owed us for life. Borrowing Cloud Nine for a midnight picnic is hardly too much to ask."

"Midnight?" Spencer moved his body halfway between Abby and the Shippers. "She's suffered an injury. Should she be up so late?"

"The man has a point," Gerry said. "Why not make it an afternoon picnic? Cedric's evening shift doesn't start until six."

"Just a minute." Spencer held up a hand. "Ms. O'Brien still needs to care for Madeleine."

Daisy spoke. "I don't mind filling in. We can go for pedicures and eat supper together. Would you like that, Madeleine?"

"Yes, Grandma," Maddie said. "What's a pet-a-gure?"

Daisy laughed and began to explain the enchanted world of foot baths and toenail polish.

"I can hardly believe it." Abby bounced on her good heel. "Cloud Nine! Thank you, thank you!"

Emily lifted her gray eyebrows at Spencer. "Any other objections?"

He shifted to Abby. "Are you sure your ankle can take it?"

"You betcha." She made a muscle. "I'm as strong as an ox. *Mooooo.*"

Madeleine giggled. Abby wrapped an arm around her and squeezed.

He cleared his throat. "Very well. As per our agreement, you have forty-five minutes."

Abby grimaced at the ugly bandage on her leg. "I hope I can find a skirt long enough to cover this thing."

Dr. Timothy Grant exited the exam room. Streaks of premature gray adorned his mahogany-brown hair. He halted when he spotted their group. "I didn't realize how popular our waiting room was. Hello, Emily. Are you getting enough exercise?"

"Yes, of course." Emily batted a hand. "How long will Abby be out of commission?"

His white lab coat lent him a distinguished air, which was counteracted by his mischievous grin. "Don't worry. As long as she doesn't sign up for any samba lessons, her ankle should be right as rain in a few days."

Emily rubbed Abby's arm. "Sorry, dear. No dancing dates in your near future."

Dr. Grant's smile teased. "I haven't heard about this, Abby. Are you dating someone?"

"Anyone who will have me," Abby joked.

An irritated huff sounded from Spencer.

"If my workaholic boss will give me the time off," she added.

"Is there a sign-up sheet?" Dr. Grant's grin widened. "I might want to get in on this."

"A date with a doctor? Be still, my heart." Abby laughed. "But talk to the Shippers. They're representing me."

"I might—"

"It's time for Madeleine's lunch," Spencer took his daughter by the hand and led her over. "Ms. O'Brien, if you'll accompany her to the room, I have some business."

"Yes, sir." Abby straightened and saluted. "On the double, sir." She laced her fingers with Maddie's and smiled at the doctor. "Hopefully the next time we cross paths won't be for medical reasons."

"Count on it," he said.

Spencer disregarded the man and herded Abby and Madeleine to the chair where they'd left their things.

Was it Abby's imagination, or had she heard Spencer mutter, "Don't count on it"?

CHAPTER 24

AMUSEMENT TICKLED EMILY'S FUNNY BONE. Spencer's futile struggle to block Abby's dating endeavors was so entertaining. The poor man had it bad and didn't even know it. She cocked her eyebrow at Gerry, who met her gaze with bland resignation.

Gerry shrugged. "Guess you're not delusional after all."

Emily basked in the triumph of an accurate deduction, but her pleasure was short-lived. She wanted to help the poor man. He'd made two things obvious with his ham-fisted attempts to keep Abby to himself. Number one, he was smitten with the delightful girl. Number two, he didn't have a clue what he was feeling.

If anyone had ever required the Shippers' help, it was Spencer. He needed their combined wisdom to make sense of his unplumbed emotions. But one Shipper disapproved.

His own mother.

Daisy had made it clear she didn't support a romance between Spencer and Abby. Without her acquiescence, Emily couldn't arrange a match for the woman's son. The Shipper code of honor forbade it.

Emily perused the waiting room. A long receptionist desk filled one side, and a woman in a nurse's uniform sat behind it. She pulled a black square envelope from her mail tray with a furrowed brow.

Emily jetted across the room. "I beg your pardon, is that note for me, dear?"

"What?" the nurse asked. "No, ma'am. This was addressed to one of our staff."

"My mistake. I have one just like it." If a person counted a paper torn into shreds and taped back together as "just like it." She turned on her best doting-grandma smile. "Did you see who left it?"

"No, ma'am. It was here when I returned from lunch."

"Thank you, dear." Emily patted the desk instead of stomping her foot as she'd prefer. Was there a blackmailing ghost on the MS *Buckingham*? How else could she explain the person's uncanny ability to leave the notes without anyone observing? If only she possessed the power to rewind time and stake out the clinic.

Emily's head snapped up. A black half globe protruded from the ceiling, indicating a CCTV camera was monitoring the room. She returned to her chair and retrieved her purse. "Daisy, are you going to spend the afternoon with your granddaughter?"

Spencer paused with tote bags in hand.

"Why, I"—Daisy looked at her son—"yes. If Spencer doesn't have a problem with it?"

He nodded his consent.

Emily gave Abby a hug. "Don't you worry. We'll arrange the incidentals for your date. Wear your prettiest outfit and be there at five."

Abby saluted. "Roger that."

Emily slipped her purse straps over her wrist and marched to the exit. "Gerry and Althea, come with me. We need to pay a visit to security."

CHAPTER 25

MR. EVERSON'S STOCKY FRAME FILLED the doorway of the security room. His glare communicated his displeasure at their visit. At least, Emily assumed he was glaring. His requisite gunmetal sunglasses blocked his eyes.

"Can I help you, ladies?" His gruff voice warned them he'd be no help at all.

"Yes, Mr. Everson." Emily peeked around his torso at a room lined with TV screens. "This place gives NASA a run for its money. Could you offer us an insider tour? Gerry is doing research for a book set on a cruise ship."

"It's not a cruise ship," Gerry objected. "It's a five-star hotel. And my villain uses the security cameras to spy on his victims."

He remained in place. "Sorry, ma'am. This area is off-limits. No passengers allowed."

Althea exchanged a glance with Emily, placed a hand to her temple, and moaned. "Oh. Oh, my head. The room is spinning. Help me, girls." She thrashed her arm.

"Don't break a hip!" Emily grabbed hold. "Help us, Mr. Everson. Her blood sugar must be low. Let her come in and sit down."

"Mike." The stone-faced security guard called without moving from the doorway. "Bring a chair out here for Mrs. Jones."

Althea lowered her hand. "You know my name?"

The right side of his mouth quirked the tiniest bit. "You ladies have been living on the MS *Buckingham* for a good while. I'm familiar with all of your names and your"—the quirk rose higher—"tactics."

His coworker Mike sidled past him with a folding chair and waited while Althea settled herself. Gerry stood as tall as the man denying them entrance. She peered over his shoulder. "Tell me, Mr. Everson. Can you hear what the passengers are saying on those TV screens?"

He locked his muscular arms over his barrel chest. "That would be a violation of their privacy. We visually monitor everyone's activity for their own safety and as a precaution against lawsuits but don't listen to their conversations. If a question arises about someone's behavior, we can check the footage."

"Speaking of footage." Emily stepped forward. "Could you check the feed for us? Someone left a note in the infirmary today, and we want to know who it was."

"Why?"

Emily shot a worried look at her friends. "I'm afraid I can't reveal the reason, but I assure you it's important."

The man did his best imitation of a statue. Only the slightest movement of his lips proved his humanity. "We respect the rights of our passengers. Whatever your newest scheme is, I advise you ladies to cease and desist." He backed over the threshold and shut the door.

Althea rose from the chair and dusted off her skirt. "Not too friendly, is he?"

Gerry frowned. "Sounds like he's onto us. We better watch what we say around him."

Emily tapped her orthopedic sandal on the floor. "We need access to those video files. How else can we discover who left the blackmail note in the clinic?"

Althea snapped her fingers. "What about Barney? He's always been nice. Maybe he'd sneak a look and fill us in."

"Great idea." Emily patted her. "Why don't we track him down? Once we've finished, we can double-check the details for Abby's romantic dinner at Cloud Nine."

Emily pictured the imaginary thundercloud hanging above Spencer's head. Did he have to make his annoyance with his nanny's dating so obvious? What a shame all that chemistry between him and Abby was wasted.

No matter. The Shippers could find their sweet client someone better. Perhaps this next date would prove they already had.

CHAPTER 26

THAT MIGHT GO DOWN AS the worst date of her entire short life.

Abby shuffled along the wide hallway leading to the VIP suites. The wispy green material of her long sundress had hidden the elastic bandage during her fancy picnic, but the effort was in vain. Perhaps she should've worn sweats to meet Cedric. The forty-five-minute date had resembled ten rounds with a kung fu master. She'd block one hand, and another appeared. Her dress wasn't the best outfit for childcare, but she was too tired to change.

Abby arrived at the Mastersons' suite and knocked. The door swung open. Her boss stood on the other side, his jaw jutting at a grumpy angle.

Why? She wasn't late. The truth was, she'd been grateful for an excuse to leave her date.

"Did you miss me?" She crossed the threshold.

"Madeleine did." He closed the door and walked to the dining room table covered with papers.

"She's here?" Abby lifted her gaze to the upper balcony, expecting to see Maddie peeking over the rail. "I thought she was spending time with Daisy."

Spencer pulled out a chair. "She was tired, and we put her down for a nap. But before she fell asleep, she asked where you were." He sat and shuffled a stack of papers. "How was your date?"

Abby moaned. "Don't remind me. The Shippers need to vet their candidates more carefully."

He stopped shuffling. "Don't tell me the almighty matchmakers picked a dud."

"Not a dud. He was just too fond of physical contact."

"What? Was he acting in an inappropriate manner?"

"*Inappropriate* isn't exactly the right word. More like overly friendly." Abby chuckled. "I haven't been out with a guy that touchy-feely since high school. Good thing I still have one good foot." She sank into a chair opposite him and swung the leg not encased in a bandage. "I kicked his knee so hard he squealed. And then I told him I'd aim higher if he didn't watch his hands."

The beginning of a smile appeared on Spencer's face. "Another gutter ball? After this many consecutive bad dates, maybe you should forgo the incompetent games of my mother and her friends."

"I don't blame them. People like Cedric have great manners until you get them alone. There's no way they could've known what a Casanova he is. I'm sure their next choice will be better." She sensed a protest coming and held up her hand. "Don't worry. It will probably take them several days to offer a new option. By then your cruise will be finished, and you won't have to work your schedule around my love life."

Spencer's forehead knotted. It was true. Soon, they'd say goodbye to Madeleine's nanny valet. Fewer than three days remained until they docked in Galveston.

Abby stood. "I'll check on Maddie."

Her gauzy green dress billowed around her figure as she carefully climbed the stairs. The color somehow made her red hair even more vibrant. The curls bounced around her soft cheeks. Her childlike air projected an innocence completely opposite of the cunning crowd he associated with. It was a shame he couldn't fire the seasick Ms. Blanchet and take this enchanting woman home to be Madeleine's nanny instead.

Enchanting?

Why did he keep applying such unprofessional terms to Ms. O'Brien? Spencer shoved back his chair and stood. After stalking to the kitchen island, he grabbed a bottle of water, twisted off the cap, and drank.

Was it all vacations or specifically cruise ships that caused a person to act so out of character? If he could set aside an hour tomorrow to convince his mother to return to New Orleans, he'd devote the remainder of the voyage to one-on-one time with his daughter.

The sound of Madeleine's giggle floated from upstairs. Spencer paused with the water bottle halfway to his lips. He hoped she still laughed when Abigail O'Brien was no longer around.

CHAPTER 27

CLAMOR FILLED THE MAIN LOBBY from one end to the other. Suitcase wheels rattled against the marble floor. Passengers hollered and laughed and complained on their way to the Galveston pier gangplank and a return to normal life.

Abby sat on a couch with her young charge beside her. Maddie gaped with wide-eyed interest at the swirl of passing people. The little girl seemed unaware that these were their last moments together.

Where had the final three days gone? A sharp, unpleasant sensation hit Abby. Almost distress. But she pushed it away. Saying goodbye was part of her job. She may have grown more attached to Maddie because of the extra hours they'd spent together, but she'd get over it soon. There'd be more children on the next voyage to take her place.

"Pink!" Maddie grabbed Abby's arm and pointed at a woman exiting the elevator with a large sun hat.

Abby faked a disgruntled expression. "Another one? Why are there so many more pink hats than green ones? I picked the wrong color."

"I'm beating you."

Maddie's merry giggle caused an agitated pulse in Abby's brain. No matter how special the new group of kids, they couldn't take this girl's place. Abby had babysat enough young passengers and taught in enough classrooms to admit the truth. This was different. Certain children claimed a room in a person's heart and lived there. Regardless of how much time passed, Abby knew she'd never forget Madeleine Masterson.

Or her handsome father.

Abby glanced at the nearby table where Mr. Masterson talked with his mother. Both sat with rigid spines, hardly a picture of familial harmony. The two stood and made their way over.

Daisy bent to her granddaughter and smoothed the girl's hair. "I was so happy to see you, Madeleine. Please visit me again soon."

"Yes, ma'am." Maddie nodded.

Daisy straightened, brushed both hands down the front of her black dress, and faced her son. "Spencer, it was good of you to visit. Please take care of yourself." With eyes averted and chin raised, she left them.

Spencer motioned to someone at the side, and the fully recovered governess joined them in her starched white shirt and wrinkle-free gray skirt. Not a hint of weakness remained.

"Ms. Blanchet," he said. "Can you please take Madeleine to the dock? I'll join you shortly."

"It'll be a pleasure to set foot on dry land again, sir." She helped Maddie off the couch.

"Wait!" Abby knelt on the ground. Tears clouded her last look at the precious girl. She swallowed the ridiculous overreaction and forced a bright smile. "I loved meeting you, Princess Maddie. I hope we can play together again sometime."

Maddie's lips turned down, and she blinked. "You're not coming with us?"

"I'm sorry. I have to stay here on the ship. But I'll miss you." Abby wrapped her in a hug and squeezed tight. The child's arms looped around her neck.

Ms. Blanchet checked her phone. "Let's go. The chauffeur is waiting." She prodded Madeleine away.

Cold air rushed to fill the empty void in Abby's arms. She drew a wavery breath and got to her feet. The somber governess led her charge to the exit. Maddie glanced over her shoulder with watery eyes before she disappeared. Mr. Masterson waited with something in his hand.

"Ms. O'Brien"—Spencer offered a white envelope—"your help was invaluable during the voyage. I've made sure to reflect my appreciation in your tip."

Abby's nostrils flared.

Her tip? He was treating her like . . .

Like what? An employee? That's what she was. If she'd expected anything more, she was the one in the wrong.

She took the envelope and fingered the flap. The evidence of his generosity bulged inside the paper. Would it be improper to slip the bills out and throw them in his courteous, unsmiling kisser?

Yes. Of course it would.

Abby extended her hand and gave him her best professional smile, the one she used at parent-teacher conferences. "Thank you, sir. I hope you enjoyed your voyage. Please choose Monarch Cruises again in the future."

His large fingers covered her own in a warm grip, and the corner of his lips lifted in an amused grin she didn't appreciate. "You can be sure I will." He released her. "Until we meet again, Ms. O'Brien."

Spencer strode off, his tall figure drawing interested peeks from more than one woman as he passed. Not once did he turn around. Clutching the envelope, Abby watched until he was out of sight. The urge to chuck it in the nearest trash can hit, but she resisted. What was wrong with accepting a tip for a job well done?

A job.

She mustn't get attached to her charges. It hurt too much when they inevitably left. She'd use the money to buy a new dress and wear it on the next date the Shippers arranged.

Love. Marriage. Babies of her own.

That's what she should concentrate on.

Emily sat between Gerry and Althea on a long couch near the entrance. They allowed the drama to play out without interfering. Abby wandered through the room. The hand not holding the envelope swiped at her eyes as she disappeared down the hallway.

In the opposite direction, Daisy rambled aimlessly near the reception desk. A man spun too quickly and bumped her. She stumbled to the side but accepted his apologies with a distracted dip of her head.

Gerry sighed. "Poor Daisy."

Althea pursed her lips. "Our girl is going to be lower than a doorstop after this."

"Can you blame her?" Emily said. "Who says goodbye to his mother like she's one of his clients?"

"In Spencer's defense"—Gerry withdrew her spectacles from a pocket—"Daisy wasn't very motherly herself. Maybe the Masterson clan does it different. Some families aren't huggers."

"Forget hugging." Althea snorted. "He didn't so much as pat her on the shoulder. If my son acted that way, I'd spank the living daylights out of him."

Gerry murmured her agreement.

Emily tapped her foot in an exasperated tattoo. Spencer irked her to no end. He'd bid an apathetic goodbye to his mother and shook hands with the woman who . . . who what? Emily had never found the right label for the closed-off man's emotions. He was attracted to Abby. Of that, there was no doubt. Telltale signs of jealousy abounded on more than one occasion. But Emily was sure it went deeper. A soul connection. Like he recognized something in Abby that was missing in himself. Yet he'd walked away after a handshake.

"Baby, please." Althea snagged Emily's vibrating knee. "You're about to beat a hole through the floor."

"Sorry." Emily laced her fingers together and eyed the decorative ceiling. Paintings of cherubs cavorting among the clouds stretched overhead. "The Lord moves in mysterious ways, but this time he's got me flummoxed. I can't spot him working at all."

"What a relief he doesn't need your approval." Gerry polished her glasses against her sleeve.

Althea nodded. "Faith is for when we don't understand God's plan.

143

Sometimes we have to walk in the dark awhile and hold tight to his hand." She poked Emily. "I know that's hard for a micromanager."

Emily could admit she liked things her way, but there was one lesson she'd mastered in her seventy-eight years. If her plan didn't coincide with God's, she'd better get a new one.

Yes. She'd learned her lesson the hard way. But that didn't make surrendering control any easier.

CHAPTER 28

ABBY TUGGED AT THE WAISTLINE of her ball gown. Her tiara pinched her head, and a dull ache pounded at her temples. Two more voyages, and she'd return to life on dry land. But that meant only two more voyages for the Shippers to find her a soulmate.

After seeing the wonderful guy they'd found for her friend Lacey, Abby had assumed the process would be easy. She'd expected her lovely matchmakers to scout the perfect man and introduce him, and then she'd start picking out the wedding colors. She *hadn't* expected the revolving door of candidates. To be fair, two men didn't constitute a revolving door. But neither Reverend Boynton nor Cedric made her heart pound like . . .

She recognized the direction of her thoughts and jerked them back to attention. No use dwelling on sweet but damaged fathers and their adorable, golden-haired five-year-olds. Spencer and Maddie were gone. She'd waved goodbye to dozens of cherished students in her teaching career, and she could put these two behind her as well.

Abby dug among the crowns, plucked a tiara from the basket, and scanned the lobby for potential princesses. She spotted a young girl by the elevators, looking at a cell phone. The child was wearing a long black dress. Maybe second or third grade. Abby hurried over, donned her best faux British accent, and presented the sparkly accessory.

"Welcome to the Monarch kingdom, fair lady."

The apathetic girl stared at the phone without response.

A woman who must have been her mother winced at Abby. "Sorry. My daughter's really into that show." The mother leaned over the girl and pointed. "The nice lady brought you a crown. Can you say thank you?"

Her daughter glanced up. "Thank you." Lightning fast, her attention returned to the screen.

Abby shifted from one foot to the other, and her sore ankle twinged. Her arms lowered. She passed the tiara to the mom. "Would you like to hold it for her?"

"Yes." The woman gave her an apologetic grimace and took the crown. "Thanks."

Abby understood why parents used the devices to help their children behave in public. But it saddened her when she saw the kids who fixated on the screens like a drug addict craving a fix. She had to give Spencer credit. Even with his parental ignorance and penchant for overworking, he'd never once passed his phone to Maddie to keep her amused.

Abby pinched herself as she walked away. "There you go again. Stop thinking about passengers in inappropriate ways."

Technically, he wasn't a passenger. His cruise had ended, and he was gone. The observation made her feel worse, and she surveyed the families milling about for any little girls without a tiara or a cell phone.

People swarmed the lobby, and the sounds of live mariachi music bounced off the marble floor. Abby hustled from group to group, bestowing crowns and taking pictures with the new group of cruisers. After an hour on princess duty, her right ankle was screaming how much it hated her. She'd worn her most comfortable tennis shoes, but her still-healing injury didn't approve.

Abby slipped behind a massive round pillar. She dropped her almost-empty basket and rotated her ankle. Who knew how she might have injured it worse, if Spencer hadn't carried—

She slapped her forehead. "No. No. No."

How much longer would she be haunted by the ghost of Spencer Randolph Masterson?

Two small arms wrapped around her from the back. It must be picture time again. She turned to see what tiny stranger was gifting her with a hug. Looking down, she found familiar blue eyes in a face wreathed with artfully sculpted blond curls.

"Maddie!" Abby sank to her knees and pulled the child close. "What are you doing here?"

"Sailing." Maddie giggled.

"We decided one cruise wasn't enough." Spencer's rich baritone wafted above her.

His voice washed through Abby and shivered her spine. She took a breath before glancing up.

He wore a fashionable black polo shirt, tan chinos, and a smile. "Surprised?"

"I am." Abby released Maddie and stood. "You finally found appropriate vacation clothes."

He shrugged. "We took advantage of our debarkation to go shopping."

Madeleine wore a pink T-shirt and jeans. "Do you like my new clothes?" She twirled in a circle.

Abby placed an arm around the child. "I love them." She turned her attention back to the father. "One cruise wasn't enough, huh?"

His gaze flicked to the ceiling. "My mother was more recalcitrant than I expected. There must be a way to talk her into returning to New Orleans. Plus, it won't hurt to spend extra vacation time with my daughter. We left Ms. Blanchet on shore this time."

"Did you find a nanny who doesn't get seasick?"

"The best. She even has experience watching Madeleine." He pointed a finger Abby's direction. "We plan to utilize Monarch Cruises' excellent VIP nanny valet service."

"Oh boy." Abby rubbed the bridge of her nose. "I'd better head to the Kids Kingdom and start buttering up my boss."

Spencer motioned for Maddie, and she slipped away from Abby to join him. "We're in the same suite as before, so it shouldn't take long to get settled."

"How did you swing that? Those suites usually book up way in advance."

"I went to school with the son of a Monarch Cruises board member. When I contacted him, he pulled some strings to offer a substantial compensation to the customers who held the reservation. It seems the family was more than happy to accommodate us."

"Must be nice," she snarked. "I hope my supervisor will be half that agreeable."

"Do you think it will take long? How about we meet you at the children's area, and you can join us for lunch?"

Abby moaned. "Twila will be spitting fire." Despite the unpleasant task awaiting her, happiness filled her voice as she held out a hand. "Welcome aboard, Mr. Masterson."

"Please"—his hot fudge sundae eyes warmed as he took her fingers in his—"call me Spencer."

CHAPTER 29

Spencer allotted Abby thirty minutes to placate her ill-tempered supervisor before he headed to the Kids Kingdom with Madeleine. They entered the cheerful open layout of the reception area, where a few parents and children milled about. A joyful squeal issued from his daughter. She bounced to a nearby bookshelf, chose a volume with a fairy on the cover, and flopped in a beanbag chair.

Spencer marveled at her laid-back manner. The first time they'd set foot in this room, she'd been like a frightened fawn avoiding a hunter. But one voyage on the MS *Buckingham*, and her comfort with the place was obvious. He suspected it had more to do with Abby than the lavish ship. The woman possessed an innate ability to set people at ease. She was partly the reason he'd committed to a second cruise. His primary objective was convincing Daisy to return to New Orleans. But allowing his daughter to spend more time with the skilled childcare worker would do her good. Who knew how Madeleine might blossom in Abby's nurturing presence?

A bedazzled brunette pixie about the same age as his daughter skipped over to him. "Can I show you my pet?"

He squinted at the strange girl. "Pet?"

"His name's Dwight." She extended her purse. The top was made of glittered plastic, and the bottom was a rainbow-colored mesh.

Spencer peered inside. Two moist yellow eyes stared at him. A frog? The child had a frog in her purse.

He cleared his throat. "Do your parents know you brought Dwight on the cruise?"

"Not yet." She giggled and threw her arms open. "Can I have a hug?"

Spencer reared back. "I . . ." None of the adults heeded the girl. Which one did she belong to? "No. No, thank you."

"Hug." She waggled her outstretched arms.

Should he call for help? He gulped. "I don't work here."

She extended her lower lip in an exaggerated pout. "Hug!" she demanded.

Spencer's eyebrows lowered. "Do I look like your teddy bear? Find someone else to coddle."

"Hello, sweetie!" Two arms caught the child from behind. Abby hovered over the precocious girl.

Spencer exhaled.

Abby squeezed the frog smuggler. "If you want a hug, come to me. That's my specialty." The child giggled. Abby bent near her ear and whispered loud enough for Spencer to hear. "There's someone else who needs a hug. Her name is Maddie, and she's sitting there on a beanbag chair."

The girl skipped away, and Abby straightened. She put her hands on her hips. "A person might presume you seriously dislike children."

"I don't dislike children. But I've little use for the things that come with them."

Abby's mouth quirked. "The smiles and giggles and hugs?"

"The dirt and frogs and runny noses."

"What's the big deal? It's just a hug."

"I don't know her." Spencer relaxed with the departure of the uncomfortable child. "I doubt her parents would appreciate a strange man embracing their daughter."

"Good point." Abby shrugged. "But I'm a big believer in the power of affection."

Spencer crossed his arms. "Do you always hug any stranger who asks?"

"If it's a child, I do. Haven't you read those studies that say people require a certain number of hugs a day to survive?"

"I've survived quite well without any."

Her expression changed. Annoyance retreated, and pity took its place. She stood contemplating him.

He squirmed under her observation. "Please refrain from feeling sorry for me. I'm not the demonstrative type."

She looked even sorrier at his statement. "Everyone needs a hug now and then."

"An admirable attitude for someone who works with children. I'm sure your sympathetic nature serves you well."

Abby pressed her lips together, nodded, and turned to leave. Spencer uncrossed his arms and reached out a hand but dropped it to his side. Why was his first impulse always to stop her? She was a temporary person passing through his life. Nothing more.

"Oh, I can't stand it." Abby spun around. "We're not supposed to hug adult passengers, but—"

Slim arms wrapped around him, trapping his own against his body. Her silky red hair rested somewhere around the area of his heart as she squeezed him tight. Her softness pressed against him and warmed his entire being.

Spencer stood paralyzed. Everything stopped—his breath, his heart, even his thoughts.

Then started again at a much higher velocity.

When was the last time someone had hugged him? He honestly couldn't remember. Another thought followed. Apart from Abby, when was the last time someone had hugged Madeleine? He certainly hadn't taken her in his arms, and Ms. Blanchet—for the short time the governess was with them and not seasick—had exuded discipline, not affection.

Abby released him sooner than he liked. "Don't be afraid to ask for a hug. Or give one. Especially to your own child."

Was she a mind reader? How did she know he was thinking of Madeleine? Before he could respond, Abby spoke.

"Let me grab something from my locker." She rushed off.

Spencer stood with his arms still pressed close to his side. An unfamiliar emotion filled his brain.

Fear.

It made no logical sense.

A suspicion hit him. Did seeing Abigail O'Brien play a bigger role in his decision to return than he'd realized? This redheaded whirlwind had bewitched him with her hugs and smiles and declarations of silver-lined possibilities. No matter how his brain tried to dismiss her as a temporary person, he feared her effect on his heart would be long-lasting and irreversible.

CHAPTER 30

GOSSAMER CLOUDS RACED ABOVE EMILY'S head. The white puffs scurried through the bright blue sky as if they were late for an appointment. A gust hit her, and she clutched her cardigan tighter around her body.

"There's a change in the wind. A storm's brewing somewhere."

She sat with her three friends at a table on the lido deck. They observed the passengers frolicking with all the excitement of their first day at sea. The chilly breeze did nothing to deter the tan-seeking sunbathers stretched out on the deck chairs.

Gerry ignored the festivities in favor of a new book, Althea offered her phone to Daisy with the latest pictures of her grandchildren, and Emily made mental notes of the people around her.

She drummed her fingers on the wooden tabletop. "We missed the new crop boarding."

Gerry droned from behind her novel. "You were the one who wanted to choose new candidates for Abby O'Brien."

"Yes, but I didn't expect it to take five hours."

"I agree," Daisy said. "The strategy meeting lasted much too long."

Althea slipped her phone in her sparkly red fanny pack. "Who knew our first two candidates would go so horribly wrong? Are we losing our touch?"

"Don't be silly." Emily bristled at the suggestion. "Unforeseen factors affected our results. Abby spent an inordinate amount of time with Daisy's son and granddaughter. Perhaps things would've gone smoother with her and the minister if she'd been able to focus."

Althea shook her head. "There was no chemistry with the preacher. Now Abby and Spencer"—she elbowed Daisy—"they could've lit the lido deck with their sparks."

"Yes," Emily said. "It's a shame."

Daisy twisted in her seat. "Y'all must imagine me a horrible mother, but I did what was best for both of them. Too many obstacles stood in the way. And there wasn't enough time for the two to form a genuine attachment. It wasn't meant to be."

Althea bobbed in her chair and hooted. "Sometimes the Good Lawd surprises us." She pointed at someone approaching their table.

Everyone's head followed the direction of her finger. Even Gerry lowered her book. Spencer strode through the crowd, carrying a small white box. Although he wore less formal attire than the last time they'd seen him, his ruler-straight posture and tall, commanding presence made him stand out like a racehorse in a herd of Shetland ponies.

"Heaven help me," Daisy murmured. She scrambled in her purse, withdrew a pair of square sunglasses, and slipped them on. Her fingers fluttered around her hair, and she rearranged her skirt.

Spencer stopped at their table, and Emily clocked the cautious set of his mouth. His face, while not unpleasant, wasn't exactly friendly. More like wary.

"Good afternoon, ladies." His gaze rested on his mother. "Daisy, good to see you again."

"I admit, I'm bewildered," she said. "Didn't you leave?"

"We took advantage of turnaround day to go shopping. I purchased vacation clothes for myself and Madeleine. And something for you too." He set the box on the table in front of Daisy.

She raised the lid to reveal the latest cell phone model in a pearly-white color. An exasperated sigh left her lips. "I thought I made it clear I don't want a phone."

"It's for emergencies"—he clasped his hands behind his back—"if you ever need to get a hold of me. Or perhaps you might want to talk to Madeleine. The rest of the time, you can leave it in your suitcase."

Althea bumped her. "Not a bad idea."

Daisy replaced the lid but didn't give the phone back. "Why didn't y'all return to Louisiana?"

Spencer spread his arms wide. "I decided another voyage might do Madeleine and me both good."

"Where is she?"

"I've left her with Ms. O'Brien."

Emily's ears perked. "You've already seen Abby?"

"Yes, Monarch has assigned her as my daughter's nanny valet again."

"What a coincidence." She exchanged a knowing look with Gerry.

"On the contrary, I requested her. Abby proved herself more than capable on our last cruise. She'll do an excellent job if you four will do me a favor."

"A favor?" Emily's eyes narrowed.

Daisy pushed her shades down an inch. "You never require help from anyone."

"A favor from all of us?" Althea leaned forward. "How fun. What can we do for you, baby?"

He widened his stance and folded his arms. "Please postpone arranging dates for Abby."

"Why?" Emily cocked her head.

"Because it's inconvenient whenever she leaves to meet some guy."

"'Inconvenient'?" Emily smirked.

"'Some guy'?" Althea wore an identical expression.

Gerry took his measure. "Sounds like someone's jealous."

He should have known better than to bring up their matchmaking. Somehow these Shippers always managed to twist things in a disconcerting direction.

"'Jealous'?" Spencer spat out the word. "You're mistaken, ma'am."

"Gerry," she reminded him. "And if you're not jealous, then this request is high-handed and unreasonable. You have no control over Abby's love life."

"I'm not trying to control her." He rubbed the back of his neck. "My interest in Ms. O'Brien is solely as an employer. After Madeleine and I leave the ship, she can date whoever she pleases."

"Now it's Ms. O'Brien," Althea said to Emily.

"He's distancing himself." She nodded. "People do that when they're uncomfortable."

"Or lying." Gerry scowled.

"Ladies." Daisy tapped her manicured fingers. "Please don't pester him. I've already told you my son is a poor match for Abby."

"Yes. Thank you, Daisy. I'm a—wait a minute. Poor match?" Spencer waved his hand down his long torso. "In what way am I lacking? I'm handsome, well-educated, wealthy—"

"Humble," Gerry inserted.

Spencer lifted his chin. "There's no flaw in giving an honest evaluation of your qualifications."

"If you're laying out your qualifications, you must be interested." Emily opened a three-ring binder. "Shall I add your name to the candidate list?"

"What? No." He had to be careful around these loony old women. Who knew what crazy schemes they might concoct? "I was merely reacting to my mother's word choice, not offering myself as another player in your matchmaking game."

"'Game'?" Emily flipped the binder shut. "I see what you mean, Daisy. There's no sense wasting our time."

"As I said." His mother took a tube of lotion from her handbag and squeezed a dab onto her fingers. She applied the liquid to the minuscule creases near her mouth.

Spencer gritted his teeth. "Abby would count her blessings to marry a man like me."

"Oh, marriage?" Emily reopened the binder. "If you have something long-term in mind, I'm willing to reconsider."

Althea smiled. "You've got my vote, baby."

"Hold it." A trickle of sweat dripped from Spencer's neck to his suddenly tight collar. "Marriage isn't an option. I've already tried the institution once, and it didn't suit."

"Surely you're not suggesting shacking up together." Gerry's eyebrows formed a hairy frown of disapproval.

"Of course not. I am saying in a forthright and unequivocal manner that I never plan to get married again—especially not to Abigail O'Brien."

"No one was offering." A new voice joined the conversation.

A female voice.

An angry voice.

CHAPTER 31

WAS STEAM SHOOTING FROM HER ears? Abby might combust at any moment. Did the man have to make marriage to her sound like the equivalent of a root canal?

From the look on Spencer's face, he recognized his faux pas. He obviously hadn't meant for her to hear his emphatic declaration, but that didn't lessen the sting.

A flush rose up his neck. "Abby, I—"

"Maddie"—she turned her back to him and squatted in front of his daughter—"why don't you give Grandma Daisy a hug? I'm sure she's missed you."

"Yes!" Daisy hastened from her chair and around the table. "I've missed you ever so much, Madeleine." She knelt and held open her arms.

"Hello, Grandma." Maddie walked into the woman's embrace.

Daisy cradled her granddaughter for a few seconds, then released her.

Althea joined them. "If someone's giving out hugs, I could use a couple." She grabbed both Daisy and Maddie, squeezing them close.

Abby noted Spencer's softening countenance. Their eyes met and she almost smiled, but then she remembered his unflattering words. How dare the man reject her as a possible marriage partner! Had he misunderstood the hug she'd given him in the children's center? She imagined he was used to all sorts of women throwing themselves at him. Was he under the impression she'd been coming on to him? If so, she'd correct the stupid assumption as quickly as possible.

"You're just in time, dear." Emily waved her over. "We spent five hours reviewing a new list of candidates for you. I expect you'll be pleased with our choices."

"Wonderful!" Perhaps Abby's response was a little too bright, but she wanted Spencer to get the message there were plenty of fish in her matrimonial sea. "Could you arrange a date for this evening? It will be a pleasure to spend more than forty-five minutes for a change."

"Hold on." Spencer took a step her way. "You agreed to a specified time in our list of expectations."

She raised her nose. "The agreement expired when our last cruise docked in Galveston, Mr. Masterson. I'm under no stipulations this time." She smiled at Emily. "Just let me know when and where."

"And who?" Gerry stopped typing.

"Right." Abby's cheeks heated. "Definitely who. That's the most important part."

Emily patted her. "We'll discuss the who after my friends and I hold a quick conference. Would you excuse us?"

The minute they left the Shippers' table, Spencer drew Abby away to an empty spot by the railing.

She remained placid, putting one arm around Maddie. "Mr. Masterson, I'd like to apologize."

"Apologize? For what?"

"I acted unprofessionally when you arrived with Maddie at the childcare center. I'm a hug-first-and-think-later type. My intention wasn't to be flirtatious—"

Spencer held up a stiff hand. "And I didn't take it that way. What you overheard was . . . I didn't mean I found you objectionable as a . . ." He looked out at the water. "I realize my words sounded harsh, and"—he faced her—"I'm truly sorry."

The tension in Abby's spine loosened a fraction. "You don't want anyone to misunderstand. I get it, Mr. Masterson."

"Spencer. And what you say is true. I wouldn't want any rumors to damage your reputation." His gaze returned to the ocean. "I've seen firsthand how ugly the gossip mill gets when an employer steps over the line."

Abby glanced down at Maddie. His daughter leaned against the rail, staring at the whitecaps surrounding the ship. The child was too young to comprehend the content of their conversation, but Abby wanted to be sure. "I get it, Mr. Masterson."

"Spencer," he reiterated. "Please allow me to say one last thing. I respect you, both as a professional and a person. When I said I didn't, that is, when I told the Shippers I never planned to marry again, it had nothing to do with you. After my first"—he noticed Madeleine and lowered his voice—"union ended, I resolved to avoid repeating the same mistake. Please don't take my words personally."

Had he really used the old *It's not you, it's me* cliché?

Abby's soul shriveled. Only an hour ago, the sight of him and Maddie had spun her heart on its axis. How quickly things changed.

Or didn't change.

That was the problem. No matter how much Spencer churned her insides, he was still immune to her and always would be. Better to concentrate on whatever new man the Shippers found. Abby wanted marriage and a family more than anything.

And Spencer was on a totally different page.

CHAPTER 32

"STILL THINK I'M CRAZY?" EMILY inclined her head toward the couple at the rail. "Spencer's working overtime to mend fences." She looked at Daisy. "You know your son better than anyone. Is this how he normally behaves?"

"I must admit"—Daisy studied him—"I've never seen him so considerate of someone else's opinion."

"Yep," Althea said. "The boy's smitten."

Daisy sighed. "Perhaps we could consider taking a personal relationship between them under advisement."

"Yes!" Emily clasped her hands and shook them. "Let's draw up a battle plan. Should we set Abby up with a random person to prod Spencer out of his comfort zone?" She opened her binder and scanned the list of names. "Who would be a good decoy match? Someone who won't be hurt when it doesn't work out."

"I don't follow," Gerry said. "How is sending Abby on a throwaway date going to help the situation?"

"I'm surprised at you." Emily flicked the novel laying on the table. "Isn't one of your favorite story tropes about fake relationships? Since Daisy has given us her blessing to arrange her son and Abby, it's time to make Spencer jealous."

"I didn't exactly give my blessing," Daisy objected. "I said we might take it under advisement. Spencer's sudden return seems to involve more than just me, and I can't ignore the truth. It's obvious the two share an attraction, but I'm still not convinced the match is advantageous. Especially for Abby."

Gerry waved her book under Emily's nose. "You also don't grasp how the fake dating angle works. Both people are supposed to be aware their relationship is phony. In your scenario, Abby would have no clue her date was a red herring."

"And what about the doctor?" Althea chewed on her smoothie straw. "We chose him after five hours of debate. Are we gonna forget about him?"

"Dr. Grant is a wonderful candidate," Emily said, "but the age difference is more than we normally recommend."

"Fourteen years?" Althea shrugged. "That's nothing. My third husband was seventeen years younger than me. He didn't mind."

Emily suppressed the frustration rising like a tide. "Do you believe the doc is a better fit for Abby than Spencer?"

"No," said Gerry.

"Nah," said Althea.

Daisy didn't answer either way.

Emily relaxed in her chair. "Then we don't want to waste a wonderful candidate like Dr. Grant and lose his trust. How about a token date for Abby to go on tonight? Let's choose someone who won't take it too seriously."

"Pick Barney," Gerry suggested. "Even though he was too scared of Everson to check the footage when we asked, we shouldn't hold that against him. He's friendly with everyone. I bet he wouldn't get too invested in one date."

"Good idea." Emily pulled out her phone. "I'll text him and ask if he's interested."

Fifteen seconds later, her cell dinged. She read his response and chuckled. "Looks like Barney hasn't been on a date in a while. He says he can be ready in five minutes."

"Excuse me." Rufus, the waiter, stood above them with his drink tray. "The bartender asked me to deliver a note to Mrs. Masterson."

The four Shippers stiffened. He slipped a black envelope off his tray, handed it to Daisy, and left. She gave an audible gulp.

"Should we grill the bartender?" Althea rose from her seat.

"Why?" Gerry said. "You know it'll be the same setup. Passed from one employee to another, and no one saw who it came from."

"I agree." Emily thumped a fist on the table. "No sense wasting our energy."

"Honey"—Althea rested a hand on Daisy's taut arm—"you want us to leave you alone while you read it?"

Daisy sighed. "No, thank you. Y'all must already suspect the worst." She slipped a manicured fingernail under the flap and withdrew the thick card inside. Her eyes jerked as she read.

Gerry leaned forward. "What does it say?"

Daisy's lips quivered as she passed the note to Emily.

Emily made sure no one was standing close enough to hear, then read aloud, "'Your beloved son returns. Pay up or confess the whole affair. Your choice.'"

"Just once," Daisy whispered. "Forty-two years ago. God forgive me." A sob racked her delicate frame.

Althea gathered Daisy up with soft murmurs and stroked her back. Gerry reached across the table to rub her arm.

Emily remained in her seat, jaw tight. "Girls, it's time to stop being so polite. Let's find out who's sending these notes and nail the creep."

CHAPTER 33

A GIANT MASS OF BROWN foam logs sat on top of the green helipad. Light shone from the middle, highlighting the red and orange cellophane flames of the faux fire. Spencer shifted in his camp chair and tugged his jacket collar around his neck. "Why did you sign us up for this?"

He scowled at his nanny valet who stood with a pillow tucked under each arm. She wore jeans and a purple Monarch hoodie. Her vibrant red hair spilled around her shoulders.

Abby seemed unperturbed by his displeasure. "Bow-wow-wow-wow glamping is a Monarch specialty. No other cruise line offers this experience."

"Well, whoever invented bow-wow-wow glamping—"

"It's three *wow*s." Abby shifted the pillows so she held them both under her left arm. "Bow-wow-wow-*wow*! It's a play on words because we pitch the tents on the bow of the ship, but it's tailor-made for the pet owners, ergo the bow-wow-wow part. The last wow is for fun."

She uttered the ridiculous nonsense without even a hint of self-consciousness. Spencer wondered at her ability to embrace any activity, no matter how absurd. He surveyed their at-sea glamour camping site. Employees passed out premade s'mores to the humans and doggy treats to the four-legged passengers sniffing around the collapsible chairs. A ring of tents surrounded them, the flaps folded back to reveal beanbag chairs and twinkle lights strung along the inside.

A brisk wind sliced through his hair, and Spencer pushed the mussed strands off his forehead. "Whoever invented Bow-wow-wow-*wow* glamping wasn't taking into account the colder evening temperatures."

"I admit it's unseasonably chilly, but Maddie's loving it."

She pointed to his daughter, who sat cross-legged in a nearby tent beside the serial hugger from the day care center. The brown-haired girl still carried her rainbow purse, and her mouth was rimmed with a sticky ring of marshmallow remains. She threw an arm around Madeleine and squeezed tight.

"Then you two stay and enjoy." Spencer stood. "I'll go to my heated suite and get some work done."

"No." Abby shuffled in front of him, the pillows hugged in front of her. "It will be much more special if you're here."

He raised his eyebrows.

She blinked. "For Maddie, I mean."

"We just finished a seven-day cruise, and this new one is nine days. Plenty of time to spend together."

"But when will you ever get another opportunity to go camping with puppies on a cruise ship? If you absolutely have to work, you can do it once the event's concluded and Maddie's in bed. Please, please, please." Abby clasped her hands. Her arms bunched the cushy pillows tight under her chin. She resembled a little girl saying her bedtime prayers.

"Fine." He crossed his arms and sat down. "Let's catch pneumonia together."

"Yay!" Abby bounded away and joined the girls in the tent.

She placed the pillows beneath them and made sure their jackets were buttoned tight. Spencer had to admit, he'd never seen his daughter smile so big. She laughed in glee as her new friend grabbed her for another hug. Daisy wandered over and knelt beside them, a thick black scarf wrapped around her silver hair.

Spencer shook his head. His mother. Camping. Even if it *was* on a cruise ship, the sight was unbelievable.

The other three members of her matchmaking crew arrived in a talkative group.

Althea spotted him and bustled over. "Hey, baby." She sat in the empty chair beside him, leaned over, and bussed him on the cheek.

He lifted his fingers to scrub at the spot but thought better of it. He didn't want to offend the tenderhearted woman. "Good evening, Althea."

"Call the papers. Daisy agreed to go camping." Her laugh was deep and throaty. "Shows how much she loves her granddaughter."

This night didn't have to be a total waste. He'd ask this woman some questions that bothered him. Like how his mother ended up on a cruise ship in the first place.

"You're from New Orleans, correct? Did you and Daisy meet there at a function?"

"A function?" She chortled. "I met your momma in a park."

"In a what?"

"A park. Those big pieces of land with trees and picnic tables."

"I'm well aware of what a park is. But it's hard to envision Daisy Randolph Masterson in one."

"Maybe that's why she was there. Because she didn't want to be *Daisy Randolph Masterson*. She wanted to be *Daisy*. Not much chance of her meeting any of her fancy friends on a park bench."

"I suppose not."

"Anyhoo"—Althea folded her hands over her stomach—"I was on a bench opposite her. My grandkids were running around the playground, having a big old time. When I spotted Daisy, she was the loneliest, most pitiful thing I'd ever seen. I waltzed over, plopped down, and asked why she was dressed head to toe in black on a stuffy summer day."

"What did she say?"

"Not much. Said she'd just come from a funeral."

"A funeral?" That was the last place he'd seen his mother until this recent trip. He recalled her rigid posture as they stood at the family mausoleum. The way she'd walked away without a word and showed up late for the reception, leaving him alone to fend off the well-bred attendees offering their eloquent, insincere words of condolence. Had she been sitting in a park?

A soft pat brought him back from his musings.

Althea withdrew her hand. "You probably already guessed. It was the day they buried your daddy." She grinned. "Daisy was pretty prickly at first—answered me with her pert nose in the air. But I could see it was a front. My philosophy is, if you want people to open up, you have to bare your heart first. So I told her about my grandkids—how Jayshawn was the mischievous one, and Bernadette was my little snuggle bear, always wanting hugs."

Her rich voice rolled out like melted fudge on a marble slab. The sweet musical tone soothed the ache in his brain. Was this what his mother had experienced that day at the park?

Althea stretched her legs out and crossed them at the ankles. "By the time I got through all my kin, your momma started to unbend. I suggested she could tell me about her family, if she wanted. I wasn't sure she'd take me up on my invite, but she did."

Spencer picked at the ends of his fingertips. "How much did she tell you?"

"Enough for me to realize I lived a happier life in my one-bedroom apartment than poor Daisy did in her big mansion in the Garden District. It was like the Lawd whispered in my ear, 'Take her on the cruise with you.'"

He squinted. "It's hard to believe you'd make such an offer to a total stranger. And even harder to fathom my mother accepted."

Althea shrugged. "It was a God thing. My oldest granddaughter bought me the cruise as a birthday present, but she had to back out because of work. I told Daisy the ticket was already paid for and it was a shame to waste it. I gave her my phone number and told her to think about it. She called me three days later."

"Did she reimburse you?"

Althea's eyes narrowed. "Baby, you got a knack for asking rude questions. I didn't request a 'reimbursement.'" She shook her head with the last word. "Her ritzy threads told me she didn't need a handout, but I wanted to offer her a gift with no strings attached. I got the impression she hadn't had many of those in her life."

Spencer squirmed in the lightweight camping chair. He knew the feeling. His father had given him a tennis racket for his tenth birthday but then required he take private lessons and enter the country club tournament. In high school, a fancy sports car arrived the day before his dad "suggested" he ask a business partner's daughter—a spiteful girl the whole class avoided because of her mean temper—to the prom. Every present he'd ever received from his father came with expectations. His mother must have suffered the same experience.

Funny. He'd never bothered to view it from her perspective.

The metal legs of the chair squeaked underneath him. "But how did one trip turn into living on a cruise ship?"

Althea's belly laugh matched her personality—large and full of life. "We met Gerry and Emily on that first cruise. They were already hard at work matching people, and we didn't want to miss the fun."

"But Daisy never uses her credit cards. How can she afford it?"

"Your momma's clever. Far more than anybody recognizes. When your father's fancy business partners gave her an expensive trinket or gifted her a designer handbag on her birthday, she saved it long enough for your daddy to forget about it, then hocked it."

"*Hocked* it?" Spencer drew back. "I can't picture her in a pawnshop."

Althea chuckled. "Imagine the small fortune she gathered over their forty-nine-year marriage."

"But why?" He scratched the back of his head. "Dad gave her everything she needed."

"Not the things she needed most. Love, understanding, acceptance."

Spencer couldn't argue. His father had never shown those qualities to anyone, including him. "Why stay, then? She could have divorced him."

"And lose the one thing she really *did* need?" Althea shook her head.

"Status?"

She smacked his arm hard. "You deserve a whippin' for that. The one thing Daisy couldn't live without was *you*, Spencer. You might not have had a close, affectionate relationship, but at least she got to see you. Your daddy ruled like a dictator. If she divorced him, he would've kept you away forever."

Spencer's brain filled with white noise. This new revelation floored him. It was true. Julius Masterson had valued control above all else. He'd chosen everything from his son's college major to the woman he married. In all things, Spencer had bowed to his father's wishes. How could he blame his mother for doing the same?

Althea stood and rubbed the small of her back. "My old carcass can't handle too much sitting. I'm gonna make a lap around the deck." She walked away with a song on her lips. "*Gonna lay down my burrrrr-dens.*"

Spencer propped his elbow on the armrest. Daisy's roommate was a shade too affectionate, but he understood why his mother chose to spend time with the agreeable woman. Perhaps he'd enlist Althea's help to convince Daisy to come home.

His mother's cultured voice spoke from his right. "Good evening, Spencer. May I join you?"

He rose and held the empty chair for her as she sat, then returned to his seat. They stayed quiet for several moments. Squeals sounded when Abby started a pillow fight with the two little girls.

"She's good with Madeleine," Daisy murmured.

"Yes."

"Were you perhaps considering—" She adjusted her scarf. "Have you determined what to do about Madeleine when you return to New Orleans?"

"If you were there, you could help me." He pulled at the cuffs of his jacket. "I mean, if you'd like to spend more time with her, I don't mind."

"Thank you." Daisy rested her hands on her lap. "I would love to be a part of her life."

Finally. Progress. Spencer forced himself not to barrel ahead. "That's hard to do when you're sailing around the ocean."

"True." She smiled. "But I'm not ready to leave just yet. God provided this refuge for me at a difficult time."

"Althea told me how she met you on the day of Father's funeral. After a lifetime of bowing to his wishes, you must have felt liberated."

Spencer paused. Did his words sound sarcastic? He hadn't meant them that way.

Daisy answered with a sad twist of her lips. "On the contrary, I felt lost. Like one of those animals that's been born in captivity and doesn't know how to survive in their natural habitat. The rest of my life stretched ahead of me, free from your father's influence, yet I hadn't a clue where to go or what to do."

"How did you wind up in a public park?"

She raised her face to the starry expanse overhead. "Someone was directing my steps. When I settled on that bench, I had no idea God was about to send me an angel. Especially such a garrulous one." Two ladylike puffs of laughter issued from her nose.

He smiled in response. "God has a way of doing that—sending the perfect person when we need them." His gaze wandered back to Abby.

"Thanks to my friend Althea, I've been happier in the past year and a half than my entire life put together."

"Couldn't you at least bring your cell phone?"

"That's one of the reasons I was happy. For the first time, I was out of touch. Answerable to no one but heaven and myself." She reached over and settled her trembling hand on top of his shoulder. "You were born in the same type of cage, Spencer. As your mother, I should've made more effort to free you. In order to buy my own peace, I sacrificed yours. It's the greatest regret of my life." Her voice grew thick. She drew a wavery breath. "Please forgive me. I know I don't deserve it. But I hope you will anyway."

Spencer stared. He knew what the obvious reply was. The Christian reply.

"Of course." Though his mouth formed the words, they felt perfunctory.

"Thank you." Her response contained the same polite, stilted quality.

Why was it so difficult for them to tear down the walls?

Daisy released him, stood, and glided off in her usual graceful manner. Spencer's heart sat like a rock in his chest. He focused on the faraway stars. When he'd drawn closer to God, forgiveness was part of the deal, and not only for himself. His new faith urged him to let go of the years of anger and hurt he'd harbored against Daisy. And to some extent, he had. But it didn't make the bad memories disappear.

"God, forgiving is hard." He lowered his gaze to the tent where his daughter sat laughing. "But I want to try. For all our sakes."

CHAPTER 34

ABBY EXITED THE TENT AND glanced at Spencer for the umpteenth time. She studied his slumped shoulders. He was a man who always said the proper words, did the proper thing, and stood the proper way. But not tonight. After his conversation with Daisy, he looked even more like a lost little boy.

Her toes twitched in her sneakers. She wanted to go over and talk to him, comfort him, find out what was wrong. But she didn't dare. He wouldn't welcome the intrusion. Her job was taking care of the daughter, not the father.

So instead, Abby wandered to where Gerry, Althea, and Emily sat by the faux campfire.

Gerry shivered. "Why is this Caribbean cruise so cold?"

"Saints preserve us, if it ain't herself," Seamus said, approaching with a cup of hot chocolate. He extended it to Gerry. "Would you care for some tasty sustenance with marshmallows?"

"No, thank you." She made no move to take the cup. "Drinking too much is a bad idea. The bathrooms aren't conveniently located."

"Ah yes." His smile drooped. "My mistake, sorry."

Seamus walked away, and Althea poked a finger in Gerry's side. "Why you gotta be so harsh, baby? It's obvious the man fancies you."

"Then it's better not to encourage his futile aspirations."

Emily thrust out her chin. "Why 'futile'? He might be your Mr. Right."

"I spent the better part of seventy years imagining Mr. Right. And in all those daydreams, I never once crouched down to kiss him." Gerry fussed with her spectacles. "Does that sound shallow?"

"Yes," said Emily.

"Not to me." Abby swooped her hand from head to toe. "I relate with the height issue, although I'm coming at it from the opposite direction. Men are too short for you. They're too tall for me." She sank to the deck and sat cross-legged. "Either way, it's a problem."

"Come on, Gerry." Althea draped an arm around her friend's stiff frame. "Give the magician a chance. He's adorable."

Gerry shrugged away from the embrace. "Do you know how many times I've been called a beanpole? People don't comprehend how embarrassing it is for me to stand next to a shorter man. It plays into my old insecurities."

"Too bad. Seamus is a sweetheart." Abby lifted her palm to stall Gerry's protest. "But I get it. You don't think of him that way, no matter how great he is. It's like me and Spencer."

"Spencer?" Emily bent closer. "How do you mean?"

"He's good-looking, industrious, intelligent." Abby checked on the man she was describing. As always, he was observing Maddie, protecting her from a distance. "Kind."

Althea's jaw dropped. "You reckon that boy's kind?"

"Not in an obvious way." Abby grinned. "You have to get past the stuck-up Southern aristocrat shell, but inside he's very caring. You should've seen him with his daughter when I took them on the ropes course. The way he spread out his arms as he followed her."

"I've heard of the type," Gerry said. "Helicopter parents. Always hovering."

"No. I know all about helicopter parents. He's something different." Abby searched for the best explanation. "He's like a . . . an undercover guardian angel. It's sad."

"Sad?" Emily said. "How so?"

"Madeleine craves love and attention more than anything." Abby caught a strand of hair and twirled it around her fingers. "But she's too young to recognize the many ways her father takes care of her. If he showed his affection more, I bet she would open up."

Daisy joined them and settled in an empty chair. She laid her hands on the armrests, a queen on a collapsible throne. Her lips parted as she watched Madeleine at play in the tent. "Abby, thank you for taking such good care of my granddaughter. I can already mark a difference in her."

"The pleasure's mine. Maddie's easy to love."

"She's such a dear." Emily shook her head. "How can her mother bear to be apart?"

"It's better for Madeleine that her mother remains aloof." Daisy's mouth pinched. "Priscilla was never the nurturing type. She was only able to get the divorce because my son supported her decision. Usually, once you're part of the Masterson dynasty, there's no getting out. Any whiff of divorce, and the whole brood descends to explain why you can't bring shame on the family name."

Althea shivered. "You make it sound like the mafia."

"They possess more similarities than you might imagine." Daisy reached over and took Abby's hand. "Please forgive me if this is an uncomfortable question, but . . . are you interested in my son?"

"Interested?"

"In a romantic way."

"What?" Abby's eyes jerked to where Spencer sat. Even though he was far away, she still lowered her voice. "Not in the least." She yanked her hand from Daisy's. "I'm his nanny—his daughter's na— You know what I mean." She sprang from the floor. "Would you excuse me? I need a bathroom break."

Yip. Yip. Yip.

A woman chased her noisy beagle across the deck. The playful puppy dashed among the chairs, knocking over camping trays and water bottles. When his owner cornered him, he howled with abandon.

A frustrated sigh rattled in Spencer's throat. He buried his hands in his pockets and reminded himself his daughter was happy. Giggles carried from the tent where she played with her friend. It made the cold and the noise and the lack of work worth it.

Abby approached him, and he stood from his camping chair.

She pointed at the tent. "Could you please watch Maddie? I need to visit the restroom."

"Of course."

He sank back to the chair and stared into the cellophane flames of the giant fake campfire. The heart-to-heart with Daisy had drained the energy from his body. He didn't have the brain space to process all he'd learned from his mother and Althea.

A forceful wind ravaged the site. It howled louder than the dogs as canvas flaps rattled. He cast a glance at Madeleine's tent and shot to his feet.

It was empty.

Spencer raced to the tent and ducked inside. The girls were nowhere to be seen, but the hugger had left her purse by the wall. The two bean-bag chairs sat desolate except for a lump of blankets in the one where Madeleine had sat. The blankets rustled, and a small foot poked from the bottom.

"Madeleine?"

Two watery blue eyes lifted above the blanket, and his heart started to beat again.

Spencer released a breath and knelt by the chair. "Are you okay?"

She shook her head back and forth.

"What's wrong?"

"It's scary. Over there. The eyes are watching me."

She pointed a shaky finger at the floor. Spencer squinted into the golden twinkle-light shadows.

Nothing.

"I don't think—"

Croak.

Spencer looked again. Two luminescent dots stared back at him from the rainbow netting on the other girl's purse. It appeared bow-wow-wow-wow glamping was for all kinds of pets.

He turned to his daughter. "Are you afraid of the frog?"

Her head bobbed, the blankets still covering half her face.

"Hold on." Spencer rose and approached the unwelcome visitor.

"Careful," Madeleine said. "It might bite."

He smiled. It was his first time playing the rescuing knight against the big bad dragon. Spencer picked up the purse. The frog made a noise somewhere between a croak and a squawk.

"Yeah, I don't like you much either." Spencer peered through the netting and into the beady, reflective eyes. He turned to Madeleine, ready to show off his conquest, but her head had disappeared under the blankets again.

Spencer didn't move. "Would you like me to take him outside?"

"Yes, please," came the muffled voice.

He took the frog out of the tent and hesitated. What should he do with it? He was tempted to dump it over the side of the boat, but who knew if it would survive the drop? Besides, its owner would be heartbroken when she found her beloved pet missing.

"Dwight!" The brunette hug monster skipped over. "There you are."

Spencer gladly passed the purse to her and returned to the tent. Madeleine was sitting in the beanbag chair with her knees hugged to her chest.

He stopped in front of her. "Is that better?"

Madeleine shrugged.

He ran a hand through his hair. "Okay . . . I guess . . . I'll go back outside."

A whimper stopped him.

Spencer tamped down his impatience. Most parents complained because their children wouldn't *stop* talking. He lowered the tent flaps to block out the other passengers and approached his daughter in much the same way he had the frog. Quietly. Not wanting to spook her. He lowered himself to the empty beanbag.

Should he pat her back? Hug her? Tell her not to be frightened?

Where was Abby? He needed an expert opinion.

Spencer cleared his throat. "I put the frog outside. You're safe now."

"I'm scared." The tremor in his daughter's voice pricked his heart.

"Scared of what?"

The wind kicked up, and Madeleine's head jerked. "It might come back."

"You don't like frogs?"

"One time," she tugged a blanket closer, "when I was little—"

Spencer pressed his lips together. It wouldn't be right to laugh at his grown-up five-year-old daughter. Not when she was confiding in him.

"A frog jumped on my arm."

He shifted his body so he could see her better. "Where were you?"

"In the park, with Nanny Margaret."

"And she didn't help you?"

"She was on the phone."

His jaw clenched. Why were all these expensive, highly vetted governesses so undependable? He forced his mind back to the present moment and his frightened daughter. How could he set her mind at ease? From somewhere deep in his subconscious surfaced a childhood memory of someone holding him and singing a silly song. He couldn't recall who it was, but he remembered feeling comforted. It was worth a shot.

"I know the perfect thing to do when you're scared." Spencer reached over and patted her silky hair twice. *Awkward.* He dropped his hand back on his lap.

Her rounded eyes stared up at him. "What?"

"Sing a song. Do you like to sing?"

Her lips pursed, and her nose scrunched. "I don't know."

"Would you like to try?"

"Yes." Madeleine blinked. "Which song?"

It was one question after another. Why was this parenting thing so hard? He tried to remember a children's song. Any song. What was the one about the rain?

"Ah"—he slapped his knee with his hand—"I've got it." Spencer cleared his throat and looked around the tent. "*Frog . . . frog . . .*" *Please, God, don't let anyone outside hear me.* "*Go away.*"

Changing an old nursery rhyme to fit the situation. *Not bad, Masterson.*

"*Don't come back another day.*"

A giggle shook Madeleine. He'd never felt so relieved to hear someone laugh at him.

Spencer grinned and sang louder. "*Frog, frog, go away.*"

He lifted his arm and gently cradled his daughter. Her body tensed and then relaxed. She cuddled against his side. Her soft voice joined his, and they sang together.

"*Don't come back another day.*"

His voice cracked, but he kept going. Abby better be somewhere out of earshot. He didn't need any witnesses.

Abby crouched outside the tent flap. The puddle of goo that was once her heart splashed inside of her. Who knew a late-night trip to the bathroom would cause such adorable father-daughter bonding? She clapped a hand over her mouth as Spencer's voice warbled. Ignoring the pitch issues, this was the sweetest song she'd ever heard.

A blast of cold air hit the back of her neck. Tent flaps rustled in the darkness. She pulled the hood of her sweatshirt over her head, crossed her arms, and wrapped her hands around her elbows.

The singing stopped.

If the ever-proper Mr. Masterson caught her, he wouldn't be happy. Abby pivoted. She tiptoed away and hurried outside the circle of tents. Spencer emerged, spotted her in the darkness, and walked over.

Abby smiled. "Hello, boss. Did anything happen while I was gone?"

A gust tumbled a thatch of his dark hair, and he pushed it away. "Madeleine spotted a frog in her room and wasn't happy about it."

"Ah yes. Dwight." She laughed. "Good thing you were nearby. How did you calm her?"

"Just"—Spencer coughed—"a little parental know-how."

Abby kept a straight face. "Good work."

The moonlight illuminated the area behind the tents, but the lights and noise and pet people remained around the campfire.

Another forceful wind whooshed and blew Abby's hood from her head. Her tangled curls swirled around her face. She grabbed the tousled mess and tried to tame it. Every time she grasped a new strand, another would fly from her hand.

Spencer stepped close. He reached with both hands and pulled the hood up.

"Thanks," she said.

Abby tried to step away, but his hands continued to hold the hood, immobilizing her. She looked up at him. Without her high heels, his face was a long distance away. Spencer stared down. He tugged, and she stumbled forward until there was barely an inch between their bodies.

Abby tilted all the way back to see him. She licked her lips. "Did . . . did you need something?"

CHAPTER 35

Did he need something?

Too many things. A list scrolled through his mind. Most of the options involved Abby, but he didn't voice them aloud. His gaze roamed the elfin face in front of him. Her bright green eyes watched him. Her eyebrows puckered. Spencer's body rocked closer. He wondered if her mouth was as soft as—

Whoa!

He jerked back and released the hood.

"I need . . ."

A jumble of stars sparkled. Far more than he saw in the city. They winked at him like they knew what he was thinking. Did Abby know too?

She sniffled and rubbed her arms.

He shoved his hands in his pockets. "I need my employee to stay healthy. Please dress appropriately for this brisk weather. Who will take care of Madeleine if you catch cold?"

Frigid air stretched between them, and not just from the evening chill. Abby squinted like he was one of her unruly kids. She raised her index finger, hesitated, and curled it back against her palm.

"Yes, sir." She tugged on the strings of her hood. It constricted until only her nose and mouth were visible. "Is that better?" Her moist lips stood out in the small circle not covered by material.

Better? Not in a million years. It was like giving him a bull's-eye.

He took a giant step backward. "It will have to do."

"Thank you for caring about my well-being, sir." Abby saluted and pushed the hood back so one eye peeped out at him. "I'll try not to let my health inconvenience you." She stomped off in the direction of Maddie's tent, yanked the flap open, and disappeared inside.

Spencer released the breath he was holding. That was close. He'd almost done something stupid. At least Abby didn't pick up on it. He must rid himself of these fleeting inclinations before people started to notice.

Emily peeked through the crack between the neighboring tent flaps. Her rear end ached from sitting on the hard ground, but their stake-out had proven fruitful. They had proof positive that Spencer and Abby were feeling more than professional admiration for one another.

"Mercy me," Althea whispered from above her. "Did you see that?"

Gerry dropped onto a beanbag chair with her arms folded. "It's hard to see anything with you hogging the good spot."

"I knew it." Emily peered out the lower half of the crack. "He had that look in his eye."

Daisy pulled her scarf closer to her neck. She lowered herself to the other beanbag chair and crossed one leg over the other. "Although I can't deny my son seems smitten, it bears repeating that Spencer is a difficult match for Abby."

"Maybe you should tell *him* that." Althea snickered.

"The poor man's in denial." Emily extended an arm from her crouched position. Althea grabbed it and pulled her up. Rickety pops sounded as her bones cracked. "I'm getting too old for these night operations." Daisy opened her mouth, and Emily held up a finger. "Not that this *was* an operation. More like a fact-gathering mission, since Daisy hasn't given her full support."

Gerry pushed her spectacles to the top of her head. "Come on, Daisy. Why do you object to Abby? Is it because she's from a different social class?"

"Hold up." Althea gathered Daisy to her side. "You're making my bestie sound like a snob."

"Sorry." Gerry dipped her head. "I didn't mean it like that."

Daisy waved a dismissive hand. "You're not entirely wrong. It's true Abby is from a dissimilar background, but I don't count that against her. I'm protecting her from the stifling, image-driven crowd Spencer associates with. Her free-spirited, loving personality wouldn't want to live in his world."

"From the sound of it," Emily said, "neither would Spencer."

Gerry tapped her chin. "Abby might be the key to liberate him from society's prison."

The ever-polite Daisy gave a rare snort. "Are you writing lines for your novel? I'm not sure Spencer wants to be liberated, and—"

"Daisy," Emily interrupted. "Do you want what's best for your son?"

"What mother doesn't?"

"Then will you admit a warm, caring, affectionate person like Abby would do him a world of good?"

"Abby is wonderful."

Althea nudged Daisy. "So why not fix Miss Wonderful up with Mr. Crabby? Don't underestimate her. I bet that girl could stare down a whole host of Mastersons without so much as blinking."

Emily slapped her leg. "Abby's partial to him. I can tell." She paced the confined space inside the tent. "How about we let them decide? If Spencer realizes the life he's missing, he might not want to go back."

Daisy bit her lip. "I still have reservations."

"I'm not suggesting an all-out campaign. Let's just create an opportunity or two where he and Abby can spend quality time alone together." Emily extended her hand. "Deal?"

Daisy hesitated, sighed, then clasped her slender fingers around Emily's hand. "Deal."

Emily's mind spun with the possibilities. Now that they'd obtained Daisy's approval, there was nothing preventing them from aiming the full force of their matchmaking arsenal on Spencer.

The poor boy wouldn't know what hit him.

CHAPTER 36

EMILY PULLED OUT THE BATTLE-PLAN binder. She settled in the desk chair of her small inner cabin and eyed her friends. "Let's get to work, girls."

Althea lowered herself to the bed with a moan. "Can't we warm up first? That campsite was like an icebox."

"And noisy," Gerry grumbled.

"But worthwhile." Emily thumbed through the binder's pages. "We know for certain now that Spencer's got it bad for Abby, and Daisy's agreed to let us match them. It's time to create a dossier on Spencer."

"Why bother with the paperwork?" Althea asked. "His own mother is right here."

Emily shook her head. "We have to follow procedure. Everyone we match gets a full workup."

Gerry remained standing. "I need to stretch these long legs." She set her computer on top of the dresser, powered it up, and clicked a few keys. "Full name of the client?"

"Spencer. Randolph. Masterson." Daisy sounded it out like she was placing an order at a staticky drive-through speaker.

Althea leaned on the headboard and propped her feet on the mattress. "Why is his middle name the same as yours, baby?"

"Randolph was my maiden name. My husband liked the idea of reminding everyone our son came from two powerful families."

Emily scrawled in the binder. *Daisy's husband was a jerk.*

"Age?" Gerry shot another question.

"Thirty-two."

"Profession?"

"Attorney."

"Personality?"

"Difficult, to say the least."

Althea tugged a corner of the comforter over her legs. "I've said it before, and I'll say it again. That boy is aggravating as a rock."

"You mustn't blame him too much." Daisy twisted the gold watch chain hanging from her neck. "His father's influence made him that way. And I was too cowardly to step in."

"Don't be so hard on yourself, dear." Emily reached to grab her friend's hand.

"It's the truth. I was very young when I married Julius and allowed him to take the lead in everything. As I grew older, I tried to assert myself more but soon found out how difficult life could be. He cut off my credit cards, canceled my appointments without telling me, refused invitations from all our friends, and spread rumors that I was suffering from depression. The term *gaslighting* has become quite popular of late, but there really were instances in that period where I felt like I was losing my mind."

A rumble of disgust issued from Gerry's throat.

Althea thumped a fist on the bed. "I wish I knew you back then. I'd have helped you figure out how to get away from that monster."

Daisy shrugged. "As long as I did things his way, he granted me a modicum of freedom. By the time I had Spencer at forty, I'd lost the will to fight my husband. My poor son was raised in a stifling atmosphere of education and expectations. When he was a child, his father wouldn't allow me to baby him or show too much affection. Julius said he didn't want his son growing up to be a sissy. He even sent Spencer away to boarding school at the age of twelve to teach him self-reliance."

Althea shivered. "I don't know how you lasted almost fifty years in that nightmare."

"By God's grace." Daisy sighed.

Silence descended on the room. The burden of their friend's painful past weighed on the other Shippers.

Gerry's voice wobbled when she tried to speak. She cleared her throat and asked another question. "Spencer's marital status?"

Daisy sat on the bed near Althea's feet and crossed her legs. "Recently divorced."

"How recent?"

"Spencer said it became official two months ago, but they were separated for much longer. Priscilla was never happy in New Orleans. She grew up in Manhattan. To her, our Southern hometown was half a step away from Hicksville."

Emily leaned forward. "How did they meet?"

Daisy gave a mirthless laugh. "Would you believe me if I said they had an arranged marriage?"

"You're kidding." Gerry stopped typing. "I thought those only happened in Regency romance novels."

"Oh, my husband didn't call it that, of course. But he was behind everything. Spencer's desire to please his father was a driving force for much of his life. When Julius took him on a business trip to New York and introduced him to Priscilla, she and Spencer hit it off. My beautiful ex-daughter-in-law can be a charming and captivating woman. She grew up in a politician's home and thrives on winning people over. Unbeknownst to my son, Julius intimated to her that Spencer would soon be pursuing a political career of his own. After the wedding, she learned how far from the truth that was. Spencer had no interest in politics. It was a source of great contention between them."

Gerry rubbed her temples. "I feel like I'm listening to the recap of a soap opera. When did Maddie come along?"

A soft smile appeared on Daisy's face. "They'd been married about two years. Madeleine was born in 2020."

"2020?" Emily lowered her pen. "You mean—"

"Exactly." Daisy nodded. "Smack-dab in the middle of COVID.

The country shut down in March, and Madeleine was born in April. To avoid the contaminated hospitals, Priscilla opted for a home birth with a private doctor. Afterward, she insisted the governess and all the staff wear masks around the baby and wouldn't even let Spencer hold her for the longest time. Needless to say, no outside visitors were permitted."

Althea swung her legs off the bed and scooted to Daisy's side. "That must have been hard for you."

A watery sheen filled Daisy's eyes. "Madeleine was almost two when I finally got to meet her. By then Spencer and his father had experienced a falling out, and Spencer didn't associate with us much. I suspect he and his father fought over the fact that Priscilla wanted to separate. I saw Madeleine only a few times before Spencer and Priscilla separated. Maddie was three years old when her mother packed her off to New York. They didn't even return for my husband's funeral."

Gerry counted on her fingers. "They were married for two years before Maddie. Your granddaughter's five. That means—"

"They were officially married seven years"—Emily scribbled in the binder—"but only lived together for five."

"If you call that living." Althea clicked her tongue. "I'd go crazy in that kind of environment."

A tear trickled down Daisy's pale cheek. "I know I've dragged my feet on allowing y'all to match Spencer with Abby, but"—her voice cracked—"please help my baby. He's suffered enough. I want Spencer to experience the kind of marriage I never had."

Emily tossed the binder on a nearby table and stood in front of her friend. "Daisy Mae Randolph Masterson"—she took both of Daisy's hands—"I swear to you on my honor as a matchmaker, I'll do everything I can to help your boy find true love."

"Me too!" Althea stretched her hand on top of theirs.

"Gerry, get over here." Emily motioned.

"Coming." Their official scribe finished entering the information on her laptop, joined them, and laid her hand on the pile. "Don't worry,

Daisy. Abby is just the girl to make up for all those hard years. Love spills out of her like a waterfall."

"'Waterfall'?" Emily's brain ignited. "That gives me an idea, girls. We need to make sure Spencer and Abby spend some quality time alone together."

Daisy's hand flew to her mouth. "Please don't tell me we're going to lock them in the lost and found."

"Of course not." Emily dug her phone from her purse and pulled up the contacts. "Abby's wise to that tactic. She's the one who let Lacey out when we used that trick before. No, this requires something new, and I know just the man who can help." Emily found the right number and hit Call. As she placed the phone on speaker, the Shippers gathered around. It rang once, then twice.

"Hello?" A young voice with a thick accent answered.

"Hello, Fernando." Emily grinned at her friends. "Do you know anywhere in Cozumel with a waterfall?"

Bam.

The battered white minivan struck a canyon-sized pothole, cracking Spencer's spine like a chiropractor. He shifted on the worn vinyl back seat and muttered low. "Why are we doing this again?"

The rough dirt road did nothing to dim Abby's natural enthusiasm. She answered with her usual bright smile. "The Shippers wanted to go on a shore excursion and asked Maddie to come. It will do her good to spend time with her grandmother."

Bam.

Another pothole jarred Spencer's teeth. "I'm well aware of the circumstances that led to this torture," he growled. "But why did it require *my* presence? I could have stayed on the ship and worked."

Her eyes widened in exaggerated innocence. "And miss the fun? When's the next time you'll get to frolic with your daughter in a Mexican waterfall?"

"'Frolic'?"

Two potholes in quick succession rocked the minivan from side to side.

"Woo-hoo!" Althea, seated in the middle row, raised her hands in the air. "This is better than a roller coaster."

Maddie giggled in the car seat between Althea and Daisy. Emily was up front in the passenger seat, conversing with their local driver like he was an old friend. Gerry sat with Abby and Spencer in the last row, attempting to read her book. They hit an extra-large pothole, and her spectacles bounced on her thin nose.

Abby leaned her head close to Spencer's and spoke softly. "Sometimes the Shippers require more supervision than Maddie. I remember once, Emily and Gerry took a trip to a lighthouse and missed the return boat. They almost didn't make it back in time for sailing. We need to keep an eye on them."

Her whispered words brushed Spencer's ear. The gentle sensations blew all thoughts of work from his brain. In fact, *every* thought vanished. He swallowed and inched away.

The van rolled to a stop, and the driver silenced the asthmatic motor and announced in a chipper voice, "We are here."

"Thank you, God." Spencer slid open the rusty door and scrambled from the vehicle.

The other passengers climbed out and looked around. A weathered wooden sign reading Tacos pointed to a run-down convenience store. Beside it sat a booth with woven ponchos, sombreros, and souvenirs.

Madeleine pointed at the colorful display. "Can we go over there?"

"*Shopping time*," Althea sang. She and Daisy took Spencer's daughter to peruse the trinkets.

Spencer took stock of their surroundings with a wary eye. "Are you sure we're at the right location?"

"One hundred percent." Emily pointed at an overgrown path running alongside the store. "That trail will lead us to the waterfall. Few tourists venture this way because it's so secluded, but our guide assured me it's worth the walk. Right, Fernando?"

"Yes." The young man winked at Emily. "You will see something amazing if you follow the trail."

Abby observed the rutted track through the grass and motioned to Emily's cane. "Can you handle the uneven ground?"

"Don't worry about me." She waved her stick in the air. "I just keep this with me to make Dr. Grant happy."

"Here." Abby moved closer and looped her arm around Emily's. "Let's walk together."

"Daddy, look!" Madeleine ran up with a pink wooden step stool. Paintings of bright purple orchids adorned the top.

Daddy?

Spencer's heart skipped a beat. Maybe two. It was the first time his daughter had called him that since the divorce.

He lowered himself to her level and examined the purchase with care. "How colorful. What's it for?"

"To stand on." She pouted like he should have already known.

Abby gave her a thumbs-up. "What a smart buy, Maddie. You can use it to reach the sink when you brush your teeth."

His daughter hugged the stool tight. "And I can sit on it. And use it as a table for my doll."

"I hope you don't mind." Daisy joined them. "I promised to buy her a gift, and that's what she picked."

"I don't mind." Spencer straightened. "Here, Madeleine." He took the stool. "I'll carry it for you."

"I wish my grandson was here." Althea walked over with a plastic bag swinging at her side. "I found something Jayshawn will love. His birthday's in a few weeks." She pulled an oval wooden mask from the bag and held it up.

Gerry yelped at the garish red disguise with black circles painted under the eyes and half-rotted teeth sticking from the bottom. "That thing is ugsome."

"Somehow I don't think that's a compliment." Althea held the mask to her face and made a wailing sound.

"Won't it give him nightmares?" asked Gerry.

"Not Jayshawn." She chuckled. "He was born for trouble. I bet he'll have a heap of fun scaring his sisters."

Lips twitching, Abby met Spencer's gaze.

"Let's not waste time." Emily pushed Abby toward the trail. "We want to visit the waterfall and get back to the ship before dark."

The ladies took off. Spencer moved to follow but stopped when their guide didn't join them.

He eyed the young man. "Aren't you going to show us the way?"

Fernando shook his head with a grin. "I must do a favor for Mrs. Emily. Do not worry. I will be here to drive when you finish."

Spencer studied Fernando as if the man were a hostile witness. Something was off. Spencer looked over his shoulder and noted the women disappearing with Maddie among the trees. He considered Fernando. "I expect to see you when we return."

"Yes, sir." His smile was a little too broad.

Spencer hesitated but took off after the women, hoping against hope the pinch in his gut was wrong.

CHAPTER 37

A TWENTY-FOOT CLIFF. BUSHES and brambles stuck from the uneven surface. A rough-hewn rock wall stood in front of an indentation in the ground that might serve as a pool if there were water flowing.

But there wasn't.

Not a drop.

Abby swatted a fly. She hoped Maddie wouldn't be too disappointed. The girl stood by her side, eating the lollipop Daisy had purchased for her from the convenience store.

Maddie stared at the dusty mountain with confusion. "Where's the waterfall?"

Spencer shifted the step stool. "My thoughts exactly." His sarcastic tone didn't help the situation.

The four Shippers huddled around a sign stuck in the ground near the wall. It was made with a piece of poster board and a thin wooden stake. The font was neat and meticulous.

Emily pointed to the words. "This explains it. We might have to wait a while."

"I hope it isn't too long." Althea waved an empty water bottle in the air. "I need to tinkle."

Abby drew Maddie closer, then walked to the sign and read the precise lettering. "It says the falls appear on certain days after heavy rains. During a dry summer, the location is an ordinary cliff. The townspeople named it Cascada Sorpresa—Surprise Waterfall. If you make a wish when the waterfall is visible, it will come true. And if a couple share a kiss in front of the pool, their love will last forever." She squeezed Maddie. "Isn't that cool?"

"Do you believe everything you read?" Spencer bent and dropped the stool on the ground. "I suspect the store owner invented a romantic story to rope in the tourists. Why is there a makeshift sign instead of a permanent one? And why is it only written in English when we're in Mexico?"

She gave him a warning grimace. Glancing at Maddie, Abby kept a cheerful attitude. "Let's wish for something."

Maddie licked her lollipop. "I wish I could eat this candy a lot." She wandered to her colorful stool, climbed up, and raised on her tiptoes to search for the nonexistent waterfall.

Ten minutes passed while they waited. The Shippers chatted. Maddie wandered around with her lollipop. And Spencer checked his email on his phone.

Abby kept her sights glued to the top of the cliff. When she spotted the first few drops trickle over the edge, she hooted. "Maddie, look!"

The girl ran and hopped on her stool again. Everyone joined her at the wall.

The paltry dribble became a stream until a gentle cascade of water poured down the cliff.

"Wow!" Maddie clapped. "A waterfall."

"More like a water drizzle," Spencer muttered.

Abby elbowed him. "Make a wish, Maddie. Ask God for something special."

Her young charge folded her hands together and bowed her head. Her lips moved as she prayed. Suddenly, her chin popped up. "Potty," she squeaked. "I need the potty."

"Here, honey." Althea scooted over. "I gotta go too. You come with me. I saw a bathroom at the store."

"I can help." Abby moved to join them but was waved back.

"Don't bother. You stay and enjoy the beautiful falls."

Spencer snorted at the inaccurate description, and Abby gave him the stink eye.

"I'm coming too." Emily hobbled toward them, leaning more on her cane than usual. "Standing around makes my legs sore."

Promising to return, every one of the Shippers headed down the dirt path with Maddie. Spencer and Abby stood alone by the rock wall, watching the spatter of water spill from the top.

Abby cringed at the awkward silence. "Care to make a wish?"

"I don't put any stock in wishes." Spencer leaned on the wall. "Prayers, yes. But a magic waterfall won't make those happen."

"True." Abby hooked a foot around the stool, dragged it over, and clambered on top. She teetered to the side.

"Careful." Spencer grabbed her elbow, then released her quickly.

"Maddie had the right idea. I can see much better with a boost." She copied the girl's earlier pose and clasped her hands on top of the wall to say a prayer.

After a few seconds, Spencer shifted beside her. "What did you wish for?"

"I wished Maddie would call you Daddy every day."

He turned at the same time as Abby. Thanks to the step stool, they were almost face-to-face. From this height, he was much easier to read. She saw an unfamiliar vulnerability in his eyes, like she'd revealed a hidden secret.

"You caught that?"

Her smile was sad. "Maddie's not exactly a chatterbox, but I noticed she addresses you in a formal way. The fact she called you Daddy today made me want to crow. You must be doing something right." She patted his broad shoulder. "Keep up the good work."

His Adam's apple bobbed, and he blinked deliberately but said nothing.

"Sure you don't want to make a wish?" She poked him in the gut.

He retreated. His sudden motion spoiled her balance. The stool tipped. Her body rushed forward. She squeezed her lids shut, but two strong arms caught her round the waist, stopping her fall.

The tips of her toes still braced against the stool, but the length of her was held against her rescuer. Abby's stomach flip-flopped at the strong body pressed to hers. She cracked one eye open.

The right corner of Spencer's mouth quirked. "You know, a wish wasn't the only thing the sign mentioned."

"Huh?"

He lowered his head. His lips touched hers with a soft but skillful pressure. His mouth rested against her own for a second before opening slightly, allowing her lower lip to nestle between his own. His large hand cupped the back of her head. Her feet lifted off the stool, adding to the dizzy swirl in her brain.

One long, slow, deliberate kiss.

His warm breath hit her face as he pulled away. Then he maneuvered her to the stool. She scrambled off. Her feet hit the ground, and she backed away.

Say something, her brain urged. Did it mean for her to speak or him? She wasn't sure.

Spencer cleared his throat. "I shouldn't have. I'm sorry."

Abby wasn't sure what she'd wanted him to say, but she was 100 percent sure it wasn't *I'm sorry.*

She despised the phony laugh that left her mouth. "I guess we checked off everything on the sign. Let's rejoin the others." She took off down the path without waiting for him.

Stupid. Stupid. Stupid.

What if he thought she was coming on to him again? In her defense, he'd initiated the kiss, but it might have been because he found her gawky and pitiable. Another gold digger throwing herself at a rich, handsome man.

But he was hard to resist when his mind-numbing, muscular torso was pressed tight against her own. She was only human.

Hadn't the Shippers said they'd found a new candidate? It was time to meet someone else and get her mind off the tantalizing man who'd just kissed the sense right out of her brain. Past time. Yep. Her alarm was ringing loud and clear.

Emily twisted in her seat and studied her watch for the third time. "Where is Gerry with our update?" She kicked the rubber tip of her metal cane in disgust. It galled her that she had to rely on someone else to investigate, but she was too tired to trek back to the waterfall.

Getting old was for the birds.

She perched on a plastic chair by a table outside the convenience store. After drawing a piece of butterscotch from her purse, Emily unwrapped it and popped the candy in her mouth. Althea took a swig from a bottle of bright orange Mexican soda and dug into a plate of tacos. Daisy sat in the chair beside her. She kept an eye on Maddie, who crouched nearby, creating a tea party on the ground with sticks and leaves.

Althea raised a bulging tortilla shell, and meat spilled from the end. She turned it the opposite way and laughed when more filling dripped. "I think they gave me a left-handed taco."

Gerry raced to the store and skidded to a stop in front of them. "Oh boy. You'll never"—she gasped—"guess what I saw. We must be getting better at this matchmaking thing." She sucked in a deep lungful of air.

Emily stood tall. "What is it?"

"He"—Gerry took another breath—"he kissed her! She was standing on top of Maddie's step stool, and he laid one right on her."

"Hallelujah!" Althea waved her taco in the air. "The romantic waterfall scheme worked. Great idea, Emily." She slapped her on the leg. "Who knew Daisy's smarty-pants son would fall for such guff?"

The thrill of success coursed through Emily's arteries, but she tried to remain modest. "All it took was creating the right setting and opportunity. We couldn't have done it without Fernando. It was providence that there was a shed with a faucet on top of the cliff."

Gerry scowled. "The waterfall was less than impressive. I'm surprised Spencer didn't guess someone was hiding up there with a garden hose."

Emily paced away from the table. "It helps that you worded the legend on the sign so poetically. It must've given him inspiration."

Daisy remained quiet, only the tiniest pucker between her eyebrows betraying her unsettled feelings. Was she second-guessing her decision to let them match Abby with her son?

Althea scooted her chair closer to her roommate and wound an arm around Daisy. "You okay with this, honey?"

Daisy shrugged. "I can't deny my misgivings. But if this will bring my son happiness, then I don't regret it."

"What a relief." Gerry collapsed in the chair Emily had vacated. "Now that we're making progress with our couple, I can get to work on my story." She pulled a notebook and pen from her bag.

"Plugging away on your romance novel?" Althea asked.

"I'm sick of romance."

"Since when?"

Gerry took out her phone and scrolled. "After a while, it starts to feel like I'm lying to my audience. How disappointed would a prospective reader be to discover the author is a shriveled-up spinster?"

"Hogwash." Emily pinched Gerry's upper arm. "You live on a cruise ship and arrange love stories for complete strangers. I imagine a reader would find that fascinating. A few months ago, you even helped capture a drug smuggler."

"Exactly." Gerry tapped her pen on the table. "That aberration stirred my creative juices. I decided to try my hand at the suspense genre. I've been reading a score of murder mysteries to put me in the mood. And I've already picked the perfect crime." She leaned forward and lowered her voice. "Blackmail."

"Sounds familiar," Emily deadpanned.

"Real life is the best place to draw inspiration." Gerry's gaze returned to her phone. "I've got a great idea for an alarm system repairman who wires the indoor cameras to spy on political candidates."

Maddie ran over with a glossy leaf in her hand, the large white petal of a flower sitting on top. "Grandma, I brought you some tea."

"Why, thank you, sugar." Daisy took the gift and pretended to drink from the flower cup. "My, my. This is the best tea I ever tasted."

"It's cupcake flavored." Madeleine climbed onto Daisy's lap, and laid her head against her grandmother's shoulder.

Althea took the last swig of her orange soda, thunked the empty bottle on the table, and made a face at Gerry's screen. "What's that?"

"Research. It looks like coaxial cables only transmit pictures, but Ethernet cables allow my villain to eavesdrop on conversations."

Althea yawned. "I miss the sixties, when you didn't wonder if your TV was spying on you."

Gerry and Althea continued their bickering, Daisy shared her imaginary flower tea with Madeleine, and Emily lounged in a chair, content to give the young people time to make a genuine connection.

Their client Abby was ready and willing for love, but Spencer's unexpected capitulation surprised Emily. She had thought he'd fight the attraction harder. She hoped Daisy's rational son could tap into his romantic side. But if he needed help, the Shippers' playbook contained more than one foolproof method for encouraging affection.

CHAPTER 38

Work was piling up. Spencer scrolled through his phone. He grabbed his sports jacket from the bed and shoved his arms in the sleeves. Nine days was a long time for a cruise. Thank God this second voyage ended tomorrow. He could return to the office and catch up on his caseload.

But there was one thing he had to do before they reached home. His pulse escalated, and he slid his cell into his pocket. Spencer had invited Abby to go for a walk on the beach before the ship pulled out of port. He'd practiced his speech as if he were preparing the closing arguments for the most important trial of his life.

How would she react?

He made his way downstairs to the living room. The back of Daisy's head was visible where she sat on the sofa, but where was Madeleine? His mother had agreed to babysit while they were gone. Jumped at the chance. It still floored him how eager she was to embrace the title of grandma.

Spencer moved in front of Daisy and saw she held a sleeping Madeleine on her lap. He paused at the incongruous sight. Silver chin-length hair perfectly groomed. Minimal makeup. Fashionable, tailored pantsuit. But there was a noticeable change. Wrinkles creased the fabric as she held her granddaughter.

His mother. The queen of New Orleans social circles. Wrinkled.

Was this boat some kind of wonderland that transformed cool, aloof society matrons into doting grandmothers?

"Fix your face. I can tell what you're thinkin'," Daisy drawled.

"What?" His eyes met hers.

"Your intimidating eyebrows squinch when you're confused. Small wonder your own child is afraid of you."

"Madeleine isn't afraid of me." His volume increased at the suggestion.

His daughter jerked in her sleep, and Daisy glared at him. "Shhhh."

He crossed his arms. "Since when are you the perfect picture of motherly affection?"

"I concede your point." Daisy rested her hand on top of her granddaughter's head. "But Madeleine is such a sensitive thing. She gets that from you."

"Me?"

"You were always a tenderhearted child. Bringing home stray animals and crying when you saw someone sleeping on the streets. It drove your father to distraction."

Spencer's eyebrows squinched further. "I don't recall behaving that way."

"No." Daisy sighed. "You were very young. And Julius made sure to punish you any time you showed 'weakness.' Love, sympathy, kindness—those were all weaknesses to him. No child of his would be a slave to silly emotions."

The suggestion his father tried to crush every softer sentiment was unsurprising. But Daisy's claim that Spencer had been tenderhearted flummoxed him. He feared he was too much like Julius Masterson. A rigid, ruthless automaton.

Madeleine stirred and lifted her sleepy head.

He crouched. "Madeleine, I'm leaving for a while. Your grandma is going to stay with you so you won't be alone."

Her lips twitched, and she yawned. "Okay, Daddy."

Daisy chuckled. "Someone's tired."

Spencer awkwardly patted his daughter's back. "Are you ready for bed?"

Madeleine yawned again.

Would she make it to the bedroom? He squinted at the long staircase. What if she tripped and hurt herself?

Spencer rubbed his neck. "I know we don't usually do this." Embarrassment rushed him. "But . . . I can carry you."

Daisy twisted her head to the side to gauge Madeleine's reaction.

Five humiliating seconds ticked.

"Okay." His daughter smiled.

The same sense of relief he'd experienced after asking his first crush on a date and being accepted overwhelmed him. He gathered her in his arms and stood. Her head settled on his shoulder, and her body relaxed. She was asleep in less than a minute.

Spencer had held Madeleine a few times as a baby, but there was always a nurse or nanny nearby to care for her as she grew. And then Priscilla had taken her to New York.

He noted his daughter's small frame. She didn't weigh much. Was she getting enough to eat? Was this normal? Perhaps he should ask Abby.

Daisy stood beside him. "Don't worry, Spencer. I'll stay in the room with her in case she wakes up. You don't have to hurry." She hesitated, then laid a hand on his forearm. "Please don't take what I'm about to say the wrong way."

Spencer tensed.

"Abby is a sweet young woman, and I'd hate to see her hurt. I hope you'll regard her with the utmost consideration."

It appeared he wasn't the only one who feared he was too much like his father. And why wouldn't his mother respond that way? After she'd watched her husband treat every woman no better than an hors d'oeuvre to be sampled, her trepidation was understandable. "I assure you, Daisy. I have the greatest respect for Ms. O'Brien and will treat her accordingly."

Spencer held Madeleine closer and headed for the stairs. There was one day left on the boat, and he'd concluded that the future happiness of both himself and his daughter rested with Abby.

He didn't intend to leave her behind.

CHAPTER 39

THE SILVERY MOON TOOK CENTER stage in the tropical sky, and grains of sand sifted between Abby's toes. She carried her sandals, but Spencer left his shoes on. He kept his head down, hands clasped behind his back, oblivious to the soothing swoosh of the waves.

After their kiss at Cascada Sorpresa and his subsequent apology, she'd been determined to put all romantic thoughts of Spencer out of her head. But then he'd invited her on a moonlight stroll. The butterflies of anticipation had been attacking her stomach en masse ever since. She stole a glance at him from the corner of her eye. He staggered in the shifting sand, and his arm flailed. She grabbed hold.

"Thank you," he murmured, his eyes swinging in a self-conscious arc.

Was he as nervous as she was? Lights from a nearby hotel helped her make out his expression. Definitely nervous. But why?

They meandered along the beach until they reached a copse of trees. As they passed the wooded area, a new scene met Abby's eyes. In the distance, a path of tiki torches highlighted a carpet of red rose petals on the sand. It led to a heart-shaped pattern of candles.

Her own heart pitter-pattered. The setup screamed proposal. Was this why Spencer had brought her here?

Giddy elation bubbled, but common sense smacked it down. This wasn't some holiday romance chick flick. It was too soon. They'd known each other two weeks.

Still . . .

There must be a reason the phrase *love at first sight* existed. Did he fall for her the day he noticed her in her purple ball gown?

His kiss at the waterfall had rocked her like a seesaw. The thought of repeating that experience for the rest of her life made her toes curl in the Mexican sand.

Could she really marry him? Besides his knock-you-dead physical attributes, his beautiful heart beckoned her. The bumbling attempts he made with Madeleine proved his sincerity.

And Maddie!

The idea of mothering the adorable girl thrilled Abby to her hot pink toenails. Marrying Spencer carried more than one perk. But she had to be rational. Two weeks wasn't long enough.

Right?

Maybe she should ask the Shippers. They were the marriage experts. Her personal matchmakers could offer wisdom.

Spencer halted, his face still pointed at the ground. "I have a proposition for you."

A proposition? Is that what lawyers called a proposal? Abby slipped her hand in her pocket and closed her fingers around a slender tube. Would it be too obvious? He wasn't looking at her. She turned at lightning speed, refreshed her lip gloss, and spun back.

"In the past two weeks, I've observed you with my daughter, and your talent and connection with her is undeniable. You treat Madeleine with a tender consideration she's never received in her entire life. The effects are startling, and there's a marked difference in her. She exudes confidence, I dare say even joy, which has also added to my own happiness." His brow furrowed. "You may be the greatest surprise God ever sent my way. And the best one."

They hadn't even arrived at the candlelight setup. He must be so crazy about her, he couldn't wait a minute longer. How adorable!

CHAPTER 40

EMILY GRASPED THE ROUGH TREE trunk and raised her binoculars. Two warm bodies leaned against her back, but she focused on the couple farther down the beach. Abby and Spencer stood ever so close together.

"Candles and everything." Althea squealed. "It's a shame Daisy missed this. Her son organized a whole romantic surprise."

"I'm flabbergasted." Gerry held the hem of her long tie-dyed skirt away from the prickly beach grass at her feet. "He's not the type for grandiose gestures."

Emily passed her the binoculars. "I guess he's improving. Take a look. Can you use this in your novel?"

Gerry accepted the binoculars. "Not bad. A little cliché. But it conveys the right message."

Althea dug a piece of chocolate from her pocket. "I like the man's get-up-and-go. Reminds me of my third husband. He proposed after one date." She popped the candy in her mouth. "Why don't we head to the ship? This may be the easiest match we ever made."

Emily steadied her phone, zoomed in, and took a few pictures. She should send them to Daisy. Wouldn't she be stunned?

"Someone else is joining them." Gerry peered through the binoculars.

"What?" Emily snatched the binoculars.

In the distance, a new couple approached, walking hand in hand. A man in jeans and T-shirt followed at a discreet distance with a camera, pausing at intervals to take their picture.

"Who are they?" she asked. "What if they spoil the proposal?"

Gerry stood on tiptoe as if that could help her see better. "Should we head them off at the pass?"

"They're too far away." Emily slapped her arthritic legs. "Why can't these old bones move as fast as they used to?"

She squinted through the binoculars. Her breath rattled in frustration at the new people approaching the couple. "We'd better return to the *Buckingham*, girls. I imagine Spencer and Abby will leave soon, and we don't want them to catch us. We can take a bicycle taxi to the ship."

Althea kept a hand under Emily's elbow as they walked along the sand until they arrived at the taxi stand. The three Shippers climbed aboard, and Emily muttered a silent prayer that the ill-timed arrivals hadn't messed up Spencer's proposal.

Abby fussed with her hair and looked at Spencer. How difficult would it be to kiss him here on the beach? The last time, she'd had the step stool. A pile of sand might give her a boost.

Spencer cleared his throat. "I realize this may come as a surprise."

Most proposals do.

"And it would be a great upheaval to your life."

Love is worth a little inconvenience.

"Perhaps it's selfish of me to hope the happiness you've brought Madeleine and me could continue." He reached for the side of his sport coat. "Is it too much to ask—"

Abby closed her eyes. She dropped her sandals and began to lift her left hand. Better to have it ready when he revealed the ring. She waited for him to utter the sweet words.

"Would you consider becoming my daughter's governess?"

A seagull squawked in the darkness.

Abby's eyes shot open. He stood with his hand in his pocket in a casual pose. Her fingers clenched. She lowered them, hoping she didn't appear as awkward as she felt. Her cheeks ignited like twin bonfires. Was the darkness enough to hide them?

"Your . . . your governess?"

A laugh floated along the breeze. Had someone witnessed her mortification? Abby's head snapped to the left, where a young couple stood in the center of the candle setup. A man with a ring box knelt on one knee. His girlfriend squealed and threw her arms around his neck.

Abby swallowed her own tears. She turned away and wished she could teleport back to the ship. Better yet, to Galveston. Anything to get her away from the most humiliating moment of her life. How had she been so delusional to presume the rich, gorgeous Spencer Masterson wanted to marry her?

After two weeks!

The breath left her nose in short, humorless puffs of laughter. She'd acted a fool, as Althea might say. Had she imagined the signals? Let the romantic ambiance get to her?

No.

She hadn't imagined the lip-lock at the waterfall either.

Abby rounded on Spencer. "Do you normally kiss your hired help?"

"What?"

"I'm sure I didn't hallucinate the kiss you gave me yesterday." She planted her feet in the sand. "Are you that affectionate with all your staff?"

"Of course not." His aristocratic nose rose even more than usual. "It was a temporary lapse in judgment." He rubbed the back of his neck. "Please accept my apology and rest assured I will always treat you with respect and maintain strict professional boundaries when you work for me. You needn't fear any unwanted advances."

Unwanted?

Abby stifled a bitter chortle. That was the trouble. She wanted them too much. But to Spencer she'd been nothing more than a lapse in judgment. A cruise ship flirtation.

"Excuse me!" The woman down the beach hollered with her hands cupped around her mouth. "We're taking engagement pictures." She made shooing motions.

Spencer gestured the direction they'd come. "It seems we're intruding on a private event. We should go."

They left the amorous couple twirling in ecstasy while the photographer snapped pictures from the sidelines.

Abby retrieved her discarded shoes. Her bare toes sank in the sand as she made her retreat. But no matter how she hurried, her steps were matched by Spencer's long strides. She huffed and puffed as she pressed forward.

Must get away.

Must remain calm.

Must not cry.

Accomplish those three things, and he might never suspect her ludicrous mistake. Abby dared a quick glance at the man beside her. He walked in silence, unaware of the storm raging inside her.

She glared straight ahead. Plenty of her coworkers indulged in onboard affairs with passengers, but she'd always been careful to reject flirtatious advances. She wasn't the messing around kind. She was the *marrying* kind. Why had she lowered her guard?

The long, mute walk to the ship allowed Abby the opportunity to replay every word, every gesture, and every interaction between them. By the time they reached the gangplank, she was certain.

She wasn't certifiable.

Spencer had sent her romantic signals loud and clear. Whether he meant them or not was another question. One she wasn't going to ask. Time to play it off.

They crossed the gangplank, and Abby manufactured a dazzling smile at the entrance. "Thank you for the exercise. I won't have to visit the gym before bed. Good night."

"Wait." He caught her hand. "About my job offer—"

"Oh, right," Abby trilled as if she'd forgotten the most unwelcome proposition of her life. "Thank you for your confidence in me, but in a few weeks, I'll be returning to the teaching profession. I already have a position lined up in Florida and have no interest in working as a governess. I'm sure you want to check on Madeleine. Good night, Mr. Masterson."

She didn't bother to gauge his reaction as she stalked away. But that was one of the disadvantages of being five foot two. With such short legs, even her widest steps took forever to get anywhere. He could catch up with her in three seconds.

But he didn't even try.

The humiliation escalated as she passed through the main lobby. Not only did Spencer not want her as his wife, he didn't even consider her worth pursuing as his employee. She made it through the public area and was almost to the stairway door when she saw them.

Sitting on a circular couch were three of the Shippers. Emily's lips lifted at her approach. She stood as Abby neared.

"How did it go, dear?" Emily asked.

"Did you make any progress?" Gerry sat with her pencil raised above a notebook.

Althea clasped her hands in front of her chin. "Did he kiss you?"

Abby looked behind her. Spencer was nowhere in sight. She sank to the couch cushion and laughed. Not a gentle, well-bred titter, but a gut-shaking, almost hysterical guffaw. She laughed so hard it shook the tears from her eyes. And once they started, they flowed in abandon. A sob broke from her lips. Anyone walking by might assume she was a nutcase.

Laugh. Sob. Laugh. Sob.

She alternated between merriment and despair. The words refused to come. Her disappointed heart stuck in her throat and blocked them.

Althea sprang from her seat and nestled next to her. Pulling her close, the older woman crushed her in a pillow-soft embrace. Smoothing a hand down Abby's back, she cooed like someone would to a baby.

"This isn't good." Gerry shut her notebook. "Those aren't happy tears."

Abby sobbed harder. She felt so very, very stupid. Why would a drop-dead gorgeous, successful, affluent man see her as anything more than a fling? It defied logic.

Emily offered a handkerchief. Abby swabbed her runny nose and made a valiant attempt to squelch the crying jag. Clamping her lips, she concentrated on taking deep, ragged breaths.

The Shippers waited with bent eyebrows and supportive expressions.

It took several minutes, but Abby pulled herself together. She pressed her palms to her overheated cheeks. "He . . . he asked me to be Maddie's governess."

"Governess!" three voices exclaimed.

Althea clicked her tongue. "That boy is aggravating as a rock."

"The gall," Gerry muttered. "Has he no shame?"

Emily face-palmed. "I'm afraid we got our bearings wrong on this one, girls." She tugged her black handbag onto her lap. "Abigail, we've let you down. Will you forgive us?"

Abby's lower lip quivered. "Don't be silly. You four have done everything I asked and more. It's not your fault I fell for the wrong man."

Emily toyed with the purse straps. "In a way, it is. We believed you two shared a connection, and we were creating opportunities where you could explore it."

Abby groaned. "We definitely explored it. But I guess Spencer is done adventuring and ready for real life." She launched to her feet. "The MS *Buckingham* docks in Galveston tomorrow, and he and Maddie will return home. All I have to do is avoid them for a few more hours." She thumped a fist against her leg. "I hate to let Maddie leave without saying goodbye, but"—her voice cracked—"I can't face Spencer again."

Emily rose from the couch. "Don't let this get you down, dear. The man is an idiot if he can't see what's right under his nose. We'll find you someone better. Someone worthy of you."

Someone better?

The idea didn't appeal at all.

She didn't want *better*. She wanted Spencer. But he'd made it abundantly clear he wanted her only as an employee.

CHAPTER 41

ANOTHER VOYAGE. ANOTHER CROP OF passengers. Another chance to help someone find true love.

But Emily Windsor's confidence lagged.

She leaned against the elevator wall, her chin as low as her morale. What a flop! Never in the Shippers' long record of coupling efforts had they gotten something so totally and completely wrong. None of them had bothered to bid goodbye to Spencer when the ship docked in Galveston—not even Daisy. That detail worried Emily. Had her misguided matchmaking attempt hurt her friend's relationship with her son? Would he let Daisy be part of Madeleine's life after this?

Emily squinted at the ceiling. "God, I'm not seeing it this time. What was the point? I can accept if Spencer and Abby weren't meant to be. But what about Daisy? The rift between her and her son is wider than ever." Her head bent again. "Is it all my fault?"

The elevator stopped at the main lobby, the doors opened, and several children in shorts and tank tops sped into the car. Their harried mother shoved them to one side with an apologetic wince, and Emily squeezed by before the doors shut.

No use wallowing. The best way to make it up to Abby was to find her someone wonderful. Might as well scope out the new batch of passengers for a few minutes before heading to her cabin. She settled in an armchair smack-dab in the center of the gigantic room. A musician from the evening shows played on the grand piano as people milled around.

Abby navigated the expansive space in her usual purple ball gown, a basket hanging from her arm. She approached a little girl standing with her mother and extended a tiara. Her warm smile showed not a trace of her misery from the previous night.

A tall man approached Abby. Emily's eyes bulged. The gentleman faced away from her, but there was no mistaking the owner of those wide shoulders.

"Oh, dear Lord," Emily muttered. "Help us all."

Someone patted Abby's elbow as she took another tiara from her basket. Her gaze met a broad chest and traveled up, up, up. Her neck bent at a well-known angle. She stopped at the square chin, unwilling to meet the eyes of the man she'd never expected to see again.

Spencer Randolph Masterson. In the living, breathing, wretched flesh.

His lips lifted. "If someone told me a month ago I'd be taking a third cruise, I'd have called him a liar. Yet here I am."

"Where's Maddie?" She looked around his tall body but didn't find her.

He pointed to a nearby couch. Maddie sat on the cushions, holding a doll. She waved with both hands.

Abby waved back before turning her attention to Spencer. "Isn't your office complaining? I doubt they expected you to take three vacations."

He shrugged. "They're not dancing for joy, but that's when being the boss comes in handy."

"Good for you," Abby ground out.

Either he missed her biting tone or chose to ignore it.

"Convincing my mother to return to New Orleans has been next to impossible. When we docked this morning, I couldn't even locate her.

The woman refuses to use the cell I bought, her roommate isn't answering her phone, and the front desk refused to tell me their cabin number. Apparently our familial problems are glaringly obvious to the crew. I had no choice but to book another voyage." He nudged Abby's arm. "Good thing Monarch has a first-class nanny valet service."

"Yes, sir." Cheap rhinestones dug into her palm as she clenched the crown she was holding. "I'm sure they'll provide you with a fabulous person. Unfortunately, I won't be available to accommodate you this time."

"What?" He inclined his ear as if he hadn't heard her correctly. "Why?"

"This is my last voyage on the MS *Buckingham*. My cruising career is drawing to a close, and I'm busy wrapping up last-minute details."

"You won't be working?"

"I'll still be performing my regular duties." Abby's calm voice in no way matched the furious pounding of her pulse. "Feel free to bring Maddie by the Kids Kingdom. I'd love to hang out with her. Now if you'll excuse me."

"Hold on."

He reached for her, and she held the basket of tiaras in front of her like a rhinestone shield. If she didn't get out of here soon, she might throw up.

"Knock me down with a feather!" Emily Windsor skidded to a stop beside them. Her curls poofed from the top of her head like a pot scrubber. "Spencer, we thought you went home."

"Not when I haven't achieved my objective. Daisy made herself scarce."

"I can help you find her, dear. We can call her on my walkie-talkie." The older woman threaded an arm around his and tugged him toward the elevators.

"Wait." He dug his heels in and glanced at Abby. "About the nanny position—"

"I'm sorry, Mr. Masterson." Abby faked a sympathetic look. "I'm not interested. At all. Goodbye."

She waved once more to Maddie before retreating. It hurt to leave the precious little girl without so much as a hug. But she had to get away from that clueless but demanding man before he suspected the pride-crushing reason she didn't want to spend time with them.

CHAPTER 42

SPENCER SCOFFED AT THE VIBRANT Welcome sign posted by the double doors of the Kids Kingdom. "Didn't feel very welcoming in the lobby."

Abby's fervent refusal to be even a temporary nanny to Maddie had thrown him for a loop. He'd counted on her to provide the same compassionate care as she had the previous two voyages. Customer service was no help, only confirming that Ms. O'Brien had removed her name from the list of nanny valet participants. His conversation with them combined with the wild goose chase Emily dragged him on in search of his mother had left him in a muddy funk.

Madeleine tugged his pant leg. "Daddy, can we go in?"

Daddy.

Abby's wish was becoming reality. Madeleine called him that more often. And whenever she did, he couldn't refuse her anything.

They entered the large public area where parents dropped off their children. A group of both adults and children crowded on the carpet around a tall, red wooden box about the size of a bicycle. A front panel sat open, showing dramatic black-and-white stripes painted on the inside.

The older man from the bingo night stood beside it with a magic wand. He removed his top hat to reveal red hair streaked with silver.

215

He quipped in his Irish accent, "I'm rehearsing a bit of magic for the big theater and could use some help. Who wants me to make something disappear?"

Energetic bodies bounced as they hollered their agreement.

"Daddy, let's watch." Madeleine tugged Spencer over to the show. They settled on the carpet with the others, and he scanned the crowd for Abby. Various employees in purple shirts and khakis serviced the guests. But no redhead.

The magician laughed. "What should we put in the disappearing box?" He placed his hat on his head. "Perhaps flowers?"

A multicolored bouquet appeared in his previously empty fingers, and the crowd oohed.

"No, no." The man waved his hands, and the bouquet vanished. "That's much too commonplace. How about"—he tapped his chin with the wand—"a human being? Do I have any volunteers?"

"Me, me, me," cried the children.

Madeleine sat up on her knees to see better.

"Ah!" The magician gestured behind them. "How about a princess?"

The audience focused on Abby entering a nearby door in her purple ball gown. She froze at the sight of every eye pointed at her.

"Wow." She laughed. "Did someone throw a party and forget to tell me?"

"It's a magic party," the magician called. "Care to be my beautiful assistant?"

Her glance grazed Spencer, but she showed no sign of recognition. He ground his molars at the slight. Had he offended her? How?

Abby's satin skirt rustled past him. She made her way to the front, bent, and looked in the empty box. "Are you sure I can fit, Seamus?"

"Don't worry, darlin'." The man winked. "You won't be in there long. I'm dispatching you straight to fairyland." He crouched and closed the front door to the box. "Let me say my special words to get the little people's attention." He tapped the sides of the red wood. "All the trees in the grove. All the fairies in the glen. Get your wings and sparkles on. I'm a'sending you a friend." Grabbing a shiny brass knob at the top of the box, he opened a new door. "Need my help climbing in? You're a wee one."

"You're not so tall yourself." She placed her hands on the lip of the box, hoisted herself to sit on the edge, and swung her legs around. "Goodbye, all." She waved at the crowd. "I'm off to fairyland." She descended into the box.

Madeleine seized Spencer's shoulder. She rose to her feet and balanced on her tiptoes. He placed a hand on her back to steady her.

Seamus waved his wand around the box. "Goodbye, dear Abigail. Enjoy your visit." He touched the short stick to the box, and a poof of smoke emitted. The magician pulled the front door open to reveal the empty striped interior.

Gasps abounded. Children whooped, and parents applauded. Seamus took an elegant bow.

"Thank ye one and all. Fairyland's so beautiful that my friend may want to stay awhile. In the meantime, my amazing coworkers are ready to check in any young passengers who want to spend more time in the Kids Kingdom."

Spencer turned to his daughter. "Do you—" His words stalled at the tears trickling down her cheeks. He grasped her by the elbows. "Madeleine, what's wrong?"

"Abby's gone," she whimpered.

People swerved around them in their rush to sign their kids in to the center. A large man bumped Spencer. He moved closer to Madeleine and wrapped his arms around her to shield her from the crush. He stared at her tear-streaked face. Dismay surged.

This was Abigail O'Brien's fault. She got a person attached and then disappeared without any remorse.

"I-it's okay." He patted Madeleine's back. "It's a trick. She's not really gone."

"Where is she?" Madeleine cried louder than he'd ever heard her. "Abby?" Her voice broke. "Abby!" She dropped her head to his chest and sobbed.

Spencer's composure crumbled. His panicked gaze darted around the room. Could anyone help him? He was completely out of his element. How did one make a child stop crying?

A thunk and then a rustle sounded behind him. Abby appeared at his side, almost like another magic trick.

"Here I am, sweetie." She knelt on the ground and wiped Madeleine's wet cheeks.

"Aaaaabbyyyyyyy," his daughter wailed. She threw herself into the woman's arms.

"Shhh." Abby hugged her. "Everything's okay. I didn't like it in fairyland, and I came home quick."

Madeleine scrubbed her eyes. "Why?"

"Because I missed you so much."

"You won't leave?"

Abby cuddled Madeleine closer. "I'm not going anywhere. I promise."

Spencer waited. Silent. A childhood memory of weeping in his closet, ever so quietly so his father wouldn't catch him and deliver another lecture, assailed him. Crying was for losers. It didn't befit a Masterson. But as the red-haired miracle worker in front of Spencer coaxed a laugh from his daughter, the thought occurred that his early years might have been very different if he'd had someone like Abby to hug him. He didn't intend for his daughter to experience the same abandonment.

His jaw firmed. "You do realize, Ms. O'Brien, you've committed yourself."

She focused on him for the first time. Her brow furrowed. "What do you mean?"

"You promised my daughter you weren't going anywhere. That counts as a verbal contract." He leaned close and whispered so Maddie wouldn't hear. "But more importantly, if you don't want to break her heart, then you'll have to be our nanny for the rest of the cruise."

Her eyes flared, and she jerked away. "I warn you, sir, those things they say about the temperaments of redheads aren't unfounded rumors. You're treading in dangerous waters."

Was it a coincidence that he was kneeling on the ground? It certainly felt like he was willing to beg.

"Please." He flinched at her furious eyes. "I wish I knew the right words, but I don't. I . . . just . . . *please*?"

CHAPTER 43

EMILY AND GERRY STOOD OUTSIDE Daisy and Althea's cabin door. A stream of passengers rambled down the hallway. Several groups swerved around a couple at the end who were arguing about where to eat dinner.

Gerry frowned at them. "They could use our help."

Emily didn't even turn. "We barely have enough time to service our current client."

"Doesn't help that two of our crew aren't answering their walkie-talkies. It would've saved us the long walk."

Emily pounded on the door. It opened to reveal a sleepy Daisy. "Where's your walkie-talkie?"

Daisy yawned. "It ran out of battery." She allowed her friends into the small cabin.

Gerry crossed the threshold. "Your son's looking for you."

"I'm well aware." Daisy ambled to her closet. She chose a black cashmere cardigan and slipped her right arm through the sleeve. "That's why I avoided him until the cruise ended in Galveston and he debarked."

"Bad news." Emily leaned her cane against the desk. "He reboarded."

"He what?" Daisy stalled with her sweater halfway on. "But . . . but why—"

Althea wandered out of the bathroom. "Did you say Spencer's back?"

"With a vengeance," Gerry said.

The soft material of the sleeve bunched around Daisy's elbow. "Why

220

can't he accept I'm not returning to New Orleans?" She yanked the sweater off and chucked it on the floor. "I've told him until I'm blue in the face."

Emily sank to a corner of the single bed on the left. "From what I saw in the lobby, you may only be half the reason for his return. He looked none too happy when Abby refused to be his nanny valet."

"Good for her." Althea's lips thinned. "That boy has twisted her heart like a kid with a piece of string."

Daisy worried her fingers. "I hope he doesn't hurt her again."

Emily grabbed her cane. "The best thing we can do is divert Abby's attention to someone else. Let's inform her of our new choice. She should be excited to learn we've arranged a date with Dr. Grant for this evening."

The Shippers left the cabin but had to squeeze past someone standing on a ladder in front of the door. They swerved around the metal rungs. Barney stood at the top. One hand held the rounded dome from the security camera, and the other gripped a screwdriver.

"There's my favorite passengers." He saluted them with the tool. "Are you making trouble again?"

"Always." Althea patted his tennis shoe. "What brings you to our hallway, baby?"

He extended the rounded glass cover her direction. Emily peered at the object. A large crack covered half the dome.

"What happened?"

He growled. "Some kids were playing softball in the hallway. No parents in sight." Barney unscrewed a metal plate above the camera. He checked the connection for each cable.

Gerry withdrew her notebook and scribbled as he worked. "Is that an Ethernet cable?" She slipped her pen behind her ear.

"It is." Barney wiggled the thick white wire. "I'm impressed, Ms. Paroo. You know your security equipment. Were you a guard in your former life?"

"Librarian." She shoved between Emily and Althea, placed a foot on the bottom rung, and hauled herself up. The metal ladder rocked.

"Whoa, whoa!" Barney propped his forearm against the wall for support, his eyes squeezed shut.

"Careful, dear," Emily said. "We don't want to order a cane for you too."

Gerry stretched to get a closer look. "I've been researching the different types of cables. Isn't it true Ethernet connections are capable of recording audio?"

"A-audio?" Barney lifted a shaky hand from the wall and ran it over his bald spot. "Well, yes. But we don't listen in on the passengers, if that's what you're worried about. The cameras are muted. We use them for surveillance. To make sure the *Buckingham* is safe and sound."

Emily pressed against Gerry and said, "But it *is* possible to hear someone through the camera? If it was unmuted."

"Well"—he leaned his head to the side—"I suppose it's possible. But cruise lines don't use the feature. Too much gray area with privacy issues."

"I knew it!" Gerry slapped the side of the ladder.

It jiggled again, and Barney clutched the dome and screwdriver to his torso with a moan.

"Can I help you ladies?" an unhelpful-sounding voice said.

Mr. Everson approached their group, his requisite sunglasses firmly in place.

"Hey, Sarge," said Barney.

"Uh-oh, time to scoot." Althea grabbed the tail of Gerry's shirt and tugged. "Leave poor Barney alone. Can't you see he's green from all the swaying? He's just a phone call away if you need more information." She glanced at the man. "Right, baby?"

"Yes, ma'am." He gave a grateful if somewhat quivery smile.

Mr. Everson marched to the ladder. Even though the sunglasses hid his eyes, he still managed to give the impression he was glaring at Gerry.

She stepped off the bottom rung, slipped her pen from behind her ear, and wrote with a hurried scrawl. "Hidden cables. Perfect for a murder."

A frustrated rumble issued from Everson's throat.

"Murder!" Barney's complexion switched from green to pale.

"Don't listen to her, dear." Emily winked at him. "You've been a great help, as always. I owe you one."

"What about the text you sent? Didn't you want to set me up with a date?"

"Ah yes." Emily rubbed her nose. "I'm sorry. That particular plan didn't come about. But I'll keep you in mind for the future."

"Great." His answer wasn't enthusiastic.

"Don't look so glum. Next time we're in port, I'll be sure to buy you some sugary buñuelos."

"Promise?" He brightened.

Althea patted his shoe again. "Barney's got a sweet tooth as big as mine."

Everson moved in front of the ladder like a barrier. "If you ladies are finished distracting my team member, he'll get back to work."

Barney sighed. "Thanks, Sarge."

Emily's nose lifted. "He's not the only one with work to do. Come on, girls. It's time to introduce Abby to her future."

CHAPTER 44

ABBY EXITED THE DOWNSTAIRS BATHROOM of the Imperial Suite and checked on Maddie. She was playing with a pair of dolls in the living room. Her happy voice chattered as she improvised their conversation.

"Sweetie," Abby called. "I'll be gone for a while, but your grandma will be here with you."

"Okay, Abby." Maddie ran over with her dolls. "You look pretty."

"Not as pretty as you." She tweaked Maddie's cheek.

Outside the windows, the last traces of sunlight dipped below the watery horizon and the more valiant stars were twinkling in the evening sky. Abby rested one hand against the couch and slipped on a pair of pink patent leather heels. They perfectly matched her new pedicure. She flexed her ankle with trepidation. No pain. What a relief.

Dr. Grant didn't tower over her like some people she knew. His lean five-foot-ten frame would be much friendlier to her neck. Especially when she was wearing heels. Would he like her outfit?

Abby passed a mirror and smoothed an errant curl into her French twist. Her white eyelet sundress was modest yet attractive. The ruffled shoulder straps lent a dainty, feminine air. *Not bad.*

Maddie's tears had suckered her into spending more time in this royal prison, but she didn't intend to miss her date. At least half the female employees on the boat had a crush on sweet and dreamy Dr. Grant.

The front door clicked, and Spencer entered, talking on the phone.

"That's right, Baptiste. Make sure he's comfortable with the switch. I've always represented their company cases. Yes, I—" He halted at the sight of her, scanned her outfit, and continued. "I'll also call him personally to soothe his concerns."

Abby settled on the couch beside Maddie. The girl pulled a cushion over and propped her dolls on top.

Spencer finished his call, settled in the chair opposite them, and sat with one leg crossed over the other. "You're all dressed up, Abby."

She smoothed her skirt around her knees. "It's my break time."

He gave a stoic nod. "I'll stay with Maddie until you return."

"Thank you, but your mother should be here soon. I'll be back in two hours."

"Two hours?" Spencer noted a tinge of desperation in his voice and cleared his throat. "You took forty-five minutes last time."

"Yes, sir. But I have important business that requires longer."

"What business?"

"The Shippers found a new candidate."

Her casual announcement raked an irritating path through his brain. Couldn't his mother and her matchmaking friends do normal senior activities to amuse themselves? Why not take up knitting? Collecting recipes? Canasta?

He feigned a playful tone. "Not another minister?"

"I've got a date with the ship's doctor."

The doctor? An attractive profession to someone with marriage on her mind. He drummed his fingers against his knee. "How can you wholeheartedly hand your future to a bunch of meddlers?"

"Don't call them that." Abby's eyes glinted. "I've seen how good the Shippers are at making matches." She glanced away. "They might not always get it right, but they don't give up." Her gaze met his. "And neither do I. In the past, I may have dated a few flops, but I still want to get married."

Spencer blinked at her unabashed statement. "Why?"

"Why?" Abby blinked back. "Do I need a reason? Most people want to get married, don't they?"

"I suppose." Spencer's upper lip lifted at one corner. "But I wouldn't recommend it. I speak from personal experience when I say it isn't the lifelong honeymoon the romance novels portray."

Abby placed her hands over Madeleine's ears. "You shouldn't say those things in front of Maddie. I'm sure she loves her mother."

"I doubt she could pick Priscilla out of a crowd. From the day she was born, Madeleine spent the majority of her time with nurses and nannies. My ex-wife was never the nurturing type. Too busy with parties and social gatherings and lunches at the country club. She remembered she was a parent when she required an accessory for the annual mother-daughter fashion show."

"I'm thirsty," Maddie exclaimed.

She waited until Abby removed her hands, then hopped off the couch and ran to the kitchen. After opening the fridge, she grabbed a bottle of water from inside, shut the door, and unscrewed the bottle cap.

Abby watched her with a smile. "I can't fathom anyone ignoring Maddie. She's too precious. I want one exactly like her."

"These days, you can have children without the old-fashioned trappings of matrimony."

"Not in my family." Abby's nose crinkled. "My father would tan my hide from Tampa to Tallahassee."

"So you want to get married for the kids?"

"Not just kids. The whole thing. The till-death-do-us-part promise that you'll have someone on your side through thick and thin. I'm not so starry-eyed that I regard myself as incomplete without my 'other half.' But if you had the choice between completing a huge challenge alone or with a partner, wouldn't you pick the partner? Is there any greater challenge than life?"

"As long as your partner doesn't end up being deadweight."

She huffed. "I can see we'll never agree."

"Well, until you find this 'other half'"—Spencer made air quotes with his fingers—"why wish for a child exactly like Madeleine when she's available? If you agree to be her governess, you can share your motherly affection with her and get paid well while doing it. Then you can take your time finding Mr. Right."

"No, thank you, sir."

Again with the "sir." What had he done to make her testy?

He propped his elbows on the arms of the chair and steepled his fingers in front of his mouth. "It hasn't escaped my notice you've adopted a more formal tone with me."

"Just maintaining professional boundaries. We've both struggled with that in the past."

A red flag waved in Spencer's brain. Boundaries. There was one definite time where neither of them maintained their boundaries. He lowered his hands and sat straighter. "Are you referring to a specific instance?"

She averted her eyes. "Let's just say you can save Maddie's step stool for toothbrushing time."

He knew it. She was still upset about their kiss at the pathetic waterfall the Shippers insisted on visiting. He must not have made his regret clear that night on the beach. A muscle popped in his jaw. He swallowed and leaned forward in the chair. "Abby, I deeply apologize if I've offended you. I didn't mean—"

"No apologies necessary. We'll split the blame fifty-fifty and leave it at that."

He might have argued, but his daughter returned, plopped down on the couch, and curled up by the woman's side.

"Be careful, Madeleine," Spencer said. "Ms. O'Brien won't want to be wrinkled when she leaves for her date."

"Sorry." Madeleine scooted away.

Abby glared at him. "Don't worry, Maddie." She placed an arm around her charge. "A hug from you is worth a million wrinkles."

Madeleine relaxed against her. "Are you going away?"

"Yes, but I'll be back." She extended a finger. "I pinky-promise I'll tuck you in bed. Okay?"

Madeleine hooked her finger with Abby's. "Okay."

The touching exchange roiled Spencer's gut. How could he ever find someone else to treat his daughter with the same amount of love? There was no one better than Abby. And he'd ruined everything. Because of one ill-timed kiss, he'd driven away the perfect person to help him raise Madeleine.

Despite his diligent efforts, he'd turned out like his father. Hurting the people around him without realizing or caring.

God? Spencer slumped in his seat. *How do I fix this mess?*

The doorbell chimed, and Abby stood. "There's my replacement. I figured this would be an excellent time for Maddie to spend time with her grandmother."

She crossed the room and opened the door, but more than Daisy entered. The whole Shipper passel invaded his suite in a noisy, unrestrained herd.

Emily led the group. "Look at this living room."

Gerry pulled her notebook and pen from her pocket. "Who knew they made cabins the size of airplane hangars?"

"This must be what heaven's like." Althea started to sing, "*Glory, glory, hallelujah! Since I laid my burdens down.*"

His mother ignored the suite and moved in a lithe, fluid motion to sit beside Madeleine.

"Grandma!" His daughter wrapped her arms around Daisy's neck.

Abby stood behind them with an approving smile.

His mother cuddled Madeleine. "Hello, sugar. You look so pretty today."

Spencer noted the lopsided bow on his daughter's dress, purple sneakers, and a tuft of hair sticking out from her head, but Daisy made no attempt to fix it. He had countless memories of his mother straightening his jacket and smoothing his hair, advising him to behave with decorum. The difference between that woman and the one who sat before him was astonishing.

"Mercy!" Althea wandered to the eating area. "Come check out this kitchen, girls. It's bigger than two of our cabins put together."

The marble-topped island in the center held a platter with an assortment of fruits, cheeses, and pastries.

"Mmm-mmm." Althea popped a strawberry in her mouth. "Where's the bathroom? I bet the commode has a solid gold toilet seat."

Abby swiped her phone from the end table. "Thanks for coming, ladies. I'm off to my date."

"We'll say a prayer." Emily took a seat in the armchair near Daisy.

"Hold on a minute." Spencer scrambled to his feet. "How long will you be gone?"

"I told you." She headed for the front door. "Two hours."

He checked his watch. "So you'll be back at 8:06 p.m.?"

She hesitated with her hand on the knob. "Yes, sir. 8:06 exactly." She winked at Maddie. "Later, alligator." Then she was gone.

Spencer fumed. Another crazy date cooked up by the Shippers. Hadn't their past candidates proved they didn't have a clue what they were doing? He scowled at the four meddlers gathered in his living room. Gerry read a book in an armchair, while the other three women fussed over Madeleine.

"You must be proud of yourselves"—he strode to their group—"finding a new date for Abby after the last dud you picked."

"Yes." Emily's lip curled. "I admit our last choice was less than impressive. We should've known better."

Althea snickered.

Daisy tweaked Maddie's chin. "You look beautiful, sugar. Did Abby let you pick your own outfit?"

"I picked it all by myself." Madeleine twirled with her arms outstretched to show off how her dress billowed. "Do you like it?"

"I love it." Daisy clapped. "It's a shame she can't take care of you all the time." Her eyes cut to Spencer. "Perhaps if *someone* hadn't made an unfortunate mistake, things might have been different."

"How do you know about that?" Spencer said. "Were you spying on us at the waterfall?"

"You poor thing." Gerry's dry voice filtered from behind her book.

"Your mother's not talking about the waterfall. Do you truly believe that's the reason Abby's mad at you?"

Not the waterfall? Was there another transgression he'd committed?

"I"—Spencer searched his memory—"I'm not sure to what you are referring."

"Show him, Emily," said Althea.

The head Shipper pulled a cell phone from her large handbag and tapped the screen. "I'm sending you a picture, Spencer. Take a look and then ask yourself what Abby assumed when she saw that setup."

His phone dinged, and he checked his texts. It took a split second to understand her implication. A picture of a couple filled the screen.

Him and Abby.

It was circumstantial evidence. But the moon shining on the waves. The candles on the beach? The anticipation in Abby's posture. They led the viewer to one conclusion. Someone was getting engaged.

Had Abby made the same deduction?

Impossible. There was no way she'd have jumped to such an assumption. After all, they'd known each other a mere two weeks at the time.

But he *had* kissed her at the waterfall.

And he *had* acted like a jealous fool when she dated another man.

Spencer groaned. There were more bridges to mend than he'd imagined. He'd start as soon as Abby returned.

At 8:06.

CHAPTER 45

SLAM!

The four Shippers jumped as Spencer closed the office door behind him.

Emily smirked. "Someone's unhappy. Why do you suppose he gets so upset about his nanny's dinner break?"

"Serves him right," Althea said. "He had his chance, and he blew it." She sashayed to the couch, settled beside Daisy, and kissed Madeleine on the cheek. "Honey, you're too sweet. You taste like candy."

The girl giggled. "Can we play hide-and-seek?"

"Oooh." Althea cringed. "My old body doesn't work so good for hide-and-seek anymore. Is there something else you wanna do?"

Maddie scratched her head. "Can we read a story?"

"Now you're talking." Althea wagged a finger between her and Daisy. "Story reading is our specialty. You go pick out which book you want."

"Okay." Maddie hopped off the couch and skipped up the stairs.

Emily eyed the long flight and shuddered. "You can keep these fancy suites. I prefer my nice, cozy cabin, where I don't have to climb a mountain before I crawl into bed."

"You and me both," Gerry said. "But speaking of stories, I need to do research for my novel. I found a great resource at the ship's library."

Stretching her long legs out, she fetched a book from her bag. The heavy hardback flopped open on her lap, and a familiar square of black rested inside.

"What's this?" she raised the envelope.

"Oh my!" Daisy's slender fingers covered her mouth.

Althea pointed. "That looks like the notes Daisy received."

Emily hurried to Gerry's side, leaned her nose an inch from the paper, and examined it. No writing on the outside. No stamp. Someone must've slipped it into Gerry's bag when she was unaware.

Gerry drew the envelope close to her chest. "It's bad manners to read other people's mail."

"I'm sorry, dear." Emily moved away. "I wanted to check for any identifiable markings, but it looks clean."

Gerry toyed with the loose paper flap. She folded it back to reveal the card inside. Her fingers trembled as she reached for it.

"Take your time, baby," said Althea.

Daisy murmured in sympathy.

"Would you . . . ?" Emily hesitated. Her curiosity was killing her. But what horrible memories might the note recall? She sank on the couch beside her friend. "Would you rather we leave you alone?"

"What for?" Gerry's brows crinkled.

Daisy rubbed her hands down her arms. "The contents might be . . . personal. We can leave."

Gerry chuckled. "I'm not nervous. This is the most exciting thing that's happened to me in a month of Sundays. If there's one fact I know better than anyone, it's how boring my life has been. There isn't a single incident someone could blackmail me for, unless you count the time I let a young girl skip the holds line because she was desperate to read a new release. And that was only once."

Althea tsk-tsked. "We need to get you a boyfriend."

Emily sat on her twitchy fingers, longing to confiscate the envelope and read its contents. Who knew what the ominous black missive contained?

Gerry's cheeks reddened as she grabbed the heavy white paper inside. Paused.

"What are you waiting for?" Althea bounced in her seat. "Open it already."

"Just savoring the moment." Gerry grinned. "I feel like a heroine in an Agatha Christie novel."

She withdrew the card, slipped her glasses on her nose, and read. Her eyes reached the bottom of the page, jerked to the top, and made another circuit of the paper. She curled her fingers and pressed them against her lips. Her body shook.

Emily reached out. "Are you all right, dear?"

"Don't worry," Althea said. "No matter what's in that note, we still love you."

"Yes." Daisy twisted the golden watch chain around her neck. "If it requires legal help, I'll instruct Spencer to represent you."

A snort emanated from Gerry's covered nostrils. She allowed the paper to flutter to the table, pressed both hands to her belly, and gave a small laugh, followed by another larger and more explosive guffaw.

"Poor thing," Daisy said. "She must be overwhelmed."

Emily couldn't take it anymore. She snatched the note and read it for herself. When she reached the end, she understood why her friend had taken a second perusal to process the message.

"What does it say?" Althea's eyebrows almost reached her scalp.

"Brace yourselves, girls." Emily's gaze slid to Gerry. "Our dear friend is being extorted for murder."

"Grandma!" Maddie's excited voice called. "I got it." She raced down the stairs with a storybook, hurried to the couch, and climbed between Daisy and Althea.

The four ladies exchanged a look, and Gerry and Emily withdrew to the kitchen.

"My, my," Althea cooed to the little girl. "You chose a good one. I love this story."

Daisy opened the picture book and began to read aloud.

Emily leaned on the island and lowered her voice. "The culprit tipped their hand this time." She pointed at the note. "It says you wouldn't want the police to go digging up your vegetable garden. Isn't that part of the mystery novel you're writing?"

"Yes," Gerry whispered. "That plot point is brand-new. I wrote the murderer's confession this morning, right before you joined me in the library. If someone didn't know better, they might mistake it for a diary entry."

Emily nodded. "Are you certain you haven't mentioned the story or shown it to anyone else?"

"Positive. When I left the library, I put the notebook in my bag, meaning to type the new paragraphs on my laptop after lunch, but we got distracted by Spencer's reemergence."

"Is it still there?"

Gerry fetched her bag and withdrew the spiral-bound notebook with the red cover. She fanned through the pages. "As far as I can tell, it hasn't been touched."

"This makes no sense. Why would someone think you're a murderer unless they've read that so-called confession?"

"And we've yet to discover how they found out about Daisy's affair," Gerry declared.

Daisy's voice faltered. Althea grabbed her hand and read the story where her friend had left off. Daisy rose and moved to join Emily and Gerry. She stood in front of them, her body blocking her granddaughter from the conversation.

"Sorry." Gerry winced. "I didn't mean to dredge up the past."

Daisy's pinched lips relaxed.

"Whooo-eee." In the living room, Althea stretched her arms. "What a good story. Why don't you find us another book to read?"

Maddie hurried upstairs.

Althea scooted to the kitchen and put her arm around her roomie. "You good?"

Daisy crumpled. "It was my error in judgment. I deserve the shame."

"Nonsense." Althea swatted her back. "We talked about this, Daisy

Mae. Once you repent, it's under the blood. The Bible promises complete forgiveness. Feeling guilty isn't part of the deal."

Emily withdrew her phone and opened a note-taking app. "Daisy, do you have any papers that mention your . . . past?"

"Mercy, no," Daisy snapped. "It's hardly something I'm proud of, and I prefer not to dwell on it."

"Did you tell anyone besides Althea?"

"No." Daisy tugged at her necklace, sliding the miniature pendant watch on the chain. "She's my only confidante. We spoke of it twice. One night in our cabin after I'd experienced a distressing nightmare and then the next day when she accompanied me to the spa. My nerves were overwrought, so I booked an aromatherapy massage."

"I sat and talked while she got the fancy stuff," Althea said.

Emily typed with both thumbs. "Althea, did you ever mention it to anyone else?"

Althea's broad nostrils flared at the implication. "What do you take me for? A snitch?"

"Forgive me, dear." Emily typed away. "I'm trying to be thorough." She set her phone down. "A crew member might have overheard you in the spa. Was anyone else there?"

Daisy shook her head. "The masseuse had already left. No one else was in the room."

Gerry wrote in her notebook. "That doesn't mean someone wasn't listening at the door. Who gave you the massage?"

"Magda." Daisy rubbed her forehead. "But it couldn't be her. She's the best spa technician on the ship."

Gerry frowned. "Her work competency has nothing to do with her trustworthiness."

"On the contrary," Daisy said. "I've found the way a person performs their job directly relates to their integrity."

Maddie's feet sounded on the stairs. The Shippers returned to the living room and met her there. With a new book, she plopped beside her grandmother, and Daisy drew her close.

Althea propped her arm on the back of the couch. "I'd be willing to bet all my bingo winnings, it isn't Magda." She snapped her fingers. "Hold up. There was one other time. I forgot because it was so short."

Daisy glanced at Maddie. "You mean that morning in the chapel?"

"Yep. We swung by after the spa. Remember?"

Gerry leaned forward. "Now we're getting somewhere. Who else was there?"

Daisy and Althea spoke together. "No one."

Emily grumbled as she made another note.

"I'll repeat what I said before." Althea rubbed her roommate's shoulder. "Tell your son. Then this scoundrel loses any power over you."

Daisy toyed with a lock of Maddie's hair while her granddaughter flipped through her picture book. "What if he hates me?" Daisy said.

The other Shippers exchanged glances. Not one of them dared to point out the relationship between Daisy and her son couldn't get much worse.

Emily slipped her phone in her pocket and stood. "Okay, girls. Let's go."

Gerry put her stuff in her bag. "Where are we going?"

"Maddie"—Emily smiled at the child—"how'd you like to read your story somewhere special? Have you ever visited the chapel?"

"What's a chapel?" Maddie asked.

"A beautiful place. We'll go say hello to God, read your story, and then eat dinner at the buffet."

"Mmm-mmm." Althea rubbed her tummy. "They have the best cupcakes. You'll love it, Maddie."

"Cupcakes?" Maddie's face beamed. "Yay!"

"Daisy, you tell Spencer we're taking Maddie to dinner." Emily retrieved her purse. "We'll stop by the chapel and examine the scene of the crime. My bones tell me that's where we'll find some answers."

CHAPTER 46

A COUPLE HOURS AWAY FROM Spencer afforded Abby a respite. Dr. Grant was charming, funny, and an attentive date. But she'd been detached.

She laughed on cue, ate her meal with relish, and grinned like an idiot when he suggested they meet for a walk the next morning. Yet, she'd checked her watch every few minutes, marking the time until her two hours were up.

She used the key card Spencer had given her and entered the Imperial Suite. Daisy sat on the couch, and Maddie spun in a rapid circle beside her.

Abby walked over. "What's going on?"

"A sugar rush," Daisy said in a soft drawl. "We took her to have supper at the buffet, and I'm afraid she overdid it. I suspect Spencer doesn't let her eat junk food often."

"Dinner was yummy!" shouted Maddie. "I had two cupcakes."

"One of which you snuck," her grandmother reminded her. "Not to mention a slushie, a hot dog, a cookie—"

As Daisy listed the many sweet concoctions her granddaughter ate, Abby chuckled. "It's nice to see her behaving like a normal child."

"Isn't it though?"

Spencer exited the office and joined them. He gaped at his little girl, who was spinning like a top. "Did I miss something?"

His mother crept from the couch with a guilty expression. "If you'll excuse me, I'm a bit tired." Without meeting his eyes, she addressed her son. "Spencer, if you have time tomorrow, there's something I wish to discuss with you."

Abby escaped to the kitchen to give them privacy. She took a glass from the cupboard and poured herself some lemonade from the pitcher on the middle island. Daisy exited, leaving Spencer alone with his daughter in the living room.

A whimper sounded. Maddie collapsed on the couch cushions and rubbed her belly in a slow circular motion.

"Madeleine"—Spencer knelt in front of her—"are you in pain?"

Abby rushed over. "What's wrong, sweetie?"

"I have a tummyegg." Maddie's lower lip protruded.

"Oh no. Those tummyeggs are awful." Abby crouched down and patted Maddie's back as Spencer hovered. "Is it a big pain or a little one?"

"Kind of"—Maddie's head tilted—"kind of in the middle."

"Does it twinge like a mosquito poking you, or is it dull like an ache?"

The girl concentrated on the ceiling as she assessed her pain. "I don't know."

"I'm calling the doctor." Spencer marched to the cabin phone and seized the receiver.

Abby straightened. "I doubt it's necessary. Maddie ate a hot dog, a slushie, a cookie, and two cupcakes for dinner."

"She what?" Spencer slammed the phone in the cradle.

"After running around in the Kids Kingdom all afternoon and then that dinner, she probably has an upset stomach. Let her rest awhile." Abby wrapped her arms around Maddie, cuddled her close, then urged her to her feet. "We'll go upstairs and get her changed into pj's."

Spencer glared at the door where his mother had exited. "The next time I see Daisy, we're going to have a discussion about Madeleine's dietary choices."

Abby headed for the stairs. "While you're planning your attack, look in my bag. You should find a box of peppermint tea, which helps with nausea."

"Not eating her weight in processed sugary foods would help more."

"Didn't you ever overindulge when you were a kid?"

"Not once."

"That's sad." Abby passed him. "Throwing up all over the floor after one of your friend's birthday parties is a childhood rite of passage."

She climbed the stairs, helped Maddie brush her teeth, and assisted the moaning child into her lacy pink pajamas. Abby had just settled her into bed when Spencer appeared at the door with a mug.

"Will this tea do any good?" he asked.

Abby was impressed he'd made it himself. She took it from him, tested the temperature of the cup with her fingers, and gave Maddie a sip.

Spencer laid a hand on his daughter's forehead. "At least she doesn't have a fever." He pulled away and studied Maddie. "How are you?"

She gulped another sip of tea. "My twinges feel better."

"Don't ever eat that much junk food again."

His stern voice came out too harsh. Abby smacked his arm before she could stop herself. Madeleine sank lower in the bed until the sheet covered her chin.

Spencer wished he could yank his tongue out of his head. Abby looked like she wouldn't mind helping him, and his daughter cowered as if he were an ogre. He'd never get this parenting thing right.

After a silent prayer, he knelt on the floor by the bed. "I mean"—his voice was getting squeaky again—"I don't want you to be sick. It . . ." He cast an alarmed look at Abby.

She must have taken pity on him. Abby smoothed her hand across Madeleine's shoulder. "Your daddy's really sad when you're sick. He wants you to be happy and healthy."

"Right." Spencer adjusted her comforter. "I want you to be happy. Very, very happy."

"And he loves you so much." Abby gave him an encouraging nod.

"Yes. I"—the long unused words didn't come naturally to him—"I l-love you. Very much."

Madeleine's smile appeared above the sheet, but it dissolved into a wince. "Oooooh. It twinges."

Abby held up the mug. "Here. Drink another sip of tea." She patted his daughter's head until she finished the tea and tucked the blankets in tight around her.

"Are you leaving?" Tears welled in Madeleine's eyes.

"Oh, no." Abby grabbed a stack of books from the nightstand. "I'm deciding which story to read first." She looked over at him. "You don't have to stay, Mr. Masterson. I'll take care of her."

An argument surged in his throat, but he suppressed it. Abby was the expert. Perhaps Madeleine would rest easier if he wasn't there. He begrudgingly rose to his feet and left the room. Behind him, Abby began a tale of a baby panda who learned to water-ski.

Spencer remained downstairs while Abby ministered to his daughter. He alternated between pacing the living room and staring blankly at his laptop screen. An occasional whimper drifted from above and threw his brain into confusion.

It was midnight when Abby finally returned to the lower level. She yawned and said, "Maddie's asleep."

She carried the empty mug to the kitchen without looking his way. He followed her to the sink and waited.

Abby washed the cup, left it upside down on a towel to dry, and folded her hands in front of her. "Did you need something?"

"I need answers." He tapped his fingers on the marble countertop. "Why would Daisy feed my daughter two cupcakes?"

"She didn't feed her two. She fed her one. Maddie snuck the other cupcake." Abby laughed. "I was proud when I heard that."

"Proud? For being sneaky?"

"Of course not. In a normal situation, I'd have a serious talk with the child. But Maddie never does anything wrong. She's always so well-behaved, it's a relief to see her acting like a regular five-year-old. To-night, she's learning the hard way that too much sugar is bad."

"I don't want her to learn the hard way. It's my job to protect her."

"That's a normal parental desire, but unrealistic." Abby stood straight, her hands still in the servile position. "Think of how many invaluable lessons you learned because you wouldn't listen when someone tried to warn you."

"Please don't marry that woman."

His mother's voice floated unbidden through Spencer's memory. She'd tried to tell him the relationship with his ex-wife was doomed, but he'd ignored her. What did Daisy know about happy marriages? Perhaps she'd recognized the looming disaster because she knew about *unhappy* ones. She'd been right. The wedding was a giant success, but everything that followed was a tragedy.

Everything except Madeleine.

And now she was sick upstairs because he hadn't safeguarded her.

He threaded his fingers through his hair and left both hands on top of his head. Why was he so wretched at being a father? As he'd prepared for Madeleine to live with him, he'd bought a stack of self-help books, subscribed to online family psychology seminars, and even hired a parenting coach.

Perhaps it was the same as being a lawyer. Some people were naturally gifted. When it came to understanding children, he wasn't. But Abby was. If he could only convince her to share that expertise with Madeleine on a permanent basis.

Abby eyed his distressed posture. Her mouth opened, but she halted. Took a step back. "If there's nothing else, I'm exhausted." Her high heels clicked against the kitchen tile. She walked to the couch and picked up her bag. "I'll report for work at eight in the morning."

Panic hit Spencer's gut. What if Madeleine woke while Abby was gone? What if she was sick again? What if she cried?

"Wait!" He bellowed the word like an ill-tempered judge.

Abby jumped. She spun with wide eyes.

Spencer cleared his throat. "Sorry. I didn't mean to be rude, but . . . but what do I do if Madeleine is sick again? What if she throws up or cries or . . . ?"

Her face softened, and a hint of amusement appeared. "I expect she'll sleep all night. But if she does wake up, I left extra tea bags in the kitchen. Give her a few more sips of peppermint tea, and she'll be fine."

Abby slipped her bag's strap on her arm and headed for the door. A sense of dread that had nothing to do with his daughter ambushed him. He didn't want her to leave. He dreaded the doubts and the bad memories and the loneliness. That last one was the worst. The ever-present loneliness.

"Wait." Spencer whispered it this time.

CHAPTER 47

WAIT. WAIT. WAIT.

The word swirled around Abby's brain, hemming her sensitive conscience like a needle and thread. She sipped her coffee and tried to forget Spencer's forlorn expression. His eyes had reminded her of Maddie's.

Bereft. Searching. Lonely.

She'd almost wavered, but a sudden mental picture had flashed in her mind of candles, a rose-petal heart, and the most unwelcome job offer of her life. This man only wanted her as an employee. If she kept spending time with him, she'd wish for more, and that made her a fool. The memory had given her the necessary boost to pretend she didn't hear him and walk out the door.

Abby thumped her menu against the white-and-chrome table. A fifties tune played over the loudspeaker to match the retro feel of the staff diner. Coworkers buzzed with early-morning chatter. She wasn't sure she could eat when she was supposed to meet Spencer in a matter of minutes.

What if he looked at her that way again? Like he was drowning, and she was the only lifeguard.

Abby dropped the menu. She wouldn't fall for his tricks again. No matter how sincere and personable Spencer appeared, he always had business on his mind.

"Do you know what you want?"

"Huh?" Abby focused on the waitress. "Oh. Just a refill on the coffee, please."

The girl made a note and walked away, leaving Abby with her tortured thoughts. She shifted in her chair, glancing around the room for a distraction. At a nearby table, a woman with kinky black hair gawked at her.

Uh-oh. Maria.

Abby had spotted the woman in the hallway when she'd left Spencer's suite shortly after midnight. Why did she have to run into a member of the gossipy housekeeping crew?

"Abby." Maria left her table and slid into the seat across from her. "Are you okay?"

"What?"

"You seem nervous." Maria latched on to Abby's arm and leaned into her personal space.

"What? No." Abby laughed. "I'm not nervous."

Maria scrunched her face. "You were exiting a passenger's cabin very late."

"I'm fine." She bit out the words. "I was helping with a little girl who couldn't sleep. No big deal."

"Oh." The housekeeper let go. "Nothing strange happened?"

Disappointed?

Abby repressed the snarky side of her brain. "It was overtime for my nanny valet duty."

"I see." Maria paused. "I'm glad you're fine."

She returned to her table, and Abby exhaled.

"Please, Lord," she said under her breath. "Don't let her go spreading rumors."

No longer in the mood for more coffee, she stopped by the counter to cancel her order. After exiting the diner, Abby met her supervisor in the hallway. Twila's face looked even more peevish than usual.

"Abigail." Twila spoke through pinched lips. "I'm relieved to run into you. There's a problem."

"Oh?" Abby got the feeling she wouldn't enjoy what was coming.

"It's been brought to my attention you're spending an inordinate amount of time with Mr. Masterson."

Good old Maria. She must've spread her gossip all night long for it to already have reached Twila's ears.

Abby forced a nonchalant smile. "I'm merely doing my job to the best of my ability, caring for his daughter."

"You were seen leaving his suite after midnight. That's in direct defiance of our policies."

"Maddie . . . his daughter was having trouble sleeping. I stayed to comfort her."

"Nanny valets are not supposed to make themselves available after eleven p.m."

"But she was sick. I wanted to—"

"Abigail." Twila's tone brooked no opposition. "I realize you'll leave Monarch Cruises soon. Up until now, you've been an exceptional employee. Don't sully your reputation in the last week."

Sully her reputation? Since when had her life become a Jane Austen novel?

Abby drew herself as tall as her five-foot-two inches allowed. "I promise you, Twila. I am not behaving in any way that would *sully* my reputation. My attitude toward Mr. Masterson is that of an employee."

"Good." Her boss gave a short, emphatic jerk of her chin. "Make sure it stays that way." She started to walk past. "And no more after-hours childcare in his suite."

Several emotions wrestled for dominance. Anger. Annoyance. Frustration. And the most unwelcome one of all—guilt.

Abby's behavior had been above reproach the previous night, but her assertion she only considered Spencer an employer wasn't exactly true. Regardless of how he'd dismissed her, she couldn't stop her traitorous heart from drawing closer like a child to a forbidden dessert.

If she knew Maria, the scuttlebutt had reached the entire crew. Good gravy! She'd better get a hold on her feelings before she ruined both her peace of mind and professional reputation.

CHAPTER 48

"So much for your bones." Althea stretched on a chaise lounge and tilted her face to the late-afternoon sky.

Emily disregarded the comment because she had no comeback. She'd been certain they'd find answers in the chapel last night, but it was calmer than a post office on Christmas Day. They'd examined every inch of the picturesque room with its short wooden pews and stained-glass windows and found all of nothing.

The four Shippers sat on the sundeck near the front of the ship overlooking the helipad. A fair number of passengers milled around, taking pictures of the calm sea. A sharp gust whipped through the open area.

Daisy shuddered and wrapped a black scarf around her head. "Why are we in this wind tunnel? My hair's getting blown to pieces."

Gerry ignored the long strands fluttering in her own eyes and wrote in her notebook. "We never sit out here. Let's tap into our senses and experience something new." She inhaled. "Smell that salty air."

"The ship's been at a standstill for the better part of an hour." Emily drummed her fingers against her chair's armrest. "If we don't get a move on soon, we'll be late to the next port. I wonder what the holdup is."

A different drumming sound drew her attention to the sky. A helicopter appeared in the distance, heading straight for the MS *Buckingham*. "Gerry, you got your wish. Something new is on its way."

The Shippers stood and hurried to the railing. Passengers crowded around, phones raised, recording everything. The helicopter drew closer and hovered over the bow of the ship. Its blades spun in a blurry circle. A light flickered on the tail. The body lowered, aligning itself to the large green circle with the white *H*. It dropped by degrees, rocking in the gusty wind. When the spindly legs finally thumped to the ground, cheers filled the air.

"Well, I declare," said Althea. "Do you think it's a medical emergency?"

Gerry scribbled in her notebook. "Either that or a company bigwig who's too important to walk the gangplank with the peons."

A short, paunchy man in a black jumpsuit climbed from the cockpit. He withdrew two suitcases, then held open the door. A taller, feminine figure descended. On her willowy frame, the jumpsuit resembled something from a Paris runway collection.

The new arrival made her way to the side as the pilot reentered the helicopter. A crew member in a white uniform rushed to be of assistance with the luggage. The woman tugged her helmet from her head and propped it on her hip. A playful ocean breeze whipped her long golden hair in a silky tumble. She struck a pose as if she knew how many cell phone cameras were pointed straight at her.

Daisy gasped.

Althea squealed. "It's like a scene from a movie."

Gerry's pencil scratched as she made furious notes. "She'd make a good heroine."

Emily observed the unfolding drama with amusement. Fifty years as a navy wife had sucked all the romance out of helicopter landings. She was about to say as much but stopped at Daisy's reaction. The unflappable composure so synonymous with their genteel member had been replaced by horror.

"Are you ill, dear?" Emily gripped her friend's arm.

Daisy pressed two fingers to her temple. "She's far from a heroine, Gerry. I'm sorry to say you are looking at my ex-daughter-in-law."

"Where is everybody?" Spencer stood at the office door and surveyed the empty space. Had Abby taken Madeleine on an excursion? She was probably still avoiding him.

He searched the suite. Would he find them in the Kids Kingdom? Or perhaps the splash pad. As he passed the dining room table, a hand reached between the chairs and grabbed his ankle. He yelped like a surprised cartoon character. A head with curly red hair poked from under the table.

"Shhhh." Abby pressed a finger to her lips. "Maddie will catch us."

"Excuse me?"

She tugged at his ankle, pulling him off balance. He hunched to steady himself and met his incorrigible nanny's face peeking at him.

"We're playing hide-and-seek. She's upstairs checking the bedrooms, but she may have heard you squeal."

"I'd hardly call that a squeal. I was merely—"

"Aaaabby." Madeleine's voice echoed from the upper landing.

"Don't give me away." Abby released him and ducked into her hiding place.

"Daddy"—the pitter-patter of Maddie's feet sounded on the stairs—"have you seen Abby?"

His daughter hopped down the last two steps and ran to his side. Spencer noted her lopsided ponytail, the faint red stain of fruit punch on her collar, and the radiant smile. She looked messy and carefree and adorable. The way a child *should* look. And it was thanks to the woman hiding under the table.

Envy pinched him. He wished he could be the one with rumpled clothing and a happy smile, forgetting the suffocating strictures of protocol.

Madeleine eyed the table and grabbed one of the dining room chairs. It seemed hide-and-seek was coming to an end.

A brisk knock interrupted the discovery.

"Someone's come to visit." Spencer took Maddie with him, drawing her away from Abby's hiding place. Might as well help her prolong the game. He reached their suite door and opened it.

A woman stood on the other side with her back to him. Tall. Stylish. Dressed in black with a large couture bag slung over her shoulder like she was shooting a commercial.

His smile faded.

His ex-wife, Priscilla Rothschild, turned with an all too familiar smirk. "Long time no see." Her husky voice greeted him.

"Mommy!" Maddie launched forward and hugged her mother's long legs.

Priscilla bent a fraction and patted her with one hand. "Hello, my darling. I hope you've missed me." Her gaze traveled to Spencer. "Both of you."

"What are you doing here?" His voice sounded calm despite the maelstrom swirling inside him.

"I've come to visit my daughter. And you too." She tapped his chest, waited for him to move, then sailed inside. "What a charming suite, Spencer. Although I imagine the decor doesn't fit your taste. Am I right?"

Maddie scampered close behind. "My room's upstairs, Mommy. I—"

Priscilla laid a finger over her daughter's lips. "The adults are speaking, darling. Don't interrupt." She turned to Spencer. "Has the porter delivered my things? I'm dying to freshen up."

His unruffled demeanor evaporated. "You're not staying here!"

A gleam entered her eye. "Where better to spend time with my precious family?"

"We're no longer family," he ground out. "You haven't so much as called Madeleine since she moved to New Orleans."

"I made sure a fabulous present was waiting at the house when you took her home." Priscilla crouched to Maddie's height. "Did you like the doll Mommy sent you, darling?"

Maddie nodded, adoration on her face.

"Marvelous. But . . ." Priscilla took stock of the little girl. "I'm not sure what you've been doing to my daughter, Spencer." She smoothed

Maddie's disheveled hair and fingered the stained collar. "Have you been dressing Madeleine yourself? A decent governess wouldn't let her leave the bedroom this way."

Abby! Spencer's eyes shifted to the table. In the shock of seeing his ex-wife, he'd forgotten all about the nanny. She must have heard the entire exchange.

Maddie pointed to the dining area. "My nanny is hiding."

"Hiding?" Priscilla straightened. "Dear me, Spencer. I hope you aren't mistreating the staff."

Maddie skipped to the table and ducked her head to peer underneath. "Abby!" She clapped. "I found you."

The chair legs squawked against the tile as Abby emerged. She crawled out and stood, tucking her polo shirt into the waistband of her khaki shorts. "I apologize, sir. I didn't mean to . . . to intrude on family time."

Family time? Even during their marriage, Priscilla and he had never been a family. He might have objected, but Priscilla spoke first.

"An employee under the table." Her laughter pealed. "How unconventional. But I'm glad you've hired someone to care for our daughter on your vacation." Her eyes narrowed. "Her uniform tells me she must be temporary. Which explains Madeleine's unkempt appearance." She flicked a dismissive hand. "Please help her tidy up, Miss—"

"O'Brien," Abby said. "I'll help Maddie change."

"Maddie?" Priscilla's lip curled. "How quaint. Yes, please help *Madeleine* change into a more presentable outfit."

Maddie grabbed Abby's hand and swung their arms back and forth as they made their way to the stairs. She giggled, not in the least concerned she was leaving her mother behind.

On closer inspection, Spencer realized the black outfit Priscilla wore was a flight suit. It suggested she'd made use of the Rothschild connections to find her way to the ship and discover his room number. "What are you doing here?"

She motioned to her apparel. "Don't you find it the slightest bit touching I commandeered a helicopter to come see you and Madeleine?"

"I would if that were your only motive, but somehow I doubt it."

She took in the surroundings. "I need to touch up my lipstick. Where's the bedroom?"

He drew himself tall. "You are *not* staying here."

"Don't be so fussy. I'm just teasing you." She tapped him on the arm. "I reserved my own suite, and let me tell you, it wasn't easy to do at the last minute. But I want to spend time with Madeleine first. Perhaps we three can have dinner together."

"Not until you answer me. What are you doing here?"

She stuck her right hand in a pocket. "I'm sure you've heard I'm running for office in New York."

"It surprised me. Don't you have to be a resident for five years to qualify?"

"Legally, I never transferred to Louisiana. Since I kept an apartment in New York, the state still considers me a resident. I even filed my taxes there."

The information pricked Spencer. After all this time, it shouldn't matter. But it did.

"That explains why you always insisted on filing separate forms. I suppose you had an exit plan from the beginning."

A flicker of hurt, so small he almost missed it, crossed her face.

"That isn't fair," Priscilla murmured. "I was raised in a politician's home. You knew it was my world. When you and I married, your father promised me your political career was in the near future."

"Perhaps you should've gone to the trouble of checking with me directly." He planted his feet, ready to enter yet another of their many disagreements. "I could have corrected the misunderstanding much sooner. I abhor politics."

Her expression cleared. "You're right, of course."

Spencer paused. Their arguments usually didn't end this amicably, especially not with Priscilla's surrender. She never admitted defeat.

Never.

"Your capitulation surprises me," Spencer said.

"You may be even more surprised at what I'll say next." She took a step closer. "I've missed you, Spence."

He forced himself to stay in place, but instinct said bolt.

God, help me.

He wasn't sure what he was asking help for. Not to let Priscilla run roughshod over him? Not to lose his temper and yell at the woman who'd caused pain to both him and his daughter?

He drew a breath before answering. "I'm sure it will pass once your campaign starts in earnest. Work was always more important to you."

"There's no denying I'm driven." She assessed him in her blunt way. "I'll even admit a happily married candidate is far more attractive to the voter than a single, divorced one. But that's not the main reason I'm going to make this proposal."

Spencer backed up. He couldn't help it. No matter how hard he tried to be unaffected by his ex-wife, there was still something charismatic about her that drew him in, mixed him up, and threw his brain in a tailspin.

He steeled himself for whatever she might say. "What proposal?"

A self-deprecating smile appeared on Priscilla's face. "I wasn't sure whether or not to get down on one knee." A hint of vulnerability lit her eyes. "Marry me, Spence. Again."

CHAPTER 49

THE MARKER TIP SQUEAKED AGAINST the paper. Maddie stuck the tip of her tongue out the corner of her mouth as she concentrated. She wore a sleeveless fuchsia top with a matching frilly skirt. Her feet swung back and forth underneath the dining room chair.

Abby stood beside her, resting an elbow on the table. "Give him a hat." She pointed at the tall, childishly drawn figure. Its long arms hung to the ground, and its fierce scowl stretched wide. Maddie chose a blue marker and drew a sombrero like the ones they'd seen in Cozumel.

"Excellent work." Abby gave her a squeeze. "You might grow up to be an artist."

Maddie beamed. "I'll put a cake beside him." She drew a giant three-layer confection with sprinkles, then shook her finger at the figure. "Don't eat it all. You'll get a tummyegg."

Spencer wandered over and squinted at the masterpiece. "What is it? A monster?"

His daughter's grin faded. "It's you, Daddy."

Abby frowned at her employer. Would it kill him to give a compliment?

"Ah yes." Spencer bared his teeth to mimic the drawing. "Looks just like me."

Maddie giggled. The happy sound twisted Abby's heart like a dishrag. This darling girl had come so far from the quiet, withdrawn child she'd been a few weeks ago. Would Maddie continue to blossom once she left the ship?

Abby's focus flicked to Spencer and returned for a second look. Tension pulsed from his core. The rigid set of his shoulders lacked the usual confidence. His whole air held a note of dread.

She didn't move or reach out. But she couldn't brush off the agitation emanating from him.

"Are you okay?" Abby asked.

Their gazes locked.

Spencer opened his mouth. "I—"

A door thumped overhead. Priscilla departed the bathroom in a white, strapless evening gown, sophisticated in its simplicity. A contemporary, artistic piece of jewelry—thin golden wires with sharp-edged onyx stones at the tips—wrapped around her neck. Her hand glided along the railing as she made her way downstairs.

Spencer walked to the front door. Maddie, blue eyes rounded in awe and adoration, scampered from her chair and met her mother at the bottom step.

Priscilla bent and smoothed the hair that exactly matched her own, followed by a quick air kiss. "You look très chic, Madeleine." She rose. "Are you ready to eat dinner with Mommy and Daddy?"

Maddie nodded.

Priscilla took her by the hand, and they joined Spencer in the entryway.

He directed his attention to Maddie. Rubbing his daughter's bare arm, he asked, "Are you warm enough?"

"Oh, here." Abby grabbed a sweater from the chair and passed it to him. "The air-conditioning does get cold in the dining areas."

"Thank you."

"Yes." Priscilla leaned closer to him. "You do your job well."

In high heels, the statuesque woman matched his height. The stunning ex-wife towered over Abby in more ways than one. An undeniable air of money and social standing pressed down on her. Priscilla's very existence highlighted Abby's inadequacies.

The woman bestowed a gracious, impersonal smile—the kind used when tipping a hotel valet. "Thank you for making our daughter look presentable."

Our daughter.

The words rankled Abby. Shamed her. Suddenly, the memory of the kiss she'd shared with Spencer in Cozumel pierced her in a new and altogether unpleasant way—like she was a home-wrecker worming her way in between a loving couple.

Priscilla slipped her long-fingered hand around the crook of Spencer's arm. It raised and tightened, as if it was used to the intimacy. He glared at her. There was no other word for it. Hardly a loving look, but he didn't remove her hand.

Spencer gave Abby a nod. "I'll watch Madeleine. Take the rest of the night off, Ms. O'Brien."

Ms. O'Brien.

Her own name had never sounded so cold. She managed a facsimile of her best boarding day smile—warm, wide-eyed, welcoming. But totally fake.

"Yes, sir. Enjoy your evening."

Her smile remained in place long after the family left, as if she were trying to convince herself she was completely fine. She put away the markers and paper, then grabbed her blue bag filled with games and toys, and left the suite.

Still with a smile on her face.

The elevator dinged as she approached, and the polished gold doors slid open. Emily and Daisy exited the car. They waved at Abby.

"We were coming to see you," Emily said. "How did your morning walk with Dr. Grant go?"

"It was wonderful." Abby cringed on the inside. She hated misleading these lovable ladies. "He's perfect." Her smiled slipped an inch. "Handsome, considerate." Her voice wobbled. "I couldn't ask for more."

Emily's sharp gaze took her in. "Are you tired, dear?"

"Mmm-hmm." Abby didn't trust herself to finish a full sentence.

Daisy spoke in a gentle drawl. "I imagine you've had a complicated afternoon. We witnessed the arrival of my ex-daughter-in-law today. Are she and Spencer in his suite?"

"No." Abby gulped. "They went to dinner with Maddie."

"I was hoping to speak with my son, but perhaps it would be better to wait. He'll be quite distracted. Priscilla was always a force to be reckoned with."

Abby's laughter sounded weak to her own ears. "Yes, I doubt anyone could deny her."

Emily studied Abby. "What type of person is she?"

Abby hated the question. Why not ask her to make a list of all the qualities she herself lacked?

"She's the sort of woman you'd expect Spencer to marry. Elegant, alluring, well-educated." Abby licked her lips. "Yes, she's kind of snooty. But she appeared genuinely happy to reunite with Spencer and Madeleine. Maybe there's hope for a reconciliation."

The statement slapped her in the heart. A physical pain spread throughout her chest. Abby pressed her lips together. What a fool she was, moping over a man who saw her as an employee. A man who was at that moment probably softening toward his beautiful and glamorous ex-wife. And wasn't it better that way? Maddie would have both parents again. Priscilla might come off a little chilly. But so had Spencer when Abby first met him. Perhaps his family only needed time and understanding to heal the breach.

Who was she to get in their way?

CHAPTER 50

EMILY MARCHED INTO THE LIBRARY. She passed the towering walnut cases filled with books and found Gerry at her favorite table by the window. The cover of the woman's latest novel featured a man in a trench coat embracing a woman wearing a fedora. The heroine's coy expression was mirrored on Gerry's face.

"How can you read at a time like this?" Emily slapped the table.

Gerry jumped. "Why? What's happened?"

"What hasn't happened? Daisy's son is spending a dangerous amount of time with his shrewish ex-wife. Poor Abby's walking around with a drooping mouth that rivals a hound dog's. And a blackmailer is persecuting our poor friend."

Gerry thumbed the pages of her novel absentmindedly. "Sounds like things are the same. We haven't any leads, and worrying won't do a bit of good."

"Doesn't it bother you that someone thinks you're a murderer and is trying to make you pay through the nose?"

Gerry's lips twitched. "That's my favorite part. I've never sounded so interesting in my entire well-behaved life."

Emily flopped into the chair across from Gerry. "I'd love to see the humorous side, but there's a criminal on the loose, and he must be stopped. Or she. We don't even know that much." She tapped her shoe against the carpeted floor.

"Fancy running into you two ladies." An Irish accent intruded. Seamus stood at the end of the bookcase row, dressed in a white shirt, plaid vest, and dark jeans. Though his words included both of them, his twinkly green eyes pointed at Gerry.

She answered with a stiff, "Good evening."

"Hello, Seamus." Emily indicated an empty chair. "Care to join us?"

"Don't mind if I do." His grin grew broader as he sat and scooted his chair closer to Gerry.

She barricaded herself behind her novel. Undeterred, Seamus propped his chin in his hands. With a good-natured flash of his brows at Emily, he focused on the former librarian.

Emily kicked her friend under the table. Gerry winced but made no comment. For a professional matchmaker, she was surprisingly resistant to any romance in her own life.

"You must forgive her," Emily told him. "She forgets her manners when there's a good book around."

"Don't we all," Seamus said. "Me own dear mother, God rest her soul, used to call me to dinner twenty times before I'd answer. I was that lost in the words of Robert Louis Stevenson."

"Oh?" Emily cut her eyes to Gerry. "You're fond of reading?"

"Can't get enough. The only thing better than a good book is a beautiful woman holding a book."

Gerry deigned to twitch one eyebrow. She turned the page with a slow, deliberate motion and lifted the novel to hide her face from view.

Emily sighed. The poor man tried so hard. "You must spend a lot of time in the library."

"A well-stocked library is as close as we get to heaven on earth."

"Funny," Gerry murmured from behind her paperback shield. "I don't recall seeing you in here. Ever."

The second kick Emily delivered swished through the air. Gerry had anticipated her. The woman uttered a triumphant "hmmph" as she turned another page.

"If I'da known you were looking for me, I'da come sooner." He chuckled. "I packed a whole duffel bag of books. I'm halfway through my to-be-read pile."

Gerry lowered her novel. "You have a TBR pile?"

"Sometimes I think it grows while I'm sleeping."

Emily's head tilted. "If you own that many books, what brought you to the library?"

Seamus coughed. "Well, paint me scarlet. You caught me." He peeked at Gerry. "Truth be told, I popped by the security room for a chat with Adrian."

"Adrian?" Emily struggled to recall a cruise employee with that name. "Is he new?"

"Adrian Everson?"

"Oh, you meant Everson. I thought he was born with a *Mr.* in front of his name and a scowl on his face. I'm surprised he let you in off-limits territory."

"Adrian's tough, but he and I get on well. We were chewin' the fat in the security room. They've got that big bank of camera feeds in there, and I beheld a captivating woman sitting alone in the library." His eyes sparkled Gerry's direction. "Would you be wanting any company?"

Gerry flipped her novel shut. "If you're a true reader, Mr. O'Malley, you should already know. A good book is all the company I need."

"Geraldine," Emily hissed.

"Oh." His reddening cheeks bunched. "Uh, yes. So sorry to disturb you." Seamus stood from the table and tugged on his vest. "I'd better crack on. It's my first time trying my new trick for the adults in the big theater tonight. Maybe I won't even need an assistant. I'm embarrassed enough to climb in me own disappearing box."

He scuttled past the bookcases, and a loud thump of the main door told them he'd gone.

Emily glared at her friend. "Honestly, Gerry"—she thrust her wrist through her purse straps and stood—"I love you, but I can't ignore stupid. It makes no sense why you treat the poor man with such contempt. He's delightful."

"I disagree. And I'd appreciate if we didn't discuss it further."

"I'm not asking you to marry Seamus. Just be civil."

"Is surveilling someone on the CCTV considered good manners?" Gerry sniffed. "In some states, it might qualify as stalking. Who knows how many times he's peered at me? A person assumes she's alone with her book, and all the time there was a pair of eyes drilling into her back."

"Don't be ridic—" Emily's head snapped up. She stared at the dark, glass half globe sitting in subtle, unobtrusive silence on the ceiling. Striding across the aisle, she found another one near the door. A third stuck high in the rafters near the balcony. Cameras abounded. Except for private cabins, almost every inch of the MS *Buckingham* was visible if someone sat in the right place.

The security room.

"Hooo-hooo-hooo." A jubilant sound escaped Emily's lips. She swiped her friend's novel.

"Hey"—Gerry grabbed for the book—"I only have sixty pages left."

Emily held the novel out of reach. "They can wait. You have something more important to do."

Gerry settled in her chair with a suspicious glower. "What?"

"You, my dear friend, are going to confess to murder."

CHAPTER 51

"Marry me, Spence. Again."

Spencer stopped at the door of his suite and looked over his shoulder, half expecting Priscilla to be thundering down on him. He hadn't seen her since they parted ways after supper the previous evening.

Again.

The word terrified him in a way no horror movie ever could. He leaned his head against the wall and moaned. "God, please deliver me from this nightmare."

It wasn't that he'd actually consider remarrying Priscilla. The hard-earned lessons from their first time were still fresh in his mind. But there was Madeleine to consider. Once Priscilla the pit bull got something into her head, she hung on till the end.

He didn't want Maddie to suffer because of her mother's ambition and ruthless determination. His breath wavered. He uttered one more prayer before entering the suite.

Quiet reigned.

Not a sign of Priscilla or Madeleine. Or Abby.

Should he try to find them or wait? Spencer paced from the door to the window and back. Two more circuits and the little patience he possessed was gone.

A delicate knock sounded behind him. He opened the door to find Daisy.

"Hello, Spencer. Are you alone this morning?"

"It appears so." He ushered her in, then closed the door. "How can I help you?"

"If you recall, I mentioned there was something I had to tell you."

She stood with the same demeanor he'd seen when cross-examining guilty parties. What subject would make his unflappable mother so nervous? Were the Shippers sneaking around again?

Spencer tried to keep a straight face. "Please, take a seat." He motioned to the couch.

"No, thank you." Her hands gripped the front of her black shirt. "I imagine you won't desire my company once you hear what I have to say."

Who was the parent and who was the child? Would he have to send her to bed without supper? "That's a shame. We were starting to get along so well." His attempt to lighten the mood was met with a sigh.

"I'm serious, Spencer."

"Okay." He crossed his arms and waited.

Daisy kept her eyes averted. Her teeth gnawed at her lower lip. She inhaled. "I have a confession to make."

Yes. It must be the meddling Shippers. He braced himself, wondering what trouble his mother and her friends had caused now.

"Once"—she gulped—"a very long time ago . . . I betrayed my wedding vows."

Her words punched him in the gut. He was well aware the union between his parents hadn't been a happy one, but he'd never expected Daisy to reveal the torrid details.

He put some distance between them. "There are certain topics a man and his mother shouldn't discuss. I may be an adult, but personal details of your relationship with my father should remain between the two of you."

"I realize this is difficult to hear—"

"Then why force me to listen? I don't. Want. To know."

Daisy stood with bowed head, her voice barely audible. "I was unfaithful to your father."

Spencer's hands clenched. If his ears had volume control buttons, he would hit Mute and free himself from this forced confession.

His mother continued in a broken wisp of a voice. "It was only once. On a trip to Europe. Long before you were born. I was angry with Julius for . . . something. But the entire experience made me want to curl up and die. I should have never—no matter what he did, it doesn't excuse my choices." She whispered the last words. "I'm so sorry."

He filled in the unspoken details. His father's infidelities had been frequent and many. Spencer had always assumed his mother was either unaware or didn't care enough to confront him. To find out she'd indulged in adultery herself drilled Spencer's soul.

An upstairs door slammed, followed by a light patter of feet. "Daddy!"

Spencer and Daisy swerved to find Madeleine peeking over the balcony. The adults exchanged dismayed glances. Had she heard their conversation?

Madeleine hurried to the steps and stopped at the top. "Is Abby down there? We're playing hide-and-seek again."

He scanned the living room, but the cheerful nanny was nowhere in sight. Was she upstairs? Or hiding in the office?

"I don't see her," he called to Madeleine. "But I . . . I have something important to do. Can you wait in your bedroom until I'm finished?"

Her golden eyebrows puckered in confusion, but she didn't argue. "Yes, sir." Madeleine returned to her room and shut the door behind her.

Spencer took Daisy by the elbow and gently propelled her to the door. "We should finish this conversation another time."

"Yes, of course, you're right."

They stopped at the entryway. Daisy kept her voice low. "I would have never told you, but . . . but someone is blackmailing me."

Would the unwelcome revelations never end?

"Blackmail?" he scoffed. "On a cruise ship?"

"I don't know how the person found out, but they threatened to reveal everything to my son if I didn't pay them in cash. I decided to disempower the wretch and confess. First, to the Lord. Then to you."

She stood with posture erect, years of Southern etiquette lending her dignity even amid the ugly circumstances. "God's forgiven me. I hope you can too."

Forgive her?

He wanted to laugh. Hadn't he suffered enough as a child? The best part of reaching adulthood was winning the right to distance himself from his unfeeling parents. His marriage to Priscilla had been the last time he'd allowed his father to exert any pressure on him. After the separation, Spencer had found refuge in the heavenly Father's unconditional love, which came without any stipulations. Learning to show that same love was a challenge, but wasn't forgiveness something God asked his children to give freely?

Spencer doubted he was capable. He opened the door. "We'll discuss this later."

Daisy cleared her throat. "I realize this is both painful and unexpected news. I'll give you time to process." She hesitated. "I don't deserve it, but I hope you can forgive me for this and all the other times I failed as a mother."

She exited so quickly that the front door caught on one of the rugs, but she didn't notice. It remained ajar, and Spencer stared at the spot she'd vacated. A tsunami rose inside him. Waves of hurt, disappointment, and fury crashed through his brain. Stomping away from the open door, he looked around for an object close enough to throw.

The sight of hot pink toenails peeking out from under the dining room curtains stopped him cold.

Abby hid behind the curtains, her hands pressed to her cheeks. She'd eavesdropped on the most embarrassing conversation a mother and son could have. It was an accident, but Spencer would *not* be happy.

Lord, I'm at a loss. How do I get out of here without him seeing me? Or should I admit I heard everything?

Spencer's footsteps sounded as he stalked to the window. She froze, lips pressed together, breaths shallow.

Hide or confess? Which one?

She wasn't the secretive sort. Before she could chicken out, she pushed the curtains aside. Her flustered hands tangled in the fabric as she made herself known.

"I-I'm so sorry." She stepped out into the room. "I promise I wasn't listening on purpose. We were playing hide-and-seek." She allowed her gaze to settle on Spencer. He wasn't even looking at her as he stood at the floor-to-ceiling windows. "I should've made my presence known, but I didn't expect you to talk about . . . I mean . . . I . . ."

She ran out of words.

Spencer remained where he was, emotion radiating like a nuclear core.

Abby backed away. "If you'll excuse me, I'll check on Maddie." She bolted upstairs and poked her head in the bedroom door. "Maddie, where are you?"

"I'm going potty," Maddie's voice answered from the side bathroom. "Almost done."

Oh, how Abby wished she'd taken a bathroom break and missed the drama downstairs. If there was a machine to erase the last ten minutes from her memory, she'd buy it.

Abby clasped her fingers together and pressed them to her forehead. *God, please. Help Spencer. Please. His heart must have a hole the size of a dump truck.*

She was tempted to use Maddie as an excuse to stay out of sight, but there were things left to be said.

"Sweetie," she called, "can you stay in your room when you finish?"

She gave a disappointed whimper. "For how long?"

"Just a few minutes. I'll be right back."

"Okay."

Abby made her way to the ground floor, where Spencer stood in the exact same spot. The whir of the air conditioner was the lone noise.

Approaching quietly, she skirted the table and stood to his left. His hands were locked behind him, his face an unreadable mask.

Abby witnessed the aftermath of this familial train wreck with shamed reluctance. "I imagine you don't want to talk about this, but please let me say one thing. Be assured I will never discuss what I overheard with anyone." She licked her lips. "I-I'll go now."

She turned away.

"Wait." His voice was quiet.

That word again. But this time she couldn't ignore it. This time she stayed.

He didn't look at her. "I know we aren't on the best of terms, but"—his jaw tensed—"I could really use a hug right now." He drew himself taller like he was bracing for rejection.

Abby ached to hold him. Still, she hesitated.

It was a bad idea for a boatload of reasons. Big trouble awaited if she fraternized with a passenger. And her peace of mind might disintegrate if she allowed this man any closer. But his tortured expression beckoned her.

Don't do it!

Her head argued even as her feet moved forward. She crossed the small distance between them, slipped her arms beneath his, and wrapped them around his waist. If she was going to throw away common sense, she might as well make it good. Abby pressed her cheek against his chest and held him close. She patted his back like a mother might do when sending her grown son off to college. Not that she felt motherly. Quite the contrary. Her body tingled where it pressed against his.

He hunched closer, his muscles providing a hard, delicious cocoon. A tremor shook him.

Abby squeezed tight and stayed there. Five minutes? Ten? She wasn't sure how much time passed, but she sensed by the straightening of his posture when he regained control. Not wanting to add to his embarrassment, she released him and leaned away, but he held on. His arms remained around her as he looked down.

Bewilderment entered his eyes. Unsurprising, considering what he'd been forced to listen to from his own mother. It was a wonder he'd managed to stay on his feet.

Abby drew a breath. "Maddie's hanging out upstairs. I'll go play with her so you can be alone for a while."

Again, she tried to step away. Again, he held her in place.

"Thank you." Spencer studied her.

"For what?"

A wistful smile appeared. "For being you."

The click of the door closing sounded behind them.

Priscilla's unwelcome voice intruded. "Isn't this cozy?"

Abby and Spencer jumped apart like a pair of naughty teenagers who'd been caught by the teacher.

"Shame on you, Spence." Priscilla approached with a blithe attitude. "I never took you for someone who'd fool around with the help."

"The *help*?" Abby cringed at the antiquated put-down. "Did I stumble into a 1950s soap opera? Surely people don't think that way anymore."

"Unfortunately," Spencer said, "it's all too common in the circles where I grew up. The old-money crowd has centuries of snobbery ingrained."

The towering Priscilla perused Abby's short figure as she addressed her ex-husband. "I suppose I can't begrudge you a little holiday amusement."

"'Amusement'?" Abby reminded herself this unbearably rude woman was a customer. "I assure you, I am not included on the MS *Buckingham*'s activities list."

The statuesque blond sat on a nearby chair and crossed her legs at the ankles. Her serene disdain disregarded Abby as if she hadn't spoken. Priscilla addressed Spencer. "Be sure not to take any pictures that might be embarrassing at a later date. My opposition has a history of digging up a candidate's dirty laundry. I've been on my best behavior"— she deigned a sideways glance at Abby—"but I'm not so sure about you, Spence."

Abby counted to four in her head. That was the number of workdays left on her contract. She wanted to finish her time on the MS *Buckingham* without any demerits on her record.

A gentle pressure on her fingers distracted her. Spencer's large hand enveloped her own. He leaned close and whispered in her ear.

"Go with me on this. Please."

With a squeeze, he released her and pulled out his phone. "Here's a picture you might be interested in." He extended the screen to Priscilla.

Her lazy lean forward came to an abrupt halt. She jolted to her feet and swiped the phone. Her cold blue appraisal pointed his way. "You must be joking."

For the life of her, Abby couldn't dream of a single thing that would make the ice queen lose her composure. The only pictures she'd ever taken with Spencer and Maddie were on the pier in Cozumel. Was Priscilla horrified at the childish pose she'd struck with her tongue sticking out?

Priscilla hurled the phone at Spencer. He caught it and tilted his head with a quirk of his eyebrow. Abby peeked at the phone. A photo showed a familiar beach setting with the two of them standing close. In the background, the candlelit heart glowed in the sand.

The reason for Priscilla's distress became clear. Spencer's ex-wife had made the same wrong assumption as Abby. Priscilla thought the romantic setup preceded an engagement.

But where did he get the picture? Abby remembered a photographer with the actual engaged couple. Had he snapped some shots when they weren't looking?

"As you can see," Spencer held his phone up, the picture pointed at Priscilla. "I made a special proposal to Abby a few days ago. She has yet to accept, but I'm hopeful."

He slipped an arm around Abby's shoulders and faced her way. His imploring gaze begged her not to contradict his ridiculous story. A dark lock of hair dipped on his forehead. It wasn't shellacked anymore like it had been on his first day aboard. He'd loosened up considerably. But this sham was outrageous.

Priscilla crossed her arms. "Are you punishing me for divorcing you? If so, don't carry it too far. What will your family say? Your friends? Your law partners?"

"I imagine they'll congratulate me on finding such an exceptional woman. Abby's smart, beautiful, makes even the dreariest of circumstances enjoyable, and is the kindest, most generous person I ever met."

"Is this true?" Priscilla turned her attention to Abby. "You're shameless enough to seduce a passenger?"

Was it wrong Abby wanted to bring this conceited woman down a peg? Probably. But still . . .

Abby hugged the solid, male body beside her. "What can I say? He's hard to resist."

"And for the record"—Spencer's spine stiffened—"I'd appreciate it if you didn't use words like *seduce*. Ms. O'Brien has always conducted herself with the utmost propriety. I'm the one who pursued her, and saying otherwise is false. A defamation lawsuit wouldn't look good for your political career."

"Consider Madeleine." His ex-wife paced. "What kind of mother would this woman make?"

"The very best." He let go of Abby. "Maddie is the one who'll benefit the most from our relationship."

The truth of his words smacked Abby in the solar plexus. Maddie was his primary concern. He'd suffer anything for his daughter. But his own affections had nothing to do with this charade. He wanted to rid himself of his ex-wife's attentions and didn't mind using a cruise ship employee to accomplish that objective.

Priscilla pressed her perfectly polished fingertips to the spot between her eyebrows and drew a breath, then another. Lowering her hand, she pursed her lips, returned to the chair, and rested her arms on the sides. Her poise recalled royalty on a throne. Even her smile was beneficent. "As I recall"—her regulated tone held none of her earlier anxiety—"our prenuptial agreement contained a clause allowing for one infidelity after marriage."

Spencer's voice matched her own. "As I recall, you were the one who insisted on it."

"Yes. Knowing the ways of men, I wanted to provide you some freedom, but I realize now I insulted you." She dipped her head. "You were the most faithful of husbands—another reason why I decided to resume our marriage. The public has grown more accustomed to marital infidelities, but scandal can still hurt a politician's career."

Abby marveled at the casual way she spoke of sordid topics. Were all rich people this cagey? Did every decision revolve around money and position?

Priscilla stood. "I've devised a solution that will benefit everyone. My campaign manager wants me in New York by the end of the week. Why don't I take Madeleine for a little visit with me? It will give you a chance to fully"—she swept Abby with a condescending look—"indulge. You always did work too hard. Relax for a few weeks. It will take that long to finish the campaign's publicity plans. I imagine the media will eat up the story of a broken family reuniting in the name of love." She raised one finger. "Why don't you visit Europe? Just make sure there's no evidence of your little holiday with the help."

That phrase again! Abby was in great danger of ruining her perfect customer service record. Her Irish ancestors must be rolling in their graves at the way this overprivileged brat was treating her.

Priscilla's unconcerned perusal traveled between the two of them. "Naturally, I'll insist you terminate the relationship before you join me in New York."

Spencer's voice remained polite. "There's one flaw with your suggestion."

Abby bristled. Only one?

An hour wouldn't be long enough to list her problems with the conversation she'd been forced to endure. She needed to leave before she said something not approved by the Monarch Cruises employee handbook. Disappointment engulfed her. She'd thought better of Spencer. The last few days had shown him as a caring father and genuine person. Yet he'd listened to Priscilla's nonsense about his and Abby's indulging in a fling without uttering a single objection. He was a lawyer, after all. Wasn't he supposed to be an expert at rebuttal? Could it be he honestly didn't see anything wrong with what she was saying?

Spencer's arm returned to Abby's shoulders. Not in the annoying way taller people had of leaning on shorter people like a prop. His hand cradled her. Supported her. Shored her up against the onslaught of his ex-wife.

He drew her to his side. "Apart from the sheer lunacy of your distasteful plan, there's a more salient problem. I'm in love with Ms. O'Brien."

CHAPTER 52

"About time you joined us, Daisy." Emily waved her key card in front of her cabin door until it beeped. She entered, followed by her three friends. "You missed all the fun."

Gerry collapsed in the chair by the desk. She kicked off her shoes and propped her feet on the edge of the full-size bed. Althea and Daisy sat side by side on the mattress.

Althea snorted. "I don't call listening to the same phony confession over and over 'fun.'"

"I hope it was worth it," Gerry moaned. "I'm sick of confessing."

"Ditto." Althea massaged her own neck. "Wasn't four times overkill?"

Emily stood by the bed and shook her head. "Who knows when the blackmailer's tuned in? I didn't want to run the risk of him missing Gerry's big scene."

Daisy smoothed the hair at her temples. "But won't he find it suspicious that she confessed to each of you twice? And in different locations?"

"I was slick," said a smug Gerry. "On my final confession to Emily, I told her my conscience tortured me. That I needed to unburden every single detail or I wouldn't be able to sleep at night."

Emily chuckled. "The melodrama abounded on the last go-round. Give them a recap, Gerry."

"*Whyyyyy*?" Gerry wailed, spreading her fingers wide and pointing them at the ceiling. "Why, God? Why did I ever have to meet that man? Oh, the bitter pain." She pounded her fist against her rib cage. "It's buried so deep, I fear it will never come dislodged."

"'Dislodged'?" Daisy asked.

Gerry straightened. "I've been rereading *Hamlet*. I'm afraid some old-timey English crept into my performance."

"Speaking of *Hamlet*," Althea said, "wasn't your performance a touch on the hammy side?"

"Not at all." Gerry's chin tipped. "I even cried a little in the chapel. Right, Emily?"

"The tears were a nice touch," Emily agreed. "We had to lure whoever is spying on the guests to the lost and found. It's remote and rarely visited. Makes perfect sense you'd hide a second corpse down there."

Daisy pressed a hand to her throat. "What a morbid thought."

Gerry brushed a stray hair from her sleeve. "But how do we catch the blackmailer without him seeing us? There's nothing but empty hallway on either side of the lost and found, and I refuse to get trapped in a closet with a criminal."

"Have no fear." Emily sniffed. "We won't be anywhere near the place." She grinned at Daisy. "I put the fancy new phone your son bought to good use." She withdrew her own cell from her purse and swiped her finger across the screen. "I downloaded one of those security apps people use to monitor their homes while they're gone and set it up so we can watch the live feed. If someone comes to find Gerry's latest so-called victim, then we've got 'em on tape."

Althea gave her a thumbs-up. "But couldn't the blackmailer argue they were there for something they lost?"

"It might not be enough evidence to convict the villain, but at least it will tell us who we're dealing with. We already suspect it's someone on the security team. They monitor everyone on the ship from the comfort of a swivel chair. Once we've identified the creep, we can tail them until we catch them in the act. But now comes the annoying part."

Emily kept her attention fixed on the phone. "The waiting. One of us must keep an eye on the camera at all times. Chances are, he won't move until later. I'll cover tonight's shift."

"You shouldn't tire yourself out," Daisy said. "We'll take turns."

"Thanks. This might be a long haul. I hope the culprit will move before your cell battery dies. If he doesn't, we'll replace your phone with one of ours. It depends on how long—" A movement on the screen caught Emily's eye. "Oh my word!" She hit Record on the app.

"What is it?" Althea scooted forward.

"Girls, you're not going to believe this. The blackmailer's already taken the bait."

"What!" Gerry bolted from her chair to Emily's side. "From his build, it looks like a man. As we expected."

The other Shippers crowded behind them. A person in an oversize black hoodie was clearly visible on the screen. A disposable mask covered the lower half of his face.

"Thank heavens it isn't Magda," Daisy said. "She's my favorite spa technician."

They watched every move the man made. The lights in the storage room were off, but the glow from the hallway partially illuminated the space. He carried a flashlight and swept the beam around, checking among the few rows of supplies.

All four Shippers held their breath.

The hooded figure riffled through the piles of junk. He swung his flashlight at the upper shelves, pausing for an extra second on a mounted moose head.

"Come on, buddy. Forget the stage props." Gerry rolled her eyes. "Looks like the blackmailer is none too bright."

"Tell me about it." Althea nodded. "How would a woman in her seventies hide a body on the top shelf?"

Emily heaved a sigh. "He may never find the mannequin on his own." She reached to the bedside table and picked up her walkie-talkie. Clicking the button, she held the receiver to her mouth and whimpered, "Help me."

"What are you doing?" Althea hissed.

Emily shushed her and whimpered again. "Help me . . . please."

The figure on the camera feed jerked, his head turning right and left.

Daisy crossed her arms. "Do not tell me you left a walkie-talkie in the lost and found."

Emily shrugged. "It pays to have a backup plan. I figured it might come in handy. Obviously, I was right." She spoke louder into her handset. "Help!"

Their culprit crept to the long, body-sized bag they'd borrowed from the ship's morgue and planted in a dark corner. He tucked his flashlight between his teeth, knelt on the ground, and slowly unzipped the bag. Bending close, he looked inside.

"Aaaargh!" His anxious cry reverberated through the cell phone speaker. He scrambled back. Arms and legs flailed. His flashlight clattered to the floor. The hood of his sweatshirt drooped off his head. He yanked the covering up and raced from the room.

The Shippers stared at the phone. A single beam of light showed on the dark screen where the blackmailer's flashlight still shone.

Emily waggled her eyebrows at Althea. "Aren't you happy you bought that horrible mask at the waterfall?"

"Lawd have mercy." Althea plopped on the bed. "I supposed criminals had more gumption."

"Bless his heart," Daisy murmured. "I told you that mask was grotesque."

"Bless nothing." Gerry huffed. "He's a thief. And an incompetent one at that. He deserves whatever he gets."

Emily set the phone on the table. "Ladies, the culprit cooperated quicker than we imagined."

"What do we do now?" Althea asked.

"Now, we set the final trap. But we're going to need help."

"Help?" said Gerry.

"From a friend of yours." Emily prayed the long-legged Shipper would cooperate. "Gerry, how do you feel about asking Seamus for a favor?"

CHAPTER 53

Spencer sat in the office chair facing the window, his elbows propped on the armrest, his forehead resting on his steepled fingers. He raised his gaze to the outline of the distant horizon against the ocean waves. Was it too far to swim to shore? Or perhaps he could steal a page from Priscilla's book and call for a helicopter?

Anything but face Abby after his spur-of-the-moment declaration.

"I'm in love with Ms. O'Brien."

Was he mad? Abby obviously thought so. The whites of her eyes had shown all the way around her irises. And his ex-wife wore a similar visage. It was the first time in their entire relationship he'd seen her speechless.

Rather than embarrass himself further, he'd done what any good lawyer would do—file a motion for a continuance. After sending Abby to check on his daughter, he'd alerted Priscilla in no uncertain terms she should leave and then locked himself in the downstairs office for the rest of the day to gather his wits.

"I'm in love with Ms. O'Brien."

It fit the cover story and picture he'd shown Priscilla. Abby had even played along. A fake relationship was the perfect ploy to discourage his barracuda of an ex-wife. So why did the statement play on a loop in his brain?

"I'm in love with Ms. O'Brien."

Because the instant the words left his mouth, he'd recognized them for what they were.

The truth.

He—logical, calculating Spencer Randolph Masterson—had fallen for a woman he barely knew. He wasn't fool enough to believe in love at first sight. But how much better was love at second sight? Or third?

They'd met two and a half weeks ago.

He spun to the desk and rested his head in his palm. A moan escaped from deep in his soul. Was Abby already sneaking out the stateroom door? He doubted she'd ever speak to him again after his crazy confession.

A knock sounded.

"Mr. Masterson?" Abby's voice carried through the door.

Still with the "Mr. Masterson." He couldn't blame her for the verbal distancing. It was a miracle she was speaking to him.

Spencer stood and opened the door.

Abby waited on the other side. "Maddie is upstairs watching a cartoon." She twisted her fingers together. "Can we talk?"

He spread his feet apart. "Go ahead. Let me have it."

"What do you mean?"

"Rail at me for my unexpected declaration. I don't blame you if you're angry."

"I'm not angry." Her calm response confirmed her words. Abby's green eyes studied him in earnest, with no hint of fury. But there was something else.

Hurt.

"Abby." He reached for her, but she recoiled. Spencer withdrew. "I didn't mean to upset you. The words surprised me too. They just"—he ruffled the back of his hair—"popped out."

She walked away from the office and wrapped her arms around herself, her hands grasping her elbows. "I get it. Your ex-wife is"—she gave a hollow laugh—"determined. You wanted to discourage her. But I can't help feeling . . ." She pivoted. "I feel used."

Spencer stepped forward. "That wasn't my intention. I honestly—"

"I know you didn't intend to hurt me. You were probably thinking of Maddie. Trying to protect her. But saying you loved me to get rid of your ex-wife—"

"I didn't say it to get rid of Priscilla."

"Then why did you?"

Oh, God, I've made a hash of it this time. Haven't I? Spencer's soul telegraphed a three-second prayer to heaven.

If he admitted he loved her, she might laugh. But if he didn't tell her, the wounded expression would stay in her eyes. He couldn't stand that.

Spencer focused on the view behind her. The ocean water rocked and crashed in turbulent waves, much like his spirit. He drew a fortifying breath.

"I said I loved you"—one more breath—"because it's the truth."

No reaction.

He abandoned the stormy view and focused on her. Abby stood with mouth open, eyes even wider than the first time he'd declared he was in love with her. She must perceive him as an unhinged lunatic.

"You"—her voice hardened—"you love me? Is this another ploy to get me to work for you?"

"This has nothing to do with Madeleine. I'm not speaking as a father. I'm a red-blooded man standing in front of a beautiful woman." Spencer stalked to the other side of the apartment. "I realize this is out of the blue. And illogical. And far too soon in our relationship. But I'd swear to it in court on a stack of Bibles. In my whole rigid, suffocating existence, I've never met a woman more caring and compassionate and captivating—" He rubbed his face. "Why am I only using words that begin with the letter *C*? I sound like a greeting card."

The woman missed her calling as a poker player. Her demeanor remained unchanged. She didn't say a word.

Spencer squared his shoulders. If he was surrendering his pride, he might as well do a thorough job of it.

"Before I make a decision, I always count the cost, weigh my options, and consider all alternatives. Yet, when I'm with you, I find myself behaving irrationally. Responding with my heart instead of my brain.

It's a completely foreign experience, and I admit I'm floundering." His chin rose a notch. "Falling in love and whirlwind romance aren't in my purview, but I'm a lawyer and I can't deny the evidence. When I'm with you . . . I'm not sure how to explain it. An emotion floods me. I don't recognize it because it's so unfamiliar. But I think it's joy. It terrifies me that I could lose it . . . lose you." He slumped. "Forgive me if I expressed it badly, but please don't doubt my sincerity. I love you."

Abby's head tilted ever so slightly to the right. She took a long, slow look from the tips of his shoes to the top of his head, as if she were testing every part of him. She glanced around the room. After spinning on her heel, she walked into the kitchen area and returned a moment later with the colorfully painted stool they'd bought in Cozumel.

With purposeful steps, she crossed the space separating them and didn't stop until she was right under his nose. Then she placed the stool on the ground and climbed on top.

"Maddie won't mind if I borrow her stool for a few minutes." She clasped her slender arms around Spencer's neck, stared at his Adam's apple, and sighed in frustration. "Even with the boost, you're still a giant. Can you give a girl some help?" Cupping her hand behind his head, she tugged his face down until his mouth was an inch from hers.

Green eyes ensnared him. He leaned closer until a mere centimeter separated them.

Abby's warm breath tickled his lips as she spoke. "Mr. Masterson, I have good news. You may not believe in falling in love, but I do." As her lips stretched in a smile, they brushed his for the briefest instant. "I accept your apology and your confession too. That leaves one thing more to say." She whispered in his ear. "It's about stinkin' time."

Spencer turned his head and captured her mouth in a passionate kiss, followed by another. His arms crushed her tight. Her petite frame fit against his and locked into place like a missing puzzle piece. The warmth of her body thawed the frozen corners of his soul, and a sense of home he'd never experienced overwhelmed him.

Love and elation and a million other emotions rushed in, drowning him in their fervor. Pesky reality intruded with questions of locations and careers and taking the proper time to get to know one another, but he pushed them away.

His heart, his mind, and his world were filled with Abby. Everything else could wait.

CHAPTER 54

SPENCER STOOD WITH PRISCILLA ON the pier. She wore an outfit more fit for a political rally than a flight—immaculate white suit with a red-and-blue designer scarf, five-inch heels, and minimal but expensive jewelry.

His ex-wife eyed him, her lips pursed. "You're sure you won't regret this impetuous decision?"

He battled the temptation to start another fight. "I can't predict the future. But I'd like to spend the rest of it with Abby. She's a beautiful, loving, genuine person. It will do Madeleine good to be around her."

Priscilla smoothed her chignon. "On that point we agree."

"Excuse me?" Spencer cocked his head.

Her gaze met his. "If this affair with the nanny falls through, I'll consider taking you back. But if your crazy gamble pays off, I can at least take comfort in the knowledge a warm, caring woman is raising our daughter." Priscilla sagged. "Perhaps she can give Madeleine the happy childhood neither you nor I lived." Clearing her throat, she drew a pair of diamond-studded sunglasses from her bag, slipped them on, and held out a hand. "No hard feelings."

He studied the long fingers with their perfectly shaped red nails, and a twinge of regret hit. They hadn't been happy together, but they'd done one thing right—Madeleine. For the gift of his daughter, he'd always be grateful to Priscilla.

He shook her hand. "Take care of yourself."

His ex-wife walked to the waiting limo. The chauffeur opened the door, and she slid inside. Spencer headed for the ship with anticipation. Whatever awaited him in the future, he was sure it would be better than his past. Because of Abby.

He checked his watch and quickened his pace. They were supposed to meet in his suite after she dropped Madeleine off at the Kids Kingdom. They'd agreed it might be better for his daughter not to be present when they revealed their new relationship status to the Shippers. She was too young to grasp the intricacies of dating.

Spencer strode up the gangplank and through the tranquil lobby. Most of the passengers must be enjoying their day in port. An elevator ride took him to the suite's floor, and his heart raced as fast as his feet. The few kisses Abby and he had shared before she left last night had only awakened a craving. If he hurried, they might be able to sneak a few more before the Shippers arrived.

He let himself into the suite and stalled as the door shut behind him. Abby stood in the same flirty green dress she'd worn the night she'd dined with the chef. At the time, Spencer had hated the outfit, but now that she was wearing it for him, his pulse tripped.

She extended a foot and waggled her gold, high-heeled sandal. "I chose my tallest shoes so we won't be totally mismatched."

Spencer bounded across the room. She giggled as he caught her in his arms. He pressed her close and bent his head near her ear. "Who says we're mismatched? You fit perfectly."

He kissed her lobe, and she shivered.

"Don't start." She squirmed from his arms. "The Shippers will be here any minute."

"All the more reason to not waste a second." Again, he reached for her.

Abby dodged right. Spencer stalked her around the living room couch. Her heel caught on the edge of the area rug, and she tottered to the side. He grabbed for her and wrapped her in a secure embrace.

"That's more like it," Spencer said.

Her emerald eyes sparkled. He bent his head, his lips a hair's breadth from her own . . . and a knock sounded.

Spencer moaned and buried his face in her neck. "Why do they have to be so punctual?"

She pushed him aside and hurried to the door.

The four matchmakers entered the room and stood in a row, his mother at the end. Identical expressions covered each face. Suspicion.

Daisy spoke first. "You asked to see us, Spencer."

"Yes, ma'am." In his current euphoric state, he could even imagine healing the breach with his mother. "Please stop throwing men at Abby."

His beloved scurried to him with a scowl. "Try to put that nicer."

"What? I said please."

Emily crossed her arms in front of her floral shirt. "It's none of your business who Abby chooses to date."

"Actually"—Abby twisted her gold sandal in the rug—"it is. Spencer and I admitted our feelings for each other last night. I mean, we decided—"

"We've decided to enter into a romantic relationship," Spencer said.

The Shippers wore identical expressions again—this time of confusion.

Emily uncrossed her arms. "I'm not sure what to say."

"Oh, Abby, are you sure?" Daisy tugged her watch necklace. "My son can be quite ill-tempered."

"Thanks a lot, Mom," he said.

"You know it's true. I'm thrilled for you and Madeleine, but I wouldn't want Abby to draw the short stick."

Hidden doubts dimmed his rosy-hued outlook. Who knew him better than his mother? Was she right? He didn't deserve someone as pure as Abby. She was summer sunshine to his winter storm. What if he froze her solid?

Abby slipped an arm around his waist. Leaning her head against him, she laughed. "Don't worry, ladies. The only short thing we'll deal with is my height. Otherwise, we'll do fine."

"Glory be." Althea launched forward and drew them both into a hug. "I'm relieved the match worked out. For y'all but also for Maddie."

"Yes"—Spencer smiled down at the older woman's beaming face—"that's one of the best parts."

"For me too," said Abby.

She released him and hugged the other Shippers. They softened in an instant from the sheer force of her exhilaration. Gerry and Emily chided Abby for not informing them right away, while Daisy dabbed her ring finger at the corner of her eye.

A pat on his back drew Spencer's attention. Althea glowed with tenderness. "You're so much like your momma."

He drew away. "I beg to differ. I'm the inverse of Daisy Randolph Masterson."

"See there. You even talk like her. Some people might be put off by the hoity-toity manners, but not me." She elbowed him in the side. "You're a beignet. Once a person gets past the crusty cover, there's nothing but sweet, squishy goodness on the inside."

His gaze returned to Abby. He hoped for her sake Althea was right. There'd been a time not long ago when darkness filled him in his neverending search for perfection and status. But God had shone a light on his soul. Highlighted the things that truly mattered.

Lord, help me not to let her down. Help me not to hurt her again.

Emily clapped with glee as another happy match was made. Granted, the Shippers hadn't been keen on Spencer in recent days, but she was willing to let bygones be bygones. After all, men struggled when it came to love. That's why so many needed the ladies' matchmaking expertise.

She tapped her cane against the suite's floor in a loud cadence. "Come on, girls. Let's leave these lovebirds to themselves. I'm sure they'd appreciate time alone."

"Good idea." Gerry shoved the sleeves of her cardigan to her elbows. "I'd like to check my room for any new blackmail notes."

"Blackmail!" Abby grabbed her sleeve. "What do you mean?"

"Yes," Spencer said. "This is the second instance I'm hearing of blackmail on the MS *Buckingham*." He approached his mother. "Yesterday, you told me someone was blackmailing you. What's going on?"

"Nothing we can't handle." Daisy waved him away.

"Don't worry, baby," Althea said. "We've got a plan in place."

"Uh-oh." Abby said. "I've seen the results of your plans in the past."

Emily brushed a gray curl behind her ear. "Successful, weren't they?"

"That wasn't the word that came to mind." Abby grasped Spencer's arm. "You have no idea what the Shippers are capable of. Truth be told, I pity the blackmailer."

Spencer squinted. "Dare I ask what you ladies are up to?"

"We made use of one of our old favorites." Emily grinned. "The lost-and-found storage."

Abby groaned. "Don't tell me you locked someone in there again."

Spencer drew back. "You locked someone in a storage room?"

"It was business." Emily propped her cane against the wall and rubbed her hands together. "We wanted a recalcitrant couple we were matching to stop avoiding each other and thought it'd be a good idea if they enjoyed some togetherness."

"It was my former roomie." Abby chuckled. "I was the one who let them out. Boy, was she livid."

Emily nodded. "But it worked, didn't it? You were on the front row at Jon and Lacey's wedding."

"This is madness." Spencer pointed at his mother. "I refuse to allow you to take part in any dangerous and possibly illegal activities. If you and your friends found information regarding the blackmailer, deliver it to the security team and let the professionals take care of it."

Althea chortled. "You don't know us very well, baby."

Gerry folded her arms. "We can't tell security because—"

Emily laid a hand on her shoulder. "No, he's right, Gerry."

"Huh?"

Emily faced Spencer. "Mr. Masterson, you have my word. We will definitely alert security."

Abby mimicked Spencer's position and pointed a finger at Emily. "And you promise not to lock anyone else in the storage closet?"

"Cross my heart and hope to die."

Abby studied her warily. "I didn't expect you to agree so easily."

"What can I say?" Emily shrugged. "I see the wisdom of Spencer's suggestion. Be assured we'll let security know without fail."

"I'm glad you're listening to reason." Spencer took hold of Abby's elbow. "It's time to pick up Madeleine." He eyed every member of the Shippers before settling on Emily. "Remember. You promised to let security handle it."

They exited the suite as a group, and Spencer and Abby walked to the elevators, leaving the Shippers in the hallway.

Gerry raised an eyebrow. "I don't recall you promising to let security handle it."

"How right you are." Emily smirked. "I said I'd let security *know*. And I made no mention of when I'd do so."

Althea clicked her tongue. "You'd think a lawyer would pay more attention to the details."

Daisy bit her lip. "Spencer will be terribly irritated when he finds out."

"That's his problem." Emily thumped her cane. "Come on, ladies. We've got a blackmailer to catch."

CHAPTER 55

THE MAIN THEATER SAT EMPTY except for the bright red disappearing box at center stage. Darkness enveloped the space, with a single spotlight illuminating the trapdoors on the top and front side of the magic trick. The front panel was open, revealing the long black-and-white stripes inside.

Emily, Gerry, and Seamus descended the middle aisle of the shadowy room. At two in the morning, most passengers were asleep in their beds.

Emily set the tip of her cane on each step as she carefully climbed to the stage. "Will it work, Seamus?"

"You can be sure of it." The sprightly redhead vaulted up beside her and clapped his hands. "People give magicians far too little respect. We can put that tendency to our favor in this instance."

"You're a dear to play along."

"Think nothing of it. I figure I might like having the Shippers owe me a favor." He wiggled his eyebrows at Gerry. "Especially the tall, beautiful one."

Gerry turned up her nose, but Emily noted the quick swipe of the woman's fingers to fix a stray hair. They should do something about poor Seamus. He was funny, clever, and an avid reader. All the qualities their dear bookworm, Gerry, should desire in a man. If they could just get their friend past her ridiculous height prejudice. Everyone deserved a chance at love, no matter their age or stature.

"We brought him!" Althea shouted from the entrance.

She and Daisy propelled Barney over the threshold, their arms linked around his. His shirt was untucked on one side, and bewilderment covered his round face.

"What's going on?" he squeaked. "I was about to get some shut-eye."

Emily squinted through the bright light. "Barney, thank heavens you're here. We need your help."

His chubby cheeks bunched in a grin. "Anything."

"Wonderful. I knew I could count on you."

He and the other two Shippers passed rows of navy-blue couches as they made their way to the front and joined the others onstage. Daisy and Althea released Barney and stood with Gerry on the right side of the red box. Everyone formed a half circle around the magic prop.

Gerry checked her wristwatch. "It's almost time. I'll stand guard outside and inform you when he's coming."

"When who's coming?" Barney asked.

Seamus scurried to Gerry's side. "I'll come with you, m'darlin'. Wouldn't want you to encounter the brute alone."

"What brute?" Barney's body constricted.

Emily laid a hand on his forearm. "Were you aware"—she lowered her voice—"there's a blackmailer on board the MS *Buckingham*?"

His cheerful countenance drooped, and his brow furrowed. "A . . . a blackmailer?"

She leaned forward. "Some scoundrel has been extorting passengers by threatening to reveal their shameful indiscretions."

He laughed. "I'm sorry, Mrs. Windsor, but that . . . that sounds unbelievable."

"Doesn't mean it's not true. We've done our research. Someone has been leaving note cards for people. Demanding that they pay five thousand dollars or else he'll reveal their"—she grimaced—"indiscretions."

Daisy rubbed her eyes with trembling fingers. "He threatened to make my marital infidelity public."

"That's harsh." Barney picked at the thinning hair on the side of his head. "Who do you think is behind it?"

Emily sniffed. "I don't have to think. I'm certain. It's—"

"This plan worries me." Daisy fanned herself. "Suppose he's dangerous."

Althea smacked her lips. "The man's a blackmailer. Of course he's dangerous."

"Who?" Barney asked again.

She grabbed his arm. "Baby, have you got a gun?"

He jerked and tried to shake her off. "A gun?"

"Yes." She kept a firm hold. "For protection."

Daisy fluttered a handkerchief. "Mercy me. I might never see New Orleans again."

Emily placed her body between Barney and the exit. "Be strong. We can catch this criminal."

His laugh sounded slightly hysterical. "I still don't have a clue who you're talking about."

"Why, Mr. Everson."

"Sarge?" Barney turned the color of leftover oatmeal. "You think he, he . . . I mean, how could Sarge be a blackmailer?"

Emily gripped the nervous man's shoulder. "It's shocking, but someone's been spying on the passengers with security cameras, and the evidence confirms it."

Barney rubbed at the freckled bald spot on the back of his head. "How is that possible? There's always two guards on duty in the control room."

"Always?" Althea squeezed herself between them. "You mean no one ever slips outside to make a phone call, goes down the hall for a soft drink, visits the bathroom to tinkle?" With each suggestion she moved closer until she was right under his nose. "Admit it, Barney. Hasn't there been a time when someone left you alone at the board?"

"I guess."

"So Mr. Everson had the same opportunity. All it requires is a few seconds to hear a deep, dark secret. He pulls out his phone, records the conversation, and makes himself a sweet bonus."

Emily flanked his other side. "It takes a despicable person to do something so low. Dig up people's painful secrets and threaten to expose them."

"Th-this is crazy." Barney's gaze swung from Emily to Althea. "You must be mistaken." He broke away and paced the stage. "Why don't you leave the investigation to me?"

"We've already investigated." Althea slapped a palm against the giant red box. "Haven't you been listening? We've got the evidence."

Barney paused. "What evidence?"

Emily lifted her chin. "We caught him dead to rights, messing around in the lost and found, hunting for a body."

"Not a real body, of course." Daisy dabbed her cheek with her handkerchief. "It was a mannequin we planted to entice him. Does anyone else find it stuffy in here?"

"You ain't kiddin'." Barney swiped beads of sweat from his forehead. "But how does that prove Sarge is guilty?"

"We recorded it on a cell phone," Emily said. "He was wearing a hoodie and mask, but I'm sure the authorities will be able to pinpoint something on the video to identify him."

"Have you got it with you?"

"It's on Daisy's phone." Emily waved to her friend.

Daisy pulled up the video and passed him the device.

Barney held the screen close. "Have you got it on a bigger screen?"

"That's the only copy," Daisy said.

He shook his head. "The lighting's too dark on this. Makes it hard to distinguish anything. I doubt the police can use it."

"Emily!" Gerry rushed into the room. "He's on his way."

Emily crossed the stage and grabbed Barney's hand. "He's coming. He's coming!"

His gaze snapped to the exit as Seamus and Gerry joined them onstage.

"Saints preserve us." Seamus shook his head. "He's mad as fire."

Barney, still clutching the phone, moved behind Daisy and Althea.

"It's not too late," he said. "Why don't we tell him it was a mistake and wait until we find real proof?"

"He already knows!" Emily stomped her sandal. "Would he be stupid enough to let us catch him again?"

"What do we do?" Althea scurried in a circle. "We can't let him get away with this."

Emily thumped her cane against the wooden floorboards. "It's now or never."

"I vote for never." Barney glanced at the phone, shoved it into Emily's hands, and headed for the stairs.

Emily grabbed him. "Where are you going?"

"I don't believe a word of your crazy accusations against Sarge."

She released him. "Could that be because you have a good reason for knowing he's innocent?" Emily brandished the phone. "Did you watch the whole video, Barney? Right at the end, the culprit's hood falls back. There's a bright, shiny bald spot with some very familiar freckles pointed straight at the camera." Emily pointed her finger at Barney's head. "You're always so self-conscious about your hair. I would think you'd have noticed."

Barney rubbed the bare patch on his head. "Wh-what? Now you say *I'm* the blackmailer? There's lots of bald guys on this boat." He swung his arms wide. "Is dementia contagious? The pack of you belong in a nursing home."

Seamus thrust himself in front of Gerry. "Stay behind me. This could get ugly."

The tall woman blinked in surprise, and her cheeks reddened.

"You're right, Seamus." Barney's easygoing smile was nowhere to be seen. "You've chosen some ugly company." He sneered at Emily. "Let's suppose I *was* guilty. If you turned me in, your friends would go down with me." He waggled his finger Daisy's direction. "Your secret wasn't illegal, but it would still be embarrassing if someone revealed it to your precious son."

A blush infused Daisy's pale cheeks. "I've already informed Spencer of my past sins. He was the only one who mattered. Inform anyone else you please."

His finger dipped. "You can't seriously want your fancy friends at home knowing you were a cheater."

"As unpleasant as the experience might be, it will provide the perfect opening to tell them, as Althea says, it's 'under the blood.' I'm sure they could also benefit from God's forgiveness."

Barney rolled his eyes. "Spare me the Sunday school lesson."

Emily glared. "You need it the most. It's not too late, Barney. God can even fix a greedy rat like you."

"Be a little nicer to me," he snapped. "The police won't care if a murderer has confessed their sins to a priest or not. That dummy with the creepy mask in the lost and found might have been fake"—he leered at Gerry—"but the corpse you wrote the letter about must still be there."

"What's he talkin' 'bout, darlin'?" Seamus's eyes held a disbelieving twinkle. "Have you got a husband buried in the backyard?"

Barney chortled. "You might not want a date so bad when I tell you what she did to her last suitor—dumped him at the bottom of a lake."

Gerry leaned over Seamus's head. "It was a wishing well, you dolt. A lake is far too prosaic."

"I don't get it." Barney waved between Emily and Gerry. "Your friend's a psychopath, but you want to send me to jail for a few black envelopes."

Althea bustled to Gerry and placed an arm around her. "She's not a psychopath. She's a writer."

"You're a bunch of fruitcakes." Barney clasped his hands to the top of his head and laughed. "Go ahead and tell everyone your suspicions. They'll think you're senile. And don't bother trying to use that video you shot. The app I installed should be finished erasing the footage."

Daisy's fingers scrambled as she swiped at her phone screen. "It's gone! My whole photo gallery is empty."

Barney shrugged. "That's what you get for accusing an honest man."

Emily rapped against the giant red box. "Did you hear, Adrian?"

"Yep," a muffled voice answered.

The false mirrored door at the back of the magic box popped open, and Adrian Everson emerged from the hidden space inside. He crawled out, brushed off his black pants, and straightened. His eyes—for once not covered by his reflective sunglasses—drilled the junior officer who cowered in front of him.

"An honest man, you said?" Emily counted off on her fingers. "You've admitted to spying on a letter my friend wrote when no one was around. The only way you could have seen it was through the surveillance cameras. You also said you checked the lost and found."

"I did no such thing." Barney held his hands out to Mr. Everson. "They're making this up, Sarge. I saw their video. That's how I knew."

Gerry stepped around Seamus. "The video never showed the mannequin we used. How did you know it was wearing a mask? It's understandable why you screamed when you discovered the repulsive thing."

"Hey"—Althea propped her hands on her hips—"you're talking about my grandson's birthday present."

Daisy patted her roommate's arm. "I'm sure he'll love it."

Emily continued. "You also mentioned the black color of the envelopes, which I didn't specify. Another unintentional slip."

The beads of sweat on Barney's forehead grew more pronounced. "I . . . I . . . uh . . ."

"And the most conclusive proof, why would an honest man delete evidence?"

Adrian's muscular arms crossed in front of his barrel-like chest. "I don't see why this skit was necessary. We've already searched his room and found the blackmail stationery."

"But a confession cinches the noose tighter." Gerry stacked her fists and clinched them together.

Barney cringed. He shouldered his way out of the Shippers' circle. "I-it was just a few times, Sarge. Really. And I never asked for much."

Everson's stony appearance matched the granite in his gaze. "You're a disgrace, Bosko."

Emily elbowed Gerry. "Get your notebook ready. I've got a feeling this guy's toast."

CHAPTER 56

Spencer wished yet again his mother would use the cell phone he'd purchased. How long would it take to locate her on this floating city? Despite their uneasy history, he didn't want Daisy to suffer. If someone was threatening to reveal salacious details from her past, it was his job as her son to protect her.

He entered the art gallery and wound his way around the standalone displays. Althea had tipped him off that he might find Daisy here. He spotted her staring at a somewhat decent copy of an impressionist painting.

As he approached, she greeted him with a hopeful smile. "Were you looking for me?"

"I was." His stomach curdled at discussing his mother's affair again, but it had to be done. "I wanted to address the blackmail problem. When we get back to Galveston, I plan to hire a private detective."

"That's kind but unnecessary." She turned to the painting. "We caught him last night."

"What? You caught him? How?"

Her voice held a triumphant note. "Don't underestimate the Shippers. We discovered that a member of the security team was spying on people through the surveillance cameras. He is currently in the ship's brig and will be surrendered to the police once we reach port."

Spencer ran a hand through his hair. "I don't even know what to say."

"How about 'nice work'?" Although her tone was teasing, her eyes remained guarded.

He lowered his arm. "Nice work, Dai—I mean, nice work, Mom. I'm relieved the man's been apprehended and you're safe."

She relaxed. "Thank you, Spencer. Would"—she toyed with the timepiece hanging from her neck—"would you care to take a stroll?"

He inclined his head. "Yes, thank you."

They walked side by side to the exit. A balmy breeze met them at the door. The pedestrian traffic grew lighter the farther they walked down the deck. He and Daisy stopped by a railing and stood in silence. Spencer balked at dredging up the past. But something inside his spirit, or perhaps he should say Some*one*, urged him to be open. Unbidden, the strains of an old song entered his thoughts.

"Do you have a favorite hymn?" he asked.

"Hymn?" Daisy turned. "It may sound unoriginal, but I've always been partial to 'Amazing Grace.'" Her head tilted. "Why do you ask?"

He ran a hand along the railing. "When I was a little boy, hymns seemed stuffy and outdated, but I've recently found comfort in the old songs. Especially 'Just as I Am.'"

His mother sang the first line in a sweet, airy soprano. *"Just as I am, without one plea."* She chuckled. "Do you think it appeals to you because of the legal-sounding language?"

"It could be." Spencer laughed. "But there's another reason." He drew a bracing breath of salty air into his lungs. "For so many years, I strived to achieve that elusive image of perfection, and I always fell short. But when I came to God, I realized he takes me just as I am."

Daisy laid a quivering hand over his. "It's all my fault. I should have tried harder to protect you." She wiped her eyes. "I'm so sorry. But I know it's not enough."

He rested his hand on hers. "It's in the past. We've both found a better way of living now."

She took a tentative step his way, then gathered him close. He honestly couldn't recall the last time his mother hugged him. Her petite frame shuddered as healing flowed through an embrace that was decades overdue. Spencer wished they could stay that way. But there was one more issue to address.

"About your past affair."

Daisy flinched and pulled away.

"I mean to say, in regard to the indiscretion you mentioned"—he reached out to her—"none of us are perfect. We all need God's grace, so who am I to judge?" He swallowed. "However, if you require some sort of forgiveness from me, you have it."

His entire body sagged. He'd gotten the words past his lips.

"Thank you, Spencer," she murmured. "With your forgiveness, I think I can move on. For too long, I've been living like I just left a funeral."

He studied her black silk blouse and matching pants, and his lips quirked. "Your attire doesn't exactly complement the surroundings."

She tugged his sleeve. "It's time we both cleaned out our closets. This time let's choose without considering anyone's opinion but God's."

Her words felt like a benediction. Permission to live his life without worry or care for what others said. As they often did, his thoughts swerved to a certain redhead.

He agreed with his mother. A whole new world of happiness awaited, and Abby was the key to getting there. She was a gift straight from a loving Creator in heaven.

He'd almost lost her once. But he'd never make that mistake again.

CHAPTER 57

"GOOD NIGHT, PRINCESS MADDIE."

Abby kissed her favorite passenger's forehead as she tucked her into bed. The lovable little girl's eyes closed when her head touched the silk pillowcase. After tiptoeing from the room, Abby peeked over the balcony. Two waiters cleaned the remainder of their room service meal from the dining table below. She waited until they left the suite before heading downstairs.

Spencer sat on the couch, perusing his tablet. He spotted her and smiled. "There you are."

Abby flopped onto the couch beside him. She'd insisted on dressing in her Monarch polo and shorts to stem any gossip the waitstaff might spread about her dining with them. But she couldn't resist wearing a too-tight platform sandal to lessen the height difference between her and Spencer, in case he tried to steal a kiss or two before she left. So far, the sacrifice had been in vain. She bent over, wedged her finger between her foot and the back of the shoe, and moaned.

"What is it?" Spencer dropped his tablet on the couch and leaned closer.

"My feet don't like these shoes. I've been running around in sneakers for the past two years in the Kids Kingdom. I wonder if I can get away with walking barefoot to my cabin."

"Unprofessional."

"Easy for you to say." Abby slid away and kicked off one shoe, lifted her leg, and pointed the other platform heel in his direction. "You don't have to wear a pair of these. Whoever invented them should be locked up."

Spencer grabbed the sandal waving half an inch from his knee. "I assure you it wasn't me. Please point your weapon in another direction."

Abby tried to lower her foot, but he held on. "You'd better let go unless"—she wiggled her toes—"you're planning on giving me a foot massage."

Spencer regarded the jerking digits. He scooted up in his seat and propped her foot on his knee. "Why not."

"Excuse me?" Abby's foot curled as he slipped the shoe off. "I was joking. You can let go."

He ignored her. His warm hands settled on her bare skin, and his fingers kneaded the sore flesh. "I talked with Daisy today."

"Good." Abby applauded. "You both need to bond."

"You must've been surprised at my mother's reaction to our dating announcement. She practically told you to dump me."

"Have you two always been so . . . forgive me for saying it but . . . *cold* to one another?"

"Mastersons aren't known for their compassion." His pressure on her foot increased. "Money. Power. Strength. We possess those in abundance. But whoever designed the family gene pool left out the softer attributes."

"I beg to differ." Abby pointed upward. "God put quite a bit of caring in the three Mastersons I've become acquainted with."

"Three?" His fingers stilled.

"Daisy, Maddie, and you."

"I can't deny Madeleine's sympathetic side." He rubbed again. "No idea where she got it from."

"None?" Abby smiled at the millionaire who was massaging her sore foot without complaint.

"Can't have come from me." He snorted. "And it definitely wasn't inherited from her mother. Maybe there's a saint hidden somewhere in the family lineage. Perhaps compassion skips a few generations."

His gentle fingers stroked the arch of her foot. The soothing pressure might have put her to sleep if the butterflies in her tummy weren't doing figure eights. If only this moment could last forever. But the ship reached home port in two days. He'd return to Louisiana, and she'd start her teaching job in Florida. Would their newfound relationship withstand the distance?

Harsh reality paralyzed her butterflies.

She pulled her foot back, tucked it under her, and locked her arms over her stomach. "I'm sorry to ruin this sweetness with cold, hard facts, but we should talk about what happens when the cruise is over."

The wary look he gave her was hardly encouraging, but she continued.

"Your job is important to you, and once I start teaching, my schedule will be more packed than ever." Abby rubbed her arms. "I'll be happy to spend all the minor holidays visiting you and Maddie in New Orleans, but would you consider coming to Florida in December? I'm from a big family, and they'd raise a ruckus if I missed our Christmas traditions."

He made a swift turn. "I've been considering the logistics, and I've landed on the best solution."

"Super!" Abby drew her other leg under her and sat on her heels. "What is it?"

"Marry me."

Abby pressed the flap of skin that covered her earhole. She wasn't sure what it was called, but if she pushed it in and out a few more times, it might fix the problem. Something had to be wrong with her hearing. "What did you say?"

"Marry me," Spencer repeated. "Now, before the ship docks in Galveston."

A half laugh, half gasp escaped her lips. No moonlit beach, no candles, no rose petals strewn on the floor. In fact, her shoes littered the living room rug. She bolted to her feet.

He followed, staring her down.

Abby's bare toes twitched on the soft area rug. Without the extra inches her sandals provided, Spencer towered over her. But he looked nothing like a giant. He looked like a scared little boy asking someone to be his friend at a new school.

She wanted more than anything to be that friend. And more. But this was crazy!

"How can we get married?"

"I know these boats have ministers since you dated one of them. Or don't ship captains have some sort of special ability to perform ceremonies? We'll ask him to do it."

Abby held her hands to her eyes like a pair of blinders, trying desperately to focus. Could she accept his proposal? They still barely knew each other.

She lowered her hands. "We've been dating one day."

He rubbed his throat. "I know it's fast."

"Cheetah fast."

"It floors me that I'm the one suggesting it. I'm always the most rational person in the room." He grasped her arms. "But I lose all reason when it comes to you. Limiting our relationship to phone calls and holiday visits sickens me. Maddie and I both need you." He drew her into a warm embrace. "We both love you."

Abby rose on her tippy-toes without realizing. She wrapped her arms around his neck and drew his face down. His head tilted, welcoming the kiss. His other hand reached around her and splayed on her lower back, urging her closer. Abby's eyes started to drift closed when she came to her senses. She jerked away and pressed against his chest.

His gaze clouded. "What's wrong?"

"I'm forcing myself to be the logical one for the first time in my life." She laughed. "Every atom in my body is shouting yes, but what if you regret it?"

"Impossible." He squeezed her in a hug and pulled her up so her feet dangled against his legs. His cheek settled on top of her head.

Rational thought dissolved, but Abby made one last, futile attempt. "Do you want to spend the rest of your life with a sore neck whenever you kiss your wife?"

He leaned back with a wolfish grin. "We'll keep a step stool in every room."

And then he proceeded to demonstrate how well he could do without one.

"Daddy, what are you doing?"

Abby dropped to earth with a thud. She and Spencer sprang apart and looked at Maddie, who stood at the bottom of the steps in her pajamas. Her wide eyes stared.

Abby wanted to race from the room and keep going till her feet hit water, but Spencer took her by the hand.

"I have a question, Madeleine. How would you like to be our flower girl when I marry Abby?"

Talk about blunt. Did he have to launch right into it without a buildup? What if Maddie didn't like the idea?

But Maddie didn't give a big reaction. Instead, she remained where she was. "What's a flower girl?" she asked

"What's a—?" Spencer scratched his head. "Well, you'll carry a basket with flowers and stand with us while we get married."

"Will there be a lot of people there?"

"No, sweetie." Abby rushed to kneel in front of her. "Just a few people you already know. Are you okay with that?"

"I guess so." Maddie blinked.

Spencer joined them and hunkered down. "We'll have a short wedding in the chapel. Grandma Daisy will be there. You'll get to wear a pretty dress, and"—he seemed to be scrambling for the right words—"and eat a big, fancy cake when we're done."

"Cake?" Maddie's face brightened. "Yay! Can we get married tomorrow?"

He laughed. "Oh, Maddie. I love you." Spencer drew his daughter into a hug. "Yes, we can get married tomorrow."

The butterflies were back. They dive-bombed from Abby's stomach to her toes and shot straight to her brain, where they drove out every thought but one.

She was finally getting married.

Tomorrow.

CHAPTER 58

"Dearly beloved, we are gathered here in the sight of God—"

Emily's smile stretched across her face like someone had fastened it to her ears with clothespins. The corners of her lips ached from holding the unfamiliar visage in place. This wasn't her normal smile. This was the painted mask of a clown who had no idea what was going on.

Abby and Spencer stood at the chapel's altar. Late-afternoon sunshine gleamed through the stained-glass windows on either side of the new honorary chaplain conducting the ceremony. He was from Dubuque, enjoying a free cruise in exchange for performing a few temporary duties on the MS *Buckingham*.

Madeleine stood between the couple, wearing one of her lacy pink dresses and holding a beribboned basket. Rose petals spilled as she sashayed back and forth. Her grandmother had styled her hair.

The bride was clad in a cream silky sheath, purchased from the ship's boutique. Her fiery curls were piled atop her head in a sophisticated bun. Spencer sported one of his many suits and a happy grin that outdid any Emily had ever seen him use.

She fidgeted as the minister finished his lengthy opening remarks. Mr. Dubuque was a wordy one. Emily drummed her fingers against her aching knee. She should be ecstatic. Never in their entire Shipper record had they matched and married a couple in three weeks. It was unprecedented.

But something was wrong.

She looked to her left. Her three comrades sat in a row with equally counterfeit expressions on their faces. Emily squirmed on the pew. It wasn't that she doubted the couple's sincerity. A whirlwind romance was entirely possible. Her own dear husband had asked her to marry him two weeks after they met.

"Will you please join hands?" the minister asked the bride and groom.

Spencer took one of Abby's hands, and they both took hold of Maddie, forming a small, adorable circle.

Tears tickled the corners of Emily's eyes. It was so sweet. So right. Maybe she was mistaken to believe something was amiss.

Mayday. Mayday. Mayday.

The prickle in her bones amplified. Drat it all! The Lord gave her an internal warning system for a reason. No use ignoring it. From the moment Spencer and Abby had announced their intentions to marry before the ship reached Galveston, Emily's insides had swirled like a typhoon. Even though this ceremony was only symbolic, they planned to board a plane and fly to Vegas once they docked and make it legal. If she hesitated much longer, it would be too late to say anything.

The minister tipped his chin to the groom. "Spencer, we'll begin with you. Do you take—"

"I'm sorry." Emily snatched her cane and pushed herself up. "I tried to wait until the 'does anyone object' part, but it's taking too long."

Madeleine stopped twisting. The wedding party pivoted Emily's direction, mouths agape.

The minister cleared his throat. "This ceremony doesn't include that line."

"Then it's a good thing I spoke up, because I object."

"Oh, thank heavens." Daisy sighed. "I was too afraid to say it myself for fear Spencer would think I was cruel."

Maddie tugged the hem of Spencer's suit coat. "Is it over, Daddy? Can we eat cake now?"

"Not yet." He ran a gentle hand over her head before directing an exasperated scowl at the Shippers. "Meddling again? Weren't you the ones who went to great lengths to encourage our relationship? I thought you wanted us to get married."

"We do, baby." Althea grabbed the pew in front of her and hauled herself to a standing position. "But you got to go about it the right way. You and me both know from experience. Divorce is like having open-heart surgery without the anesthetic. It's better to be sure before tying the knot."

"Yes." Gerry stood as well. "Falling head over heels is great in the novels. But real life lasts a lot longer than three hundred pages."

Abby gawked.

Spencer flourished their interlocked fingers at the Shippers. "Three hundred pages or three hundred years, I want to spend them all with this woman."

"Awwwww." Joint murmurs of approval poured from Gerry and Althea.

Emily swatted at her friends. "Don't let the pretty dialogue distract you, girls. We've lived on this planet long enough to recognize when something ain't right." She slipped from between the pews, marched down the aisle to Spencer and Abby, and took each of them by the hand. "Please don't misconstrue my actions. It's a blessing from above that you two found each other." She gestured to Maddie standing between them. "You three. And I want you to have every possible advantage on your side when you marry."

Abby squeezed Emily's fingers. "I love him, Mrs. Windsor. Truly."

She and Spencer looked at each other in that intimate way couples had that automatically excluded everyone else in the room.

Emily's heart hurt to be the one interrupting them. "I'll make you a deal. Give us ten minutes. I'll talk with Abby. And Daisy will talk with her son. If you two still want to continue with the ceremony afterward, we won't make a peep."

Spencer withdrew his fingers. "Do we have your word? Ten minutes and then no more objections?"

Emily crossed her heart and held up her right hand. "On my honor as a matchmaker."

♥⚓♥

Abby stood by the railing on the lido deck. Her formal dress hardly fit with the bikinis and tank tops of the sunbathers. Amari was monitoring the splash pad alone. He eyed her outfit with curiosity.

Why had Emily insisted on talking here?

Abby turned to the woman who'd sidetracked her wedding. "You have less than ten minutes left. Lay it on me."

Instead of speaking, Emily motioned to a nearby table. The two settled in the empty chairs, but the older woman still didn't speak. She bowed her head. Her lips moved, but no sound came out. After a few seconds, she faced Abby. "You shouldn't marry Spencer."

"What?" Abby's jaw slacked.

"Oh, I don't mean never. But not right now. It's too soon for both of you. He's recovering from his divorce, and you need to rediscover your own passion in life."

Abby's stomach churned like she'd eaten a dozen cupcakes. "But . . . but I love him."

"You can love someone and still take your time marrying them. Trust me. I speak from experience. My poor husband, Bill, had to wait a year after proposing before I shopped for a wedding dress."

Emily's words clattered inside Abby's head. They resurrected her buried doubts. She gnawed her lower lip, realized what she was doing, then licked her upper teeth to remove any lipstick marks. Mustn't ruin her makeup. She had a wedding to get back to.

Or did she?

"Aaaaaahhhhh!" A dark-haired boy hollered inside a jungle gym to their left. The child's upper half hung from a circular opening near the top.

Abby raced over. With careful hands, she rescued him from his uncomfortable position and set him on the ground. A little girl barreled through the spurting jets. Her heavy steps splashed water onto the wedding gown.

Abby checked the stains and moaned. Oh well. It was a job hazard. She returned to the table, and Emily nodded.

"See there? You're in your element around the children. No matter how busy you are, you keep an eye and ear tuned to what's going on around you. It's time you rejoined the real world and put your God-given abilities to better use. You were born to be a teacher."

Abby plucked at the wet hem of her dress. "Spencer didn't ask me to give up teaching."

"I'm sure he didn't. He's not an idiot. But the best marriages take place when each partner knows who they are and what they can bring to the relationship. Spend time getting to know each other. Then you'll be all the stronger when the two of you come together."

Abby covered her face. She managed a shuddery breath, and her voice wobbled. "You're right. But"—she swallowed hard—"what if Spencer isn't willing to wait?"

"Pish-tosh." Emily patted her shoulder. "Don't underestimate the man. I imagine he'd fetch you a piece of the moon if you asked him. Postponing the wedding isn't too hard a request, as long as you help him understand you're not abandoning him." Emily thumped the table. "Besides, I'm not telling you to join a convent. I'll bet New Orleans is dying for good teachers. If you took a job there, you could see each other seven days a week."

Abby raised her head. "You think so?"

"I know so. It's obvious Spencer didn't get much care or affection in his previous marriage. Take some time enjoying your courtship."

"I was looking forward to being Maddie's mother." Abby brushed impatient fingers over her watery eyes. "She deserves to be showered with affection."

"Maddie's another good reason to wait. Her father needs to be the one to shower that affection first. Allow them the opportunity to get close. It will make it even sweeter when you join the family."

Abby sat on her hands and rocked in her seat. "How do I break this to him?"

"With lots of love." Emily grabbed her purse and stood. "And it won't hurt to throw in a few hot-blooded kisses. Give him a preview of how much fun it will be to date you."

Fun? Abby suspected her conversation with Spencer would be anything but fun. What if he decided she wasn't worth waiting for?

CHAPTER 59

Eᴵɢʜᴛ sᴛᴇᴘs.

It took exactly eight steps to cross the outer balcony opposite the chapel. Spencer knew the distance well because he'd paced it for five minutes. Where was Daisy? Considering he'd given the Shippers a mere ten minutes to change his mind, the delay confused him. His brain had calculated every argument his mother might use and prepared a proper response. No one and nothing would talk him out of marrying Abby.

The door opened, and Spencer braced himself. Daisy's pink suit matched the shade of Madeleine's flower girl dress. This doting grandmother in no way resembled the cold, proper woman of his childhood.

He firmed his jaw. "Well? Let me have it."

A tender smile adorned her lips. She walked over, slipped her hands under his arms, and wrapped him in a warm embrace. The subtle scent of magnolias teased his nostrils.

Spencer froze. Two hugs from his mother in one week. It must be a record.

After a few seconds, she drew away and captured the decorative timepiece around her neck. She yanked hard. The delicate gold chain snapped. Extending her fist, she unclasped her fingers to reveal the watch.

"I remember when your father gave me this *gift*." Her tone hardened at the word. "It was on our wedding day. Naive, starry-eyed girl that I was, I presumed it symbolized his never-ending love for me. I soon learned differently."

The broken necklace strands swayed in the sea breeze. Daisy's fingers closed. She faced the billowing waves. "When he and I were courting, he waited for me without complaint as I primped and powdered. But after the marriage ceremony, his patience ended. This gift was his way of telling me he wouldn't wait again." Her head bowed. "You're more than aware of your father's insistence on punctuality."

Spencer's shoulders constricted at the very mention. As a child, he'd spent many hours locked in his room because his lateness had affected his father's schedule. The controlled Julius Masterson never once hit him, but the emotional punishment he'd inflicted was acute.

He studied his mother's profile. The wind whipped the sides of her sleek silver bob against her cheeks. Her sophisticated nose wrinkled in a sniffle.

"I'm so happy you've found Abby," Daisy said.

"If you're happy, why are you interrupting our wedding?"

"She's not ready." Daisy turned. "And neither are you." She opened her fist. The miniature clock face glinted in the sunlight. "It's not too late, Spencer. Your father browbeat every kinder emotion out of you. Or tried to. But I believe my sweet, sensitive little boy is still in there somewhere."

She spun and pitched the watch. Spencer reached out. Too late. It sailed through the air and disappeared into the wavering deep surrounding the MS *Buckingham*.

He clapped a hand to his forehead. "That was a family heirloom. Dad stated in his will it should go to Madeleine."

Her eyebrow lifted. "Doesn't it strike you as odd that your father bequeathed other people's possessions in his last will and testament? I suppose he never truly gave the piece to me. Just loaned it awhile for his own convenience. Everyone and everything in Julius Masterson's family belonged to him. He intended they should adhere to his well-ordered, punctual routine, even beyond the grave."

The cold sting of fear Spencer used to experience at his father's censoring glare crept through him. His neck prickled as if a ghostly, disapproving specter stood behind him.

Daisy placed two hands over his. Her skin was cool. Soft as cashmere. With so many more wrinkles than he remembered.

"Sugar, don't live in the cage your father built." She caressed his thumbs. "It's not too late for you. Or Maddie. You can live a happy, disorganized, hectic life if you choose." She laughed. "Abby will certainly help with that. But you must allow her to do it at her own pace. Time is one of the greatest gifts you can give a person you love."

She embraced him again. Spencer hesitated. Five seconds. Ten. Then he returned the hug and clung to her. His mother's words battered his conscience, but he shut his mind.

There must be some other way to give Abby time than canceling the wedding. He'd agree to whatever she wanted to do after their marriage. Even if it required moving to a different city. He'd relinquish his home, his connections, his business. All to be with her.

The door beside them opened, and his bride stepped onto the balcony. There she was in her cream dress, her red hair glinting in the sunlight. Abby. If he loved her this much after three weeks, how would he feel in fifty years?

His mother pulled away and smoothed her hair. "I'll leave you two alone." She entered the chapel and closed the door behind her.

Spencer walked the eight paces to the end of the confined space, his back to Abby. "Well? Did they convince you what a bad risk I am?"

Footsteps drew close. Her arms encircled him from behind. Her warmth enveloped him as it always did. He relaxed and laid his hands on top of hers.

Perhaps the wedding would still happen.

Abby spoke. "You're mighty fine in your fancy suit."

He swiveled, caught her close in almost desperation, and lowered his head for a kiss.

She tasted sweeter than a cupcake. But no matter how many kisses she gave him, he knew he'd never be full.

He allowed an inch between their lips. "You look even better in that dress than your princess costume."

She smacked him. "Stop." A flicker of apprehension entered her gaze. "I'm afraid we'll have to save these outfits for another day, Spencer."

His muscles grew taut. So the Shippers had done their worst. The wedding was off.

Abby smoothed her fingers against the lapel of his jacket. "I wanted to ignore Emily's arguments for postponing, but the more she talked, the more I realized she was right. We need time to get to know one another. Rushing into things might hurt everyone. Especially Maddie."

The bitter taste of rejection swelled in Spencer's mouth.

God, I can't do this. Not again!

He tried to remember the Bible verses he'd read to calm his nerves before the ceremony, but instead his mind recalled the doubts.

Abby didn't want him. Like every other woman in his life. His mother. His ex-wife. What was it about him that drove people away?

At least Priscilla had the decency to give it a try before she dumped him.

Abby's voice drifted into his consciousness. "I'm not saying I don't—"

"I comprehend perfectly." Spencer nodded once. "You've decided you don't want to marry me. Thank you for coming to the realization before it got messy."

"That's not what—"

"If you'll excuse me, Madeleine and I should prepare for our arrival in Galveston."

He lowered his arms and attempted to leave. Abby locked her hands behind his back.

Spencer kept his eyes averted. "Please release me."

"Where do you think you're going?" She pressed closer. "I can't hear the cynical mumbo jumbo running through your brain, but you'd better tell it to shut up."

He zeroed in on her face. Her smile held adoration and understanding and, dare he hope, love? Abby pressed her cheek against his body.

She groaned. "I'm probably smearing makeup all over your coat, but

I don't care. I love you, Spencer. I'm not rejecting you, and I'm not letting you go. I'm just asking for a little time."

That word again. *Time.* The first piece of motherly advice Daisy had ever bestowed upon him turned out to be correct.

He rubbed the heels of his hands against his eyes. "I know. The fact I want to marry someone I met three weeks ago floors me. It's only possible because"—his fingers brushed the vibrant curls on top of her head—"because it's you."

She snuggled closer. "Then could you please participate in this hug?"

He crushed her to him, an odd mixture of sadness and peace swirling inside. He knew they had to wait, but now that he'd admitted the unhappy truth, the Lord's gentle voice echoed in his spirit, confirming it was the right choice.

"I love you too," he whispered. "What do we do now? Am I going to rack up the frequent-flier miles between Louisiana and Florida?"

She propped her chin on his chest. "They have schools in New Orleans. I bet one of them would love to hire someone with my unique talents."

His spirits lifted. "You'd be willing to move?"

"Try and stop me. Maddie begins kindergarten this year. Who's going to help her buy new clothes? If I left it to you, she'd always be dressed like it was picture day."

A school wardrobe? He hadn't thought that far ahead. Parent orientations. Homework. Girl stuff he knew nothing about. A wave of father fatigue ambushed him.

Abby giggled. "Wipe that panicked look off, mister. I'll be there to help. And if Maddie ever has another 'tummyegg,' I can rush over and make my special peppermint tea."

Spencer cupped her cheeks and rewarded her with a lingering kiss. The shorter curls that had escaped from the bun tickled his nose. He raised his head with a moan. "We won't wait long, will we?"

Her answering grin was a mixture of innocence and mischief. "Not one day longer than we have to."

Spencer shot a glance at the sky. "God, give me strength."

She grasped his lapels and tugged him down. Her lips met his in a passionate promise for the future. Spencer allowed his worries to dissipate in the force of her overwhelming love.

No doubt about it. They might need a step stool in every corner.

CHAPTER 60

Ten Months and Fifteen Days Later

"Look what came in the mail." Emily joined her friends at a table on the upper deck. She waved an envelope of expensive cream linen paper. "I bet it's a wedding invitation."

"We already know Spencer and Abby are getting married." Gerry typed on her laptop. "Daisy told us a week ago."

"But this makes it official." Emily slipped her finger under the flap. "Besides, we can add it to our trophy collection."

"Gerry's suggestion about scanning invitations to her computer was smart. Who knows how many we'll end up with?" Althea wiggled her flowered shawl from under her thighs. "Can you imagine toting a scrapbook around in our suitcases?"

Daisy tapped the invitation in Emily's hand. "I'm relieved they chose the off-white. It's so much more elegant. Don't you think?"

"I think we shouldn't claim credit for this one." Gerry kept typing. "Abby and Spencer found each other with minuscule help from us."

"What are you talking about?" Emily tossed her gray curls. "Who arranged their first kiss at the waterfall? Who convinced them to strengthen their relationship before saying 'I do'? Us. That's who."

"Quite right." Althea nodded. "But I wonder how they held out this long. I'm sure if Spencer had his way, the wedding would've been much sooner."

Daisy pulled her phone from her pocket and swiped the screen. "I'm afraid I have to agree. He was none too happy when Abby said she wanted to finish the school year before she could enjoy the bridal festivities." She turned the phone to show her friends the wedding photos. "They decided to take their pictures before the ceremony. Less to do on the actual day."

"How unromantic." Gerry clicked one last key and shut the laptop lid.

"Makes sense to me." Althea accepted the cell from Daisy and studied the photo. "They already saw each other in their wedding duds on the ship. The surprise is gone."

"Still." Gerry crossed her arms. "I hope Abby gets a new gown for the ceremony."

Emily took the phone and beamed at the evidence of another successful match. The picture showed the couple posed on a winding wrought iron staircase. Spencer sat in the back with his arms around Abby, one long leg stretched to the side. Abby nestled against him while embracing Maddie. The little girl's mouth was open in an abandoned laugh.

Emily sniffled. "Well done, Shippers. Well done." She dabbed her sleeve to her eyes and returned the cell to Daisy. "I'm glad you decided to use the phone Spencer bought. It makes operations so much easier."

"All 'cause Daisy wanted to talk to her grandbaby." Althea chortled. "She jumps for that phone whenever Maddie calls."

"Whatever the reason, it's a lot more convenient than the walkie-talkies."

"What happened to those things?" Gerry asked.

"I stored them in the lost and found in case we ever hit a storm and get bad reception on our phones. It always pays to have a backup plan."

A nervous voice rang out, "Mrs. Windsor!" Peter scurried to their table. His crisp first mate's uniform matched the whites of his wide eyes as he joined them. "You haven't forgotten it's turnaround day, have you?"

"I'm not senile, dear." Emily rose. "I was just about to fetch my purse."

"Really?" He beamed and grabbed her in a wiry hug.

She gave him a quick pat before he raced away to hurry the passengers loitering on the lower deck. The almost-finished cruisers swarmed the lido deck, rushing to take last-minute pictures before they returned to normal life. Emily spotted a face in the crowd and paused. Her head tilted.

"What?" Gerry asked. "What is it?"

"My bones are telling me something."

"Heaven help us." Daisy pressed a hand to her chest.

Althea moaned. "I hope it's not another warning signal."

"On the contrary"—a smile broke across Emily's face—"I've found our next client, girls. Right over there." She pointed below.

Her friends peered over the railing, and Daisy gasped. Althea chuckled and shook her head.

Gerry sighed as she reopened her laptop. "I don't know about this one. Are you sure you heard your bones right?"

"Loud and clear." Emily rubbed her hands down her arms. "They're tingling like crazy. What can I say? The Lord moves in mysterious ways. Come on, Shippers. Let's get to work. This is going to take extra planning."

"Maybe Peter will let us stay aboard," Althea said.

"Not much chance of that." Gerry started typing. "It's turnaround day."

"Poor Peter." Daisy took her sunglasses from her handbag. "He is persistent. Bless his heart."

Emily marshaled her friends around the table and started to map out their next battle plan. The identity of their new client surprised her. But God gave her noisy bones for a reason. Who was she to argue with the Ultimate Matchmaker?

ACKNOWLEDGMENTS

MY LIFE OVERFLOWS WITH A wealth of people who help make my stories a reality.

Thank you to my agent, Cynthia Ruchti. Both your patience with all my questions and the wisdom you share make the journey easier.

The ACFW Writers on the Storm have brought joy to my life. I appreciate the knowledge, support, and encouragement I've gleaned from this group and hope all the members will find great success with their writing.

Kregel Publications has been wonderful to me, and I value their commitment to sharing God's love with the world. Thank you especially to the editors who filed down the rough edges of this novel: Rachel K., Andrea, Lindsay, Jeanna, and Rachel O.

My stories wouldn't mean much without the awesome people who read them. Thank you to all the book dragons out there who laugh along with my Shippers and leave kind reviews that bolster my confidence. You rock!

I don't have the right words to express how wonderful my parents are. They've supported my dreams without fail and held me up during the hard times. I love you, Mom and Dad!

And, of course, I saved the best for last. My heavenly Father has lifted my head when it hung low and filled my heart with sweet visions. Bless the Lord, oh my soul! Let all that is within me and my writing bless His holy name. God always keeps His promises.

ABOUT THE AUTHOR

SHANNON SUE DUNLAP EARNED AN MA in journalism from Regent University in her beautiful home state of Virginia. She enjoys traveling, chocolate, K-dramas, and singing obscure songs from classic movie musicals. She currently lives in hot and humid Houston, Texas, where she writes stories of love and laughter—always with a happy ending. You can learn more about her books and sign up for her email list at shannonsuedunlap.com.

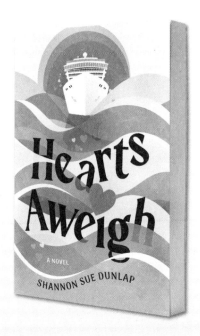

YOU CAN KEEP THIS BOOK MOVING!

Give this book as a gift.

Recommend this book
to a friend or group.

Leave a review on Christianbook,
Goodreads, Amazon, or your favorite
bookseller's website.

Connect with the author on
their social media/website.

Share the
QR code link
on your social
media.